TOO TOUGH TO TAME

Storm ran a forefinger along the lace-edged neckline of her chemise, making her blazingly aware of her scanty coverings. "Freckles," he noted in a purring tone that made Tess's heart race.

"Yes, well, that's what happens when a lady goes outside without her bonnet," she said breathlessly.

One corner of Storm's mouth quirked up. "I like freckles."

"You—you do?" Tension squeezed her chest and she had trouble breathing, thinking. She was mesmerized by the shape of his lips.

"I like freckles very much." His gaze dipped. "Where else do you have them?"

A high laugh tumbled from her. "Nowhere else. Now, you should sleep—"

His fingertip stroked her quivering skin again, slipping under the chemise, tugging the fabric lower. "I would like to look for myself," he murmured.

TOO TOUGH TO TAME

DEBORAH CAMP

AVON BOOKS ◆ NEW YORK

TOO TOUGH TO TAME is an original publication of Avon Books. This work has never before appeared in book form. This work is a novel. Any similarity to actual persons or events is purely coincidental.

AVON BOOKS
A division of
The Hearst Corporation
1350 Avenue of the Americas
New York, New York 10019

First Avon Books Printing: February 1996

AVON TRADEMARK REG. U.S. PAT. OFF. AND IN OTHER COUNTRIES, MARCA REGISTRADA, HECHO EN U.S.A.

Printed in the U.S.A.

RA   10 9 8 7 6 5 4 3 2 1

Never trust a wolf for dead until he's been skinned.

—Cowboy saying

Chapter 1

Montana, 1878

His chest and back were leaking from the bullet wound as Storm-In-His-Eyes wiped dust from his face and looked back once. He could see the hulking figure of the marshall, but he could no longer see the slender form of his sister. Had Willow-Bends-Woman fled? *Good. Run, sister, run.* Shouldn't have followed him anyway. She was always looking out for him since he'd returned to the Blackfeet.

Damned crazy marshall. Shooting at him when the son of a bitch knew damn well he was unarmed. A man doesn't strap a gun on when he comes a courtin'. And where the hell had Millie been? She was usually home alone during the day when her tin-starred father and her deputy brother were at the town jail, where they presided over the resident drunks, moonshiners, and petty thieves. Knowing Millie, she'd probably been hiding in the house, shivering like a rabbit 'cause Papa had come home unexpected, leaving Storm to face her fuming, gun-toting, Indian-hating father alone. But not

Willow-Bends-Woman. His little sister had shown courage by falling into the fray, begging the marshall not to shoot him, to let him go, giving him a chance to spring onto a horse and ride like the wind. He had almost gotten away clean—almost.

All this trouble over a gal he didn't even fancy all that much. White women. Would he ever learn to stay away from the pale-haired witches? Maybe this would teach him. Either that or kill him.

He rode up into the mountains, stopping his winded horse beside a stream to let the poor animal drink and catch his breath.

Storm considered getting off the horse, but then thought better of it. The way he was feeling, he might not be able to haul himself back into the saddle. He tore away his blood-soaked shirt and groaned when a red-hot poker of pain burned through his chest. The world spun before his eyes, and it took all his concentration not to faint dead away.

Yanking off the shirt and wishing he had the strength to tear the pants off as well, he balled it up and tossed it into the stream. His hat went with it. White men's clothes. He didn't belong in them or in the white man's world. And he sure didn't belong with a white woman. Experience had certainly taught him that. He'd never tangled with one yet who hadn't tried to stab him in the back or get him thrown in jail.

Never again.

He felt the life seeping from him and the cold breath of death on his heart. Kicking the tired horse into a lope, he made for the high ground, wanting to go home to the Blackfeet but worried that he'd lead the marshall there. The crazy old goat had been yelling something about how Storm had robbed and shot at some white settlers.

Trying to hang some kind of crime on him, get him hanged, Storm decided, and then his thoughts began to blur along with his eyes and other senses. The world seemed filled with hollow sounds and harsh light and blazing pain.

Can't lead the marshall back to the Blackfeet. . . . Rat bastard might burn them out just looking for him. Marshall Long had a list of reasons to hate him. He'd killed one of his deputies in that gunfight a few months back, and then there was that time Long caught him rolling around in a hay stack with Millie. Hell, he hadn't thought to ask Millie's last name. How was he to know she was the marshall's only daughter?

His thoughts staggered back to the marshall's rantings. *Robbing white people . . . of what?* They *were* robbing his *people. Lock the white ones up. . . . Hang the lot of them.* He grinned, felt it stretch his lips to a slanting smirk. His head buzzed and he knew he wasn't making much sense. Had to hide before he fell off this horse and the buzzards and wolves found him. . . .

Looking up at the ragged mountaintops, his thoughts staggered to a cave he and his sister used to play in when they were children. Red Deer Cave. Willow-Bends-Woman would make her way back to the Blackfeet camp and tell them he'd been shot. When he didn't return, she'd try to think where he might hide. *The cave; yes, she'd know.* Maybe they'd find him still clinging to life—maybe not.

He coughed and blood rattled in his chest. He tasted it on his tongue. The cave would be a good place to die. But to die at the hands of a bastard like Long, and all because of a flip-tail like Millie! There was no honor to it.

White women. Should have obeyed the elders who had told him not to listen to the call of the white blood flowing in his veins, for that blood was tainted.

He slipped off the horse and gave its rump a whack, sending it down the mountainside again. With grim determination, he climbed the bumpy, rocky ground to the cave, invisible to the eye even from this short distance. His booted feet slipped on stones and rolling pebbles, but somehow found enough purchase to propel him to the wide ledge and into the cave—the cave of his people, the ancient ones.

Pitching forward, he fell onto cold stone, his life leaking out of him in crimson drops. He closed his eyes and dreamed of his home, of tepees and communal fires. He'd missed it all and had come back to the Blackfeet. But the white people refused to let him live in peace. So they wanted war? Then war it would be. Clinging to the last embers of life, he decided he would cheat death and wage war on those who would try to destroy him, starting with False Hope's lying marshall.

Death approached the back room of Dr. John Summar's home in False Hope, Montana, hurrying to arrive before dawn. The sky was already getting lighter, and the breeze that had been softly blowing the lace curtains at the window had stilled. Crickets awakened and a tree frog cleared its throat. A few minutes later a whippoorwill called across the field behind the house.

The young woman, lying so still in the single bed, stirred as if she, too, felt the approach of the Grim Reaper. Her leather dress lay in a heap on the floor. Splattered with blood, it told a sad tale of what a bullet could do to a young, vulnerable body. The doctor had removed the slug and stopped the bleeding, but his efforts had been futile.

Perspiration dotted the patient's forehead and upper lip as she raised one hand to grasp the sleeve of the attentive woman standing near the bed. To the dying woman, the slim figure could have been a beautiful spirit with her halo of golden hair, her kind blue-green eyes, and her heartfelt smile.

Tess Summar squeezed water from the washcloth and placed the cool cloth against the young woman's forehead. "Rest now and don't be afraid. I'm right here, and I'm not leaving you."

Dark eyes, bruised eyes, stared up into Tess's face, and the fingers on her sleeve tightened. The woman's parched lips moved. Tess trailed her wet fingertips across the cracked skin, then dribbled water into the woman's mouth, hoping to fight the fire she knew raged in the frail body.

"I am Willow-Bends-Woman." The voice was weak, but the words were carefully enunciated. "And you must promise to save my brother."

"First we must save your life," Tess said, patting the hand clutching the sleeve of her white blouse.

"No, please . . ." The young Blackfeet sucked in a breath as pain shot through her. She trembled and tears filled her eyes. "You know that I am near death." She shook her head slightly to ward off Tess's automatic denial. "I have no time left for . . . listen, please. You must listen."

Acknowledging the determination on the woman's face, Tess nodded and sat on the side of the bed. "Very well. I'm listening, Willow-Bends-Woman."

"I was not shot by my brother. It was the lawman. The marshall."

Tess furrowed her brow, thinking the woman was delusional. Not knowing the marshall very well, Tess still couldn't imagine him shooting this harmless creature. Such a beauty! She was younger than Tess. Maybe eighteen, she thought, seized by the tragedy of this short life.

"The marshall . . ."

"Yes, the marshall was there. We know that. He's the one who brought you here to be doctored. I'm sure your brother wasn't trying to harm you. Marshall Long said your brother was aiming at him, but you stepped into the path of the bullet. It's criminal that you have to suffer for—"

"*He* sh-shot me," she interrupted Tess. "The marshall, not my brother. The lawman aimed the gun at me when I stopped him from killing my brother."

Tess blinked, trying to envision such a scene. "By accident, you mean. You got in the way—"

"No accident. I stopped him. He turned to me, aimed at me, shot me." Her voice rasped and her words ran together. "No accident. He wounded my brother. He will kill him now. You must save him. You must go to him. Quick. Before it is too late."

Compassion welled in Tess's heart. The fever again, she thought. It had rattled the girl's perceptions. Marshall Long wouldn't have shot her deliberately.

"My brother is injured. I saw him slump in the saddle as he rode away. The lawman shot him through the back. I believe he rides to the cave above the springs." The fingers tugged at Tess's sleeve, pulling her down to hear the whispered words. "My people call it Red Deer Cave. He is there. It is where he hides when trouble seeks him. I beg of you . . . *please.*"

"You don't have to beg me for anything," Tess told her, stroking the young woman's straight, black hair, tangled and smeared with dried blood. "I'm here for you."

"Promise me. Promise you will save my brother."

Tess sighed, reluctant to be roped into a situation that could prove dangerous. If this brother of hers was the outlaw the marshall claimed, Tess certainly didn't want to have anything to do with him. But the girl's dark eyes implored, and her feeble fingers gripped Tess's sleeve as her lips formed the word *please*, again. Tess's heart melted like ice in August.

"I promise," she vowed, and the slender, dark-brown hand slipped down Tess's sleeve to lie motionless on the white muslin sheet.

Willow-Bends-Woman closed her eyes, drew in a breath, and smiled. "I hear the drums," she whispered. "The rattle of the gourds . . . the pounding of hooves." She swallowed with difficulty. "I see my people of old . . . waiting." Peace settled upon her face, and her breathing became more regular. "They come for me." Her voice weakened. "And I hear the drums." Her final breath left her body. Her chest did not rise again.

A cock's crow shattered the stillness. Blinking away sudden hot tears, Tess turned aside and crossed to the window. She opened the shutters wider and drew misty air into her lungs. Pink and lavender crept up from the horizon. Dawn had come for the night just as death's riders had come for the spirit of a young Blackfeet maiden, an innocent victim of man's inhumanity to man.

In the five years since she'd been assisting her brother in his medical work, Tess had noticed that death often claimed the soul minutes before darkness gave way to dawn. It was eerie, but somehow fitting. Tess stared at the rugged, saw-tooth mountains while she fought to control her emotions. Death was never easy to witness, but this death was particularly difficult to bear because of the promise Tess had made to the girl. And then there was her account of how she'd been fatally injured. Tess scraped her teeth over her lower lip, pondering the scenario and having difficulty believing that a lawman would intentionally shoot an unarmed female.

The doorknob rattled, and Tess glanced over her shoulder to see her brother's gaunt face as he stepped into the room. His sleeves were rolled up to his elbows, and his blond hair was a nest of matted curls.

"Betty Lomax had a girl."

He'd been called away a few hours ago to deliver a baby, this after frantically working on the doomed Willow-Bends-Woman. His gaze darted to the bed, then to Tess.

"She died a minute ago."

His shoulders sagged and his mouth dipped at the corners. "I expected that, but still . . ." He shook his head. "Her family is outside. They'll want to take the body. I'll help you with her."

"Her family?" Tess pulled the sheet away from the body; the gruesome task of preparing the dead was second nature to her.

"Yes. Several of them. All savages. I made them wait outside."

"John!"

"Don't you scold me, Tess. This is my home, after all. And my wife lives here."

"Ah, yes, and Camilla would faint at the sight of an Indian, I suppose."

"She doesn't want them parading through our home, and who can blame her?" He lifted the body while Tess swept aside the soiled bedding.

They fell into silence while they finished their ministrations. Tess cautioned herself not to complain too fiercely about Camilla's unfounded fears; she did so detest women who swooned at everything and everybody out of the ordinary. Of course, that was one thing John loved dearly about his young wife. Camilla's need for him as a protector acted like an aphrodisiac on John.

Certainly, if she asked, Tess knew that John would tell her that she could learn a few things from Camilla. At twenty-four, Tess was considered a spinster in False Hope. While other girls her age were attending socials and learning the fine art of courting and being courted, Tess had been battling severe cramps and an insidious weakness that often left her bedridden for days on end. John had diagnosed poor blood. Whatever the ailment, it had disappeared when she was twenty-two. By that time, however, her girlfriends had married and Tess had discovered that she was considered a woman past her prime. Past her prime, indeed!

"Tess?"

John's voice cut through her reverie. "Yes? Yes, what is it?" She saw that he'd tucked a clean sheet tightly around the body.

"Will you gather her belongings?"

"Of course. There isn't much." Tess retrieved the ruined leather shift, a necklace of beads and feathers, a pair of beaded moccasins, and a braided leather belt. She placed the items in a clean flour sack and carried it out to the porch, walking behind John, who held the body in his arms.

Five Blackfeet men and three women waited by the hitching post, all chanting softly, but the volume and the sorrow increased when their loved one's body was placed in the arms of the broad-chested Blackfeet who stepped forward. Tess handed the sack to one of the grieving women.

"I did what I could for her," John said. "She died minutes ago. I'm sorry."

Willow-Bends-Woman's words circled in Tess's head. Should she tell John about the accusation against Marshall Long?

"I am Chief Eagle Talon, her father." The sad-faced man looked at the sheet-draped figure in his arms. "She was my youngest daughter."

"I'm terribly sorry," John said. "Being shot by her brother . . . that makes it worse. I understand he was firing at the marshall but hit her instead."

The Indian's features hardened, but he said nothing as he turned away. The others moved aside for him. He draped the body over his horse, tied it down, then climbed to sit in front of it. He rode sedately toward the majestic Rockies. John shrugged and went back inside, but Tess lingered to watch the Blackfeet, clad in leather and beads and feathers, move slowly to their horses, their faces streaked with tears, their voices broken and hoarse with grief.

One of the men, a stocky and rather bow-legged brave, paused beside his spotted pony and studied the house. Was he committing to memory the place where his family member had died? He frowned and made a move to mount his horse, but Tess lifted a hand to stop him. She blinked in surprise, feeling as if her hand had moved of its own volition. Or was Willow-Bends-Woman directing her from the spirit world?

"Pardon me," Tess ventured, and the Blackfeet looked startled. "Might I have a moment?" She moved to the edge of the porch and motioned for him to come nearer, then wondered if she was daft to do such a thing. After all, he was sturdily built and barely civilized. His face was smeared with dark-blue paint—war paint? She swallowed her misgivings and reined in her wild imagination.

"Willow-Bends-Woman told me something I think you should know. Something about her brother."

"Storm-In-His-Eyes?" The Blackfeet left the horse and came forward on bowed legs. He kept his gaze directed away from her, as if he was loathe to look her in the eye. It crossed her mind that he might be shy or as uneasy around her as she was around him. "What did Willow-Bends-Woman say?"

"She told me her brother was wounded, and she believes he is in Red Deer Cave. You know the place?"

He nodded guardedly, his gaze still averted from hers.

"She was afraid he might be injured and in need of your help. I promised I would do what I could." Tess removed a handkerchief from her skirt pocket and twisted it, needing something to do with her hands. The Blackfeet regarded her furtively; snatching glimpses, his gaze never rested on her for more than a few seconds. His shifting eyes and wariness made her apprehensive, ill at ease.

"She also said something about the marshall. . . ." No. That was ridiculous. Why get into that with this Indian, who appeared to be anxious to leave? "Anyway, I think you should go to this cave and see if her brother is there." She retreated but paused as curiosity nibbled at her. "What's your name? Are you related to Willow-Bends-Woman?"

He nodded. "I am her brother." His lips tensed. "You would say I am her cousin. Among the Bloods there are only brothers and sisters. I am Brown Otter."

"I'm Miss Summar, the doctor's sister." Tess smiled quickly, feeling like a dunce. How did one talk to an Indian? She had little practice at it. "I'm sorry about your cousin . . . or rather, sister. She was beautiful."

After a few moments of awkward silence, he whirled and sprang lightly onto his horse. Without another word or glance, he rode away as if the hounds of hell were after him. She hoped he was heading for Red Deer Cave.

Tess entered the quiet house. A weight seemed to have lifted from her since she'd shifted the responsibility of locating Willow-Bends-Woman's brother to the Blackfeet. Storm-Whatever was their problem, after all, not hers. And he was an outlaw, which was another good reason to wash her hands of the incident.

Camilla descended the stairs from the second story. She wore a pink wrapper, and her hair had been brushed but not yet styled.

"Everyone is up early. Where's John?"

"Washing up, I think," Tess answered. "There was a shooting last night."

"Not another one," she said with a sigh. "I suppose some cowboys got liquored up and had an argument over a saloon trumpet."

"No, a Blackfeet girl was shot by accident. She died a few minutes ago."

"An Indian?" Camilla's eyes widened with alarm. "Why was John called for her? Why not let their own doctors tend to them?"

Before Tess could retort that John had taken an oath to protect *all* human life, he emerged from his office down the hall. He wore a freshly laundered shirt, and his curly blond hair had been tamed by a thorough wetting.

"Ah, I thought I heard your voice," John said,

coming forward to embrace his wife. "Good morning, dear heart." He kissed Camilla tenderly and ran a finger down her cheek. "I was just coming to ask my sister if she'd be good enough to prepare breakfast. I'm glad you're awake so that you can eat with me."

"You've had a busy morning," Camilla said, walking her fingertips up the front of his shirt. "You know how I hate to wake up without you beside me."

Feeling like an interloper, Tess cleared her throat and edged past them. "How do eggs and grits sound? I'll put on a pot of coffee." She didn't wait for their approval, knowing they'd eat whatever she cooked.

John had married Camilla almost a year ago, changing Tess's role in his house. Now the house was Camilla's, and all the things in it were hers as well. Tess had begun to yearn for her own possessions, her own furniture and lace doilies and rag rugs. And, yes, her own husband.

When her parents had died, all their possessions had gone to John, the eldest, and Tess resented it. Her situation hadn't bothered her until John had married, which had usurped her role as the lady of the house. Now Tess felt like a servant, waiting on John and Camilla as a way of earning her keep. She didn't like the arrangement, but she felt shackled to it and could see no way to freedom other than through marriage. But there was no handsome hero for her in False Hope. She'd searched and had come up empty-handed, empty-hearted. Of course, that didn't stop John from trying to find her a beau, which only served to make Tess feel that he, too, would be glad when she moved into her own house.

As Tess prepared breakfast, her thoughts kept

returning to Willow-Bends-Woman and the story she'd told. Had Marshall Long lied about how the shooting had happened? Maybe Willow-Bends-Woman had only *thought* the bullet had been fired by Marshall Long. The woman's retelling of the incident haunted Tess, stubbornly persisting. When someone pounded on the back door, she nearly spilled the skillet of scrambled eggs she was mounding into a bowl on the table.

The top portion of the Dutch door was open, and Marshall Chester Long poked his head in. His flushed face was in stark contrast to his white mustache, eyebrows, and shirt. She motioned him to come inside.

"You're just in time for breakfast, Marshall."

"Oh, thanks, but I've had mine. Is your brother around?" He removed his cowboy hat and ran a pudgy hand over his hairless head and down the front of his boiled shirt, his fingertips brushing a point of the silver star pinned to it. A gun belt hung low on his hips.

"Yes, he is. Sit down, won't you? I'll fetch him."

"No need for that," John said, striding into the kitchen, one hand outstretched. "Good morning, Marshall."

The marshall shook hands with him. "I hear that Indian squaw died on us, doc. Thought I'd come by for the body."

Tess winced at the lawman's disrespect for the deceased, but John didn't seem to notice.

"Sorry, Marshall, but her people collected her body awhile ago."

Marshall Long squinted one beady eye. "That outlaw brother of hers wasn't among them, was he?"

"Can't help you there. I'm afraid I don't know one from the other when it comes to Indians."

"He wasn't with them," Tess said, and the men seemed startled to discover that she was still in the room.

"Are you saying that you know this character, Tess?" John demanded.

"No, but I don't think he'd be stupid enough to come into town for his sister's body when everyone knows he's a wanted man."

The marshall chuckled, pulled aside his shirt collar, and scratched his ruddy neck. "I wouldn't bet on that, Miss Summar. Most Indians ain't that smart, and this one I'm after is plain loco. He's dangerous, and I'm warning everybody to be on the lookout for him. The sooner he's locked up, the better it will be for the whole town, if not for the whole territory."

"He's that bad, is he?" John asked, his brow wrinkling with worry.

"Yes, sir, he is. He not only shot his own sister, he's been stealing horses and robbin' folks of their cash and family heirlooms. He's a gunslinger, to boot. No tellin' how many men he's killed."

John glanced toward the hallway where tapping footsteps could be heard. "Please, Marshall Long," John said, lowering his voice, "let's not speak of this in front of my wife."

The marshall nodded, giving a wink. "Sure thing. I'll be on my way. Y'all take care." He ducked out the door just as Camilla breezed into the kitchen.

The scent of lilac trailed her as she swept past Tess and took her place at John's side. Her buttercup-colored dress hugged her curves and paid compliment to her fair complexion and light-blue eyes.

The scent of bubbling fat spun Tess around to the stove. She grabbed a potholder and lifted the skillet off the fire just in the nick of time.

"John, go ahead and pour the coffee and fetch the milk. Breakfast is ready." Facing the table again, she wasn't the least surprised to see that Camilla was seated and helping herself to the bowl of grits.

Lovely but useless, she thought, partly taking the blame for Camilla being treated like a queen instead of a small-town doctor's wife. After all, she allowed her sister-in-law to treat her like a servant.

Gazing out the window at the sun-dappled mountains, she wondered if Willow-Bends-Woman's brother was out there somewhere, dead or dying.

"I'm certainly glad to have that Indian riffraff out of the house," Camilla said.

"Me, too, dear," John agreed.

"Promise me you won't bring such people into our home again, Johnny. Why, I shudder just to think of it."

"I promise, dear heart. I promise."

Tess pressed her lips together, feeling as if her tongue had been cut out. She might as well be mute, she thought, for she often felt as if she had no voice in this house anymore.

"Tess, did you know that Marshall Long has a good-looking son? A *bachelor* son?"

Not this again, Tess moaned inwardly. John, the relentless matchmaker, had no idea of what constituted husband material. If a man was single and breathing, John tried to foist him on her.

Tess sat down and threw her brother a barbed glare. "I've met Red . . . and he has met me. End of discussion."

"You should be trying to catch a man's eye, little sister. You're past marrying age."

Tess stiffened. "I am not *elderly*, John. I'm younger than you."

"But I'm married," he pointed out needlessly.

"Which makes you no better or worse than me." Tess frowned. "Eat your breakfast."

"Tess, I'm only trying to look after you."

Her gaze strayed again to the window and the view of the purple white-capped mountains. Melancholy drifted over her like a silky shroud. Of course, she wanted marriage, but not to just anyone who would have her for a wife.

Her dreams were of a strapping, courageous man, as ruggedly beautiful as the mountains; a man who would look at her as if she were the only woman in the world, who would desire only her, who would want only her to have his healthy, strong children.

But it was a dream . . . only a dream. Was she too choosey? Her thoughts veered to the Blackfeet outlaw. Wonder if he's married . . . ?

Tess rolled her eyes in utter disgust—*My stars and gold bars!* Next thing she knew she'd be eyeing the WANTED posters in the marshall's office!

Chapter 2

❝Now, Mrs. Bishop, I want you to follow doctor's orders and take this medicine as I've directed." Tess set the dark-brown bottle on the bedside table of the elderly woman's bedroom. "That cold of yours has hung on all summer, and we must get rid of it before winter sets in. This elixir will do the trick, but only if you take it three times a day. Promise me now."

Lying in bed, a lacy cape around her shoulders, Mrs. Bishop patted Tess's hand. "I promise. My, you do look out for me, don't you, dear? It warms my heart."

"Every patient of John's is special to me," Tess asserted as she adjusted the woman's wool bed cap. "But you're extra special because you were Mother's best friend."

"That's right. Why, I remember the first day she and your father rode into town in their overland wagon. They'd journeyed all the way from Memphis, Tennessee. That was, let me think, a dozen or more years ago."

Tess nodded. "They came here in July of 1866. Father wanted to set up his doctoring practice here.

18

That was back when there were rumors of a railroad head going in."

Mrs. Bishop chuckled, then coughed, her eyes watering. "That's why we call it False Hope. Before that, it was Hope, Montana."

Tess laughed with sudden realization. "I'd forgotten it was called that when we arrived."

Mrs. Bishop nodded. "Weren't too many years after that the railroad decided to run their track in a different direction. Lots of folks packed up and moved, but your family stayed on, bless them."

"We're stubborn that way, I suppose. We Summars dig in our heels and set our jaws once we've made up our minds. The only time John left was to attend medical school. As for me, well . . ." Tess sighed, wishing she had clearer memories of her family's journey overland. It had been a big adventure for them, but her recollections were spotty. Mostly, she remembered eating around a campfire and sleeping in the wagon.

"As for you, what, dear?" Mrs. Bishop asked.

Tess shrugged, retrieving her dangling statement. "As for me, I never had an occasion to leave False Hope."

"Good, because I would miss you if you left. We need you here, dear." Mrs. Bishop's smile warmed Tess's heart.

It was good to be needed, she thought. And it was even better to be appreciated. Sometimes John took her for granted. Tess had spent many hours studying his medical books so she could assist him ably. He often praised her knowledge in private, but he diminished her contributions in public, always quick to point out that she had no formal training. Still, Tess believed in her heart that she had an aptitude for doctoring. Once or twice when her diagnosis had differed from John's, she'd been proven correct. Of course, John attributed this to "dumb luck."

Tess snapped shut the black bag and gave Mrs. Bishop's shoulder one last pat. "See you next week."

"Good-bye, and send John my regards." She left her brother's patient resting comfortably. Closing the front door behind her, she stood on the porch and slipped on her gloves, tied her bonnet. The house was situated outside of town on a three-acre plot, and Tess could see a dot that was the farmhouse of Mrs. Bishop's nearest neighbor.

The early-August sun crept steadily up, inching toward its zenith and charging the atmosphere. Bees droned and flies swarmed around chicken droppings. Tess noticed a ceramic jug sitting near the front door and decided to fill it with water for Mrs. Bishop. She placed her medicine bag in her buggy, then took the jug around back to the well. There were no more appointments today, and she thought she might visit an old friend. Selma Kinder was a few years older than Tess and lived with her husband and parents about a mile east of Mrs. Bishop's, on the road that also led to Tess's Aunt Mattie and Uncle Elmer's spread in Pleasant Valley.

Hoisting the bucket up from the well, Tess took a long drink of the cold water before pouring the rest into the clean jug she'd found on the front porch. She set the filled container inside the back door for Mrs. Bishop. Starting for the front of the house again, she nearly jumped out of her skin when a shadow fell across her and she found herself staring into the stark black eyes of an Indian. In the next instant, she recognized him.

"Brown Otter." Tess fanned her face with one

hand and laughed at her own bout of fright. "You startled me."

"You must come with me." Although his tone was forceful, he refused to meet her gaze, his acute shyness preventing him from fully confronting her.

"Where? Is someone hurt?"

"Storm-In-His-Eyes needs you."

"Storm . . ." Tess sucked in a quick breath. "Th-the outlaw? So, he's still alive?" She retreated a few steps, her initial relief tempered by her good sense. "I'm sorry, I can't. My brother might accompany you, if the marshall goes along to protect him, but I simply can't—"

"He is dying." His voice rang with alarm, and he spoke through tense lips. "He will not see our own medicine woman because he doesn't want to bring more trouble to our people. You must come."

Tess shook her head, feeling as if she had slipped into a penny novel. Modern civilization surrounded her, but the Indian in front of her defied it in his buckskin leggings, beaded vest, long braids, and slashes of rust-colored paint highlighting his round face.

"I'll get John."

"No." He closed a hand on her forearm. "You will use your medicine on my brother."

"You don't understand." Tess tried to remain calm, but his tight grip ate at her resolve. "I am not a doctor. I only assist my brother. What we should do is talk to him. Maybe I can make him understand—"

Brown Otter shook his head firmly, and in the next moment the world tipped upside down before Tess's eyes as she was resolutely picked up and flung over the Indian's shoulder.

"Storm must not die."

"Let go of me!" Tess struggled as he carried her

across the yard. Although he was short—her height, in fact—his physical strength was immense. She was ever so relieved when he set her on her feet again. Brushing wisps of dark gold hair from her eyes, Tess smoothed her dress into place and prepared to lambast the insolent Blackfeet. Before she could utter another word, however, he stuffed a rag into her mouth and blindfolded her with another. Tess's scream burned her throat, but emerged as nothing but a gurgling groan, stifled by the gag.

Again, she felt herself being lifted. She kicked and tried to land blows with her fists, but all she managed to do was twist her petticoats and skirt around her, further inhibiting her movements. She smelled horse sweat, felt the shifting of hide beneath her, and knew she sat astride a steed—*astride* as if she were a man!

The next minutes blurred as a myriad of emotions and impressions crisscrossed in Tess's brain. The horse settled into a gallop as she was whisked away, held in place by a beefy arm wrapped around her waist and the press of a hand on her right thigh. Besides the muffled thunder of hooves, Tess could hear the rattle of buggy wheels and realized that her horse and buggy were being towed, leaving no sign that she'd been abducted. She grew hot from panic and the intensifying summer sun. Her clothes stuck to her body, wrinkled and bunched. The Indian sitting behind her smelled of wood smoke and animal fat, as if he'd been near a cooking fire recently. She knew where he was taking her. Whether she wanted to or not, she was going to meet his outlaw cousin. Well, she wouldn't save the rascal's life. He couldn't make her do that. He could gag her, blindfold her, throw her upon his horse, and make off with—

Dear Lord! She'd been *kidnapped!* A heart-rattling shiver attacked her body, and tears stung the corners of her eyes behind the cloth.

"You will not be harmed," Brown Otter said, and Tess realized he must have sensed her sudden shock. "You will help my brother, and then I will let you go."

Such gratitude, she thought sarcastically, wishing she'd never laid eyes on Willow-Bends-Woman or, at the very least, kept her stupid promise to the girl. Oh, she'd landed herself in a mess this time. John would have fresh fodder for his lectures to her about how she was too headstrong, too impulsive. Providing she ever saw John again. Why should she believe this dangerous Indian? He cared nothing for her or he wouldn't have trussed her up and taken her against her will.

The discomfort of the galloping horse and her bondage began to worsen as the wild ride continued. Tess felt as if they'd traveled for hours, but time was as confusing as place with her sight stolen from her and her other senses dulled by fear. Her back began to ache and her leg muscles quivered as the unaccustomed seat on the pad saddle began to test her endurance. Little by little, her bonnet slipped off and her hair pins gave way as the warm breeze plucked and ruffled her tawny mane. A lump of fear and self-pity formed in her throat, but she stubbornly swallowed it.

She'd get out of this mess, she told herself. Her head ached with questions and plans of escape and scenes of struggle and doom. She thought of trying to fight Brown Otter while he attempted to control the horse, but she sensed he was a natural equestrian and any such battle would result in her tumbling from the mount and breaking her fool neck.

Sweat rolled between her breasts and down her

inner thighs, and her nerves began to fray. She couldn't recall ever being so miserable, so vulnerable.

Suddenly, the arm around her tightened as Brown Otter jerked on the reins. The horse slowed to a canter and then stopped. Tess whimpered against the cloth, now wet with her own saliva and sweat. The Indian slipped from the horse and dragged her down with him. He took her by the shoulders, turned her, then gave her a push. Tess grunted her aggravation, but he only pushed her again, making her walk ahead of him. His hand closed on her upper right arm, keeping her his hostage and also helping her traverse an uneven ground she could not see. She stumbled, cursing him with her mind and praying for an end to the ordeal. He placed his other hand on her head and pressed down, forcing her knees to bend. She crouched and walked into a cooler place. A cave? Red Deer Cave? From the echo and air flow, she guessed they'd reached a large inner chamber.

In swift succession the blindfold was removed, then the gag. Brown Otter called out something in Blackfeet to someone in the darkness beyond.

Tess glanced around, her eyes wide and searching but refusing to focus or recognize anything in the dimness. She wiped at them with the heels of her hands, feeling the grit left by dirt and trail dust. Finally her senses adjusted and she could see the smooth walls of the cave, the smooth rock under her feet, the sunlight falling through the opening behind them. Something touched her hand. She looked down to see that Brown Otter held out her medical bag to her.

"You will save his life," he whispered.

Tess sighed as Willow-Bends-Woman's words seemed to reverberate in the Blackfeet beside her.

"Why should I even try after being treated in such a fashion?" she whispered back, wondering why they were talking in hushed tones.

"Because you cannot watch death come and do nothing to stop it. I see this in you. I know this." He raised a hand and pointed ahead to the shadows. "He is there. I will light a torch for you to see by, but you must work quickly so we aren't discovered by our enemies."

"*Your* enemies," Tess corrected, giving an exaggerated sigh. "All right. Let's get this over with so I can return home."

She walked with Brown Otter to the back of the cave. She saw only shadows at first, but then the man in the corner moved into the light and Tess could make him out. She held her breath and stared; her heart sputtered and her mouth was suddenly as dry as chalk.

He was magnificent, this Indian outlaw. Sprawled on a pallet of brightly colored blankets, he wore only a breechclout and a necklace made of leather and silver. His bare chest was broad and gleaming like polished mahogany, and his stomach rippled with muscles. His long, ebony hair of uneven lengths hung past his broad shoulders. His eyes glittered in the darkness like stars, and his teeth flashed like lightning as he raised one fist. A wicked knife blade glinted, slicing through the air.

"Who are you?" he demanded, his voice deep and thundering.

Tess amazed herself by not cowering, not even flinching from this knife-wielding savage. She felt no fear, only fascination. He sat up, his back coming away from the rock wall, and showed his teeth again. White, straight teeth. Teeth bared in a warning snarl. A shiver, deliciously erotic, licked up her backbone.

The next words were in the Blackfeet tongue, guttural sounds and harsh syllables to Tess's ears. Brown Otter answered in the same language, and the Indian outlaw snarled again.

"Get out of here, white eyes, before I cut you!" He carved an S into the cool air, then tensed as if the exertion caused him pain.

Pain! He was injured, near death according to Brown Otter. Looking at him, all gnashing teeth and manly bellows, she'd clean forgotten that he was supposed to be her patient.

Tess forced her attention away from his gleaming teeth and glinting eyes to his body, bulging with muscle. A large square of blood-stained cloth covered one shoulder and half his chest. Rusty streaks ran from under the makeshift bandage. Tess sharpened her gaze and studied the face before her again. The eyes glimmered, but not so much from anger as from fever; the thin veneer of perspiration would probably feel hot to her touch. She would also probably feel a slight trembling running just beneath his skin, because he was sick—terribly sick. Despite his vicious wielding of the knife and the booming threat of his voice, he was in no condition to do battle with anyone, not even a defenseless doctor's assistant.

"Go, before I cut out your heart. One thing I don't need is another white woman trying to kill me or get me killed."

Tess gave a scoffing laugh. "This white woman isn't here because she wants to be, I assure you. Let's not make this any more difficult than it already is, shall we? Lie back and let me see to your wound. I can't promise anything because I'm—"

"I won't let any white eyes touch me," he said, his voice a dangerous growl. "White eyes' hands are unclean."

Tess arched a brow. "True, they are unclean because I've been led a merry chase this morning, thanks to your cousin here. I'd wash them if I could, but I see no basin in here."

"I can bring water," Brown Otter said, stepping forward. "I can bring whatever you need."

"I doubt that, but I will be in need of water at the very least."

The outlaw spoke again in Blackfeet to Brown Otter, and the two engaged in a heated argument.

"Please, won't you hush, both of you?" Tess interrupted, just as heatedly. "Stop snapping at each other and let me do my work. I have a life I'd like to get back to sometime today. You," she said, poking a finger into Brown Otter's forearm, "go get the water. And you—" She pointed the same finger at the snarling outlaw, though her courage wavered in the face of his menacing visage. She realized she could never browbeat such a man or scold him as if he were a child. Such tactics might work on her brother, but not on this dark stranger. "I am here to help you, at the request of your sister, I might add, and I wish you would—"

"My sister?" He straightened, winced, then squared his shoulders in an impressive display of male pride. "You knew my sister?"

"I was your sister's nurse. I was with her when she died." Tess's opinion of him softened when she observed the grief blanket his features and pull at the corners of his wide, full-lipped mouth. His reaction placed a new weapon in her diminished arsenal. "She made me promise to help you, if I could. If you refuse my aid, then you refuse to honor your sister's last wish."

He glanced away from her to mask his discomfit, and Tess knew she'd won this battle; but the war was far from over. After setting her bag near him, she began rolling up her sleeves. He sat back against the wall again—gingerly, Tess noted.

"You were shot in the back?"

"Yes."

"Is the bullet still in there?"

"Brown Otter got it out yesterday." He laid a long-fingered, brown hand above his heart. "It had lodged here. It had almost gone clean through."

"That's good." She didn't try to disguise her relief. With no bullet to remove, her task would be less complicated. "Are you stiff? Do you feel feverish? Has there been drainage? You're not still bleeding, are you?" She brushed a lock of hair from her face, realizing she must look as if she'd been in an all-day sack race.

"I am dying. The white man's bullet has poisoned me, just as his lies have poisoned my honor." He gritted his teeth and spoke through them. "But I will exact my revenge. I will restore my honor, my sister's honor, and my people's honor."

Not knowing how to respond to that, Tess knelt on the blankets near him just as Brown Otter returned with a canteen of water.

"Good, let me have that." She took it from him and set it against the wall within easy reach. "You said you could light a torch?"

"No light," the wounded Blackfeet ordered.

"I can't even see your injury, much less treat it in this black hole. Be reasonable." She glanced up at Brown Otter. "Please?"

Ignoring the other man's murderous glare, Brown Otter lit a torch and shoved it into a crevice in the wall. The sputtering flame threw golden light across Storm-In-His-Eyes, revealing to Tess just how he got his name.

His eyes were gray. A stormy, tempestuous gray.

She realized with a spurt of amazement that he must have white relatives in his family tree. How else could he have gotten those mesmerizing eyes?

"What are you staring at, white woman?"

Tess jerked her gaze from him and frowned. "Stop calling me that."

"It's what you are. You're ashamed of your white blood?"

"No, are you?"

He flinched, but not from the pain of his wounds. She'd struck a nerve. Narrowing his eyes to smoky slits, he burned her with his outrage. Tess shivered, a little scared, a lot fascinated. The power within his body reminded her of a panther's: deadly, but contained within a graceful form. She knew she shouldn't challenge him, shouldn't anger him, but she couldn't help herself. The deep growl of his voice and the silvery glints in his eyes made her pulses leap.

"Why don't you just turn me over to the marshall, Brown Otter? Once this white witch gets back to town, she's going to break her pretty neck running to him and spilling everything she knows."

"We will keep her then. We will keep her until you are far away from here."

Tess whirled around to Brown Otter. "You will not! I don't want to get involved in this trouble. I gave Willow-Bends-Woman my word that I'd help her brother, and I will do that. Besides, I couldn't turn him in because . . ." She glanced from beneath the veil of her lashes at Storm-In-His-Eyes. *Because you are like a dream. Because you are strange and beautiful. Because you are a thunderstorm and I am a desert.*

She swallowed the naked confession, shocked that she would even think such things about an outlaw. What was wrong with her? She knelt beside him on the many-colored blankets and something bit into her knees. Inching back, she spotted a string of red and black beads. She picked them up, examined their craftsmanship for a few moments, and set them on top of her medicine bag. Gathering in a deep breath to calm her fluttering nerves, she prepared herself for her first obstacle. She'd have to touch him—*wanted* to touch him— and that, in itself, alarmed her. "All right. Let me do what I can for you."

He leaned away from her, his expression wary, his eyes cold. Tess lifted her lashes, meeting his gaze with confidence, she hoped. His brows met slowly as if he found her puzzling. Finally he sat straight again.

"Be quick."

"I shall be thorough," she informed him archly as she began to remove the bandage. His skin was hot, but only moist. She worried, realizing his fever was climbing, peaking. He was hard and his skin was scarred from many wounds. A warrior, she thought, and a peculiar spiraling sensation erupted in her stomach.

"There should be a pint of whiskey in my medicine bag, Brown Otter. Please uncork it and hand it to Storm-In-His-Eyes."

The patient stirred. "Whiskey, eh? Give it over, my brother." A hint of a smile lightened his gray eyes as he took the tin flask from his cousin and swallowed some of the strong brew. His breath whistled past his lips, and he screwed up one eye in a wince of appreciation. "That's *good* medicine." Raising the bottle in a toast, he issued a nod. "I will let you call me Storm, white woman. It was my name among the pale faces when I lived with them."

Her anger flared briefly, lit by his use of denigrating names, which she knew he wielded like his knife to keep her away from him. Tess yanked at the material that was stuck to his wound with dried blood. He jerked and uttered what was probably a foul curse in his own tongue. Tess smiled with saucy retribution. "And you, brown man, can call me Miss Summar."

Chapter 3

The white medicine woman had made him swallow some bitter liquid along with half the pint of whiskey, so it was no wonder that his vision blurred around the edges and lead weighted his limbs, his eyelids, his thoughts. Storm tested his shoulder and found that his wound ached but fire no longer shot down his body and burst in his chest with every infinitesimal movement. The woman was talking with Brown Otter in hushed tones, their words buzzing in his mind like pesky flies, too quick to grasp.

Through a squint he observed the woman. Her blue gingham bonnet hung against her back, held around her neck by knotted ribbons. Her skirt and blouse were wrinkled and smudged with dirt. Animated by what she was saying, she gestured expressively, her delicate, white hands fluttering like wings in the semi-darkness. The torch had been extinguished, leaving only daylight to illuminate the pocket where Storm had spread his blankets to mourn his sister and plot his revenge.

That fateful day ballooned in his mind again. He felt the bullet tear through his flesh and nearly unseat him. He'd hung on and had heard the marshall's gun spit fire again. Looking back, he'd seen the marshall, but not Willow.

Willow—his beautiful young sister. He'd thought she'd run away, but when Brown Otter had found him in the cave, Storm had seen the tragedy on his brother's face and had felt the deadening of his own cold heart. If he could beat the odds and this poison attacking his body, he would seek his revenge on the lawman. He would put the bastard in his grave and then spit upon it.

The woman moved her head and the meager light caressed her tawny hair, picking out strands of bright gold and warm ginger. He remembered her changeable eyes—blue one moment, green the next. She was most beautiful, and she possessed two things he found nearly irresistible in females— pluck and freckles.

She glanced at him with finely shaped eyebrows pulled into a V and a full mouth forming a moue. Pretty, she was. Yes, pretty with her dark-gold hair, pouting lips, and the splash of dots across her nose and rosy cheeks. The Blackfeet women had no freckles. He'd seen the sun spots only on the whites, like this one. This medicine woman intrigued him. She stood straight and proud, talked sternly to him as if she had no fear even when he growled and snapped at her. Her hands had been sublime upon his skin, her touch a tonic, a revelation. She had dealt with his wound swiftly, certainly; her expression revealed nothing to him except that she was used to viewing torn, rotting flesh.

But he wished she hadn't taken the flask away. He would like to drink the firewater until he passed out, never to awaken to the pain again. He would like to open his eyes and see his sister before him, holding out her arms, smiling brightly in eternal forgiveness. But that was a selfish dream, he knew. He wanted this vision to alleviate the guilt he carried in his heart. Storm shut his eyes and rolled his head from side to side against the rock wall. Willow, Willow, why didn't you stay away? Why did you tag along after your big brother?

. . . go part of the way back with me. I'll try to return in a few days.

Storm sharpened his senses, realizing that the woman was preparing to leave. "She can't go," he managed, his voice sounding hollow, foreign. Had he spoken in his native tongue or English?

"Don't you fret," the woman said, leaning down so that her eyes were level with his. "I'll be back to see about you."

Fret? He was not a baby. He was a man. Foolish woman.

Her face swam before him like a moon in a gray sky. He used all his strength to wrap his fingers around her narrow wrist. Her skin felt cold—or was he hot? The fever made his thoughts scatter like embers. "You will stay," he said, forcing each word out, then looking toward Brown Otter. "She'll bring the law on us, my brother."

"No, I won't. You have my word." She tried to wrench free of him, but he wouldn't let go. "I must get back to False Hope before I'm missed."

"Can't trust her," Storm insisted, but Brown Otter stepped into view and shook his head.

"We must trust her, brother," he said in Blackfeet. "I believe her when she says she will not talk of this. She says she will return with more medicine to give you back your strength, your life."

Storm released her with a burst of frustration. The fool! Believing a white eyes! What choice did he have? He was too weak to fight or argue. Let her go and tell the lawman where to find him. He'd be ready for that weasel with a star. A bullet or knife in the heart is what the marshall would get if he came snooping around Red Deer Cave.

The woman cradled his chin in her hands and dribbled cool water over his lips. He drank, his throat as raw as freshly butchered meat, his body blazing, inside and out. She let him drink his fill, then wet her fingers and smoothed them across his brow. Her touch held magic in it.

"Go then, *AnadaAki*," he murmured, falling to his side to slumber. "Leave me."

Tess looked at his scarred, muscled body, and her heart constricted in her chest. Would she be able to save his life? Would the medicine she'd given him keep him alive until she could return?

"What did he call me?" she asked.

Brown Otter refused to meet her eyes. "*AnadaAki*." He seemed uncomfortable and shuffled his feet as a shy smile lingered on his mouth. "It means, pretty woman."

Tess felt her skin flame from her throat to her hairline, followed quickly by intense pleasure. So, he found her pretty, did he, this raging panther of a man? She regarded him again; the white scar under his ribs testifying to a knife fight, another jagged line on his thigh making Tess wonder if a spear or a dirk had made it. His legs were long and powerfully sculpted, and she knew from experience that he possessed great strength. Even in his weakened state, he could clutch her so tightly she couldn't shake him off.

But he had another strength as well. He could hold her fast with a look, a steady stare and the sheer power of his spirit. He shifted again, revealing his other leg more fully to her gaze. A red gash crossed his thigh. Tess gasped, touching the new wound.

"What's this? When . . . ?"

"He did it to himself," Brown Otter explained. "It is a custom with our people. The wound is to show his grief over his sister. It is also why his hair is unbraided."

Tess nodded, thinking of her own custom of wearing black following a death in the family. She dabbed at the gash with a wet rag, cleansing it as best she could.

"We should go now," Brown Otter said.

"Yes." Tess turned her back on the fascination of Storm-In-His-Eyes. She pulled her bonnet onto her head and tied a bow under her chin. "You'll remember to give him plenty of water? And sponge him off every chance you get. His fever must be broken."

Brown Otter nodded. "When will you return?"

"Tomorrow. Day after tomorrow at the latest. I'll have to make up something John won't question. I don't usually disappear for hours on end, you know." She flapped a hand, dismissing her own petty problems. "I'll think of something. He's a man, so he can't be that hard to fool." She laughed at her little joke, then realized her audience probably wouldn't appreciate it. However, she needn't worry, she thought, watching Brown Otter stride to the front of the cave and hearing Storm's soft snores behind her.

Tess scrambled down the steep incline, the going much rougher without Brown Otter to steady her. Once she reached level ground, she looked back to find that the cave wasn't visible. Locating the overhang, she realized that at this distance it didn't appear to harbor a cave. Shadows and fallen boulders tricked the eye into believing that the overhang didn't jut out far and didn't form a ceiling for a deep crevasse in the mountainside.

She realized hours had expired and that it was much later than she'd thought. Brown Otter appeared, leading her horse and buggy and his own pony from a copse of aspen. He helped her climb into the buggy, then sprang onto his prancing pony with its braided mane and tail. He led the way across the rough terrain until they reached a road Tess recognized. She waved at him after guiding the buggy horse onto the trail. Brown Otter emitted a high yipping sound, reined his pony around, and set off for the mountain ranges again.

It was another hour before Tess entered False Hope and urged the horse and buggy toward the familiar white-framed house where a signpost by the front gate proclaimed: JOHN T. SUMMAR, DOCTOR OF MEDICINE.

Tess drove the buggy to the side yard. Slipping one hand into her medicine bag, she removed the string of red and black beads she'd taken from the cave when Brown Otter wasn't looking. She'd wanted something tangible from this adventure, something to remind her of the Indian outlaw, so she'd sneaked the beads into the bag. The irregularly shaped balls, strung on a thin leather strip, spilled over her fingers. A silver arrowhead hung in the center. Smiling, she pushed the necklace into the pocket purse tied around her waist. Her little secret, she thought, wishing it was already tomorrow and she was returning to her patient.

Her patient.

Glancing up at the blue sky, she thought of his stormy eyes and irascible disposition. He was too stubborn to die, she told herself, but she knew that if she didn't get some strong medicine in him soon, he wouldn't survive.

"Tess." John rounded the corner of the house, his face set in a scowl, his arms pumping, his fists clenched. Aggravation burst from him. "Just where the devil have you been?"

"Visiting," she said, thinking it wasn't entirely a lie. "And don't yell at me as if I'm a recalcitrant child."

"You could have told me you'd be gone all day. I've been worried."

"Why? I'm a grown woman, John. I don't need looking after."

"Don't be ridiculous, Tess. You're a woman alone without even a weapon to defend yourself. You were supposed to see one patient this morning and then return home." John helped her from the buggy, but his attention was on the horse. "Cameo is lathered. Where have you been with her?" He swept her up and down with a narrowed gaze. "Look at you. You're dirty and your hair is all—"

"I've been here, there, and everywhere," she rejoined, moving quickly away from him and his persistent questions. "I'll throw something together for dinner. I suppose you're hungry and that's why you're so cross."

"I *am* hungry, but I want an answer. Where in heaven's name have you been all—"

Tess went into the house and closed the door on the rest of his tirade. She glanced at the examination room, thinking of the cabinets of medicine inside, but restrained herself. She'd sneak in late tonight when John and Camilla were fast asleep. If she was careful, John would never suspect a thing. He left the replenishing of the medical supplies to her and rarely paid any attention to them.

Two days later, Tess knelt beside Storm's fevered body and forced medicine down his throat. Brown

Otter held him fast. Even ravaged by fever and pain, Storm fought valiantly, thrashing at Brown Otter, cursing, snarling like the wounded, dazed animal he'd become. He grabbed a sleeve of Brown Otter's leather shirt and ripped it clean away.

"He's much, much worse," Tess said, sitting back and watching Storm's heaving chest, hearing his laboring breaths. She touched his fiery brow.

"I do what I can," Brown Otter said, examining his own ruined shirt. "He is a bull of a man. Yesterday when I came, he was wandering in here, stumbling around, out of his mind. He had thrown aside the bandages and he was bleeding again."

"Yes, I noticed you'd applied new dressings." She backhanded a stray lock of hair from her eyes. "The marshall had a posse out yesterday looking for him."

Brown Otter nodded, a frown darkening his face. "They came to my people's camp and searched. They brought bad spirits with them, and we all had to cleanse our bodies and our lodges after they left. We are fasting and dancing as the holy ones guide us. Maybe I have brought the bad spirits with me to this cave."

"A poison caused by the bullet is what is attacking your cousin," Tess said, trying to describe Storm's predicament in a way Brown Otter could understand. "If I could stay with him and nurse him night and day . . ." She wondered how she could leave home without arousing suspicion. What if she told John she would be staying with their uncle and aunt in Pleasant Valley? He wouldn't raise an eyebrow at that, and he wouldn't have occasion to check out her story.

Storm moaned and flung out an arm, which landed heavily in her lap. As if seeking her comfort, her essence, he rolled onto his stomach and across her thighs. He wrapped his arms around her waist and buried his face in her skirts. Glancing at Brown Otter, Tess shrugged helplessly before giving in to her desire to stroke Storm's back. Her fingertips tingled, sensitive to the flame burning under his skin. He murmured something in his native tongue and snuggled closer, his arms like steel bands around her, his mouth moving against her stomach, the top of his head nudging the undersides of her breasts. She thought she might die.

"Can you stay with him?" Brown Otter asked. "Can you stop the fever?"

"I don't know. . . . " She ran her fingers through Storm's inky hair and spread the ends of it across his shoulders. He needed her. Isn't that what she wanted? To be needed by a patient she could nurse back to life? He was so helpless in her arms—yet so powerful, so strong. She wanted to make him well again. She wanted to see him standing straight and tall, and she wanted to know him better. Who was he? Where had he gotten those gray eyes? How long had he lived among white people, and why had he returned to the Blackfeet?

"Yes," she said, her tone unrelenting. "I'll stay. But first I have to go back to town and cook up a reason for my absence. You stay here with him. I'll return tomorrow morning loaded with medicine and all the know-how I can muster."

She knew she should wriggle from Storm's embrace, but she didn't. She imagined herself washing his hair, combing it, twining feathers and beads among the straight black strands. This beautiful, brave warrior's life was in her hands, and she was scared to death she might fail him.

Maybe she should speak to John, tell him the truth and beg him to save Storm's life, yet not give him over to the marshall. But she knew John would never agree. Just last night he had told her of the posse and how he hoped they were successful in capturing Storm-In-His-Eyes. No, he would never help her. She must depend only on herself. She must believe in herself.

Reluctantly, she dislodged herself from Storm's tenacious hold and rose unsteadily to her feet. "He needs plenty of water, remember," she advised Brown Otter. "And don't let him move around. Keep him still. I'll be back in the morning."

Brown Otter sat beside his fallen cousin and soaked a rag with water. He ran the cloth over Storm's face and chest. "The spirits are near, aren't they? I will fight them, if they come for him."

His fierce promise touched her. "You do that. Keep them away until I can come back and help you." Tess hurried from the cave, her mind in a whirl.

Before she saw the buildings of False Hope again, she had rehearsed her lies thoroughly and was prepared to give the greatest performance of her life.

Luckily John hadn't returned from his home visits. Avoiding Camilla, Tess went to the kitchen and prepared a supper of pork roast, boiled potatoes and carrots, oil and vinegar slaw, and peach cobbler. She had finished setting the table and was removing a sheet of yeast rolls from the oven when John came in the back door.

"What are you up to?" he asked, admiring the banquet on the table.

"Just fixing supper," Tess said, flashing him a smile. "Wash up and fetch your wife."

John gave her a peck on the cheek. "You've outdone yourself, Tess. Care to tell me what's inspired you?"

"I thought I'd give you a good last meal."

"Last meal?"

"I'm going to visit Uncle Elmer and Aunt Mattie for a few days. You'll have to muddle through without me." She straightened his shirt collar and sensed he was getting ready to argue, so she took a different tack. "You won't mind being without me underfoot for about a week. I'd say it's about time you and your bride were alone together in this house."

John closed his mouth and gave her a considering look. His eyes twinkled with the possibilities. "And how are you planning on getting to Pleasant Valley? Surely, you don't think you're going there alone."

"No. Selma and her family are heading that way. We'll travel together. When they come back next week, I'll meet up with them again." This, of course, was her biggest lie, and she prayed she wouldn't give herself away. Afraid he might read something in her face, she turned and busied herself at the table.

"Where are they headed? I didn't know the Kinders were acquainted with—"

"John, I thought I heard you," Camilla said, coming into the kitchen and offering up her lips to him for a tender kiss. She sniffed and directed her attention to the supper. "My, my! Doesn't this beat all? Why, I do believe Tess has been as busy as a bee in here."

"She's fattening us up so we won't starve while she's gone."

"Gone?" Camilla asked, looking from John to Tess.

"I'm going to visit Uncle Elmer and Aunt Mattie for a few days. I need to get away from town. I so love the country. And you and John can have the house all to yourselves. Won't that be nice?"

For an instant, Tess thought she had under-estimated her sister-in-law. Would she object? Perhaps she dreaded having to cook . . .

"You can try out the dining room that opened in the hotel," Tess added quickly. "It's very posh, I hear."

Camilla's face lit up. "What fun! I can buy a new dress . . . and there's that church social at the end of the week, John. Oh, and this Sunday is the pie social at the church. Tess can bake one for us to take before she leaves. Her mincemeat ought to put everyone else's to shame."

Laughing, John gathered Camilla close and swung her around. "Anything you want, my darling."

Tess felt giddy, light-headed at having accomplished such a feat. Now if she could just as easily stuff a medicine bag full of bandages and other necessities without John noticing. Oh, well, if he caught her she'd tell him she wanted to be ready for anything on her trip to the valley. If he didn't believe her then she'd . . . she'd throw a temper tantrum and make him wish he'd never opened his mouth.

Nothing was going to keep her from Storm. Her place was with him until she was sure he could survive without her.

A telltale tremble raced around her heart as she recalled how he'd snuggled into her lap, seeking her stroking hands and whispered words. When John said grace, Tess added her own silent prayer for a certain Blackfeet outlaw.

Chapter 4

Brown Otter stood at the mouth of the cave when Tess arrived the next day. She knew by his gaunt expression that Storm-In-His-Eyes was worse.

"Has he been ranting again?" she asked, hitching up her skirts to step over rock and pebbles as she climbed. When the Indian offered his hand, she let him pull her up the rest of the way.

"He does not move. Not even to open his eyes."

"Have you been giving him water?"

"He will not drink."

She gritted her teeth to keep from yelling at him. He wasn't trained in caregiving, she reminded herself. He couldn't be expected to know how to handle a patient. Instead she pointed to the area where she'd tied up her old mare below them.

"Is there a place to hide Cameo?"

He looked confused until he spotted the horse, then he nodded. "I will tether her with mine in the hiding place I use."

Tess went into the cave, moving slowly to allow her eyes to adjust to the changing light. She carried her black bag, a satchel, and a roll of bedding. The snarling, spirited creature she had left yesterday was a motionless heap against the wall. Blankets lay around him, but none on him. His skin was dry and dull. His hair looked lifeless as well, lying in black streaks across his shoulders and down his back.

Gasping in dismay, Tess dropped to her knees beside him and swiftly removed her gloves. She automatically reached for the rag and shallow bowl of water nearby. She bathed his face, arms, chest, skirting around the dressings, noting they were clean, proof that Brown Otter had followed some of her instructions. Storm's breathing was fast and shallow, his skin dry and hot. Tess tore off her bonnet and flung it aside. Grabbing up the canteen, she uncapped it and slipped one hand under Storm's head to lift it. His lips were tense, pale, cracked. She pushed two fingers between them and forced his mouth open, then poured a small amount of water onto his tongue. He sputtered, but drank.

"No . . . no," he muttered.

"Yes . . . yes," she replied, forcing him to drink more and then even more of the tepid water. He was burning with fever and listless. The weakness bothered her more than anything because she knew his spirit to be gigantic and his strength, impressive. He lay inert, only his chest heaving with each rapid breath.

She traced the scars on his body with her fingertips. Aside from his recent injuries, including the one he'd given himself to demonstrate his grief over his sister's death, she counted fourteen old wounds. The ones on his chest were the worst, puckered and irregularly shaped.

Her brave warrior. She yanked hard on her emotions, warning herself that this man spared no fondness for white women and that she shouldn't get all dreamy about him.

When Brown Otter returned, she instructed him to light the torch and hold it close while she examined Storm's wound. The infection had claimed some of the flesh around the hole in Storm's back.

"I'm going to cut away that dead tissue," she announced. "Hand me my doctor's bag, please, and hold the light steady."

She removed a leather wallet and opened it to reveal an assortment of instruments from which she selected a scalpel. With Brown Otter watching her every move from over her shoulder, she cut away the decayed skin to give the healthy tissue a chance to reproduce, all the while conscious of the man she worked on, watching for any sign of pain. But there was none, and that troubled her. If he had flinched, she would have felt better, but he didn't move an eyelash.

After cleaning the wound thoroughly, she applied fresh bandages she'd soaked in a salt solution and then checked on the chest wound Brown Otter had made to remove the bullet. It showed signs of healing. She cleaned it, too, and dressed the area. When she'd finished, Storm's upper body was almost completely swaddled in white cotton gauze.

She slipped a hand under his head and brought him closer until his head was in her lap. When she tried to get more water into his mouth, he roused and struggled away from her. Determined, Tess grabbed him by the chin, used her fingers to pry apart his lips, and poured the water into his mouth. He swallowed. Brown Otter made a sound of wonder.

"He tried to bite my fingers off when I did that."

"He probably knows that if he bites me, I'll bite him back," she teased, pushing midnight hair off

Storm's forehead. At least he still had some fight left in him, she thought. That was a good sign. "He needs water and lots of it, Brown Otter, or he will surely waste away." Glancing toward him, she caught Brown Otter looking at her provisions. "I brought my bedroll, medical supplies, some clothing, and a few odds and ends. I didn't know what to pack in the way of food, other than some dried rice and beans, coffee, and a few pieces of fruit."

"I will bring you fresh meat, already cooked, and I will keep the water buckets full." He squatted beside her, his face full of worry as he looked at his cousin. "I thought he would die before you returned."

"I'm here now." She stroked a hand down Storm's dry, stubble-roughened cheek. His fringe of black lashes fluttered slightly, but he didn't open his eyes.

"How long can you stay?" Brown Otter asked.

"A week or two, give or take a few days. I told my brother I was off to visit relatives in the valley."

"I must return to my people, but I'll be back."

She nodded. "I'll be fine here with him." In truth, she wanted to be alone with him so that she could touch him, care for him without someone else watching her every move.

"If the spirits come for him while I am away—"

"Let's not talk of that," she said, quick to cut him off, but not before her heart froze for a moment at the thought of Storm dying in her arms.

"No, we must." He stood and went to the cave opening, then motioned for her to follow.

Reluctant to leave Storm, Tess heaved a sigh and carefully let Storm's head rest on her bedroll. She joined Brown Otter outside and he pointed straight ahead.

"Can you see the forked tree?"

She shook her head and shaded her eyes with one hand. "No. Which one?"

"Stand up on this rock and look where I point." He waited for her to obey. "Do you see the forked tree in the distance? The one on the rise of land? Straight ahead."

She located it. "Yes, yes, I see it. It's a huge, old thing." The tree was leafless and looked to be dead.

"It is easy to climb. If he is taken from this world, you will tie this to a high limb. I can see this tree from a hill near our camp. I will look every day." He pushed a red bandanna into her hand.

Tess stared at the crimson square of cloth and nodded. "Very well. What about my horse?"

"I will take her with me. You can't care for her out here. I'll bring her back when it's time for you to go."

She didn't like the idea of being without ready transportation, but she could appreciate the wisdom in Brown Otter's plan. She couldn't tie up poor Cameo where anything could get at her. Yes, Brown Otter should take the eighteen-year-old mare with him, even though that would leave her virtually stranded.

Tess sighed and stepped down from the rock. "Once your cousin recovers, I think he'd better stay low. The marshall will surely put him in jail or hang him if he tracks him down."

"The marshall will be the one who should lay low," Brown Otter assured her. "Once he is well again, Storm will not rest until the marshall is dead."

"Can't you talk sense into him? If he kills a law officer, he'll be in bigger trouble than ever."

"I was told the other day that the lawman says I ride with Storm-In-His-Eyes and I also steal horses. He says he saw me and Storm riding away from a ranch where horses were stolen and money was taken from white people."

She tried to read his expression, but couldn't. "All of this isn't true?"

His dark gaze flashed to hers and fury blazed in them. "I want no money from the whites. I want nothing they have. They bring suffering to my people. Their soldiers lie, telling us we have no rights to this land and we can no longer live here."

She'd heard of worthless treaties and stories of horrific battles where scores of whites and Indians were slaughtered. The wars had fueled distrust and confusion. Even John had changed his mind since the wars and had begun to see all Indians as enemies, something less than human. Appalling, since she and her brother had been raised in a household where everyone was treated with respect. They'd never even owned slaves because her parents had found the practice barbaric.

"I must get back to him," she said, emerging from her reverie. As she moved toward the opening, her attention was captured by a streak of color on the rock wall. She paused to admire the drawings of elk, buffalo, figures of men, fires, lightning bolts, and a herd of red deer . . . *ah, Red Deer Cave.*

"Who did these?"

"Our ancient ones," Brown Otter answered. "It is a place that was once holy, we believe, but white men spoiled it during the big war."

"How did they . . . spoil it?"

He ran his fingers over the markings. "The magic . . . the holiness left. The white men chased it away. They were soldiers who had run from their battles. They died in here. Some of my people found their bodies and buried them, but the holy ones said the place was no longer pure. No one comes here anymore."

"No one except wounded outlaws," she added with a quick smile. "That's what he is to my people, you know. An outlaw. The marshall says he not only shot and killed his sister, but he also has killed many others in gun battles."

Brown Otter shook his head vigorously. "He lies. We steal no horses, no money, nothing. And my brother would turn a gun on himself before he would harm his own family."

She believed him. She *wanted* to believe him. "You said he's come back to the Blackfeet. Where had he been?"

Brown Otter gestured to indicate a long distance. "He went on journeys because he wanted to live among the whites, but he came back and was happy until the trouble in town."

"What trouble? You mean when his sister was shot?"

"Before when he and a white man faced off. Storm-In-His-Eyes shot the man dead. The man wore a star."

"*He's* the gunslinger who shot Marshall Long's deputy last winter? He's been back that long? I'm surprised I didn't see him around town."

"He stays with the Blackfeet, but he's been wearing white men's clothes. The spirits have guided him back to the heart of the Blood now. I feel this in him. He will forever be a Blood and shed all white ways."

"I heard about that gunfight with Jake Wilhite. Everyone said it was a fair gunfight, but Marshall Long was livid when his deputy died." She kicked at a pebble, wondering about Storm and his divided life, living with the Blackfeet but dressing like a white man. Obviously he was a man torn between two worlds, no matter what Brown Otter believed or wanted her to believe. "Is Storm's mother or father white?"

"No. Both were Blackfeet."

Were. So they were dead. "But he has white blood . . . his eyes and—"

"That happened long ago. He is a Blood." Brown Otter's expression and tone warned her not to argue.

She heard a shuffling and a soft groan deeper in the cave and jerked to attention. "Sounds like he's thrashing about again. I'd better go check." She turned and went toward her patient, the same man folks in town claimed had a lightning quick draw and had shown not an ounce of remorse when he'd killed the marshall's best deputy. But the same gossips had admitted that the deputy had been a fool to bully the gunslinger and insist he meet him outside the saloon for a shooting match.

The story floating around town was that Jake Wilhite had coveted the gunfighter's pearl-and-silver-handled six-shooters. Wilhite had offered to buy them, but they weren't for sale. The gunfighter had said the only way anyone would get the guns was when he was dead. The deputy had said he would be more than willing to hasten him to his grave and take the guns from him. Thus, another brutal, meaningless gun brawl had commenced.

Standing beside the tumble of blankets and the sprawl of brown limbs, Tess stared at her patient for a few moments, transfixed by his manly beauty. Brown Otter moved to tuck the blankets around Storm, but Tess stopped him.

"But he will get cold."

"No. Until his fever breaks, he needs to be uncovered." She uncapped the canteen to give Storm another drink, but it was almost empty.

"I will fetch fresh water." Brown Otter took the

canteen from her, then picked up the two wooden buckets and went outside to fill them at the nearest water source.

Tess ran a wet rag over Storm's face, neck, and arms, admiring his high cheekbones and boldly masculine nose. She liked his hands, too. Even with their nicks and scars, they were beautiful. She placed one palm flat against his, and her hand looked small, white, delicate. Suddenly his fingers flexed and curled as he threaded them between hers and squeezed gently. Startled, her gaze flew to his face and she half-expected to find him staring at her. But his eyes were closed, his features relaxed in a fever-induced sleep. His fingers loosened their hold, and his hand fell back to the blankets.

Tess released her breath and shook off the shimmer of excitement dancing inside her. He hadn't even been aware of his actions, she chided herself. It was a reflex, pure and simple. A reaction triggered by the deep recesses of his mind. *He doesn't know it's you.*

Looking at him, she tried to imagine him in a pair of trousers, white shirt, vest, boots, and a hat, with a gun belt strapped recklessly around his lean hips. But the image refused to take shape in her mind. She liked him as he was now—with only a loincloth and beads for decoration.

Beads. Tess reached into the satchel and located the necklace she'd taken before. Her private little treasure, she thought, thinking how the touch of them had brought her a sense of purpose when she'd needed it. Whenever she'd faltered or doubted her decision to help Storm and Brown Otter, she'd fingered the beads as if they were a rosary and had found the self-confidence she'd needed.

Now she lay them on top of Storm's sheet-draped chest and sent up a prayer for his well-being.

Brown Otter returned with the water and a parfleche full of unleavened bread, dried buffalo strips, and wild berries. Tess examined one of the berries.

"What are these?" she asked.

"We call them saskatoons."

"They look like serviceberries."

"I have heard that name, too."

She popped one into her mouth and smiled. "Delicious. Thank you, Brown Otter. You've left us with good provisions. When you return, I hope you will find your cousin—er, brother—much improved."

"He *is* my cousin," he assured her.

"Yes, but you told me that the Blackfeet—"

"Among our people, we are brothers," he finished for her. His gaze flickered to Storm and his expression was a mixture of worry and hope. "Why do you help him?"

The question gave her pause, then she realized his curiosity was sensible. He couldn't know her circumstances, her desire to prove herself. "I promised Willow-Bends-Woman I would help her brother and . . ." She smiled before giving up the real reason. "The healer in me won't allow me to turn my back on him, and it seems this is my destiny, my fate. My heart tells me to do what I can for him."

Brown Otter turned away from her, suddenly reticent again. He cleared his throat, glanced at her, and raised a hand in a solemn farewell. "I am beholden to you." Then he strode from the cave, his leather-encased feet nearly silent, his stocky body as agile as a mountain goat's.

Tess listened until she could no longer hear his

soft tread or the scattering of pebbles or the startled calls of birds. She listened until there was nothing to hear but the sigh of a breeze and the beating of her own heart. She listened until she heard loneliness all around her.

Self-doubt crept up on tiny feet. Was she too prideful in thinking she could heal this man by herself? If he died, could she live with the guilt that she knew would consume her?

Closing her eyes, she reminded herself that she had little choice in the matter. She had to trust her know-how and quit allowing her self-confidence to wane. She had assisted John in treating gunshot wounds and high fevers for years. She could do this—all by herself.

Armed with her own resiliency and intelligence, she set to arranging an efficient sickroom. She unpacked, spread her bedroll next to Storm, and set out her medicinal aids, then she prepared something to eat. She anticipated a sleepless night spent fighting the fever that had laid claim to her patient.

Her patient.

Wicked pleasure coursed through her. If John had even an inkling of what she was doing, he'd bust a gut.

At daybreak, Storm dreamed. . . . He was staked outside, spread-eagle, his ankles and wrists bound by leather thongs to pegs driven deeply into the hard earth. Naked, he stared up at the bright disk of the sun, which was baking his skin and drying his mouth. He could feel the sweat running in rivulets down his thighs, his arms, his stomach, and ribs. Why was he here? What had he done to deserve this torture? He thought of Willow-Bends-Woman. Perhaps this was his punishment for coming back to his people and bringing trouble.

White blood flowed in him and the mixture was bad. He should have stayed true to his people's ways and not sought out the white eyes, lived among them, taken their money. They had tainted him and he had brought the sickness with him to infect those he called the Blood, the Blackfeet.

He heard a rustling of wings. The death birds had come to pick his flesh. A cool shadow fell across him, shielding him from the relentless heat of the sun. He squinted and a vision of a milky white face swam before him. Ah, it was the white woman. *AnadaAki*. Her blue-green eyes were cool pools, and he wanted to dive in. She appeared to him as a spirit—or as the whites say, an angel. She moved her hands over his wrists and ankles, and his bonds became like water and rolled off his skin to disappear in the sand.

Moving back from him, she stood in a green place with trees and shade and sparkling water. She motioned for him to rise and come to her.

He rose effortlessly, no longer thirsty or in pain or blistered from the sun. Strength flowed into his limbs, and he walked to the green place where a breeze combed through his wet hair and cooled his brow. Her hands floated before him, long-fingered and delicate, and then framed his face. They felt like clouds, light and airy. Her lips beckoned, her beauty enticed. She moved away from him and he followed, eager to hold her, to kiss her. Her mouth was yearning and soft beneath his, as sweet as a newly opened flower. Intense wanting consumed him like a fever, and he felt her body yield to his. . . .

Nice dream. So real. So—

Tess awakened with a start, realizing that her dream had somehow become reality. Masculine lips moved insistently against hers. Tess stared at

Storm's blurred features. Was he crazy? She pushed at his uninjured shoulder and he lifted his mouth from hers, murmuring strange words as he nuzzled her jawline and then settled his lips against the curve of her neck.

Shivers of awareness skittered down her arms and across her breasts. His mouth osculated against her skin and she closed her eyes and told herself that if she were a decent woman she would push him away this instant. But decency seemed a trivial concern while his hands closed upon her shoulders and one of his hard thighs separated hers.

Oh . . . oh . . . his mouth was doing wondrous things. And the tip of his tongue, teasing her flesh, made her breathless with delight. His large hands moved down her arms and back up. He shifted until his lower body rested intimately upon her, so intimately she could feel his manhood stirring, growing firm, thickening even as her blood thickened and her nipples firmed and her own desire stirred to life.

His body was a revelation. She skimmed her palms across his warm back. She thought to push him away, then it seemed more sensible to embrace him. Either way, she might hurt him, anger his tender wounds. *Embrace him!* What was she thinking? He was her patient and clearly out of his head with fever. *Push him away. Force him to come to his senses. Tend his wounds.*

The medical wisdom buzzed like a gnat in her ear, and she waved it aside to concentrate on the feathery sweep of his lips across her cheek. His mouth found hers, enveloped hers, and his tongue flirted lightly and then lavishly until her lips were seared, swollen and throbbing. She parted them and touched the tip of her tongue to his. He groaned and deepened his kiss, sucking gently, seeming to pull her soul up, up, up to merge with his.

Her fingertips danced over his ribs and lower to his hips which undulated slightly so that he rubbed himself against her thigh. He was hard, hot. She lifted her hands to his head and threaded her fingers through his sleek hair.

With the advent of night, she'd removed all her clothing except for her chemise and lace-edged drawers. These proved to be flimsy barriers to his wandering hands. Somehow one of those marauding bandits stole inside one leg of her drawers and smoothed across her inner thigh to the very folds of her femininity. Tess stiffened and stilled, her eyes wide, her breath caught in her lungs.

Something long and hard and alive rubbed against her most private part. She closed her eyes, telling herself she must stop him or be doomed. His mouth roamed over her face, pressing hot kisses to her eyelids, her cheekbones, her chin. One hand covered the left side of her head, angling her face sideways so that his lips could slant across hers. His other hand . . . oh, that other hand! Massaging her, his clever fingers delving inside, slipping in, slipping out. And then she felt him trying to enter, felt the fiery tip as his plucking kisses rained down upon her.

"Spirit woman," he murmured. "*AnadaAki.*"

Spirit Woman? Pretty Woman? A ghost, an image. He didn't even know her. She was no more than a feminine creature to him. Nameless. Faceless. With a groan of self-deprecation, Tess swept his hands from her body and rolled away from him. She sprang to her feet, shivering and aching all over. Pressing her fingertips to her throbbing lips, she watched as he tossed fretfully before lying on his back, his chest rising and falling as if he'd run a mile. He kicked at the blankets, muttered dark words and then relaxed. His eyelids twitched, but his breathing slowed and settled into a soft snore.

After a few minutes of berating herself and struggling to bring her emotions under control, Tess wet a cloth and bathed his arms, neck, and face. She rested a hand on his brow. His fever was high, so she forced him to drink more water. He trembled, chilled by the battle being waged inside him. Tess thought of lying next to him, taking him in her arms to keep him still, keep him safe from his own restless movements, but she had lost all trust in herself. She sat away from him, her back against the rock wall, her knees pulled up to her chest, her chin quivering as she fought back tears of humiliation.

Never had she been so close to abandoning herself to a man. His kisses and caresses had laid to waste her morals, her firm belief in chastity before marriage.

Thankfully she'd come to her senses before she'd made a complete fool of herself. Her body burned where he'd touched her and she felt damp and achy. Closing her eyes, she acknowledged to herself that she didn't regret the desire he'd awakened in her. No. She only regretted she hadn't awakened any in him. His desire had been fueled by images in his head, by fever-induced dreams, not by her and anything she'd done.

She was only "woman" to him. In his right mind, he'd have nothing to do with her, she reasoned, for his attitude had been anything but cordial. He hated white people. For all she knew, he might have a wife worrying about him in the Blackfoot camp.

That possibility placed a bad taste in her mouth

and a weight in her heart. She reached for the flask of whiskey and took a swig. The liquid burned all the way down, but created a warmth in her stomach and cleared her head. She cushioned her cheek against her folded arms and closed her eyes. She hoped she wouldn't dream anymore.

Chapter 5

O n the third day his fever broke.
    A ray of sunlight speared Tess where she lay near the wide cave opening. Squinting against the intrusion, she reluctantly awakened to peer at the buttery light falling warmly on her body. She raised onto one elbow and looked out at the wedge of sky and tree tops visible to her, then she heard a shuffling behind her and whirled about. Storm-In-His-Eyes shifted to his side, curled his body into a ball, and settled into sleep again. But there was something different about him, she thought, raising up from her tumble of blankets. She draped one about her shoulders and crept closer on bare feet.

His breathing seemed more normal, no longer rapid or shallow. Touching his shoulder, she found that his skin was damp with sweat.

"Thank the Lord," she murmured, glancing up in divine gratitude. She let him sleep, moving away to eat her breakfast of apples, raisins, and hardtack biscuits. She drank sassafras tea while sitting in the pool of sunlight and breathing in the aromas of a new day.

The days and nights had surprised her in that

she'd found them pleasant and not as boring as she'd imagined they'd be. Taking care of Storm had consumed her, and several times she'd been called upon to exercise strength and cunning to keep him flat on his back when he'd been out of his head with the fever. Her voice, soothing and cajoling, had seemed to instill peace in him, lulling him back to his fitful sleep after brief struggles when she'd flung herself upon him, using her weight as an anchor.

The fever had broken and she had her sweet reward. She hugged herself, seized by her own accomplishment. Of course, there was more to do, but he had definitely turned a corner.

And when he was well, then what? She sighed, troubled that she wasn't looking forward to returning to her life in False Hope. This adventure had proved more than that she could successfully treat a patient without her brother's help. Her time away from False Hope had also proved to her that her place there wasn't vital enough to pull her back. In fact, she dreaded returning to the same problems, the same situations. She dreaded it so much that she found herself plotting ways to break out of her routine.

Since she couldn't move into a place alone without ruining her reputation, perhaps she could find other accommodations. Would someone like Mrs. Bishop allow her to rent a room and give her kitchen privileges in exchange for light housekeeping? A bubble of excitement broke through her muck of dread, and she hugged her knees more tightly against her body.

She would have more freedom to live as she pleased without John's reminders that she needed to find a suitable gentleman to marry. As if that kind of man was as common as chin whiskers!

"Do you see someone out there?"

Tess jerked in surprise, then twisted around to find her patient staring intently at her. He'd risen up on an elbow and one hand rested on his knife lying sheathed beside him.

"No. I was just watching the clouds and enjoying the fresh air. Your fever has broken." She fetched him a cup of tea. "You should drink something. It's important to keep plenty of liquids in you."

He moved as if preparing to stand, and Tess flew to him.

"No, no. What are you doing? You aren't mended enough to go anywhere yet."

"Help me up. I won't go far."

"You won't go anywhere."

"You want me to wet my blankets like a babe?" He gave her a speaking glare. "I must pass water, woman. Now help me to stand."

She decided he wouldn't want to hear that he'd already passed water several times and she'd cleaned it up, so she hooked her hands around his elbows and gave a grunt as she hauled him up. He staggered, swayed, and then miraculously found his balance. Tess admired his fortitude, watching while he gained his bearings and moved with lunging steps to the cave opening. She turned her back, giving him a measure of privacy, and slipped into her own petticoat, shirt, and long skirt. When he returned, she picked up the cup of tea again.

"Come back to bed now and drink this."

"I am weak. What have you done to me?"

She glanced back at him and saw the glint of deviltry in his eyes. For an instant she wondered if he remembered anything about their intimate encounter the other night, but that worry soon passed. If he did recall anything, he would no doubt believe it had been a dream.

He navigated his way to the sprawl of bedding like a man who was seeing triple, his hands splayed out in front of him, his eyes wide and bleary. He walked stiff-legged, and when he lowered himself to the blankets, he did so slowly, gingerly. Tess pushed the tin cup of tea toward him. He made a face and turned away.

"You will drink this," she said, firmly.

"How long have you been here?" he demanded.

"A few days. Drink."

"Gather your things and leave."

"Drink, please."

His hand flashed out and knocked the cup away, sending it clattering to the cave floor. Most of the strong tea splashed across the front of her white blouse, staining it dark-brown.

"You must learn to listen when a man talks, white woman."

Anger swept through her like a stampede. "Look what you've done!" She brushed at the liquid seeping into her blouse and the chemise underneath. "I'm trying to save your ornery hide and you behave like a spoiled little boy."

"Take your white medicine with you when you go," he drawled in a tone of voice intended to irritate and insult.

"My white medicine plucked you from the jaws of death, you ungrateful lout," she seethed. "I've wrestled with you, bathed you, cleaned you when you messed on yourself, combed your hair, forced medicine down your gullet, and taken a few blows when you were out of your head." She pointed to a purple bruise under her chin and then, goaded by her mounting fury, hiked up her skirt to display an apple-sized bruise on her left thigh, just above her knee where he'd kicked the stuffing out of her last night. Letting her skirt drop back into place, she straightened, hands on hips, and trembled with outrage. "I demand your respect, sir. What's more, I've earned it."

Her trembling crescendoed into a long shiver that sluiced down her body from head to toes. Yes, she was angry, but she acknowledged a shard of fear deep inside. After all, this man had been quite a handful when he'd been unconscious, and now he was alert. He continued to stare at her bruised leg, although her skirt now covered it. Finally he swallowed hard and lifted his silvery-gray eyes to her face. The thoroughness of his perusal made her feel like a mouse shivering before a crouched timber wolf.

Shifting his attention, he looked at himself and unfortunately so did she—at his long limbs, his scarred chest, the skimpy square of cloth covering his privates. Memories of his body pressing upon hers teased her. He'd been out of his head, making love to her in a dream, in a stupor. Good Lord, what would it be like to be loved by him when he *knew* what he was doing?

Shoving aside those sinful thoughts, she jerked her eyes away from his tempting body. What was he thinking? she wondered, steeling himself for whatever new threat or accusation he was certain to toss at her. He lay back, resting his head on a bunched blanket and letting go of a long sigh. He closed his eyes.

"You're a good-looking woman. Do you have a husband back in False Hope?"

That, she didn't expect, and she could only stare at him for a few moments, her mind temporarily stalled. "A husband?" The query tweaked her anger for it reminded her of the many times she had been called upon to defend her unmarried status. Why was this a major concern for *every* male who crossed her path? "No, I do not. What has that got to do with anything? Do *you* have a wife back in your village?"

He smiled faintly. "I almost did, but she died when she was twelve. Got swept away in the river."

"Oh, I'm . . . she was twelve?" Tess waited for his nod. "How old were you?"

"Sixteen."

"You marry that young in your tribe?"

"Sometimes much younger. We hadn't married yet, but she had been picked out for me to wed. Another girl was chosen for me, but I decided to leave and explore the world. A trapper said I could ride with him, so I did. Otherwise, I would be married with many children by now."

"I see." She brushed at the tea stain on her blouse again. "Where did you travel with this trapper?"

"Many places. I became a guide for white people from the east who came to this country to live or just to hunt the buffalo. But that work sickened me, so I quit."

"Why did it sicken you?"

"The white hunters kill for sport, not to eat. And there are too many white families coming here. They all want the Bloods to go away or to die."

"Not all of them. I don't want that." She glanced away nervously when the intensity of his eyes took on a predatory glint. "So did you go back to trapping?"

"For a while, but then I was called home."

"Called home?"

He gestured around him. "By the spirits, the gods. I wanted to live in peace, to settle down and start a family, but trouble dogs my footsteps." He tilted his head to one side, examining her, his gaze

playing over the front of her damp, stained blouse.
"What happened to you?"

She looked at him, wondering if his fever was
back and had fogged his brain, since he surely
should recall how he'd knocked the cup out of her
hand and spilled . . . She brought herself up short,
contemplating his faint smirk, his slitted eyes. He
wasn't talking about tea stains.

"Nothing happened to me," she replied, then
turned away to retrieve the tin cup.

"Then why have you not found a husband for
yourself?"

"I have had other matters to occupy my time."
She was glad her back was to him so he couldn't
see her grimace of censure. Pouring more tea into
the cup, she schooled her features before facing
him again. "I am offering you more tea, and I
would appreciate it if this time you put it *in* you
instead of *on* me."

He propped himself up on one elbow again to
accept the cup she offered. His long fingers
brushed hers. He drank the contents, then handed
it back to her.

"I would rather have whiskey."

"I'm sure you would, but the whiskey is all
gone."

"You drank the rest of it?" He reclined again and
closed his eyes.

"No, you did. When you became simply impossible, thrashing and kicking like a wild animal,
whiskey was the only thing that would settle you
down." That and her stroking caresses, she
thought, but kept it to herself. Those minutes in the
dead of night, when his fever had spiked and her
soothing hands upon his brow and lips and eyelids
had gentled his spirit, would be hers to treasure
forevermore.

His skin glistened with sweat, and she knew she should run a cool rag over his fevered flesh, but now that he was conscious, she hesitated. *Go on,* a voice urged her. *He needs medical attention. He is a patient not a suitor.* Definitely, not a suitor, she thought with an inner grimace as she wet a rag and approached him. He didn't open his eyes until she knelt beside him. Wariness fairly radiated from him. He drew back as if she held a revolver instead of a damp rag.

"What are you doing?"

"Nothing that will harm you." She ran the cloth down his arm, across his breastbone, and then wiped his beaded brow. "Now that the fever has broken, you'll be drenched in sweat," she explained. "It's important to keep you dry and not allow you to get chilled. You're shivering. Bundle up." She pulled at the blankets, throwing one over his long legs.

"Where is Brown Otter?"

"With the Blackfeet. He should return today or tomorrow."

He raised a hand and she stiffened, but his fingertips merely brushed her bruised chin. "I have never hit a woman before."

"You were out of your mind."

"I must have been to do this."

She realized it was as close to an apology as she was going to get, so she shrugged and wet the cloth again. "Could you eat something?"

"Not now. I'm—I'm tired." He relaxed, his arms falling to his sides, his eyelids drooping. "I will sleep now."

"Yes, you do that." She placed the cool cloth on his forehead. Picking up a light blanket, she draped it across his upper body, then stood back to watch him drift off to sleep, his chest moving rhythmi-

cally. A measure of cautious elation stole through
her, and she allowed herself to rejoice in the moment. He would make it, she told herself. In a few
days, with her care, his strength would return and
he would no longer need her.

The momentary jubilation subsided with that so-
bering thought. Tess sat near him and thought of
the glimpses of tenderness he'd reluctantly revealed. His grief over his sister was most touching,
and then his confession that he'd never before laid
a hand in anger on any woman. Oh, he wanted so
to be fierce and unpleasant, totally wild and dangerous, but no heartless beast would feel any com-
pulsion to state that he wasn't the sort of man to
bruise a woman's tender skin. He might wave a
knife to frighten her, but slap or kick or punch her?
Never.

Tess yawned and curled up near him. She'd close
her eyes for only a few moments, she thought, but
she was fast asleep within minutes.

The light seeping into the cave was fading.
Brown Otter wouldn't be around today, Storm
thought, then staved off his disappointment. It was
best if Brown Otter stayed far away. All of the
Blackfeet should keep their distance. He'd brought
nothing but trouble to his people since he'd returned from the white man's world.

Testing his shoulder, he grimaced as pain radiated between the twin wounds, back and front. Noticing the crumpled cloth the woman had used on
him, he snatched it up and dipped it into a shallow
basin full of tepid water. The wet coolness felt wonderful as he dragged the cloth across his forehead,
down his face and neck and chest. He looked at the
woman, curled like a kitten near his feet.

A piece of a dream floated through his mind like

a plume of smoke. *AnadaAki*. She'd been a spirit in his dream, a white man's angel lying at his feet. Her golden hair tumbled about her shoulders, framing an oval face. He smiled to himself, admiring her pouting lips, the sweep of her dark-gold lashes, the dash of pale freckles across her nose and cheeks. Her white blouse and dark-blue skirt were wrinkled and tea-stained. He grimaced, regretting his actions. She was right. Her devotion to him deserved his eternal gratitude, not his temper.

She'd rolled up the sleeves of her blouse, and he saw a bruise above her left wrist. Had he put *that* there, too? He narrowed his eyes, pummeled by guilt. The woman had tolerated more than anyone should have on his account.

Why had she stayed? Why had she insisted on saving his hide, a worthless Indian wanted by every white man in the whole county? She should be with a white man, not holed up with a Blood.

Storm sighed away the wistful thinking, but not before an image of himself standing at her side taunted him. She might doctor him, but she'd never allow him into her life. Not this woman. In his years living among the white people, he'd discovered their women saw Indians in one of two ways—as curiosities or as beasts. Some had flirted with him, even asked to bed him. He'd taken a few at their words, giving them a ride, making them moan for mercy beneath him. One white lady had followed him after he'd delivered her family to the valley where they were to build a log house and mission church. Moon-eyed and rattle-brained, she'd slipped off and tracked him down that night when he'd made camp. Her family had been embarrassed when he'd brought her back to them and she'd tried to sneak off again to be with him. Last he knew, they had tied her to her bed.

Other white women had spit on him, had hidden behind their men when they saw him, had quaked in his presence as if they expected him to leap on them like a ravaging animal.

He'd begun dressing like a white man, talking like a white man as much as possible. Hoping the whites would accept him and not always see him as an enemy, he'd been disappointed. His dark skin and shiny black hair could not be hidden, no more than his less than fluid speech.

He'd been goaded into gunfights over white women, but he'd never wanted to draw his gun to win any of them. Wanting no wife or permanent bedmate, he'd tried to keep from stepping in a woman's trap, but he hadn't had much luck. Seemed like he always found himself facing a jealous man on a dusty street, guns at the ready. He'd had a belly full of shoot-outs and crazy white women.

Arriving back in the Blood country, he'd sworn off any contact with the white eyes. But somehow he'd gotten himself tangled up with Millie Long, a red-haired vixen, bursting with questions about him, his tribe, his reputation as a gunslinger. Once again a white woman had dropped trouble at his feet. Because of Millie, he found himself on the run again, his sister dead, and a poison raging in his body.

Shifting restlessly, he examined the new white woman in his life. So pretty. Night painted her face silver and shimmered over her hair. He swallowed hard and reached for the canteen. Uncapping it, he drank until he'd emptied the vessel. He was hot, sweating rivers; then he was cold, shivering until his teeth chattered. He hated being helpless, depending on a woman to do for him, a woman he had no business admiring or wanting.

Frustration went off in him with the power of lit dynamite, and he flung the canteen past the woman's inert body. It slammed against the wall and clattered to the floor. The sounds reverberated in the stone cavern and the woman bolted upright, her blue-green eyes wide with alarm, her mouth working as if she wanted to scream but wouldn't let herself.

"My stars and gold bars! What did you do *that* for?" she demanded, her voice rapping like knuckles against his forehead. Scrambling to her feet, she snatched up the canteen and shook it at him. "Listen to me, mister. If you want more water, you ask me nice. Don't you *ever* throw anything at me again, you understand? Am I making myself as clear as a bell? I hope so, because I will not tolerate such behavior."

Lounging back, he seized a few moments to appreciate her high color, snapping eyes, and quivering countenance. Pluck, he thought, and his loins stirred.

"Quit staring at me as if you can't understand English and answer me," she insisted.

He grinned, finding her both amusing and beautiful, a powerful combination. "Yes, ma'am," he replied, dutifully. "I wasn't aiming at you, though. I generally hit what I aim for."

"So I've heard," she rejoined, bending over to dip the canteen into a bucket of water.

"What have you heard? What are they saying about me in town?"

"You know," she said crossly. "I'm not going to recount your dubious achievements so you can preen over them."

Irritated with her refusal of his every request, he kicked viciously at the blankets covering him, flinging them off his legs, scattering them across the stone floor. "Answer me, woman. They talk behind my back, not to my face, and I want to know what crimes the white-eyes marshall has pinned on me."

Fury pumped red color to her neck and cheeks. Bending over, she gathered up the blankets and threw them in his face and over his head.

Stunned by her actions, Storm was reduced to fighting off the grasp of wool blankets clinging to his sweaty face and arms and hands. Ignoring his paining wound, he flung aside the last blanket and stared up at her. He felt his upper lip curl even as he watched her breasts rise and fall with her agitated breathing. For a moment the air fairly sizzled between them, but then he saw a glimmer of mirth in her blue eyes. The stupidity of their blanket battle engulfed him.

He lay back exhausted, defeated by the woman's temerity, and he laughed—laughed until tears rolled from the corners of his eyes, until his stomach muscles burned, until he almost choked on the joyous sounds. And she joined him, her laughter throaty and melodic. She sat cross-legged beside him as if her muscles had liquified and she could stand no more. Doubled over, she giggled and struggled for a decent breath. Her eyes glistened like rain-washed jewels, and her hair tumbled over her shoulders in golden profusion. The ends touched his thigh, caressed his skin. He wanted to bury his hands in her hair, but he resisted the wild desire. It was enough to laugh with her, to share the hilarity they understood, although it made no sense.

"We're a pair, aren't we?" she asked, breathless, blushing. "Is this any way for two adults to behave?" She looked around at the cave, almost dark now, save for the blessing of starlight filtering in. "I suppose we deserve to act like a couple of children, considering what we've gone through the past few days." She backhanded a stray lock of her dusky gold hair, but it fell back to curl against her cheek. "I'm sorry. I shouldn't have buried you in those blankets. You're my *patient*, for goodness sake!"

He liked her voice and the way she talked. Yes, he liked the slight huskiness in it, the deep richness of it. And he liked the way she looked at him— straight in the eyes. Most white women wouldn't do that. They were afraid, timid, even around their own men sometimes.

"I wasn't trying to strike you," he explained. "I only wanted . . . I want to know what they are saying about me behind my back. And I want you to know that . . ." He drew in a breath, his pride rising up to smite him.

"What? What do you want me to know?" she asked, concern etched on her features. She wiped moisture from her eyes and gave him her full attention, her sky-eyes searching his face.

"I wanted you to know . . ." Why should he tell her? Why would she care? His need to confess overcame his misgivings. "I didn't kill my sister. The marshall shot her."

Her eyes reflected the tragedy of his statement. "Oh, dear," she whispered. "Your sister told me the same thing, but it was difficult for me to believe that Marshall Long would do such a thing."

He stiffened, his heart and mind wincing. "You think I lie."

"No." She reached out a hand, her fingertips stopping short of his shoulder. "I believe you."

He blinked incredulously. "You do?"

"Yes. I didn't like the idea that you might have shot your poor sister by mistake. That would be a terrible thing for you to live with."

"Her death is a burden I will never lift from my heart," he murmured, sadness and grief falling over him. "She was innocent. She was trying to help me. I didn't know that she'd tagged along when I went to the Long house. It was only after the marshall confronted me and started talking crazy about arresting me that my sister showed herself. She defended me and got his attention long enough for me to spring onto my horse and ride away. I thought—I thought she'd run away, too."

He swallowed the rest, afraid his voice would break and show too much of his heart to this woman. After all, she was a stranger . . . and she was white. When sides were drawn, she would leap to join her own people and leave him to the law. Right now he was an adventure, but it would not remain so. Eventually the lawmen would find him and want to kill him. Unlike his brave sister, this woman would not stand between him and the marshall's gun.

Not that he'd want her to. She had no business being here. Brown Otter was crazy to let her stay in the cave alone with him.

"When Brown Otter returns, you should go back to False Hope," he said, and she looked at him as if he'd slapped her. "Your medicine has worked," he added, wanting to spare her feelings.

"Not entirely. Your fever has broken, but your infection hasn't been brought to an end. You could take a turn for the worse at any time. I hope that doesn't happen, but I'm staying another day or two to make sure. My brother isn't expecting me back until next week anyway."

"Your brother?"

"Yes, I live with my brother and his wife in our family home. My parents are dead. I assist my brother in his medical practice."

"You aren't a medicine woman?"

"I . . . no, I guess . . ." She squared her shoulders and a fierce light entered her eyes. "Yes, I am. In a sense, I *am* a medicine woman."

"There are many great medicine women among the Blood."

"The Blood? The Blackfeet, you mean?"

He nodded. "Minipoka is a powerful medicine woman."

She drew her knees up under her chin and carefully draped her skirt over her legs so that not even her toes peeked out at him. "John is an excellent doctor. He could improve his bedside manner, but one can't fault his medical knowledge." She gave a little sigh. "I'd like to know more than I do. My father was a doctor, too."

He started to ask why she didn't simply ask her brother to teach her more about medicine. That's how the Blackfeet learned, passing knowledge from one to another. However, the faint sound of a pebble rolling underfoot outside closed off his throat. He held up a hand, motioning her to be silent. Her eyes widened, and she twisted around to stare at the cave opening.

Rising to a crouch, Storm strained to hear the slightest noise. The wind sighed, the trees answered, another pebble skipped down the mountainside. Reaching for his knife, his wound tight and throbbing, Storm slipped the blade from its leather sheath just as a shadow fell like a black finger on the moonlit ledge.

Chapter 6

⌒◠◠◡◠⌒

With her heartbeat booming in her ears, Tess was amazed she could hear anything else. But she did. The soft snuffling sound had to be made by an animal. She looked at Storm, wondering if he'd heard, and she saw by the sudden relaxation of his shoulders that he had.

"Coyote?" she whispered.

"Maybe even a goat."

A gray-coated coyote stepped into the moonlight, its eyes glowing momentarily. Sniffing, it caught their scent, and its hackles rose. With a soft yip, the scruffy-furred animal scampered away. Storm chuckled as he settled back on the blankets.

Tess placed a hand over her laboring heart. "That old coyote sure knows how to get a person's full attention."

"It's dangerous for you to be here. I want no more innocent blood spilled on my behalf."

"This place is well hidden. It's doubtful we'll be found."

"But possible."

"Anything's possible," she allowed, sitting on her own pallet a couple of feet from his. Now that

76

he was feeling better, she wondered if she shouldn't widen the distance between their beds. "Would you let me take a look at your wound without a fight?"

He shrugged one tan shoulder. "Do what you like. It is the same as it was yesterday."

"Does it hurt? Is it a constant pain?"

"It pains me when I move. I feel weak. Perhaps I should eat."

"Yes, after I take a look at your wound." She knelt beside him and removed the bandages. The wound on his chest looked good, but the back wound had not improved. She dabbed at the clear seepage around it. The bandage she'd removed was damp.

Tess cleaned the wound again and covered it with treated bandages. The chest wound would leave a scar, but nothing compared to the ones already there.

"Is this from the Torture Dance the Blackfeet are so famous for?" she asked, touching one of the puckered masses of scar tissue. She'd heard the stories of the young Blackfeet men skewered and tethered to a pole. They danced around the pole until they tore themselves free. Horrible images flitted through her mind and she flinched.

"Yes, but it is called the Sun Dance, and it is a holy tradition," he explained, his brow furrowed as if he didn't like that she'd winced when she'd spoken of it. "The Sun is our symbol of the Creator. It is in the Sun that we are born and prove ourselves." His glance hardened. "White people can't understand our ways."

"I'd like to understand," Tess ventured, curious about his life, his customs. "I'm sure things we do seem very odd to you. Every community or race has its symbols and rituals."

"These scars might look ugly to your eyes, but they are my medals. Instead of fancy ribbons and gold stars, I wear these on my chest to prove my worthiness, my bravery."

She nodded as if satisfied with his explanation and opened the parfleches to remove hardtack biscuits, jerky, and a pear. She handed them to him, along with the canteen.

"What will you eat?" he asked. He bit off some jerky, white teeth flashing in the dusky cave.

"I boiled some potatoes and rice yesterday, and I have some of it left. I'll finish it up."

"You lit a fire?"

"A small one, and only long enough to soften the potatoes," she assured him. "Actually, we're getting low on food. Brown Otter said he'd bring us freshly cooked meat when he comes." She frowned, wondering what was keeping him. "I was sure he'd show up today."

"He is careful. He won't come unless he's sure he won't be followed or watched." He ate slowly as if the very act of chewing required a major effort. "When will I be well enough to ride?"

"Not for quite awhile yet," she informed him. "Just because the fever has subsided doesn't mean you are free of the poison. Your body is still fighting it off and that's why you feel weak."

He finished one of the biscuits, but handed her the other, shaking his head. "No more." Then he fell back and closed his eyes. "Did my sister suffer?"

The question gave her a glimpse into his heart, and compassion tightened her throat and made her wish she could reach out to him, place a consoling hand on his shoulder and give it a squeeze. Instead she clutched her hands in her lap and strove to ease his conscience.

"My brother and I did everything we could to make her comfortable. She died in the back bedroom of our home, and she seemed to be at peace."

"She spoke to you about me?"

"She made me promise I would help you. She knew you'd been shot, and she suspected you would be here in Red Deer Cave. I told you that she'd related to me how it had been the marshall, and not you, who had shot her. Anyway, I gave her my solemn vow I would do what I could for you, and then she died. She said she could hear drums beating in the distance and that the riders were coming to take her to see all those she loved who had passed on before her."

Gauging his reaction to her recounting, she saw him swallow hard and suspected that he struggled to keep his emotions hidden from her. Any man who would dance with skewers stuck through his skin and muscles certainly wouldn't cry over the death of his sister, she surmised with a good measure of sarcasm. Men, she thought with a small shake of her head. Men and their foolish notions of pride and virility.

"She was the bright moon shining in my dark soul, and I would rather die than have her taken from me," he said, and Tess felt her eyes widen, startled by his naked admission. "My sister never harmed a creature in her life. She wouldn't even go on hunts with us, as other women of the Blood often do, because she wanted no part of killing. I teased her about it. She would eat the buffalo, but she would not watch while it died. She would roast the fowl, but she would not have any part in its capture and death."

"I must admit that I can understand her qualms." Tess curled her legs to one side and tucked her wrinkled skirt around them. It was getting so dark she could only see the gleam of Storm's eyes and the flash of his teeth. "I can dress wounds with no problem, but I can't bear to witness violence of any sort. How women can watch gunfights is beyond me." A memory floated to her, vivid enough to make her shiver. "Why, once when I was twelve or thirteen, I saw a man beating and kicking a dog. I ran to him, tore the whip from his hand, and preached him a sermon he'd never forget."

A deep chuckle emanated from Storm. "I have no trouble believing this of you. You, with a will of iron and a heart of plenty."

His compliment worked on her like a potion. Feeling her skin warm pleasantly, she averted her face, even though he probably couldn't have seen her in the gathering gloom. The moon had deserted them, flying higher into the sky and taking its milky illumination with it. Her thoughts skipped to when he had sought her in the night, his feverish kisses persuading her, his hands exploring places no man had touched before. And she had allowed it. No, she had *enjoyed* it.

Shoving aside such thinking, she focused on the rumors she'd heard about him. "Do you think the marshall dislikes you because you shot his deputy?"

He frowned, his eyes still closed. "That added to my problems with him, but our war really started when I met his daughter."

"Millie?" Tess asked, picturing the petite redhead who was too forward and man-crazy for Tess's taste.

"When I hit town, she followed me like a lost puppy wanting to be petted."

Tess had no trouble believing this. "Millie chases lots of men," she told him, aiming her pointed statement at his overly large arrogance. "Do you like her? I mean, you aren't sweet on her, are you?"

One corner of his mouth lifted. "No, I am not *sweet* on any woman—especially a white one."

"Why, *especially* a white woman? We're not devils, you know." She resented his tone and attitude.

"I came back to live with the Blood as a Blood. I've tried living in the white world, and it didn't work. I felt as if I was caged. I didn't like being shackled."

"If you had sworn off white women, why did you sport with Millie?" she charged. "For heaven's sake, didn't it occur to you that flirting with the marshall's daughter might get him riled at you?"

"I didn't know she was the marshall's daughter at first. Besides, it is not easy for a man to turn his back on a lovely, willing woman. No matter what color she is."

"It's obviously not too easy for you. Maybe you should ask your spirits to give you more common sense and the ability to refuse certain women's attentions."

His eyes opened to slits and Tess felt herself blush. Why was she snapping at him, fussing at him? Who he saw and what he did were none of her concern. But why had he succumbed to Millie Long? She was such a tart!

"Are you through with your tongue-lashing?" he drawled.

She nodded, pressing her lips together and wishing she hadn't spoken her mind.

"The marshall caught me with his daughter one evening and branded me an outlaw, then and there. He has been hounding me ever since, blaming me for every crime in the territory. After I shot his deputy, he was really mad. Even after all the witnesses told him it was a fair fight, he swore he'd send me to prison or see me swing from a rope."

"What did he catch you and Millie doing?" she asked, that one item clinging tenaciously to her active imagination.

His lips curled into a grin. "What do you think?" He chuckled at her heightened color. "We were kissing, that's all. And rolling around in the hay. I'd just met her at a dance and we'd found a quiet place to get to know each other a little better."

"I thought you said you weren't sweet on her."

"That's right, I'm not. Haven't you ever kissed someone you weren't in love with?" His gaze sharpened. "You *have* kissed a man, yes?"

"Of course!" she huffed, her mind skipping to the night when his lips had made love to hers. Leaning back into the shadows, Tess hoped he couldn't read anything in her expression. Did he remember anything about that night?

"Just wondering . . ."

Wondering what? She stared at him, waiting for him to say more, to give her more insight into his life, his feelings or lack of them for Millie. Men were strange creatures. Willing to flirt and kiss and even bed women they cared little or nothing for! Well, maybe that was all right with Millie, but Tess expected more than a dalliance.

In the ensuing silence, his breathing deepened and Tess cocked an ear. Was he asleep already?

"Storm?"

Nothing. Only deep, steady breathing. Tess crossed her arms and stared at his dark form. Asleep, just like that. He makes sure she's been kissed, and then he falls asleep. Ah, well. He needed his rest. But why had he made think about kissing and spooning before he dropped into dreamland? There was something about him that made her senses riot and her imagination run away

with her. She found she couldn't even look at him
without remembering his mouth on hers, the rough
caresses of his hands . . .

Absently, she fingered her wrinkled blouse and
wanted to be out of it and the equally rumpled
skirt. Tomorrow she would don the other skirt and
blouse she'd brought. They, too, were in need of a
scrub board and a hot iron, but they weren't in as
sorry a state as her blouse, which had once been
white, and her black skirt with its torn and dirt-
caked hem.

Rising from the cool, hard rock floor, she
stretched and moved a short distance from Storm's
sleeping form. Relying mostly on touch, she un-
buttoned her blouse and shrugged out of it, then
unfastened her skirt and let it fall to her ankles.
Wetting a rag, she ran it over her arms and neck
and face, all the while longing for the big, claw-
footed tub in the small room off the kitchen back
home. For an instant the tiny hairs at the back of
her neck lifted and she spun around, certain she'd
find Storm watching her. But his eyes were closed.

Wishful thinking? she chided herself, removing
her petticoats, but leaving on her lacy drawers and
chemise.

Restless and not yet sleepy, she went to stand at
the front of the cave. The night breeze caressed her
and a hoot owl sent a throaty greeting. She wondered how John and Camilla had fared without
her. Perhaps she'd be pleasantly surprised when
she returned home to find they had managed quite
nicely. But she doubted it. That Camilla could become a competent housewife overnight was highly
unlikely. Why, she couldn't even fry an egg without—

Behind her came a strangled groan and then a
spate of garbled words, half Blackfeet, half English.

Tess spun around and advanced on the writhing shadows. Storm tossed and wrestled with the coverings. He called out again, his voice full of anguish. Tess dodged his flailing arms and grabbed his shoulders, giving them a quick, hard shake.

"Wake up, Storm!" She laid a hand alongside his face and his eyes popped open, wide and searching. "Storm, it's me. It's Tess. You're having a bad dream."

"AnadaAki."

She felt herself blush, flustered that he insisted on calling her by that name. Reaching for the canteen, she uncapped it and placed it to his lips.

"Here, drink some water." She cradled the back of his head with her free hand while he drank. Before he finished, his glinting eyes focused on hers and sexual awareness burned hot, passing from him to her. He ran a forefinger along the lace-edged neckline of her chemise, making her blazingly aware of her scanty coverings. The pad of his finger brushed her skin, dipping lower to skim across the top of her breasts. She shivered uncontrollably and felt her nipples tingle.

"Freckles," he noted in a purring tone that made Tess's heart race.

"Yes, well, that's what happens when a lady goes outside without her bonnet." Her hand slipped from the back of his head to his shoulder, and she would have drawn away from him, but he eased an arm about her waist and held her in place. His eyes moved, taking in her freckled features and one corner of his mouth quirked up.

"I like freckles."

"You—you do?" Tension squeezed her chest and she had trouble breathing, thinking. She found herself mesmerized by the shape of his lips—the upper one wavy and the lower one full and glistening.

"I like freckles very much." His gaze dipped. "Where else do you have them?"

A laugh, high and flutey, tumbled from her. "Nowhere else. Now, you should sleep—"

His fingertip stroked her quivering skin again, slipping under the chemise, tugging the fabric lower. He inched up so that he could look down and see the swell of her breasts. Tess gathered in a shaky breath, his willing captive.

"No other place?" he murmured, his voice lazy and deceptively cool. "I would like to look for myself."

Again her laugh was high with nerves. Is this how he had been with Millie Long? If so, she couldn't blame Millie for being caught in the haystack with him. He was a hard man to turn down. Somehow she formed the words, although her heart wasn't in them. "I won't allow it, so you might as well stop this and—" The rest of her admonishment clogged in her throat as he swayed closer, infinitely closer, and the arm around her waist cinched more tightly.

The touch of his mouth on her skin was as light and soft as a moonbeam. He kissed the valley between her breasts then the rosy swells, then up, up her throat to her chin, which he gnawed gently. Tess's eyes closed. Never had she been kissed in such a fashion. Her head swimming, she clung to his shoulders, adrift in emotions too terrifying, too glorious to ponder or deny.

He tugged her chemise off her shoulders and kissed and licked the exposed skin. His mouth flirted across her cheek, teased her ear, and claimed her lips. He combed her hair with his fingers, dragging them through her long locks and burying deep until he found her scalp. He didn't just kiss, he courted, nudged, plucked and nibbled. With her eyes closed, Tess was lost in her own simmering pool of desire.

He was hot, so hot, and he peppered her shoulders with quick kisses and tiny, arousing bites. She gathered the ends of his silky hair in her hands and brought his lips to hers again. She slanted her mouth more fully beneath his, and he drew her lower lip between his, and sucked gently. Tess moaned, drowning in desire.

The invasion of his tongue plunged her deeper still, and she clutched at him, arched against him, gasped for breath when his mouth finally left hers.

"Yes, yes," he groaned. He clutched handfuls of her hair, and his kiss verged on being savage, his tongue taking and plundering. He kissed her neck and throat and murmured Blackfoot words of passion.

"My dream was of you," he whispered, his breath warming her skin. "I dreamed that you unfurled your wings and flew away from me." He gazed at her breasts where the fabric was stretched taut just above her diamond-hard nipples.

She smiled, her body humming. "I have no wings."

"True, but you will leave." He bestowed a feather-light kiss on her lips and straightened away from her. "You must leave."

Was it her imagination or did she see sadness in his eyes? His hands fell away and she could tell that he'd decided not to continue his gentle assault of her senses. What had changed his mind?

"You have been good to me," he said, lying back on the blankets and staring at the darkness above him. "I don't wish to dishonor you."

Tess edged away from him, chastising herself for once again allowing him liberties she had never allowed any other man. He was right, of course. She would leave him soon and probably not see him again, so any intimacies were out of the question. The least she could do was to return to her former life with her honor intact. A relationship with him was impossible. She chided herself for even thinking such a thing. Surely Storm had never even suggested that he was interested in her in that way. A few kisses and a fever-induced seduction were hardly signs that he cared deeply for her. He was beholden to her perhaps, and found her attractive, but he certainly would rather take up with a beautiful Blackfeet maiden.

Lying on her side, the pallet beneath her adding a thin cushion from the hard, cold stone, she stacked her hands beneath her head and shut out the sight of Storm, lying tantalizingly near. Remembering the tough tenderness of his embrace, she wished she had the courage and audacity to fling herself at him and ask him to finish what he'd started.

The very thought made her wince with self-consciousness. She'd better go back to False Hope soon, she thought, or she'd return a fallen woman and a spinster for life.

In the gray of dawn, Brown Otter arrived. Tess stood just inside the deep crevice and waited for him, but she was more interested in the slight, bent-over figure trailing behind him, a light blanket shawl over the head and rounded shoulders. Tess finished dressing as the two drew nearer, and she could see by the long, fringed shift and beaded leggings that the other Indian was a female.

Brown Otter nodded at Tess, then turned to his companion. "I have brought a medicine woman from our tribe. She will heal my brother."

Tess smiled at the old woman. "He's much better." She turned and indicated Storm, who was sitting up, his back braced against the wall. "See for yourself."

Storm didn't seem at all pleased with their company. "Why have you brought Minipoka here?" he demanded of Brown Otter. "It's not enough that my sister is dead? You want others to die because of me?"

"No one saw us, and Minipoka wanted to come," Brown Otter said. "I couldn't refuse her."

The old woman removed the lightweight blanket from her head and shoulders and folded it carefully. Her gray hair was braided in two long ropes that she'd looped at the sides of her head. She wore a green and black bandanna lengthwise around her forehead, the knotted tails fluttering at the back of her neck. Up close, Tess realized the woman didn't wear leggings, but knee-high moccasins of buttery leather and intricate black and yellow beading. Her long dress, also of leather, was deeply fringed at the hem and sleeves. Belted with a band of heavily beaded cloth, the dress had a colorful yoke, all green and yellow and red beads and quills forming horizontal bands. Low down on her skirt, she'd sewn a triangular piece of trading cloth and outlined it in green quills. Several beaded necklaces swung from her neck and disk-shaped earrings of white bone dangled from her pierced lobes. She was exotic and beautiful; her face lined with years and wisdom, her eyes as gentle as a doe's. Tess reached out a hand to her in a genuine gesture of welcome.

"Hello. I'm Tess Summar. I'm glad you've come, Minipoka."

The old woman smiled and grasped Tess's hand, although she didn't shake it. "You are the white medicine woman. Has your medicine worked?"

Tess could see why this woman was revered among the Blackfeet tribes. Her voice commanded, her touch warmed and comforted. Her very presence seemed to embody eternal hope.

"Storm's fever has broken, but he's very weak. This morning he seems to have fever again. I tried to get him to eat something, but he refused. I'm troubled that he's suffered a setback. I had hoped he'd be feeling much better today."

"I can hear and speak for myself," Storm bellowed, and Minipoka made a face at him.

"Do not shout at me, boy," Minipoka said. She shuffled toward Storm-In-His-Eyes and untied a pouch from her belt. Removing a red and yellow beaded band from it, she tossed it into Storm's lap. "Put that on your right arm. It has power that will strengthen you." She eyed him carefully. "I see that you have demonstrated your grief by using your knife on yourself."

Storm nodded and tugged the arm band up onto his bulging biceps. "You should not have come, Minipoka. You're too important to the Blood. If something happened to you—"

"I have brought this," she interrupted, and held out a long eagle feather. "Braid your hair and place this among the twined strands."

"I mourn my sister. I won't wear a braid for at least another moon phase."

"A small braid," she said, waving the feather at him and making him accept it. "This will give you courage to fight your sickness. The bird of prey's spirit will make you strong."

He raised his arms to begin fashioning the braid and grimaced. Realizing that the action aggravated his wound, Tess stepped forward and knelt beside him.

"Let me do it . . ." She paused, looking from one

Indian to the other. "Unless that's forbidden."

Minipoka smiled. "You are not afraid of this growling wolf, eh?" Her eyes almost disappeared in the mass of wrinkles when her smile grew. "Go ahead, but just one small braid. Storm-In-His-Eyes is right; he must continue to mourn for his loss is great." She took Brown Otter by the arm and used him to steady herself as she knelt on the other side of Storm. "I will ease your pain, my noisy one. I will ask the spirits to blow out the fire in your wounds. You will see. Soon you will be glad old Minipoka came to your lair."

"I'm honored you've come," Storm said, then cut his eyes sideways at Tess when she selected strands of his hair to braid.

Ignoring his edginess, Tess plaited the dark strands, secretly thrilled to participate in this ritual. His hair was so black it shone blue. Straight and silky, it grew in several lengths. She wondered if he'd cut it while living among the whites. He relinquished the feather, and she tucked it in the tightly woven hair. Finished, she sat back to watch Minipoka remove a bundle from her pouch. Peeling away the cloth, the woman exposed a dozen or more sharp quills and cactus spines. The tips were shiny as if they'd been sharpened.

Minipoka selected one, blew on it, then leaned toward Storm. He closed his eyes and the old woman pierced his cheek with the quill. Tess gasped, staring at the quivering quill Minipoka had left in Storm.

"What's that supposed to do?" Tess asked.

"It will ease his pain and allow the fire in his body to blow itself out." She selected another sharp needle and stuck this one in Storm's neck, twirling it, blowing on it.

Not knowing what to think of this odd practice,

Tess sat back and simply watched. Storm showed no discomfort, so she surmised that the insertion of the quills was painless. The places Minipoka selected in which to place the needles seemed precise, as if their locations held significance. His cheeks, his neck, his chest, his upper arms, even his forehead and temples. When she was done, some twenty-three quills quivered on Storm like insect antennae. Tess realized she had much to learn about medicine—especially Indian medicine. John, she sensed, would not approve of this cure, but Tess found it absolutely enthralling. If it worked ... why, she'd know something John didn't know!

"Now I will sing," Minipoka announced, "and I will dance."

A current of excitement sluiced through Tess. She'd heard of such rituals, but to witness one thrilled her. Sitting straighter, she observed the old woman's preparation of what must surely be a most sacred endeavor. Brown Otter sat off to one side and Storm remained still, his eyes closed, his expression one of repose. He seemed utterly relaxed and at ease.

Taking another bundle from her pouch, Minipoka laid it in the center of the area. She danced around it, her moccasined feet whispering on the stone, her voice rising in a high, eerie cadence as she circled the bundle. Brown Otter crouched, his gaze latched on her, his lips moving with the words, but he didn't sing. Only Minipoka's voice, wavering with age, filled the cavern. Storm began to quiver, his limbs jerking, a muscle ticking at one corner of his mouth. Minipoka stood in one place now and bounced at the knees, her voice rising and falling to a whisper. Then she retrieved the bundle, opened it, and dipped her fingers into a greenish, sticky substance.

"Remove the bandages from his wounds," she instructed, and Brown Otter leaped forward to obey before Tess could even bat an eyelash. Swiftly, he stripped the white gauzy cotton from Storm-In-His-Eyes and then stepped back. Minipoka blew softly on the green muck, murmured Blackfeet words, and applied the goo to the wound. The stench of mold rose in the air. Tess wanted to question the woman and ask the ingredients of this strange medicine, but she felt that it wasn't her place and that it would be tantamount to whistling in church.

The Blackfeet medicine woman rubbed the sticky salve into the wound. Storm knitted his brows and grunted once in pain, prompting the old woman to tweak the quill protruding from his left temple. At once Storm relaxed, the lines in his brow dissolving.

When the wounds were saturated with the smelly stuff, Minipoka gestured to Tess.

"You can put the white cloth on these places again," she directed. "He will heal now. I feel his spirit growing and fighting the poison."

Tess fetched her medicine bag and the roll of bandages in it. She dressed the wounds, her gaze straying to Storm's serene expression.

"Are the quills dipped in some kind of numbing agent?" she asked, but she could tell by the old woman's expression that she hadn't made herself clear. "The quills . . . are they coated with anything special? Any kind of medicine?"

"No. They direct the poison to them and let it out."

The whole process was a mystery to Tess and one she realized she wouldn't solve easily. But she could certainly attest to the quills' power. When Storm had experienced pain, the old woman had merely touched one of the quivering needles and his relief had been immediate.

"And the salve . . . it smelled like mold."

The old woman nodded. "That, too, is an ancient cure."

"Mold?" Tess smiled. "There is so much I could learn from you. I only wish . . ." She shrugged, knowing it was foolish to think that this woman would even care to teach her about Blackfeet medicine.

Minipoka ambled around the cave and studied the parfleches and black medicine bag, eyeing the contents of each. She sniffed at one of the tin cups and smiled.

"Willow-bark tea."

"Yes," Tess said. "Do you use it, too?"

"It is good for many ailments," Minipoka acknowledged. "You could teach this old woman a few things, too, maybe." Her smile was pure kindness. "Brown Otter has brought more food. You should eat and keep up your strength. By this evening, Storm will know hunger again and will be anxious to fill his belly."

"I certainly hope so."

The old woman smiled and her eyes shone with certainty. "The fire on his skin has been put out. He will sleep now." She removed each quill carefully, slowly, pressing a fingertip to each tiny hole before going to the next. Storm never moved. He seemed to be in a deep trance.

While Minipoka bundled up the quills again, Tess laid the back of her hand against Storm's cheek. His skin had cooled considerably.

"Why, that's the most remarkable thing I've ever seen. However did you do it?"

Minipoka chuckled. "It is old medicine."

"Would you teach me?"

"Maybe." The old woman studied her for a few moments. "You would be a good student. You would learn quickly." She rested a wrinkled hand on Tess's shoulder. "Your medicine has been powerful, too, child." Her nut-brown eyes reflected truth and infinite wisdom. "We will share a meal with you and then be on our way back to our people."

Glad for their company, Tess nodded happily, but something in the old woman's expression gave her pause. In a moment of clarity, she realized that her patient no longer needed her and she was being dismissed.

"You'll take him with you back to the Blackfeet camp?" she asked, already knowing the answer before the old woman nodded slowly.

"I will ride part of the way back to False Hope with you," Brown Otter said. "Then I will return for my brother and my grandmother. Our people will never forget your kindness . . . ma'am."

Sadness crept into her, unbidden and uncalled for. "Call me Tess."

"*AnadaAki,*" Storm said, his voice clear and strong.

Tess turned to him, surprised to find that he was awake, no longer in the trancelike state. His eyes were silvery and warm as he regarded her.

"Is this your Blackfeet name?" Minipoka asked with a cagey smile.

"My name? No, of course not." Tess darted a glance at Storm, catching his slow grin.

"It fits you, pretty woman," he said. "And it is what I have named you in my tongue. AnadaAki."

She had no rejoinder for that. Tess ducked her head, seized by a sensuous pleasure.

Chapter 7

⟨⟨◦𝒪𝒟◦⟩⟩

Sitting in a circle, Storm, Brown Otter and Minipoka conversed heatedly in Blackfeet. Glancing occasionally at Tess, Storm could see that she was becoming increasingly irritated at being shut out, but he decided this might be best. After all, the sooner she realized her place was in False Hope with her own people, the better.

They'd shared the food, and talk had centered on Minipoka's insistence that Storm return to the Blackfeet camp. Strongly opposed to this, Storm tried to make the old woman see that his presence among the Blood would be disastrous.

"My medicine is already giving you back your strength," Minipoka contended, shaking her head when Brown Otter offered her the last piece of Bannock bread. "All the people want you to come home. It isn't right for you to be here alone when you are suffering and grieving. It dishonors us."

"No." Storm shut his eyes for a moment, striving to keep a cool head although the old woman was goading him to fight. "I mean no dishonor. I'm trying to help the Blood." Why couldn't she understand that he would bring the law down on the

Blackfeet if he returned now? He was filled with a need to avenge his sister's death, and he would only poison those around him with it.

"You'll come home and send this white medicine woman back to her people."

He looked at Tess. Her lovely mouth was pursed in consternation and she flashed him a scathing glare. She didn't like to be closed off from them, and she was too naive to see that this would always be so. He'd lived among the whites and knew that as a Blood, he would never be accepted fully and would always be treated with wariness—just as he had learned to be wary of the white eyes and their forked tongues and lying smiles.

"She should go back to her people," Storm agreed. "But I should stay away from mine. I am unclean from living too long among the whites. They want to end my life and they will not rest until I am gone from here."

Minipoka grunted and folded her arms in a defiant gesture. "I am old and don't want to sleep on this hard stone, but I will if you won't leave with me. I go where you go. I have seen visions and have been told by the spirits to stay with you, to heal you. I would rather sleep in my lodge upon my soft skins and furs. Will you make this old woman suffer, too?"

Storm sighed, weary of her ploys. "Leave me to the white medicine woman. She will remain a few more days and see to my sickness. By then, I'll be strong enough to travel on my own."

Minipoka pointed a wrinkled, shaking finger at Tess. "Her medicine is good, but her place is not here. You must make her leave. She is stubborn, can't you see? She wants to stay with you, but each day away from her people brings her more trouble." Her eyes snapped with determination.

"What is she saying?" Tess demanded. "She's looking at me as if I've done something terrible."

Brown Otter rose from his seated position on the ground. "She says her medicine will heal Storm-In-His-Eyes. It's true, my brother," he said, addressing Storm. "You will mend quicker among the people and with Minipoka's care. Already you are better. It is clear to my eyes as it should be to yours."

Tess sat straight, as if her spine were made of iron. "I beg your pardon, but *my* medicine broke his fever. It flared up again, as it will do from time to time, but he's on the mend because of what I've done for him, and he'll be as good as new with my continued care."

Storm eyed her speculatively. Her possessiveness made him wonder if Minipoka was right. While he was grateful to Tess for staying with him and tending to him through the worst of his illness, he didn't want her to remain with him. He'd have to return to the Blackfeet, he thought with resignation. He certainly didn't want Minipoka to stay in the cave with him, and he didn't want Tess to remain with him until her family or friends formed their own posse and came looking for her.

She'd done so much for him, this freckled beauty, this stranger who had fought for his life. She'd done enough. It was time for her to take the path home, even if it meant he must give her a not-so-gentle push. He set his jaw with determination and tried to ignore the sharp regret in his heart at the thought of never seeing her again.

"Minipoka is right," he said, making his voice cold and daunting. "Her medicine is powerful and will heal me. Yours takes too long. I might die before it starts to work again. I'll return to my people until I am strong enough to ride, then I'll go far away from them and stay gone this time."

"Well, I never." Tess scrambled up, dusting her hands on her skirt, her actions full of affront, her blue-green eyes blazing in her pale face. "This is a fine thank-you. I give up my normal life to come here and honor your sister's request and this is my reward? To be told that I've done nothing?"

Storm wanted to tell her she'd restored his faith in people outside the Blackfeet, but he firmed his jaw again and stared blankly at her, refusing to give her any reason to stay a moment longer. He wanted her gone, back to safety and the life she'd known before his sister had extracted an unfair promise from her. He caught Brown Otter's eye and gave a quick nod toward Tess and then lowered his brows, using the silent language they'd forged since they were boys. Brown Otter nodded and composed an unrelenting scowl.

"It is best that you leave now, white woman," Brown Otter announced, then surged to his feet. "Gather your things and I will take you partway. Minipoka is right. The sooner we return my brother to the Blood, the sooner he will heal."

Storm felt Tess's questioning gaze on him, but he ignored her. Scooting backward, he propped himself against the wall, his pulse beginning to pound in his head, his heart heavy for her.

"I'm being sent home, is that it?" Tess asked, a quiver running through her voice.

"We are obliged to you," Minipoka said with a smile. "We will not forget your kindness, but now you go back to your own people."

Tess shrugged, and Storm sensed she joined him in an attempt to disguise true feelings.

"Very well. I don't stay where I'm not wanted." Stiffly, she turned and began stuffing her belongings into the medicine bag and her satchel.

Storm turned his face away and closed his eyes. Her imminent departure brought a fresh pain to him that had nothing to do with his injuries.

"What you do is wise," Minipoka said in Blackfeet, and her dry hand ran down his arm, shoulder to elbow. "She is a good woman, but this is not her battle to wage."

"I never wanted her to be here anyway. It was Brown Otter who brought her."

"And he did what he thought was right. But you will come back to us now, Storm-In-His-Eyes, and this old grandmother will ask the holy ones to lift you up on your feet again and give you the strength of the grizzly bear."

"I suppose that's all . . ." Tess said, mostly to herself as she looked around the cave.

"Come then." Brown Otter motioned for her. "I have brought your mare and hidden her with our horses. They are only a short distance from here."

With a jerk of her chin, Tess followed Brown Otter to the cave opening. Storm watched, admiring her proud carriage and her graceful strides. She paused and looked back at him, her eyes huge and glistening. Storm's heart kicked and he doubled his hands into fists. He knew a moment when he wanted to reach out for her, bury his hands in her thick hair and taste the sweetness of her mouth again.

"Good-bye, Storm," she said, the sadness in her voice tearing at him like talons. "And good luck. I'll—I'll be praying for you."

Storm stared at her, the war within turning him to stone. Finally she turned and moved out into the sunlight, the beams striking her hair, burnishing it, changing it to a flowing crown of gold.

"AnadaAki," he whispered, and Minipoka began chanting, eyes closed, her small body swaying.

Storm found the sing-song chorus strangely comforting.

After awhile the chanting stopped abruptly and Minipoka's eyes opened. Her hand closed on his upper arm, and her face revealed concern—no, terror.

"A vision . . . a vision of the white medicine woman!"

Instantly Storm was on his feet, swaying, his heart thundering, his own sixth-sense sending a gut-chilling fear through him. "Tell me more."

"We must go. She rides to danger."

Not affording Brown Otter even a cordial glance when he bid her farewell, Tess flicked the reins to urge Cameo into a quicker pace. She tightened her leg around the side saddle pommel to keep from sliding off as Cameo summoned a trot. Tears burned her eyes and her throat ached. Looking around to make sure Brown Otter was good and gone, Tess allowed the tears to well in her eyes and spill onto her cheeks.

Those ungrateful brutes, she fumed. After she'd slaved over Storm, after she'd dragged him from death's door, after she'd wrestled with him and suffered his stinging blows when he'd been out of his head with fever, after all that, *this* was her reward. To be thrown out on her ear, told to run on home because the *real* medicine woman had arrived with her smelly green mold and porcupine needles, no less!

When a sob broke through her thick throat, she pulled herself up short. Okay, that's enough, she told herself firmly. No more blubbering over an Indian outlaw and his unfeeling relatives. She'd had her adventure and she knew—she *knew*—that it had been her medicine, not Minipoka's, that had broken Storm's fever. But it was over. The Blackfeet would return to their tribal camp and she would return to—to what? False Hope, yes. But could she go back to the same old life?

She shrugged. Of course, she'd have to for now. However, her time away from John and Camilla had opened her eyes to other possibilities. Mrs. Bishop might consent to letting her use a room in her house in exchange for—''

Cameo snorted, shook her shaggy mane, and veered off the byway. Tess knew the signals.

"You're thirsty, are you? Smell water? Okay, go ahead then." She loosened her hold on the reins, allowing the mare to pick her way off the road and between stands of trees. They came upon a wash where a trickle of water glistened from mountain-top runoff. Cameo dipped her head and slurped until she'd had enough. Giving a shake, Cameo turned herself around and went back toward the road.

Laughing to herself at the mare's independence, Tess didn't bother to clutch the reins more tightly again. Obviously Cameo was in charge and needed no instructions from any human. They took to the road again, but Cameo seemed edgy and pinned back her ears. When they reached a clump of trees offering deep shade, Tess pulled on the reins, thinking she would check the mare's feet to make sure she hadn't thrown a shoe, but then she heard the rumble of other horses' hooves. Twisting around in the direction of the approaching thunder, Tess spotted two riders racing toward her, but they were riding some ways off the road, parallel to it. The riders wore fringed leggings and quill vests. As they drew closer, Tess saw they wore Indian ceremonial masks, frightening in their stark colors of white and red and in the depiction of grotesque expressions. The sun slanted over their hair—not black, but light-colored—and then Tess noticed their skin—not teak, but also light-colored. White men dressed as Indians!

Glad for the concealing pool of shade, Tess tried not to move and to make herself as inconspicuous as possible. She was about to breathe a sigh of relief as they drew even with her and started to pass, when Cameo chose that moment to snort and whinny. One of the riders turned his head, spotted her, and reined his lathered horse in her direction.

"Hey, look who's here," he shouted to his partner, and the other pulled his mount to a high-stepping prance.

Plain, good sense told her to run and Tess obeyed. She dug her heels into Cameo's side and took off, but that same good sense told her that old Cameo was no match for the younger horses already catching up, flanking her, overtaking her. One of the men, the one wearing a mask with a harsh grimace and pointy teeth painted on it, reached out and grabbed a handful of her hair. Pain shot through her scalp and Tess cried out. She clamped a hand around his wrist and felt herself falling. She screamed before the ground came up quickly to pound her chest, hip, and hands. Dust caked her face and coated her tongue and throat. Coughing, she struggled for breath even as the men pounced on her and dragged her off the road and into the high grass alongside it.

The nightmarish masks hovered above her. One of the men held her legs to keep her from kicking and the other held her by the hair and throat.

"I know you," he rasped. "And I'm aiming to know you a whole lot better before we're through."

The other man laughed and yanked her legs apart. Tess screamed, but the shrill sound was cut off by a hand clamped over her mouth. She tried to fight, but the two men overpowered her. One of them flipped up her skirt and Tess's mind snapped. Desperate noises clawed up her throat as she strained every muscle to find movement, to find an opportunity to flee.

Suddenly a shrill war whoop rent the air, and the men abandoned their wicked intent to stare bug-eyed behind them. Tess managed to struggle upward enough to see a swell of land in the near distance . . . the forked tree . . . and beside it a lone rider with one arm raised above his head and a lance in his fist.

"Damn it to hell," one of the men muttered. "Let's shoot the summabitch and then take a poke at this girlie."

Another shout sounded from a different direction. The men loosened their holds. Tess sat up and spotted another rider, this one pointing a rifle at them. He fired and a bullet plugged the earth, sending up a spray of grass not two feet from them. Tess screamed, realized she was no longer being held captive, and scrambled to her feet. She didn't know if the real Indians would be friendly or hostile toward her, and she didn't want to wait around and find out. But she didn't get far. She'd run only a few steps toward her horse when one of the masked men grabbed her from behind and flung her to the ground. The breath left her body and she gasped, trying to fill her lungs again.

"No more screaming, bitch. You brought trouble down on us already, so shut up."

Tess blinked in bewilderment as a hand swept toward her in a vicious arc. Pain shot through her head, hot and blinding, and she fell back against something sharp. A scalding, crushing agony filled her skull, and then cold darkness swept over and through her.

*   *   *

Wood smoke permeated the void. Aromatic and comforting, it curled through her senses, awakening her, stirring her memory, jostling her into woozy consciousness. Tess heard a rustling nearby, then a rhythmic rattle accompanied by a melodic chanting. She tried to open her eyes, but her lashes seemed impossibly heavy. Her temples throbbed and her spine felt stiff. Disoriented, she knew she wasn't in her bed, wasn't in her house, possibly wasn't even in False Hope. Where had she been . . . the cave? But hadn't she left there?

Finally able to open her eyes to slits, Tess saw orange light, a cone-shaped peak overhead, and a painted sun and moon and stars. An arrow of pain shot from the back to the front of her head and she moaned, the sound hoarse, rasping, ringing in her ears. The chanting and rattling stopped, and a seamed face peered down at her.

"Who . . . where . . . ?" It was too difficult to speak. She closed her eyes, not caring where she was anymore. The aching in her head, down her spine, at the back of her neck, became her only existence.

Moisture dripped onto her lips, the touch of the drops making her realize that she was incredibly thirsty. She parted her lips and a cup's edge tapped against her teeth before water flowed into her parched mouth. She drank and drank, the cool liquid making her feel alive again. The cup was taken away and someone ran a wet cloth over her face and neck and arms. She sighed and relaxed. The darkness came again and she put up no resistance.

"Tess? Tess?"

"John?" Tess tried to prop herself up on her elbows, her eyes popping open. "What time is it?"

She blinked, trying to make her eyes focus. An ache twisted around her backbone and a drum pounded in her head. "Oh, what happened?" She laid a hand across her forehead. "Where am I?"

"You're with the Blood. You're safe."

That voice wasn't John's. She knitted her brows. Something wasn't right. Moving her hands at her sides, she felt fur and wool and—was she lying on the ground? She tried to sit up, but her back protested and she gave up, lying flat to stare at a peaked ceiling supported by poles. Poles . . . a pole lodge.

"The Blackfeet," she murmured.

"Yes, we brought you here after the men attacked you. They knocked you down and kicked you before the cowards sprang to their horses and ran. We were too far away to catch up with them. We brought you here."

That voice—like aged whiskey, like rubbed chamois—that voice could belong to only one man. Tess looked sideways and saw him.

Storm-In-His-Eyes crouched beside her, his face set in gloomy lines, his ebony hair spilling over his shoulders, a single feather swinging from a narrow braid at his temple. He wore leather pants and moccasins and a quill breastplate over a faded red shirt. A necklace of shells and bear claws hung around his wide neck.

The pain throbbing in her head lowered her defenses. She smiled at him. "You're beautiful. Wild and beautiful." Had she spoken aloud? When he ducked his head, she knew she had. Oh, lord. She'd embarrassed him. "My head hurts," she blurted out.

He looked at her again. "I'll get Minipoka. She's been doctoring you." He rose up, up, up, and his head seemed to poke at the pointed ceiling. "Don't move. You rest."

She had no choice, she thought. She honestly didn't think she could even sit up, much less stand and move anywhere. Her head felt as if it weighed a ton, and the throbbing pain intensified until she wanted to scream.

A breeze played over her skin and then Minipoka's face appeared above her. The old woman peered at her with watery eyes, then drew a symbol in the air, her gnarled hand moving gracefully. She chanted a phrase several times.

"You got pain?" she asked in English.

"Yes, my head, my back."

"Very bad?"

"Very bad," Tess agreed. "I must have struck my head against something. I might have a—"

"A rock," the old woman said. "You hit your head on a rock and made a big bump. Time will heal that, but I can make the hurting go. You drink."

"What is it?" Tess asked, watching a battered, hollowed-out gourd swing toward her.

"Powerful medicine. You drink."

A mixture of scents—licorice, cloves and tar—assaulted her nose before the warm liquid entered her mouth. Tess sputtered as the stuff went down her throat; a vile brew fit for a witch's cauldron. She coughed and made a face she hoped conveyed her utter disgust.

Minipoka chuckled lustily. "You'll sleep now, AnadaAki, and you will dream of what's in your heart."

The words were no sooner out of the old woman's mouth than Tess felt herself drifting away . . .

*   *   *

. . . to a sun-struck stream. She was sitting on Cameo, letting the old mare drink her fill from the sparkling water.

"AnadaAki."

She turned in the direction of the voice. Storm-In-His-Eyes sat astride a huge chestnut stallion, its blazed face and socks a startling white. A loincloth covered Storm's privates and backside, but every other part of him was hers to admire. And she did.

He urged the stallion closer. Somehow she found herself standing with Storm's arms around her. He wore a buttery leather shirt now and matching pants. Colorful beads decorated the front of the shirt and lay in loops around his neck.

"Pretty woman," he whispered.

"Do you think I'm pretty?"

"Yes. Oh, yes."

And then his mouth moved over hers like a cloud over the moon. His hands cupped her breasts. She arched closer to him, seeking his hard strength. He lifted his lips from hers, and his eyes were smoky gray.

"I am your heart. You are my hope. Is this not so?"

She nodded, but then a gunshot shattered the beauty and a blood-red stain blossomed on his chest. Shock registered on his face before he disappeared. Marshall Long materialized, laughing and reaching for her.

Retreating, she screamed when someone wrapped his arms around her from behind.

"Tess, don't be ridiculous."

John. John was holding her! She twisted from his embrace and saw that he stared at her as if she were naked. Looking down at herself, she gasped when she saw that she was wearing a beautiful white leather dress, decorated entirely with tiny, white shells.

"You don't mean to marry that heathen, do you?" John demanded.

"I don't know." Confused, she looked around. "Where did he go?"

"To jail, of course. He'll rot there, or they'll hang him. You want to be a widow? You want to spend the rest of your life alone, scorned by decent folk? That's what will happen if you go through with this, Tess. You'll be a loincloth widow."

"He hasn't even asked me to marry him, John."

John placed a hand on her shoulder and his expression was painfully serious. She knew that look; knew it well. Her heart lurched.

"He's dead, Tess. I'm sorry. I did everything I could for him."

Marshall Long laughed behind her. "So did I, girlie! I did what I could. I put a bullet through his black heart. Killed him like I killed his split-tailed sister. The less of them, the better, I say."

Tess screamed and John's hand flashed, landing a blow on her cheek. Tears sprang in her eyes as she stared at her brother, not recognizing him anymore. It wasn't John standing in front of her . . . it was . . . oh, who was he? She'd seen him, met him . . . red hair like his sister. Red.

"Red Long, the marshall's son?"

He grinned, then his face changed again. This man's hair was dirty-blond, slicked over his head with buffalo fat. Tall, thin, gangly. A thin mustache gracing his upper lip. Looked like a caterpillar. She shivered, wanting to brush it off him. She knew this man, too, but his name was out of reach.

"Who are you?" she asked him.

He leaned forward and she smelled sweet cologne. "I'm your man, honey lamb. I'm your man."

Shivering, she tried to run, but discovered that she was bound and gagged and couldn't move. Two men came toward her, both wearing masks. One drew back his foot and kicked her.

Tess screamed until her throat was raw. Hands caressed her, cool water played over her lips, sweet words slipped into her ear. Ah, that voice. Storm was with her again, his arms enclosing her, his lips moving against her temple.

She relaxed, finding a safe place in his arms, away from those other men.

"I shouldn't stay," he said.

"Stay, stay," she begged, clutching him. "Promise me you won't leave. Those men . . . they'll be back."

"Men? Tess, those men are far away. They can't hurt you now."

"Not while you're here."

Was she dreaming or was she awake? She rubbed her cheek against his arm—his bare arm. His skin was warm, vibrant. She remembered how he'd snuggled into her lap back at the cave, and she did the same to him, inching closer to hug his waist and lay her head in his lap.

"What are you doing? Ah, Tess. You torture me. All right, I'll stay. You don't have to squeeze me so tight." His fingers combed through her hair. "How can I leave you, Tess? How can I turn my back on my AnadaAki?"

She felt his lips on her cheek, and she thought she heard tears in his voice. Perhaps she was dreaming, after all.

Chapter 8

With her head feeling like a hollow drum and the room spinning before her like a whirligig, Tess sat up and tried to pry her tongue from the roof of her mouth.

Surely death could be no worse than this, she thought, her distorted vision beginning to steady enough for her to see a container of water within reach. She grabbed the pottery jug in both of her trembling hands and brought it to her lips, bumping the edge against her teeth. The water sloshed over her chin, down her chest and, *thank the Lord*, into her mouth.

Choking a little, she swallowed and coughed and swallowed some more of the delicious water. After washing away the paste coating her mouth, she poured the rest of the water over the top of her head. Her senses revived and her head cleared. Miraculously the room stopped spinning.

Ah, Tess sighed, feeling more like she belonged in the land of the living again. Looking at her strange surroundings, she remembered that she'd been brought to the Blackfeet camp, but she had no idea how many days she'd been in the skin lodge.

She examined the leather dress she wore and the
bear claws sewn across the bodice and down the
sleeves. Lifting the blanket, she saw that the dress
was long, stopping at her ankles. Her feet were
bare. Touching her bodice, then her stomach, Tess
realized she was naked beneath the shift.

Where were her clothes? Where was her horse?
Who had saved her? Must have been Brown Otter.
Couldn't have been Storm because he would have
been too weak—but she'd seen two Indians on
horseback challenging the white men who had decided to rape her.

Confused, she ran a hand over her hair, and got
another surprise. Her hair had been braided into a
thick rope that hung down her back.

"Minipoka," she murmured, grasping at a vague
recollection of the old woman practicing her
strange medicine on her. Well, it had worked, Tess
thought. She was alive. Touching the back of her
head with careful fingers, she examined the lump
there. Next, she gingerly massaged her spine,
which felt bruised and stiff. She remembered being
told that one of the men had kicked her.

The cruelty, the viciousness of the attack sent a
shudder through her. Who were those men? What
were they doing dressed up as Indians and—oh, of
course. She pressed her fingertips to her lips as she
fit the pieces of a puzzle together in her mind.
These white men dressed as Indians must be the
same ones sought by Marshall Long! Not Storm or
Brown Otter, but two men *impersonating* Blackfeet
renegades.

And those two outlaws had been ready to rape
her and then murder her.

She closed her eyes, struggling not to cry. But
the fear was real. The two men knew her, but she

didn't know them. What if they lived in False Hope?

The lodge flap opened and a smiling young woman came inside. She carried a bowl of something that smelled wonderful.

"Good, good!" The young woman moved lightly to Tess's side and extended the bowl. "My English not so good as my brother's. You eat, thank you?"

"Yes, thank you." Tess took the bowl and examined the contents which looked to be some kind of stew. "Is this Minipoka's lodge?" she asked, glancing at the neatly folded blankets stacked nearby, lances leaning against the hide wall, a gun belt hanging—gun belt?

The other woman shook her head and said something in her native language, then she frowned in concentration. "I think of the words . . . Eyes Like . . . no, Storm Eyes . . ."

"Storm-In-His-Eyes?" Tess offered, then gasped when the woman nodded. "You mean, this is where he lives?"

"Yes." She seemed relieved to have communicated that much.

Tess stared at the pallet she'd been sleeping on. His pallet. Where had he been staying since she'd taken over his home? She looked around but found no other sleeping pallet.

"I am called Many-Smiles-Woman."

Tess grinned. "And I can see why. I'm Tess."

"AnadaAki," Many Smiles said. "It is what Minipoka and the others call you . . . Tess."

Tess averted her gaze, uncomfortable with the flattering name. She tasted the stew and her stomach clenched. Suddenly she was ravenous and the boiled vegetables and venison were the best she'd ever tasted.

"Brown Otter is my brother," Many Smiles said.

"He teaches me English." Spotting the empty water jug, the Blackfeet maiden picked it up. "I fill." Then she went outside, leaving Tess to devour the stew.

Setting aside the empty bowl, Tess leaned back, only then realizing that a tripod-shaped backrest was there to support her. Relaxing, she stared at the depiction of a sun high above her, and the moon and a few stars. Zigzag designs of red, yellow, and black bled through from the outside. The interior was draped with gauzy sheets, wafer-thin skins, and some furry buffalo robes.

Many Smiles came back inside, followed by Minipoka. The old woman beamed at Tess as Many Smiles poured Tess a cup of water.

"My medicine has chased the clouds from your head?" Minipoka asked.

"Most of them, yes," Tess agreed, taking the cup from Many Smiles and drinking the cool water. "I'm grateful to you, Minipoka." She drew her brows together. "How long have I been here?"

The old woman hitched a blanket shawl more tightly around her bony shoulders. "Two days. Not so long."

"Where is Storm-In-His-Eyes? I'm told that this is his home."

"He stays with Brown Otter while you are sick," Minipoka explained. "He is much worried about you and will be happy to know that you are no longer cloudy-headed."

Tess placed a hand to her own forehead. Her skin was cool. "Other than a slight headache, a few bruises, and bumps and a healthy dose of fear, I suppose I'm fine."

"Fear?" Minipoka knelt beside her. "You know the men who hurt you?"

"No, I don't think so. But I was thinking that—"

Whatever else she'd been about to say evaporated as the tent flap rose again, this time to admit Storm-In-His-Eyes.

The mere sight of him made Tess's foolish heart leap for joy and wedge itself in her throat. His black hair streaked over the shoulders of his doeskin shirt. Fringed leather leggings climbed up to his dark-blue loin cloth. An eagle feather bobbed at the back of his head, and rawhide strips of bright yellow and blue wove in and out of the narrow braids at the sides of his head. He approached her, his beaded moccasins whispering on the soft, hide-and-fur-strewn floor. She wanted him to smile, to beam at her, but he didn't. His expression was taciturn, his eyes furtive, meeting hers for brief seconds.

"Ah, so you're finally awake." He crouched beside her. "Do you remember what happened to you?"

"Yes, of course." Tess inched up, straightening her back and tamping down her giddiness at seeing him again. Obviously the feeling wasn't mutual.

"Do you know the men who attacked you?"

"They were wearing masks."

"Yes, but I thought you might have known them from their voices or by what they said to you."

She shook her head. "But I'm sure they're the outlaws the marshall is after. He's blaming you and Brown Otter for what those two white men are doing."

He shrugged. "But he won't believe that."

"I'll tell him," Tess asserted. "He'll have to believe it once I've told him of their attack on me."

Storm exchanged a speaking glance with Minipoka. Standing again, he looked down at Tess. "You will stay here until Minipoka says you are fit to travel, and then you will be taken back to your people."

"That's very kind." She noticed his erect posture and clear eyes. "You're feeling much better, I see."

He placed a hand on his chest, over the wound. "I am healing, yes. The sweating and chills are gone."

"That's good." Feeling awkward with Minipoka listening to every word, and Storm treating her as if she were an obligation, Tess folded her arms and waited for him to leave. She resented his cool manner toward her, but she knew what was behind it. He wanted her to understand that he was well and she was no longer needed. The sooner she left, the better he'd like it. That message pierced her heart and she fought the sudden urge to cry.

Sentimental fool, she called herself. Don't waste a tear on this ungrateful renegade. She plucked restlessly at the blanket covering her. When Storm made no move to leave, she darted a searing glare at him.

"Is there anything else on your mind?" she snapped.

He seemed surprised by her cutting tone, but he recovered quickly and shook his head. "No. Nothing." Then he turned on his heels and stalked away, out into the sunlight and away from her.

Tess sighed and closed her eyes. Terrible masks floated through her mind. Frightening masks. Indifferent masks. Faces that laughed, mocked, ridiculed, hid the reality, the heart.

She hated masks. All of them.

Venturing out of the lodge, Tess remained in the shadows as she approached the communal campfire, where many of the Blackfeet had converged. Hugging the edge of the darkness, Tess tested her

legs and stepped lightly in the unfamiliar moccasins. She felt like an interloper, an enemy stealing
into the Blackfeet camp to be pounced upon at any
moment. But those who saw her didn't pounce.
They smiled, they nodded, they gave her a wide
berth.

Several dogs stopped to sniff her before running
off, chasing each other's tails, tongues flapping out
the sides of their mouths. She passed a woman
about her age, sitting quietly while she nursed a
baby who couldn't have been more than a week
old. The young mother gave Tess a gentle smile
that was part pride, part wonder.

The mountain breeze stirred life inside of Tess
again, and her knees stopped shaking. Even the
ache in her back and head eased, whisked away by
the sighing wind carrying the smell of pine and
cedar and wood smoke.

Pausing beside a darkened lodge, Tess studied
the seated figures around the campfire until she
found the one she wanted. Her heart skipped. Her
knees quivered ever so slightly. Fool, she thought.
You're a fool for him.

Storm-In-His-Eyes spoke avidly with Brown Otter, seated on his right. The two men used their
hands, gesturing with short, stabbing arcs and jab-
bing fingers. She knew they conversed in Blackfeet
by the flexing of their throats around the guttural
sounds and the stillness of their lips, which were
hardly required to form the words. The tongue and
the throat did most of the work, she'd noticed.

Still dressed in his leggings and loincloth, Storm
wore no shirt this evening. His bare chest glistened,
the scars shining white, a two-inch wide bandage
ran over his shoulder and back up under his arm,
shielding his fresh wounds. He sat cross-legged, his
elbows propped on his knees, his face lit by the fire

glow. Even from the distance, Tess could see the sultry set of his wide mouth, the hooded intensity of his eyes. She shivered, watching his hands move, wanting them to move over her body; then watching his lips, wanting them on hers. A sweet craving spiraled through her, making her knees quiver again. Did he have any idea how much she cared? Would he be amused to know that she wanted to cry when she thought of leaving him?

A pretty Blackfeet maiden strolled into the firelight and stood behind Brown Otter. She said something and Storm looked at her, a ready smile finding his lips. He held her gaze and she held his.

Tess stepped forward, her heart tugging her even as her legs and feet tried to hold her back. She felt the warmth of the campfire on her face. Was this sienna-skinned beauty Storm's betrothed? she wondered, and something cold and hard dropped through her, landing in her stomach before sliding lower. Cold. So cold. She shivered and would have turned away, but Storm chose that moment to look in her direction.

Looking across the campfire at Tess, Storm-In-His-Eyes was momentarily transfixed. She was a beautiful spirit rising from the ground, undulating before his eyes as smoke curled around her. When he'd seen her earlier, he'd wanted to crush her to him, rain kisses over her face, and thank all that was holy for her recovery. He'd been so afraid that she might not awaken from the attack.

Watching her, he bunched his hands into fists and swore vengeance on the men who had harmed her. They would suffer. He would see to it.

If Slow-Riding-Woman hadn't rested her hand on his shoulder, he might have stared at Tess for hours. Giving a start, he glanced at the woman behind him, saw her uncertain smile, then looked back at Tess, who wasn't smiling. Her gaze lifted slightly and he knew she was looking at the Blackfeet maiden. Regret seemed to shimmer around her like the undulating air. Turning, she walked toward his lodge, her steps laborious, her head down.

Storm muttered a dark oath that brought a gasp from Slow-Riding-Woman and a frown from Brown Otter. He surged up, telling himself he shouldn't go to her, but blatantly ignoring his own advice.

"Where do you run now?" Brown Otter asked.

"I run nowhere. I have to see someone."

"Her." The word was laden with accusations. Brown Otter shared a quick glance with Slow-Riding-Woman. "Stay here with us. The white woman should rest. She needs no visitors tonight."

"You speak wisdom," Storm agreed, but he left the camp fire anyway and followed Tess.

He thought of how strength had flowed into him when he'd thought she was in danger, of how he had commandeered one of the horses and had ridden with Brown Otter to find her; the blind rage he'd felt when he'd seen the two men hovering over her, one straddling her and trying to unbutton his fly while the other held her by the throat—his AnadaAki, prone on the dirty ground with her skirts pushed up and her eyes glazed with fear and confusion.

He had wished for the rifle, but Brown Otter had held it and finally fired, missing both men on purpose but scaring them away. If only he'd had the rifle, Storm thought, the fury boiling in him again. Those men would be dead and buried by now and he wouldn't have to worry that they might find Tess again and hurt her.

Standing outside his lodge, he paused to gather his self-will around him like a shield. He didn't want her to think that he had a wife or wife-to-be here among the Blackfeet, although that might happen someday. It was important that she not think of him as unfaithful. After all, he'd told her about being with Millie Long. She'd think he had placed his hands on a white woman even though he had a Blackfeet woman waiting for him.

He shifted uncomfortably, the loincloth rubbing him. The truth was he couldn't look at Tess without getting hard, but she was not to know that. She was to know only that he was an honorable man.

Cursing darkly again, he cleared his throat so she'd know he was about to invade the lodge, then threw back the flap and ducked inside.

She hadn't lit a fire and the light was pearly gray inside. He didn't see her at first, not until she moved to show that she was standing near the sleeping pallet, her hair shining around her head and down her back like a river of gold.

"You want something?" she asked, her voice striated with so many emotions he couldn't possibly know them all.

"I wanted only to . . ." *To taste you with my tongue and bury myself so deeply inside you that I will be lost.*

"To what? I don't want to keep you from your . . . friends."

"She is only that." He told himself not to move toward her, to keep his distance. Somehow he found himself standing near enough to see the freckles on her cheeks. "Out there, what you saw. You don't understand it. That woman, she is—"

"What's her name?"

Name? For a moment all he could remember were her names—Tess Summar, white medicine woman, AnadaAki. "Her name," he repeated numbly before it popped onto his tongue. "Slow-Riding-Woman."

She made a humming noise in her throat and swept one beaded moccasin in a graceful half-moon. "She didn't seem slow to me. Seemed she moved pretty fast."

The jealousy in her tone wasn't hard to miss. "She isn't my woman or my intended."

"Who is she intended for, then?" Her gaze lifted to do battle with his and wring the truth from him.

"Me, maybe. Maybe not. It hasn't been decided, but there has been talk, there have been signs." He shrugged one shoulder, trying to make her understand that what he felt for Slow-Riding-Woman was dust, and what he felt looking at Tess in the filtered moonlight was as solid as a gold nugget. "But I've made no promises to anyone about her. I won't take a wife until all trouble is behind me."

"Ah, but you won't go without either, will you?" Her blue-green eyes challenged him, taunted him. "You won't suffer each and every night, will you, Storm? Will you strap on the chastity belt until you are proven innocent?"

Her challenging tone licked at him like a whip. Reaching for her, he wrapped his arm around her waist. "You mock me," he nearly growled at her.

"No, I merely doubt you."

"I am an honorable man."

She blinked at him, her eyes wide and coy. "Whatever you say. Who am I to question—"

Her mouth was too close, too fetching. His lips stopped her nonsense words and she made that humming noise in her throat again, except that this time she sounded like a cat purring. He growled in response and slanted his mouth over hers as he pulled her up tight against him.

Nudging her lips insistently, he rubbed them

apart and stoked her fires with his tongue. She tasted clean and bracing like mountain water. Her tongue touched his, softly stirring, gently probing. He caught her up against him, pushing himself against her so that she might know how she affected him, so that she could take pleasure in being right about him. Yes, he hungered. Yes, he craved. Yes, he wanted to have her here and now.

He felt her hands in his hair, moving and stroking, grabbing strands and wrapping them loosely around her fingers. Smoothing his palms over her head, he framed her face and deepened his kiss until she groaned and sagged against him.

Together they dropped to their knees on the soft pallet of buffalo robes and wolf furs. Her hands felt like cool rain on his heated skin, skimming over his scars and bandages, kneading the muscles in his shoulders and upper arms. He blew softly in her ear and cupped her breasts. They filled his hands and he moved his thumbs across the beaded bodice of her leather dress until he found the softer, sensitive beads beneath. He chased those nubs with his thumbs, feeling them grow, opening his mouth wider to accept her thrusting tongue.

Tearing his mouth from hers, he stared at her face until she opened her eyes. "I have yearned for this," he whispered to her.

"I know," she replied, a dreamy smile gracing her swollen lips.

He licked her glistening mouth, tasting the mingling of their juices. She lay back, stretching out, her hands resting lightly on his bare shoulders.

"How do you know?" he asked, smiling at the simmering pleasure in her eyes. She was steaming with desire and it seemed to rise up off her like curls of smoke that only he could see. The leather dress was bunched at the waist, probably by his hands, and he could see her long, pale legs. They were slim and shapely, her thighs creamy in the moonlight. He hardened even more and winced. He'd never been so hard, so full of wanting. He could barely hear her above the gushing of blood in his ears.

"You tried to . . . well, make love to me one night when you were still funny in the head with fever." Spots of color bloomed in her cheeks. "Of course, you didn't know it was me, so I'm not suggesting that—"

He swooped down and kissed her quiet. She wrapped her arms around his neck and arched her body into his. The cloth covering him rode up, exposing him, allowing that throbbing skin to slide against her thigh, so soft, so virginal.

Expecting her to turn to stone, he lifted his mouth from hers to meet her gaze. She smiled and moved her leg so that her thigh caressed him. His organ pumped, throbbed. His moan burned up his throat and sounded to his ears like a wounded animal's cry.

"You are so untouched," he whispered, dropping kisses upon her freckled cheeks, her pouting lips. "I have no right to take from you what you don't know how to give."

"I know how," she asserted.

He studied her, seeing no artifice. "You have been with a man already? That's what you're telling me?"

She giggled like no Blackfeet woman could. Her laughter was musical and floated through his head like a song. "Of course not. No one, but you. But I know about men and women and . . . well, mating. I know what is expected of me."

"How do you know this?"

Hooking her hands at the backs of his upper

arms, she raised herself up to whisper in his ear. "I'm a medicine woman. I *know* these things. I've read all about them."

He stiffened his lips to keep from grinning and grasped one of her hands. Pushing it down between their bodies, he placed her palm against the length of him. She gasped and tried to snatch her hand back, but he held her in place as her fingers stretched and tried not to touch him.

"You know what those two men were trying to do to you, yes?"

"Y-yes."

"Same thing I am trying?"

"No!" Anger blazed like twin flames in her eyes. "I might be a spinster, but I'm not a ninny. Rape and what I thought we were going to do together ... well, they are two quite different acts. And I shouldn't have to explain this to you, Storm. You should *know*." She turned her head, averting her gaze from him. "Now let go of my hand."

He grazed her flushed cheek with his lips. "I do know," he whispered. "I'm trying to understand why you would allow me to do this to you. You have remained innocent for so long, and now you are willing to give yourself to a Blackfeet warrior, a man with a price on his head?"

Her lower lip quivered. "Perhaps I was wrong."

He grasped her chin and hauled her face around to his again. Her eyes were wide and winsome, brimming with disappointment and lingering desire. "And perhaps your head tells you what mine tells me, that you are crazy to want me, that you must not touch me, that you must not think of me. And perhaps you can't help yourself. Perhaps you can't stop yourself from feeling and touching and—" With a groan, he kissed her again, his lips grinding relentlessly against hers, his tongue surging in with wild desperation.

Her fingers caressed his hot, swollen flesh and he squeezed his eyes shut as a tremble shook him and all the blood in his body seemed to pool in that place between his legs, that aching, heavy, throbbing place.

"Yessss," he hissed and her hand surrounded him, moved up and down the length of him, squeezed him. He bucked and his mind froze, went black as colors exploded behind his eyes and hoarse cries burst from his throat. Her lips spread fire down his throat, and the tip of her tongue trailed sweetness across his shoulder. The world seemed to fall around him like pieces of a dream, and then he felt her shift and her hand came away slowly.

He bowed his head, hiding his face in the curve of her neck and feeling like a boy for the first time since he was allowed to dance with the other men in the circle.

"I'm sorry," he mumbled against her sweet-smelling skin. "I didn't mean to . . . I'm sorry."

Her other hand drifted over his hair. "It's all right."

But it wasn't. He had emptied himself, ruining the bedding and the dream of how it would be for them the first time.

A voice drifted from outside. "Storm-In-His-Eyes? I know you are in there. Answer this old grandmother."

He groaned softly before lifting his head, but still unable to look Tess in the eye. "I am here. What do you want?" he called in Blackfeet.

"I want you, my grandson. I have had a vision. Come to my lodge and hurry."

He sighed, his eyes closed.

"What did she say?" Tess asked, moving a little to one side so that his weight was no longer on her.

"I have to go." He stood up and made sure his loincloth covered him. His glance, although fleeting, proved him right. The spoilage was on her dress, maybe even some on her thighs, and on the blanket beneath her. "Forgive me." Embarrassed, angry at himself and trembling from the passion that had erupted in him so suddenly that he'd had no time to think, only to be taken by it, consumed by it, he wheeled around and did everything but chase his own shadow out of the lodge.

Chapter 9

Stopping off at a water barrel to splash himself and cleanse the residue of spent passion from him, Storm tried not to think about what had just happened between him and Tess. Wanting her was wrong, so why couldn't he put her from his mind and from his heart? He had done so with other females, women who belonged to other men or who only wanted to use him for their own twisted means. Not that Tess was guilty of those things. It was wrong to want Tess because nothing but grief could come from it.

Their union couldn't be permanent, and he wanted nothing less than that with her. She wouldn't live with the Blackfeet, and he refused to live among the whites again. Once this war with the marshall was over, Storm wanted to surround himself with his Blackfeet relatives and enjoy being part of a whole. In the white world he had felt so alone. He never wanted to feel that soul-crushing solitude again.

Yes, it was but a dream to think of him and the white medicine woman together. Maybe for a night

but not a life. He could have her in his dreams—
and he often did—but that was all.

He'd have to keep his distance, he resolved, running a hand down his face as he tried to block out
thoughts of what had happened in his lodge. Ah,
but it had felt so good to be touched by her, to taste
her and feel her respond to him.

Perhaps they could handle a few nights together.
If he made her understand that their union was a
flickering flame not a long-burning one, they might
. . . no. He shook his head sadly and regretfully.
She would be hurt. He knew enough about women
to know that when they took a man into their beds,
they usually took them into their hearts as well.

He wouldn't want Tess to feel that he had used
her. He knew that pain. When he'd lived with the
white eyes, he had mistaken curiosity for caring
and had bedded a woman who had pressed money
into his hand when they had finished pleasuring
each other. She'd tried to *pay* him, *buy* him. When
he'd refused the money and had told her what he'd
thought of the gesture, she'd spit in his face and
called him a heathen.

Beating down those demeaning, mean-spirited
feelings, he vowed never to inflict them on Tess.
He would rather disappoint or frustrate her by not
making love to her than be hated for selfishly using
her.

Finding himself outside Minipoka's large skin
lodge, he pushed back his shoulders and laid a
hand against his bandaged wound. The skin
around the hole burned and was tight, but he knew
that healing was taking place. Soon he would be
able to fight to clear his name, avenge his sister's
death, and track down the men who had attacked
Tess.

"Old grandmother," he called out, using the

term of respect and endearment. "It's me, your grandson Storm-In-His-Eyes."

"Enter and sit by my fire," she responded in the cracked voice that could be downy soft or flinty hard.

He found her sitting beside her cooking fire, her shoulders hunched, her gray head nodding as she hummed to herself. The lodge smelled of incense and bear fat. His eyes watered slightly, stung by the aromatic smoke. Picking his way across the rush-covered floor, he sat opposite the old woman and waited for her to speak, as was the custom. She took her time, her eyes closed, her body swaying as she continued humming an old song Storm had heard since boyhood. He was beginning to think he might spend the rest of the night here by the fire with the old woman when her song dwindled and she smiled faintly. Her stubby lashes fluttered and lifted to reveal charcoal eyes, the whites now yellowed and filmy with age and disease.

"I have been visited by the spirits," she said. "They have given me visions, mostly about you and the way you must follow."

Storm rested his elbows on his knees and listened intently. Minipoka's visions were true and only fools would ignore them. Storm had always respected the old woman and obeyed her, although sometimes her directions were odd and seemed pointless. Always they had proved wise, and Storm believed that Minipoka did commune with the gods of the Blackfeet because her medicine was all-powerful. Even the great chiefs of the Blood tribes listened when Minipoka spoke.

"You are tainted by the white men," she said. "You must remove this bad medicine from your body. Tonight you will go to the sweat lodge and you will stay there until the spirits speak to you and tell you what must be done. You will take nothing but water into your body."

Dread tumbled through him. He'd already spent time in the sweat lodge, ridding his body of the impurities. It was a lonely vigil, and one he didn't want to repeat. But if Minipoka said it must be done, then he'd obey. Would Tess be gone by the time he emerged from the lodge? Would he be deprived of a last good-bye? Maybe that would be best. Perhaps the gods wanted them to part as strangers.

"I have been shown a two-headed white snake," Minipoka said, her voice taking on an awed, hushed quality. "The gods put this vision in my head. And I saw you." She closed her eyes slowly, folding into herself as he watched, her shoulders drawing forward, her chin dropping to her chest. A small hump of a woman.

Storm waited, his nerves thrumming. What could it mean, a two-headed snake? What were the gods trying to tell him?

Minipoka stirred and lifted her head, but she kept her eyes shut. "One of the heads sank its fangs into your neck."

Storm resisted the urge to cover the side of his neck with his hand, but he felt the bite.

"The other head attacked it, killed it. And, of course, killed itself, too, so that you might live." She opened her eyes again and the pupils were dark and fathomless. "You are important to the gods, my grandson. They have guided you back to us, blocked your passage to their world, and now they tell me of your fate."

"But what does the vision mean?" he asked, unable to keep the questions inside any longer. "And why was I brought back here when all I've done is rain trouble on my people?"

Minipoka chuckled silently, her shoulders and throat moving, but no sound emerging. "You ask, you ask, but you ask the wrong person. *You* have the answers, my grandson. They are all in you." She stared at the fire for long moments before speaking again. "Some of the answers you will find after the poisons have leaked from your body and your head is clear again. Other answers you already know, but you are willful and won't take them into your heart."

He shook his head. "I long for answers. Why wouldn't I embrace any that came to me?"

"Why? Yes, why, my grandson?" Smiling, she motioned for him to come closer and patted the ground beside her. "Come to old grandmother, boy. Let me lay my wrinkled hands on you and speak to you through them."

Pushing to his feet, he moved around the fire to sit by her side. It had been a long time since she had communed with him with only her hands. He loved her hands. His eyes closed on their own as her warm, dry fingertips stroked across his forehead and to his temples. He realized only then that a sheen of perspiration covered him and he was cool, almost cold. But her hands, they warmed him and brought him a glimmering peace deep, deep in his soul.

As a young boy he would sit for hours and let this old woman comb his hair with pine cones and tell him of her childhood. She'd been married when she was six to a man of thirty-three, who already had two other wives. But it had been a good marriage for her and her family because the man was respected and had wealth. She didn't need to scrub or clean because the middle wife did all of that. The oldest wife saw to the man's physical needs, leaving Minipoka to play with his children, some older and some younger than she. That's how she was given her name. Minipoka, the favorite one.

When the man died some twenty years later, the wives went back to their tribal families. Minipoka was taken in by her oldest brother, who had become a powerful leader and holy man of the Blood. She told him of the visions she had known since she was a child, and he saw that she was touched by the gods and the higher spirits. He saw that she was their favorite, too. And so her power became legend among the Blood, and she reigned over many Sun Dances for she was a woman of true virtue. No man had ever lain with her. Even to this day, Storm assumed, for she had taken no other husband.

Now her hands moved lightly over his face. She flattened one against his forehead and the other over his heart. Instantly he felt a change within him. A light glowed in his mind and his heart heated like a stoked fire. He saw, clear as daybreak, AnadaAki, and his heart swelled.

A beauty, she was, walking through golden light; her hair like a sunrise, her smile alone giving him infinite pleasure. She stopped and turned toward him, and her eyes glowed with recognition and love. Holding out one hand, she beckoned and he felt his whole body jerk forward in response.

"Take me," his AnadaAki said. "Make me yours."

Blood boiled in his loins and shot fire to his organ.

Minipoka chuckled and the vision dissolved. Storm opened his eyes to see the old woman's gap-toothed grin.

"You got that white woman on the mind, eh, grandson?"

He started to shake his head, but froze when the

hand covering his heart suddenly darted beneath his loincloth to find his bobbing man-root.

She laughed. "The spirits have placed a different kind of fever in you, Storm-In-His-Eyes. This fever can be doused only by mating with the white medicine woman."

Her hand slipped out from under his loincloth, and he released a long sigh of relief. Twice he had been embarrassed by a woman tonight. It was almost too much.

"Hear me, big stick." Her eyes danced with lights, and Storm knew she was making reference to his organ. "Are you listening?"

"I am," he assured her, his pride pawing; his very maleness flinching from her jesting.

"The cure, making love to the white woman—"

"I won't," he said. "That is no cure. That is a curse."

"You listen," she said, and the twinkles went out of her eyes. The corners of her mouth dipped downward with displeasure. "The cure could cloud your judgment and could lead to your death. You must be careful," she warned, grasping his forearm with both hands. "You must weigh all risks, all dangers, and then decide if the cure is worth the price. I tell you this not to push you in one direction or the other. I tell you only because it is my duty."

Her hands slipped away and she faced the fire again. Storm remained seated beside her and waited. Obviously she wasn't through with him. There was more, but she took her time as elders often did. Their age gave them the luxury, the privilege of moving at their own, comfortable paces.

"When I was a girl . . . maybe seven or eight summers old, I saw a doll that I very much wanted. This doll belonged to one of my husband's children—an older child, and one I had to give over to because she was the first daughter. This doll was made of corn husks and real human hair. The hair was red like those coals." She nodded to the fire. "It was the most beautiful doll, and the first daughter knew I wanted it more than anything, so she hid it from me and never allowed me to even touch it."

Minipoka picked up a long stick and poked at the fire, encouraging flames to leap and firewood to break and send embers flying up through the smoke hole.

"First daughter has since joined the spirit world," she said in her way of explaining why she didn't use the woman's given name, lest the woman's ghost might return, thinking she'd been called back to this world. "Back then she did not like me so much because I was the youngest wife, and my husband thought me very pretty. He treated me as I wanted to treat first daughter's doll. Finally first daughter grew tired of the doll. She had so many others, you see. So, she offered the doll to me if I would do one thing." Her eyes shifted sideways to glance at him. "I must sew her a new dress and decorate it with the many shiny beads and shells from the dress that I wore on my wedding day. This dress I prized, and it tore at my heart to think of stripping off the colorful beads and white shells. It would ruin my beautiful dress."

She tossed the stirring stick into the fire and watched as the flames ate hungrily at it. After a few minutes she sighed and her eyes glimmered with old tears.

"But I wanted the doll. The dress had given me pleasure, but I would never wear it again. I cried as I removed the beads from my dress and sewed them onto the one I made for the first daughter.

And I cried when I gave that dress to first daughter. But my tears dried and I had my doll, which gave me many, many days of happiness. So it was a hard trade but a good one, and my regrets were fleeting like snowflakes in the sun." She turned her head and smiled at him. "Some trades seem too harsh, my grandson, but they will give pleasure for a long time to come. Some trades are easy, but the thing you've traded for loses its value in the blink of an eye, and you are left with drops of water instead of beautiful snowflakes."

He nodded, understanding that she was talking about the decision he would be forced to make concerning Tess. He couldn't deny his craving for her, but he must think carefully before acting on it. Would the pleasure be worth the trouble such an action might cause? Would loving her once be worth the pain of losing her forever? The gods had warned him to be careful not to bring about his own death by reaching for something that might not be his to take.

"Just because she is white does not make her evil," Minipoka said.

"I know she's not evil," he allowed. "She has a good heart and a fine spirit."

"And she has a heart that beats in time with yours. Some unions can't be imagined. Who could have known how my own marriage would serve a higher purpose in my life?" She sighed wistfully, he thought. "We cannot see so far ahead, my grandson. Not with our eyes, anyway. Maybe with our hearts. Many times our eyes deceive us but not our hearts." She patted his knee. "Go now, young buck. Leave this old woman to smoke her pipe and dream her dreams."

Storm rested a hand on her hair, gray and coarse and stretched tightly across her head in a thick braid. He kissed her wrinkled cheek and love crowded into his chest.

"Thank you, old grandmother. As always, I will heed your words. I will live by your wisdom."

He rose to his feet and left the woman who could always bring peace to his warrior's heart. For a moment he thought of telling Tess of his destiny with the sweat lodge, but then he decided to leave that to Minipoka. She would find the right words to explain to Tess, and he felt empty of words. What he had dreaded—all those lonesome hours in the lodge with his body bleeding sweat—he now hurried toward.

When the light changed in the lodge, Tess whirled toward the opening, thinking it would be Storm returning to her. He'd been gone for hours, having been called away by Minipoka at a most inopportune moment. She'd used the time to tidy up, secretly pleased that he'd lost control with her. Surely this was a good sign. A man like Storm certainly had experience with women and knew how to pace himself. But he had trembled violently in her arms and . . .

Her thoughts stumbled as she stared at the woman who entered her lodge. Slow-Riding-Woman? Now what did *she* want? Tess schooled her expression carefully, determined not to show the young Blackfeet a hint of the jealousy and self-doubt surging through her at the sight of the pretty maiden with her jet-black hair and copper-colored skin.

"Storm isn't here," Tess said.

"I know. He has been sent away from you."

Tess's heart bucked, then settled. She regarded the other woman for a few moments. "He's visiting Minipoka."

Slow-Riding-Woman walked further inside, her movements as graceful and precise as a doe's. "He has gone to a sweat lodge to remove the poison placed in him by"— her dark brown eyes moved, raking Tess from head to toe—"white people." The last two words she spoke with heavy venom. "Once Storm-In-His-Eyes was an honorable warrior, but a white man tempted him and he left the Blood to explore beyond the great mountains. When he returned he was broken, his spirit weak. He will regain his courage and his strength, but he must first be rid of the white eyes' bad medicine."

Tess listened, impressed with Slow-Riding-Woman's grasp of English, but not so impressed with what she said. "Who taught you my language?"

"My father. He was a scout for the blue coats during the great war. They taught him, and he taught his children to know when the white eyes' plot against us and when they lie."

"I see." Tess refused to rise to the bait the Blackfeet maiden dangled before her. Keeping her smile civil and her temper firmly in hand, Tess motioned to what she thought could be a couch on the north side of the tepee. "Won't you sit down?"

Glancing with derision at the mounds of skins and furs, Slow-Riding-Woman moved to the opposite side and sat on a brightly colored blanket. "It is our way that men sit at the north."

"Oh." Tess shrugged. "I didn't know."

"There is much you don't know."

Sitting across from the insolent young woman, Tess arched a brow. "And there is much *you* don't know as well," she rejoined. Guessing that she was older than Slow-Riding-Woman by a few years, Tess determined to use that advantage. "You obviously don't know that this particular white eyes used good medicine on Storm and made him well again."

"Minipoka's medicine healed him."

Tess gritted her teeth and forced herself not to yell. "He was half-dead when I found him and it was *my* medicine that removed him from death's door." Sitting cross-legged, she pulled the leather skirt over her knees, then noticed the Blackfeet woman was looking at her with disgust. "Now what? Obviously you find something displeasing about me."

"The way you sit. No woman of respect would sit with her legs spread apart." She glanced at her own posture, her legs tucked neatly to one side, her buckskin skirt hiding everything except her beaded moccasins.

Sighing, Tess adopted the same pose. "You know, we could spar like this all evening. I could point out to you my superior knowledge of medicine and the ways of the world outside this camp, and you could annoy me with your knowledge of the Blackfeet tradition. Is that how you want to spend our time together, or have you another purpose in mind?"

For a moment Tess saw pure hatred in the woman's eyes, but then the Blackfeet looked away as if she knew she'd revealed too much. "You must leave while Storm-In-His-Eyes is in the sweat lodge. Staying here will harm him. He needs to be away from all white eyes."

"I'll leave when Minipoka says I should. I'm under her care."

"You can't think for yourself?" Slow-Riding-Woman snapped, her lips drawing into a tense line.

"Yes, and I think I'll stay until I'm ready to ride. I was viciously attacked, as you must know, and I haven't regained my strength yet. It's a long ride back to False Hope, and I want to be sure I can make it."

"You fool others, maybe, but not me. I know you stay and think that Storm-In-His-Eyes will choose you. He will choose a woman of his own kind, not a white eyes."

"His own kind . . ." Tess recalled the silvery-gray of his eyes. "Doesn't he have white blood in him?"

"Very little and from long, long ago. No one even remembers which of his forefathers took a white woman for a wife. Even Minipoka cannot remember, and she is the oldest here. Storm-In-His-Eyes is needed here. He has wisdom and has seen many things about the world. He has lived among the whites and knows their lies, their tricks. We look to him as one who can show us the true way, one who could guide us. You must remove yourself from his sight so he won't be tempted by what can only bring him much trouble."

Tess didn't like the lecture one little bit. She eyed the woman, amazed at her cheekiness. "Did someone send you in here? Brown Otter, maybe?"

"I came on my own. I thought you would listen to a woman who knows Storm-In-His-Eyes in ways you will never know him."

"Oh, is that right?" Tess sized up her adversary, wondering at the wisdom of engaging in a verbal brawl over a man neither one could claim. "You'll forgive me if I doubt you. From what I saw out by the fire, I don't think you have any romantic past with Storm. He looked at you as if you were his little sister." He hadn't, of course, Tess allowed, but one good lie deserved another. Slow-Riding-Woman was no more important to Storm than any other Blackfeet maiden in this camp. Storm, himself, had told her as much.

"You are wrong." The young woman leaned forward, jutting out her chin, her dark eyes glimmering. "You think your white skin and yellow hair can lure him, can keep him away from what is in his heart, but the Creator will not allow it. The spirits will guide him back to his people, and you will not be able to stop this." Her hand shot out and she grabbed Tess by the wrist. "If you care for him, then leave."

"Now look here, I know why you're doing this and I..." Tess heard the scrape of feet on the ground and felt the breeze from outside. She turned to confront a wide-eyed Many-Smiles-Woman. The newcomer looked from Tess to Slow-Riding-Woman and her eyes narrowed.

"I bring Minipoka's tea and bread and butter," Many Smiles said, coming inside and approaching the other two women. "What bring you, Slow-Riding-Woman?"

"Tall tales," Tess responded with a cheery smile. "I'm so glad to see you. Won't you join us?"

"I am going." Slow-Riding-Woman stood, and in a fluid motion, was heading for the lodge flap, held open for her by Many Smiles.

"Too bad. I love girl-talk," Tess said. "Thanks for stopping by and bringing such glad tidings." She gave a wincing smile that was not returned.

"You mock, but you will see that I'm right." Slow-Riding-Woman spared a menacing glare for Many Smiles before ducking and disappearing into the darkness outside.

Many Smiles let go of the flap and released a sigh. "She says she belongs to Storm-In-His-Eyes, yes?"

"Yes, she did, in so many words." Tess accepted the tin cup and hunk of bread, smeared with salted butter. "But, don't worry. I didn't believe a word of it."

Many Smiles suddenly looked sad.

"What's wrong?" Tess asked. "Has something happened to Storm? Slow-Riding-Woman said he has gone to a sweat lodge or something like that. I assume it's a ritual of sorts, but it's not dangerous, is it?"

"No, no." Many Smiles patted the air, placating Tess. "Sweat is good, but . . ." She shrugged helplessly. "Slow-Riding-Woman makes mischief, but she does not lie. She belongs to Storm-In-His-Eyes."

Chapter 10

The night and following day seemed endless to Tess. Getting only a few hours of sleep after Many Smiles left her alone, Tess had gone over and over in her mind the newest catastrophe in her life.

According to Many Smiles, Slow-Riding-Woman was in line to marry Storm-In-His-Eyes. Since her oldest sister had been the one betrothed to Storm as a child and had died young, the next unmarried daughter in line must honor her sister's betrothal.

Throughout the restless night, Tess had wrestled with this idea, finding the custom bizarre and comforting herself with the knowledge that Storm had sought *her* out earlier, not Slow-Riding-Woman. He had demonstrated his preference, which woman he wanted.

However, the next day her self-confidence waned as she rested and drank Minipoka's strong tea and felt her strength return after a delicious noon-day meal of roasted elk ribs, boiled greens and potatoes, and berry pudding. Perhaps she was placing too much importance on his actions last night, she argued with herself. He might have been flirting with her, playing with her, but not taking her seriously. After all, hadn't he told her he had contempt for white people? Of course he would marry a Blackfeet. She was foolish to think he'd even consider making a white woman his wife.

Later she remembered his kisses and how he had trembled so violently in her arms when she had caressed him. There was no denying the way the air almost sizzled when they were together. And when they touched . . . all else seemed small and insignificant. She knew he felt these things just as keenly. He might have a Blackfeet bride waiting patiently for him, but he also had a passion for a white woman.

During the meal she had learned more about the sweat lodge where Storm had taken himself on Minipoka's advice. She likened it to forms of meditation she'd read about in some of John's books about Far East practices and beliefs. Observing the Blackfeet had given her many insights, and she realized she was beginning to understand them and that they were generally maligned by white people, who made fun of or feared their mystic ways instead of simply accepting them.

After eating enough for two people, Tess curled on the pallet and slept. When she awoke hours later, she found Minipoka sitting near her, a peaceful smile on her aged face. Tess sat up and rubbed her eyes, wondering how long the old Blackfeet woman had been watching her.

"You must think I'm a lazy lay-about," Tess said, pushing aside the covers and glancing toward the open flap. The sky was deep purple. Night was falling. "I didn't mean to sleep so long."

"Sleep is good." Minipoka moved to sit against the south wall of the tepee. She took a pipe from her pocket, lit it from a twig near from the fire, and sat back to smoke, extreme pleasure apparent in her expression.

Tess brushed her hair and straightened her clothes, wondering if she should offer something to Minipoka, but what? This wasn't her lodge and she didn't know where anything was kept in the way of tea or coffee or any utensils. So far all food had been brought to her, and the fire in the lodge was small, apparently used for heating and not for cooking.

"What do you think of us?" Minipoka asked, her eyes squinted against the pipe smoke.

"You've all been very nice to me," Tess answered, rather lamely she thought.

"You may speak from the heart to old grandmother. You think we are full of foolish notions, eh?"

"No, not really." Tess paused, choosing her words carefully so as not to offend the woman she'd come to respect. "I think the Blackfeet believe in magic, in gods and spirits, in other worlds beyond this one."

Minipoka nodded her gray head. "It is true. We believe in the great Creator."

"So do we," Tess said.

"Have you heard any talk of Napi?"

"No. Is he the chief?"

Minipoka chuckled and smoke poured from her mouth. "He is the first chief. Napi—it means 'old man' in your language—is one of the children from the first man and woman. He is most cunning and made great blessings for us and great tragedies. He taught us our ways."

"How were the first man and woman made?" Tess asked, wondering if it would be similar to the biblical stories of Adam and Eve.

"The Creator made them from a buffalo bone

and mud. He blew on them, bringing them to life, and taught them how to make others of their kind so they wouldn't be lonely." Her eyes twinkled. "A wolf happened by and wanted to help. He blew on the woman, then howled. This is why women have higher voices. They are trying to sound like their helper, the wolf."

Enchanted by the stories, Tess moved closer so as to catch every word. Minipoka nodded as if she were pleased by Tess's interest in her legends and religious beliefs.

"A serpent tempted our first people," Tess told her.

"Yes, I have heard these stories of the white people. Many white men and women have stayed with the Blackfeet. Trappers, traders, holy men. Our stories are not so different from the white eyes' stories."

"I'm sure you're right. They're meant to guide us in the right directions, to keep us honorable and respectful."

Minipoka nodded slowly and regarded Tess for a few moments. "I see that you open your heart and your head to that which is different. It is like when the elk called the buffalo his brother and the buffalo said, 'I am not your brother. I am different from you.' And the elk said, 'I look at you and see a brother. You look at me and see a stranger. But when men look at us they see meat and hide. We are not so different, depending on who is looking and what they want to see.' "

Tess laughed softly. "I must remember that story so I can tell my brother. Maybe he'll learn something from it."

"You aren't happy in the town called False Hope."

Tess gave a start, wondering how the old woman

had discovered this. "I'm not unhappy," Tess amended. "It's just that . . . well, I need to find somewhere else to live. My brother and his wife should make a home without me in it."

"You could marry."

"Yes, if I could find a man I love."

"What if this man was not loved by your family?"

Tess's heart quickened and her breath shortened. Was the wise woman talking about Storm? Did she know that Tess had never felt so alive as when she was in his arms? "My family would have to accept my decision, I suppose. I'm old enough to know what I want."

Minipoka blew smoke and watched it circle and twine above her head. "You have a waiting heart."

"What do you mean?"

"A heart that waits is wise . . . and lonely. But, often, the ones with waiting hearts make the best matches. I know a certain Blackfeet warrior who also has a waiting heart." She glanced at Tess and her eyes laughed. "Napi taught us that men and women didn't get along for ages. Napi finally met with the chief of the women and said something must be done so that men and women can live together."

"The women had a chief?" Tess asked, liking this story more and more.

The old woman nodded, smiling around the pipe stem. "Women need leaders, too. The chief of the women said Napi could make the first decision as long as she always got the final word. Napi said this was okay with him, and so it was and still is between men and women."

"Compromise," Tess said, smiling, and Minipoka nodded in happy agreement. "What else did the men and women compromise on?"

"Many, many things. Men and women were both told to cook, but the men decided they would cook quick over open fires, and the women said that was fine. The women would cook slow and use utensils, and their food would not be burned and would taste better. And so it was and so it is."

Tess laughed softly, finding the tales of compromise so much more appealing than strict rules and iron-clad verbatims. The Blackfeet ways seemed simple and gentle.

"When a Blackfeet man decides, you must know that you do not have to obey. A Blackfeet man sometimes decides what he thinks will cause no quarrels; but he knows his woman will have the last word, and he trusts her to follow her heart and do what is best for both of them, though it might not be the easy path and others might shake their fingers and wag their heads and talk bad talk about them."

Tess sobered, realizing she was being given sage advice. "So the Blackfeet man will be happy with his woman's decision because he expects it?"

Minipoka drew deeply on the pipe, making a whistling noise as the tobacco fired and crackled in the bowl. "When the others call him a fool, he can point to his woman and save face. He can say, 'She is the one who wants this, and I go along because it is how Napi teaches us.' But in his heart, he is glad."

"So it was, and so it is," Tess said, exchanging a knowing smile with the old woman. "I'm glad you shared this with me, Minipoka, because I very much want to understand the Blackfeet." She drew a circle in the thick wolf's fur rug she sat on. "Minipoka, what does it mean if a woman is promised to a man? Must the man marry her?"

"If the families have agreed, then he must honor the agreement."

Tess closed her eyes, stricken by the news.

"If he changes his mind, he can make a new agreement with the family. Maybe he agrees to give the family goods and valuables if a dowry was paid, and this will free the woman to find someone else and does not disgrace her or her family." Little puffs of smoke escaped with her words. The air was redolent with the aroma of tobacco. "It is not so uncommon for a girl to be promised to a much older man. Our people know that a man is not fit to marry until he is full-grown and has had his adventures, his battles with death. Sometimes these men decide they do not want the young girls as wives. Maybe his heart is stolen by another during his adventures, so he breaks the agreement in an honorable fashion and everyone is satisfied. It is the way of men and women."

Tess released her pent-up breath slowly as a flicker of hope glowed in her mind and heart. Gazing at the old woman's profile, she felt a sudden, overwhelming desire to speak her deepest secret. "Minipoka, forgive me, but I think . . . I've never felt for any man what I feel for Storm-In-His-Eyes. Am I a fool?"

The medicine woman checked her pipe. She tapped it against the sole of her moccasin, knocking out the burned tobacco.

She held out both hands to Tess. "Help me to stand. I must go now."

Tess's heart plummeted. She'd spoken out of turn, should have kept her mouth shut. Standing up, she grasped the old woman's hands and pulled her to her feet. Minipoka couldn't weigh more than ninety pounds, Tess thought, scrutinizing her bent shoulders, humped back, and scant hips. Tess walked with her to the tepee opening, wondering if she should apologize or just leave well-enough alone.

"The next time you see him he will be different," Minipoka said as she stood in front of the opening and looked out at the banked communal fire and starry night. With a start, Tess realized she was talking about Storm. "He will have seen things, and he will know things that he will not share with you for they are private between him and the spirits. But one truth he will know when he looks at Slow-Riding-Woman is that she will be a good wife to him, but she will never be a sits-beside-him wife."

Tess shook her head. "I don't know what that means. Sits beside him?"

"The sits-beside-him wife . . . her place is beside her husband and no other wives may sit there. Not all men take more than one wife. If their main wife is all they need, all they desire, then it is enough. Only one can be his equal. Other wives he takes for other reasons, to sit near the door or the cooking fire, but not beside him. Never beside him." Minipoka turned her head and lifted her gaze to Tess's. "Already you sit beside him, but he might not see this. You might want to show him, AnadaAki. Sometimes, as Napi knew, we Blackfeet must be shown the way."

Tess closed her eyes for a moment, seized with sudden, piercing joy. "If he chooses my path, it will be a difficult journey."

Minipoka rested a hand on her shoulder. "That grandson of mine has always chosen such paths. He is a child of the mountains and expects the road to be rocky and twisting." She patted Tess's shoulder slowly, then gathered her shawl around her stooped shoulders and left the lodge.

Tess watched Minipoka's halting progress to her lodge, a big one that always seemed to have children around it. Stepping outside, Tess took in the sweep of the village, the conical shapes poking into the night sky, the smoke from the fires hovering like gray clouds, the glisten of a mountain stream on the edge of the camp. She could see the dark shapes of horses at the stream and the darting of bodies, young Blackfeet, who guarded the herds at night.

The air had a bite to it, sliding down from the snow caps, and Tess shivered and went back inside. She closed the flap, content to be alone with her dreams of Storm-In-His-Eyes. Lying on the soft pallet, she went over all the fascinating tales Minipoka had shared.

"Sits-beside-him wife," she whispered, then laughed softly and stretched like a cream-fed cat. Ah, yes. She liked the sound of that.

Slumping against the lodge wall, Storm breathed shallowly. Sweat rolled off his body in big, fat drops. He wanted to open his eyes, but he couldn't. His strength depleted, he could no longer fight the visions, the dreams, the thoughts of *her*. He groaned in desperation. He'd come to the sweat lodge to be rid of the white eyes' poison, but all he could think about was a white woman with freckles and dark gold hair.

His lips moved, forming Blackfeet words of prayer, of salvation. He begged the Creator to give him a vision that would show him the true way.

Immediately he saw the two-headed white snake Minipoka had told him about. It was a strange, fascinating creature and, oddly, he felt no fear or revulsion. He reached out and stroked one head. The eyes were blue. The other head's eyes were brown.

He jerked back his hand. The serpent wrapped it-self around his ankles and slinked up his body.

The head with brown eyes lifted and its fangs glinted in the sun. Storm let out a cry, realizing that he was a fool to let the snake come close for it would surely bite him. But before it could strike, the other head, the one with blue eyes, sank its fangs into its own body. The long, smooth length shivered and went limp, falling like a white ribbon to his feet. Then it disappeared entirely, swallowed by the earth.

He cried out again, this time a cry of anguish because the serpent was gone. But in its place there appeared a plume of smoke, white and delicate, and then the smoke became solid and made the shape of a woman. A woman with blue-green eyes.

Storm groaned. Not her again. What did this mean? Why couldn't he escape her? Was she, in-deed, his destiny? Is that what the Creator was try-ing to tell him? But how could this be? His troubles had always been with the white eyes. What made this white woman any different from all the others?

A vision of a powerful stag came to him, and he knew he was the stag. With his big rack, he roamed the hills and valleys, marking his territory and leaving his scent to attract a mate. A doe appeared in the mist—a fine, young doe with big, brown eyes and a gentle temperament. She stood still for him while he mated with her. And it was good and she conceived. And as stags do, he left her and wandered alone while the offspring grew in her belly. Even when the twins came, he stayed away while she raised the fawns. He hunted alone. He slept alone. He lived alone for the rest of the year until it was time to mate again.

Now the vision of a wolf bloomed before him. He was the wolf, and he trotted proudly and marked his territory. He howled, calling for a mate, and a beautiful white woman-wolf answered his call of the wild. She danced with him, showing him new leaps and different ways of stalking and pouncing. And when it was time, when he was breathless from the chase, she flipped up her tail and whined softly, telling him she was ready and wanted him.

And his wolf-person mounted her and it was better than good. They joined and howled and whined and pleasured each other many times, even after her body had received his seed and his offspring began to grow in her belly. But he did not leave her as a wolf. He stayed, he hunted and brought her food, as wolves do. He groomed her and she groomed him. They loved each other and protected each other while their babies grew.

Even after the cubs were born, he stayed with his white mate. They raised the pack together, sharing the hunting and feeding and grooming and teaching. And they mated and made more babies and never left each other except to hunt and guard their home. He, as a wolf, did not know loneliness.

Storm opened his eyes and steam rose in great gusts in front of him.

Which do you want, Blackfeet son? a voice asked, emerging from the center of him, from his soul. *Would you rather live as a deer or a wolf?*

"A wolf," he answered and closed his eyes again to embrace the vision of AnadaAki.

He saw himself holding her, kissing her and burying himself deeply into her, to the root. The peace that enveloped him was tranquil, serene, like none he had known before. As he emptied into her and her hands moved like a warm tide over his skin, he realized he was cleansed of all his demons.

Storm released a long, head-clearing sigh and

opened his eyes. He flexed his hands, stretched his legs, and felt like a new man. The poison was gone.

Even his wound felt better, no longer tight and throbbing. He ran a hand through his wet hair and filled his lungs with the damp heat. Yes, he was his old self. The Creator had swept all the evil spirits from him and had shown him the true way.

Outside the lodge the sun burned low in the sky, painting everything orange and gold. Brown Otter came toward him, smiling, extending a hand in greeting. Storm opened his arms and hugged his cousin, his brother.

"You saw wondrous things?" Brown Otter asked, standing back to examine him with a sweeping glance.

"I am healed, brother. Inside and out." Storm tipped back his head and stared at the silvery clouds and the twinkle of early stars. "I can face anything, anyone. I have no fears, no qualms. I am the wolf, and I am not meant to travel the path alone."

Brown Otter rested a hand on his shoulder and gave it an affectionate squeeze. "We will do the Ghost Dance tonight, my brother. We will drive the white eyes' troubles from our camp. Will you dance with us? Will you share your new strength and your new wisdom?"

"Yes. I will wear the wolf's head tonight, and I will chase down the trouble and gobble it up just as my spirit animal would chase a mouse and eat it. By dawn we will all be stronger, Brown Otter."

Brown Otter draped an arm around his shoulders, and they walked toward the flaming heart of the camp.

"The white woman is still here."

Storm nodded, his gaze roving, hungry for the sight of her. "I know."

Brown Otter frowned. "How do you know?"

"The Creator kept her here for me." Storm felt Brown Otter's uneasiness. "There is a fork in the road—on up ahead—and she must take one side while I take the other. But for now, my cousin, our paths converge and we must not veer from the way."

"And will you keep to different paths once you part ways, my brother?"

Storm shrugged, his mind flinching from that twist of fate. "I can't see that far ahead. And neither can you." He lengthened his stride, outpacing his disapproving cousin.

Chapter 11

❦❦

"It's the Ghost Dance," Many-Smiles-Woman whispered to Tess as they sat together in a big circle of Blackfeet and waited for the dancing to commence.

The central bonfire threw sparks high into the sky and painted everything and everyone with gold and yellow. Long shadows writhed as women and children and old men approached the circle, found a place, and settled down to watch the Blackfeet braves perform.

"You must forgive, but this dance is to rid our land of white eyes, our enemies," Many Smiles said, worry erasing her customary pleasant expression.

"I'm not your enemy," Tess said. "And I'll try not to be offended. Should I even be here?"

"It was decided. The elders talked and Minipoka told them you are friend to us. Our dance is meant for those who harm us."

"I can certainly understand why your people don't trust my people. But the path goes both ways, Many Smiles. Indians have not always been fair to my people either."

"We were here first," Many Smiles said, facing the fire again. "And we should not leave."

Tess decided to change the subject. "Who will dance tonight? Is there anything I shouldn't do? I don't want to upset anyone by doing the wrong thing."

"It is great honor for you to sit in the circle with us. Our dances are sacred and not for others." She motioned to the inner circle. "All the warriors dance. The women sing. The very old men play the drums. You sit." Many Smiles patted Tess's arm. "No dance."

"Don't worry about that," Tess said, laughing. "I wouldn't dream of it. I can barely manage a slow waltz, so this sort of dancing will be out of the . . . oh, my." Tess stared at the men approaching the inner circle, their heads covered in feathers, their bodies painted, their clothing heavily beaded and deeply fringed.

Hands tapped and thumped on drums and tom-toms, generating a rhythm that kept pace with Tess's heartbeat. The dancers broke into the circle and pranced slowly around the perimeter, their fringed leggings flowing, their white and red and yellow painted faces sending shivers down Tess's spine. The women began to chant as the men whirled toward the fire, tomahawks clutched in their fists, their shadows dancing wildly across the ground.

A smile bloomed on Tess's face as she continued to take in the spectacle. More dancers joined the original four. Young and old and in between, the painted men seemed lost in their footwork, their tradition, their purpose. And Tess was lost with them. The color, the grace, the solemnity captured her immediately and mesmerized her as the night wore on.

Occasionally the drums would stop and some of the dancers would leave the circle to sit behind the drummers, while their fellow warriors started up another phase of the Ghost Dance. The women around her sang, then chanted, then began another song, their voices blending beautifully. Beside her, Many Smiles's sweet soprano climbed and soared, making Tess wish she could join in.

Once again the drums stopped and the whole world seemed to hold its breath along with Tess. Was it over? she wondered, glancing at Many Smiles, whose face suddenly lit up with pride. Tess followed her eyeline and saw two men coming forward, out of the shadows—one short, one tall. The shorter one pranced into the circle and the drummers took up the beat of his moccasined feet. Dressed in a pale-yellow breechclout and quill vest, the man's face was painted so heavily that Tess didn't recognize him until he was right in front of her.

Brown Otter! She blinked, then smiled as he pranced on, lunging at the bonfire, then holding up his arms as if beseeching the gods to hear his shrill cry. The women chanted softly while Brown Otter continued his lunging pattern. He carried a lance in one hand, and he shook it in time with the drumbeats. The feathers decorating it shivered and trembled. Brown Otter picked up his pace, his brown legs pumping. He moved in Tess's direction and shook his lance at her. Some of the men sent up war cries, and Tess stiffened, realizing that Brown Otter had made her the symbol of the very enemy this dance was meant to vanquish.

Leaning away from him, Tess met his fierce expression with one of her own. Narrowing her eyes, she smoked him with her glare. He shook his lance again. Cries went up, but Brown Otter looked confused by the shouts and he turned around, moving out of Tess's way so that she could see the dancer who had entered the ring of Blackfeet.

He was the tall one. He was Storm-In-His-Eyes.

A ribbon of pleasure unfurled within her and Tess swayed forward, her eyes fastened on him, her whole body yearning for his. Of course, he was magnificent in tight, white leggings and a leather shirt like none she'd ever seen before. Bedecked with white stars on a gray background, the shirt had a fringed hem and sleeves, also fringed, that stopped at his elbows. Four bird shapes, their wings outspread, had been cut into the front, giving glimpses of his bronze chest. The deep V-shaped neckline also exposed his throat and part of his chest. Only a corner of a white bandage could be seen on his chest, and the shirt completely hid the bandage on his back. Soon, she knew, he'd stop wearing the gauzy wrappings altogether, eager to be done with the healing process.

The head of a wolf sat on top of his, its eyes glazed and fierce, its gray fur ruffled by the breeze. Storm certainly didn't move like a man who had been deathly ill only days ago, Tess thought. His steps were light and airy. It seemed that his white moccasins barely touched the ground as he pranced around the bonfire, his knees nearly bumping his chin with each high step. The leggings reached to above his knees, leaving six inches of brown muscled thigh naked to the eye. Tess swallowed hard, her mouth suddenly as dry as cotton. The full moon could have tumbled from the sky, the trees could have uprooted themselves and performed cartwheels, the shadows could have come to life and made for the hills, and Tess wouldn't have been able to tear her rapt gaze from Storm for one precious second.

His steps quickened and he whirled and twirled, the fringe on his leggings and shirt flying around him. Brown Otter gave a war whoop and danced backward out of the circle, leaving it to his more flamboyant, more beautiful cousin. The drums pounded like a lover's pulse, and the night grew warm. Storm-In-His-Eyes held a red tomahawk in his right hand and a small shield in his left. The beads and quills on his shirt ranged from snowy white to smoky gray, like his eyes, and bright yellow like the sun, symbol of his Creator. White ermine furs fell over his ears, mingling with his ebony hair. He cut fancy designs in the air with his tomahawk, reminding Tess of the first time she saw him when he'd threatened her with a knife. A delicious tingle worked up her spine, and she felt her lips curve into a smile.

Twirling in tight circles, he kicked up dust devils and his moccasins tapped out a beat that matched the incessant tap of the drums. The air seemed to vibrate around him. Tess realized that no one was singing. The women were silent, all eyes on him. Not even a baby cried.

As he high-stepped around the fire again, his slashing tomahawk speaking of fallen enemies and bravery beyond compare, Tess caught sight of Slow-Riding-Woman. She didn't sit but stood with a few other young women, all entranced by the fancy dancer, all bouncing gently to the beat of the drums. Slow-Riding-Woman was a Blackfeet warrior's vision in a dark-blue dress festooned with red and white ribbons and dozens of white shells. She swayed from foot to foot, swinging her long braids, tempting Storm-In-His-Eyes with her parted lips, her adoring eyes.

He danced near her, then past her, whirling fast like a tornado. Tess released her breath, realizing only then that she'd been holding it. Beside her, Many Smiles suddenly made a yipping noise, startling Tess. Many Smiles closed her eyes and released the high, short cry again. Slow-Riding-Woman echoed the sound, then other young women joined it, sounding like a pack of wolves to Tess. The cries crescendoed as the drums picked up the pace and Storm's feet flew across the ground. The wolf's head bobbed, its long snout flashing with dangerously sharp teeth. The birds on his chest came to life, moving with his rapid breathing.

In a final flourish, just as the women's cries diminished, Storm flung up his arms, tipped back his head and sent up a hair-raising howl. The women yipped in response. Storm spun like a top before falling to one knee, his body draped over it, his chin touching his chest.

Silence, except for the crackle of the fire and the loud boom of Tess's heart in her ears.

After a few quiet moments, Storm's head lifted and he stared straight at Tess, his gray eyes glinting, his paint-streaked face that of a wild animal.

And then he winked, slow and deliberate, giving a nod to the other blood flowing in his veins. Tess raised a hand to her smiling mouth to keep from giggling aloud.

Storm rose up to shouts of jubilation. The other dancers swept into the inner circle to a round of hearty congratulations. Tess felt a hand at her elbow, and she turned reluctantly toward Many Smiles.

"All finished. The men go to smoke in the sun lodge."

"And the women? What do we do?"

"We talk about the men." Many Smiles issued

one of her namesakes, and Tess couldn't help but
return it in kind.

After a couple of hours in Minipoka's big lodge,
where the young maidens had gathered to giggle
and talk in hushed tones about the dancers, Tess
decided to take her leave. After all, the conversa-
tions were in Blackfeet and Tess could only guess
at most of what they were saying to each other.
She'd learned that Many Smiles was to be wed
soon to a young man from a neighboring tribe, the
Kootenay, and would go live with them. She'd also
heard Storm-In-His-Eyes's name several times
when the maidens had spoken to Slow-Riding-
Woman.

As Tess moved toward the opening, she caught
Minipoka's eye and waved. The old woman lifted
a hand and nodded, a smile touching her lips. Tess
gave an answering nod, feeling a warm regard for
the woman who had befriended her and talked the
other Blackfeet into accepting her, even at their sacred dance beseeching the gods to rid the land of
the white eyes. The irony wasn't lost on her, and
it was this conflict and contradiction that made her
restless.

Ducking outside, she stood beside the lodge and
examined the camp around her. Most of the tepees
were dark. Only two or three pulsated with inner
light. Although the people had stayed up half the
night to celebrate, Tess knew they'd rise at dawn,
for they were industrious. They tended their herds
and their crops, tanned hides and made clothing
and shelter, hunted and harvested. The days were
filled with activities, while the nights were mostly
quiet, spent in small family circles.

She'd be sad to leave them, but Tess knew that's
exactly what she'd be doing soon, if not tomorrow,

she thought as she walked toward Storm's lodge. Having sensed tonight that the elders had also discussed her departure, she had figured out that her inclusion in the Ghost Dance had also been the Blackfeet's way of thanking her for what she'd done and giving her a fond farewell.

And so she was restless, restless with a faint yearning for home and the familiar—but hating to leave the Blackfeet, and one Blood in particular. Storm. Would she see him again? Would he be one of the Blackfeet to escort her home? Probably not. He was a wanted man and had to keep hidden.

Tears burned the backs of her eyes at the thought of not seeing him, of not having even a minute alone with him so that she could tell him . . . Tell him what? That she was smitten with him? That her body ached for his? That he had stirred feelings in her she'd never even dreamed about before? Oh, how could she tell him such things without him laughing in her face? Perhaps it was best if she didn't see him again. Perhaps . . .

Slipping into the lodge she had made her own, she blinked in the darkness. The fire had died to embers. Tess went toward the fire pit and reached for the stirring stick, then jumped and smothered a scream when a brown hand closed on her wrist. Her gaze bounced up along with her heart, and then she released a slow, hissing sigh.

"Storm," she whispered, smiling. "I didn't see . . ." She straightened to look at him. He'd removed the war paint, the wolf's head, and the fancy shirt, but he still wore the tight leggings and breechclout. The bandage on his chest was gone, but a large square one covered the wound on his back, which had been the worse of the two. Tess touched the swollen skin around the puncture three inches above his right nipple. "This is healing nicely.

He held her by the wrist and reached for the other one. Pulling her closer, he placed her arms around his waist. "Tomorrow you will leave."

She nodded, her mouth as dry as dust. "I know."

"It's for the best."

"Yes, of course."

"I am grateful to you for all you've done."

"I wanted to."

"And I know you want to be back with your people and away from us . . . from me."

"No."

"No?"

"I must go home, of course. If I don't, John will send a posse out looking for me and that will only bring your people more woe. But I . . ." She raked her teeth over her lower lip, wondering if she dared tell him the truth.

"Yes?"

Tess placed her hands on his smooth back. His skin was warm, the muscles hard. Looking up into his eyes, she found the strength she needed. "I'll miss you terribly, Storm. You've come to mean so much . . . oh, please kiss me once more."

With a tortured groan he swept her up against him and his mouth swooped to hers. He kissed her hungrily, greedily, as if he were starved for her touch, her taste. His tongue courted hers, and his hands roamed her back and hips before rising up to capture her head. Tearing his mouth from hers, he gazed into her eyes with a searing intensity.

"I have no right to ask this of you, but I must. I have dreamed of you, I have had visions of you, I have cried out in the night for you. Will you let me love you tonight, AnadaAki? Even though you must ride away come morning, will you be mine tonight?"

"Yes, yes." Tess stood on tiptoes and pressed kisses against his chin and jawline before he dipped his head so that her mouth could find his again. "There has never been another, Storm," she told him.

"I know. That is why you must be certain. I won't take what you don't want to give."

"Take all of me," she heard herself saying.

In his arms, she found a liberation from what was expected of her, what was demanded of her by others. Light-headed from the freedom, she arched her body into his and wound her arms around his neck. His tongue slipped between her lips, smooth as silk, and he kneaded her backside. Tess snaked one leg around his, stroking his calf with the back of her heel. She didn't know what was keeping her upright because her limbs trembled. He dropped to his knees before her and gazed up into her eyes. His hands slid under her skirt and stroked up her shins to her knees, then to her thighs. Tess caught the hem and brought it up and over her head. She tossed the dress aside and stood before him in her torn chemise and ribbon-and-lace-edged drawers.

Easing herself down, she knelt in front of him. He placed his hands over her cotton-covered breasts and smiled.

"You are so pretty . . . and look." His fingertips eased the straps off her shoulders and the chemise off her breasts. "Freckles. I knew they must be other places besides your nose." He cupped her breasts in his hands and examined each puckered nipple before he took one hard, pink bud into his mouth.

The sensations that shot through Tess took her

to a whole different world of experiences. She flung back her head and, somehow, found herself lying on soft bear skins and wolf furs with Storm's mouth suckling one breast as his fingers teased the tip of the other. Her body attuned to his, she rubbed her heels against the backs of his thighs and ran her hands over his smooth shoulders, up his wide neck, to the bold planes of his face. She thought of that other time when his emotions had bubbled over before she'd even known he was reaching his boiling point, and she leaned up to whisper in his ear.

"Now, Storm. Now. I want you to be satisfied."

He smiled, turning his head to kiss her cheek. "You surprised me the last time we were together," he told her softly, his hands stroking over her hair, which was loose and thick and curling at her shoulders and down her back. "But this time I will surprise you. I will wait for you, my AnadaAki, and we will climb the highest peak together."

Sliding his hands along the length of her thighs, he nuzzled the valley of her breasts as he peeled away her drawers and chemise. She trembled, vulnerable but anxious to please, to be claimed by him.

Gazing at her, Storm felt a clutching in his chest. Her pale limbs, her slightly rounded stomach, her high, soft breasts were all beautiful, but it was her face that made his heart buck. Her sweet, oval face would forever be embedded in his mind. He loved the shape of her mouth, the upward tilt of her nose, the determined set of her chin, and the sandy-colored dots dancing across her creamy skin. And he loved the way she looked at him—unflinching, unfailing, unequaled.

Yes, he wanted to take his pleasure from her, but he also wanted this to be perfect for her, something by which to remember him when she was back among her people.

With his hands, he guided her. With his eyes, he encouraged her. With his mouth, he courted her. By the time he touched between her legs, she was wet and clinging. Her feminine folds cleaved to his fingers. A good sign.

Inching down, he nuzzled the damp triangle of dark golden curls. He heard her quick intake of breath, but kissed her there anyway and located the button of flesh with the tip of his tongue. She quaked violently and made sounds of wonder that spurred him on. Using his mouth and tongue on her, he brought her to another shivering, trembling, moaning plateau of rapture. His erection throbbed painfully, and he pushed aside the square of cloth covering him. He bobbed up, stiff and dark and shiny-tipped.

"Wrap your legs around me," he told her. "That's right." He slipped his hands beneath her backside and lifted her up to receive him.

Still in a partial swoon from the magic his mouth had worked on her, Tess didn't feel the penetration until it was met with resistance. Her eyes flew open and she tightened her legs around him and grabbed at his forearms. A sliver of fear sliced through her.

"Storm?" she whispered, and in that one word she asked for his indulgence, his care, his tenderness.

Holding her gaze, his body tensed and glistening with perspiration, he paused another moment, then drove through her shield in one swift thrust. She cried out, but the sound was muffled by his mouth on hers. His tongue coaxed hers into a seductive dance, but he didn't move inside of her. She felt him, so big, so foreign, and her body smarted and twitched. Gradually the bullet of pain receded, leaving her vaguely uncomfortable and hoping he wouldn't move again other than to pull out of her.

He trailed the fingertips of one hand down the side of her face. "You want me to leave you alone now, I know this. But you must trust me."

She wanted to make love, but her body felt raw and she thought she might even be bleeding a little. "But, Storm, I . . ."

"Shhh."

And then he moved inside of her, and she clutched at his arms and bit down on her lower lip to keep from crying out. He withdrew, only to enter her again. She closed her eyes, remembering that her mother had once confided to her that making love wasn't always pleasant. Oh, why must women endure this? To please their men, of course, a voice inside her answered. And to get babies. Otherwise, no woman in her right mind would . . . ahhhh. She opened her eyes, her inner muscles softening, tightening, softening, tightening, in tempo with Storm's advance and retreat. Passion erupted in her stomach and spread flames to her thighs. She hitched up her backside and found a more solid purchase around his waist with her legs. He nodded, his ebbing and flowing coming faster, his guiding hands loosening their hold as her body caught fire with his.

All coherent thought lifted away from her mind like smoke, leaving only the fire raging through her body. Inarticulate sounds escaped her and she clung to Storm, letting him take her higher and higher to a place that shattered around her like diamonds to dust.

His release was violent, exciting and life-changing. Tess chanted his name and he kissed her lips tenderly, devotedly.

The next thing she was clearly aware of was her own breath sawing in her throat and the rapid beating of her heart. Her fingertips moved gingerly over Storm's back and across the bandage that covered his healing wound. His skin was damp, slick. So was hers.

He pressed his face into the side of her neck, and she felt his lips purse and brush her skin. After another minute or two, he withdrew from her soft folds and lay on his side against her. He trailed his fingers across her blushing breasts and spread his hand on her stomach.

"Already I mourn tomorrow," he whispered, his voice hoarse and deep.

Tess closed her eyes against the tears that sprang to them. "So do I." She was glad her voice didn't break. "What are you planning on doing? Will you track down those men who are dressing like Indians and robbing people?"

"I must. They hurt you."

She framed his face between her hands, panic building inside her. "Storm, don't put yourself in danger for me. What they did . . . it's not that important."

"It is to me. If we hadn't gotten there when we did, they would have . . ." He gritted his teeth and anger blazed in his eyes. "And there is the marshall. He killed my sister and he will die for that."

Fear struck her heart. The tone of his voice brooked no argument. "Was she your only sibling?"

"Yes. My parents died when my sister was about ten years old. We looked out for each other."

"Storm, I know you want to avenge her death, but I'm afraid for you. You'll be careful?"

He tried to smile, but it was brief and never reached his eyes. "Always. And clever."

She brought his lips down to hers and whispered against them, "Leaving you is one thing, but having you taken from this world . . . I couldn't bear that, Storm."

He shifted until they were lying side by side, facing each other, then he flung a leg over her and pulled her up closer to him. He still wore the leather leggings and they felt soft and warm against her skin. His hands strayed over her waist and back and the curve of her buttocks. She caressed the tautness of his waist, the bulging muscles of his chest, the pale scars on his chest. Leaning closer, she kissed the puckered skin, evidence of his bravery.

"Heaven knows, I'll miss you."

"And I you." His lips rubbed hers, setting off sparks.

"I want you to clear your name so that you can remain here. Your place is with the Blackfeet."

"You think so?"

"Yes. You didn't like living among the white people. You seem more comfortable here."

He caught a lock of her hair and wrapped it around his index finger. "I learned many things while living with the white people, but most of the time I felt closed in, as if I was surrounded by fences. Among the whites, I had to follow too many rules. They expected me to be something I did not want to be."

"What?" she asked. "What did they want you to be?"

"A savage."

An arrow of pity pierced her heart when she thought of him struggling to be accepted, but seen by most white people as an oddity, a heathen. How could anyone see him that way? How could anyone look at him, so proud and fiercely loyal and resolutely honorable, and think of him as a savage?

"Storm," she murmured, kissing his shoulder. "You are the most noble, most gentle gentleman I've ever known."

His eyes glistened and a smile, slight and tinged with shy pleasure, poked at the corners of his mouth. He sat up and twisted around to attend to something at his waist. She realized he was loosening the ties of his leggings and she helped him, unknotting the other set from the waist cord of the breechclout. He peeled the leggings off his long, bronze legs, folded them and set them aside. His breechclout followed. After glancing at her and giving her a quick smile, he removed a string of red and black beads from around his neck and dropped them over her head.

Fingering the circle of beads, Tess smiled. They were the same ones she'd taken from the cave that first time.

"Keep these," he said. "Keep them and remember me."

"Always." Sliding her fingers through the sides of his inky hair, she pulled him back down to her, her mouth opening beneath his, her thighs parting to make a cradle for him.

"Do you regret what we have done together?"

"I have no regrets about this night," she told him, emotion thickening her throat. "Dawn will be here too soon. Hold me until then, Storm."

"I will let you go only when the sun rises to claim you," he promised, his lips brushing hers.

Tess gave herself to him again . . . and once more before the sun came for her.

Chapter 12

To Tess, the ride back to False Hope seemed more like a death march. Escorted by the chief himself, Eagle Talon, and two of his sons, Tess rode in the middle of the entourage and wrestled with what she was going to tell John.

She'd certainly have to tell him something.

Dressed in a wool skirt made from a Hudson Bay blanket, a green blouse decorated with shells and beads, moccasins, and the necklace Storm had given her, it was obvious she hadn't been visiting relatives in the valley. John would never understand, and she dreaded the confrontations.

When she'd awakened earlier that morning, she'd found herself alone in Storm's lodge, making her wonder for a confused moment if she'd imagined the night of passion. Her body's tenderness and the scent of Storm still clinging to her skin told her it had been no dream. She'd been unhappy that he'd slipped away from her, but later she was glad. Saying good-bye in the light of day would have been too wrenching. Her ride away from the Blackfeet had been difficult enough with Minipoka and Many-Smiles-Woman waving a sad farewell to her.

At the edge of town, very near Mrs. Bishop's house where Brown Otter had kidnapped her, Eagle Talon and his sons reined in their horses. The chief pointed ahead to the sprawl of False Hope.

"Go in peace," he intoned.

"Thank you," Tess replied, tears gathering in her throat. She tipped up her chin, suddenly feeling ridiculous for being such a bawl-bag. These people valued honor and dignity, and she would not disgrace herself by giving the appearance of a weepy bride of regret. "If I can ever be of any help to the Blackfeet, please don't hesitate to contact me. I believe we've forged a lasting friendship, Chief."

The handsome Indian nodded, reined his horse around, and started back at a canter for home, his sons flanking him.

Urging Cameo onward, Tess steeled herself for the barrage of questions and admonishments awaiting her. Her heart felt like a lead weight in her chest. Suddenly prickling warmth spread across the back of her neck. Something sweet nudged her leaden heart, and she glanced around, hope rising within her. *Yes, there!* Her hungry eyes latched onto the silhouette of a solitary horseman on a distant ridge. She lifted a hand as tears welled in her eyes. It was him. Storm. He'd followed her for one last look. *Thank God!*

He raised his hand, answering her. She felt his sadness as keenly as her own. Her heart came to life again, beating frantically as sweet sensations of yearning tumbled through her. She released a soft cry when he reined his horse and disappeared over the ridge. Gone. Gone forever?

She jerked her mind from such a possibility and wiped the tears from her eyes. Giving Cameo a kick in the sides, she tried to compose herself before she reached town and was just barely able to do it. A wild yearning blossomed in her and whispered in her ear to return to the Blackfeet, return to her one true love, Storm-In-His-Eyes. But reason prevailed, keeping her to the road that led back to her life in False Hope.

The moment she entered the town proper, she felt the shocked stares. Several people called out to her.

"Hey, there, Miss Summer! Where you been, to a powwow?"

"Tess Summer? Are you all right?"

'Why, is that you Miss Summer? Whatcha dressed for?"

Tess ignored all the comments, the questions, the snickers and chuckles and kicked Cameo into a trot. Oddly, she was almost glad to see her neat, cared-for house with its blue shutters and rooster weather vane. At the back, she slid off Cameo and led the old mare to the barn. As she unsaddled the mare, she noticed that John's buggy horse was lathered and the buggy seat was still warm. He must have just returned from his morning rounds, she thought. Had he missed having her around, helping take the work load from his shoulders? Maybe he missed her so terribly he'd forgive her anything —even lying to him. Hmmm. She shook her head and dumped some oats into the feed trough for Cameo.

Rubbing the beads of the necklace Storm had given her for comfort and courage, she walked slowly to the Dutch door. The top half was open and she peeked inside. John was in the kitchen, up to his elbows in dishwater. Around him was a sea of dirty pots and skillets and tableware. On the table sat a bowl of grits, a plate of toast, and a glass of milk. The grits looked gummy and the toast was burned around the edges. He turned his head toward the hallway that led to the stairs.

"Cammie, honey! Hurry now. I've got your breakfast on the table and it's getting cold."

Tess inched back, taking in the scene before her. Her brother had taken over her duties, adding to his already full schedule. Poor John. She wondered if Camilla had even attempted to cook or clean while she'd been gone. She doubted it.

Placing her fingers on the handle, Tess pushed open the door and stepped into the kitchen that smelled like burned toast. "Good morning, John."

He whirled and a grin broke over his face. "Tess! Thank God." He came forward, arms extended, but stopped just shy of her, his gaze dropping before lifting to her face again. "Why in heaven's name are you dressed like that?"

Tess gave him a quick hug. "It's a long story. First, tell me how you've been." Stepping around him, she eyed the pitiful excuse for breakfast. "Have you become a cook and bottle washer?"

"Uh ... well, Camilla isn't ... that is, she tried, but after the fire, she—"

Tess turned to face him again. "Fire? What ..." She looked toward the cookstove and the black, scorched wall behind it. "My stars and gold bars! What happened?"

"Nothing tragic," John assured her. "Camilla just let some bacon fat simmer too long on top of the stove and—well, it caught fire. The poor dear threw water on the flames and that made the fire spread to the wall. Luckily I was home and managed to put the fire out. I've hired a man to come in next week and repair that wall."

"I'm glad you were home, or I might not have had a home to come back to."

"How are Uncle Elmer and Aunt Mattie?" He

examined her clothes again and a frown pinched the skin between his eyes.

Tess weighed the tall tales she'd cooked up on the ride home and decided none of them would do. Only the truth would suffice, she told herself.

"I don't know, but I'm sure they're fine."

"You don't . . ." He looked past her shoulder and his eyes lit up. "Camilla, look who's home."

"Tess!" Camilla came forward eagerly and embraced Tess. "It's so good to have you back. John and I couldn't seem to get that old stove to work for us. I think you've cast a spell on it." She held Tess at arm's length, and her eyes narrowed. "What are you wearing? Is this how they dress in the valley?"

"No." Tess turned toward John. "I must talk with you, John, but privately, if you please."

"I have nothing to hide from my wife," John said, jutting out his chin.

Tess patted Camilla's shoulder. "Camilla's breakfast is getting cold, and what I have to tell you would only make her swoon and take to her bed." Not waiting for him to agree or disagree, she swept out of the kitchen and down the hallway. "We'll talk in your office. Excuse us, Camilla. You go ahead and enjoy your . . . uh, delicious breakfast. Don't you worry about all those dirty dishes and that filthy kitchen floor." Tess glanced back with disgust. "I'll tackle them shortly."

Pacing in his office, John kept raking his hands through his hair until the front was standing straight on end. "You *lied* to me," he repeated. "I would have never believed that you would look me in the eyes and lie."

"Yes, I'm sorry for that," Tess said, staring at her hands clasped tightly in her lap. "But I knew you wouldn't help him, and so it was left to me."

"Why?" John demanded. "Why didn't you either leave him be or tell the marshall where he was holed up?"

"I told you, John. I promised his sister I would do what I could for him."

"You're not a doctor."

"No, but I nursed him back to health."

"An Indian," he said, his upper lip curling. "You've been off chasing Indians."

"I beg your pardon," Tess said, her voice rising with her temper. "I was *not* chasing Indians. Two *white* men dressed as Indians attacked me and the Blackfeet saved me."

"And you've gone . . . native." He scorched her with his insulting gaze.

"You haven't heard a word I've said. All you hear is what others—"

"Oh, no. I've listened to you and I've listened well." He stood before her, hands riding his hips, a superior air enveloping him. "And I've heard the inflection of your voice when you talk about this Indian outlaw. Like every other female, you've a romantic streak which has led you to folly, my dear sister. You fancy yourself besotted with this Indian, and he with you." John shook his head slowly, deliberately frowning at her as a father would at a disobedient child. "We can spare your feelings and salvage your reputation by not speaking of this again, Tess. Anyone outside this house will be told that you visited our aunt and uncle and those clothes are gifts from Aunt Mattie, who is a bit dotty."

"She's not!"

"Better her than you," John said, scowling darkly. "Do you want to be the laughingstock of False Hope? Do you want people whispering behind your back?" He folded his arms against his chest. "If you won't save your own reputation, kindly consider mine."

His damning words doused her flare of temper. Tess shrugged, deciding what he offered was tolerable. She didn't want the whole town talking about her anymore than they already were, and she didn't want to distress John further.

"Fine," she agreed, tight-lipped. "We'll speak no more of it."

John gave her another long, stern glare. Stiffly, Tess left his office and headed for the stairs. She fumed inside but decided any further discussion would be useless.

Her bedroom seemed a safe, comforting place. Removing the clothes, she folded them neatly and placed them in the bottom dresser drawer, then she prepared a basin of water and washed off the trail dust. The bruises at her back and ribs were fading but still tender. The bump on her head was gone, but when her brush touched it she winced. Funny, how none of them had bothered her last night with Storm. Of course, he'd been so gentle, so considerate . . .

She sighed away the memories. When she was once again in her usual long black skirt and crisp white blouse, she went to the mirror to brush her hair and sweep it up into a neat bundle at the crown of her head. She left the bead necklace on, but when she examined her reflection in the oval mirror, she tucked it under her collar. The beads felt warm against her skin. Warm and intimate.

In her town clothes with her hair tamed and her mother's brooch pinned to her high collar, Tess recognized the woman in the mirror. Tess Summar, False Hope's most eligible spinster and Dr. John's able assistant. She had left AnadaAki with the

Blackfeet, back where she belonged. But she'd left her heart back there, too. She felt hollow, numb.

She traced the irregularly shaped beads with a fingertip. They reminded her of what she had been with the Blackfeet and what she couldn't be here— an equal, a true partner and helpmate. Yes, she thought, the beads would remain out of sight, but they would always be with her. Like her memories of her night with Storm, they would be hers alone, private and intensely personal.

"You're a fool," she whispered, looking at herself in the mirror again. "You're just an old-maid spinster with stars in your eyes, an easy target for a virile, young buck used to having women fall at his feet."

She frowned. Those were words John would like for her to say to herself, but she didn't really believe them. Not anymore. She had changed and she was glad.

Whirling away from the mirror, she started to tidy up her room when she heard a commotion outside. Glancing out the window, she saw a covered wagon pulled by two lathered horses charge down the street toward the house. The man at the reins tugged the wild-eyed horses to a stop and leaped down from the wagon seat. Tess sucked in a gasp when she saw arrows sticking out of the canvas cover.

"Doc! Doc!" the man yelled, reaching out to take a girl's limp body from the arms of a woman, who was probably his wife. "Help us, please!"

Tess whirled and ran downstairs where John had already thrown open the door and had darted outside. John carried the girl inside while the man helped his woman into the house. The woman was round with child. From the looks of her ruddy face and grimly set mouth, Tess guessed that she might be in labor.

"What happened?" Tess asked, entering the office to help John place the girl on the examination table. The child's cries echoed off the high ceiling.

The girl wore a simple, blue dress and blood had soaked one shoulder of it. John tore the fabric away to reveal the wound. A broken shaft of an arrow stuck up through the split skin.

"Indians attacked us," the child's father said. "They took our spare horses and what little jewelry and money we had on us."

"Indians?" Tess repeated, stunned. "How many?"

"Two. They was wearing Indian masks."

"Probably your friends," John muttered.

"Probably not," Tess shot back with a pointed glare. "Is your wife in labor?"

"Yeah, I guess so."

"Please, sit down," Tess said, reaching out to guide the woman into a chair. "Take deep breaths."

"Don't mind me," the woman insisted. "Take care of our little Nugget."

"Nugget?" Tess glanced at the squirming, crying girl. "Is that her name?"

"Her name is Cassie Mae," the man said. "But we call her Nugget. We're heading for California to strike it rich in the gold fields."

"Oh, I see." She fetched the woman a glass of water, then went back to the table to help John with the wounded child.

"The Indians shot this child?" John asked, preparing to remove the arrow.

"Yeah, but I'm not sure they meant to. They was shooting them arrows willy-nilly, like they weren't too sure how it was done, and Nugget there popped up in the back of the wagon and got plugged with one."

"It makes no difference if it was an accident or not. They shot her, an innocent child." John's glance at Tess was sharp and accusing.

Tess narrowed her eyes at him, knowing full well that he was blaming Storm and Brown Otter for this. "Sounds to me like the same two men who attacked me. White men dressed as Indians."

John gave a derisive laugh. "White men? Not likely."

"Very likely," Tess insisted, but the howl of the child made her drop the argument. "Hold on, honey. Doctor Summar is going to get that old arrow out of you and then you'll be all well again. How old are you, Cassie?" She took one of the child's hands in her own and gave it a quick squeeze. The girl turned large brown eyes up to Tess's face.

"Tw-twelve."

"Is that right? Why, you're almost a lady." Tess smoothed a hand over Cassie's clammy forehead and white-blond hair, while John cleaned the wound.

Surreptitiously examining the girl's parents, Tess noted their soiled faces and hands, their wrinkled and tattered clothing, their yellow teeth. The woman slumped in the chair, her hands resting on her swollen stomach.

"John, I'll let you see to Cassie while I take her mother to the back room where she can lie down."

"Yes, go on." John glanced at the pregnant woman. "Make her comfortable and then come back here. I might need you."

Tess helped the woman up from the chair. "I'm Tess Summar, the doctor's sister."

"We're Ben and Maybelle Little," the woman explained haltingly as she walked with Tess to the back room. "We tried homesteading here, but then we heard about them California gold fields and Ben decided he'd rather bust sod for gold than for potatoes." She glanced over her shoulder and knitted her pale brows. "My girl's gonna be okay, isn't she?"

"She's in good hands now," Tess assured her. "Lie down on the bed and rest. Let me put a cool cloth on your brow. Are the pains coming faster?"

"Not faster. Harder."

Tess placed a wet cloth on the woman's forehead and a glass of water on the side table. "If you need anything, just shout. I'll be right in there with John and your daughter."

The woman nodded. "Thanks. I'm obliged."

As Tess returned to the office, Cassie let out a fresh howl. John held up the arrowhead and stubby shaft. Hurrying forward, Tess gathered the sobbing child in her arms and rocked her gently.

"There, there. The worst is over. We got the arrow out, angel, and we're sorry it had to hurt so bad."

The girl's sobs subsided to sniffles and she snuggled closer to Tess, her arms tightening around Tess's waist.

"You smell good," Cassie said. "Like flowers."

Tess laughed softly and chucked the girl under the chin. "Thank you, little charmer. Feeling better?"

"My shoulder still h-hurts."

"Yes, I know. The doctor hasn't quite finished with it."

"My rifle jammed on me or I woulda killed me some Indians," Ben Little grumbled. He sat in the chair his wife had vacated and looked worn out.

"Are you sure they were Indians?" Tess asked.

"Huh?" Mr. Little looked at her blankly. "I told you they was shooting arrows and wearing redskin masks."

"Yes, but was their skin red? Not white?"

"Tess, enough!" John scowled at her. "They were attacked by Indians, no matter how badly you don't want to believe—"

"The one that shot me had hair the color of Pa's," Cassie spoke up.

Tess and John stared at Ben Little's yellow hair, and vindication shone through Tess.

"Blond, you mean?" Tess asked, relief flooding through her.

"Uh-huh, but it was stuck to his head. It was real dirty, I guess."

"Or maybe it had hair tonic on it," Tess ventured with a smile of satisfaction as she faced her brother again. "How many Indians do you know with blond hair, John? And hair tonic?"

John firmed his jaw. "The child was hysterical. How could she be sure of such a thing? Clean this wound while I check on Mrs. Little. I'll be back in a minute to stitch it up," he instructed coldly, then marched from the office.

"Poor loser," Tess whispered. She ran a hand over Cassie's soft, shimmering hair. "I'm going to clean that blood off you."

"While you do that, I'll check on my other kids," Mr. Little announced, rising from the chair.

"Other children?" Tess echoed.

"Yeah. We got four others out there in the wagon."

"Well, for heaven's sake, bring them inside! They must be scared and worried. Just take them into the parlor. When we get your wife and daughter seen to, we'll make sure your other children are all right."

"Nobody else got hurt," Mr. Little said. "You sure you want me to bring them inside?"

"Yes, I'm sure," Tess said, smiling.

"Okay." Mr. Little paused and looked at his daughter. "Nugget, honey, how did you see that bad man's hair? They were wearing hats."

"His hat blew off. I saw it, Pa. I saw it." She stuck out her lower lip in a stubborn pout.

"Okay, okay," Mr. Little said. He shook his head sadly. "Lord, lord, what's this old world coming to when white men act like wild Indians and rob poor dirt farmers like me?"

Tess nodded in agreement, but rejoiced in Cassie's observation. Of course, Tess had known that the masked men hadn't been Storm and Brown Otter, but she was ever so glad to have Cassie confirm it.

She cleaned the girl's wound as Mr. Little herded his other children into the parlor.

"Tess?" John stepped into the office, his features tense with worry.

"Yes?" Tess stiffened, recognizing the signs of trouble.

"Come in here. I need you. And bring the smelling salts."

"Okay." Tess patted Cassie's hand reassuringly and motioned for Mr. Little. "Could you make sure your daughter stays right here while I help my brother with your wife?"

"Yeah, sure. That baby wasn't supposed to come for another month."

Tess nodded. "Well, it seems to be coming today instead."

Chapter 13

❧

The next day before sunup Tess trudged out to the barn where the horses shared space with ten hens and a bantam rooster. The house had been overtaken by the Little family yesterday after catastrophe followed calamity.

Mrs. Little had finally delivered the baby, but it had been a stillbirth and had left the distraught woman exhausted and weak from loss of blood. After Tess fixed supper for all of them, Mr. Little and his three sons had bedded down out front in their wagon, while his wife and two daughters had slept in the house.

It would be another long day, and Tess had risen earlier than usual to get a head start on it. She dressed and tiptoed out, careful not to disturb Cassie, who snoozed on a cot next to Tess's bed.

Grabbing a bucket off a nail just inside the barn, Tess started toward the shelf where the hens had made their nests. The rooster stirred and crowed, making the hens cluck nervously and ruffle their feathers.

Tess sighed. Now why was she thinking of Storm? Was it because of the pride the rooster displayed or because the hens seemed flustered by the cock's attention? Probably it was because the rooster was being protective of his females, and Storm was also known for protecting the women he valued.

Oh, how she missed him! Her spirit seemed to be a gray, lifeless shadow inside of her without Storm. She'd returned to False Hope with a new appreciation for its name. If she could only see him one more time, she'd tell him how much he meant to her and that she would go to the ends of the earth if he would only—

"Tess?"

The deep voice sent her heart into her throat. Tess whirled, a startled cry escaping her as she stumbled backward. A man separated himself from the shadows. Tess gathered in a breath, intent on screaming if she had to, but then she recognized the cut of his shoulders, the timber of his voice, the glitter of his gray eyes. The air whooshed out of her lungs and she dropped the bucket and threw herself into his arms.

"Storm! Oh, thank God!"

He felt so good and strong she didn't care that she was wearing her heart on her sleeve by embracing him and showing him how happy she was to see him again. His arms were bands of steel and velvet around her, powerful but gentle. His lips touched her temple, cool and light. He lifted her until her feet left the ground. She felt as if she were a feather, floating in his arms. Holding her thus, he retreated into the shadows again before he set her back on her feet.

"I had to see you," he murmured, running his hands over her hair as his gaze played on her face like a flame. "I rode in during the dead of night and hoped you might come outside so we could be together, if only for a few minutes."

"I'm glad you did." She framed his face in her hands and ran her thumbs across his high cheekbones. He was so handsome she wanted to cry, so dear to her heart she wanted to hold onto him forever.

"Are you glad?" He knitted his brows. "I should stay away, I know. If you're caught with me—"

She pressed her fingertips to his lips. "I don't care. All I care about is being with you, Storm." She lifted her lips to his and wound her arms around his neck. His mouth moved insistently, and she parted her lips to accept the strokes of his tongue. Her limbs trembled and her breath shortened. She thought she might faint before he ended the passion-filled kiss.

"I saw the wagon outside and I—"

"John was convinced it was you and Brown Otter, but I knew he was wrong."

He inched his head back to give her a confused frown. "What are you saying?"

"The Littles ... they were attacked and—" She sucked in a breath. "You mean, you don't know what happened?"

"No."

She stepped out of his embrace and laid a hand to her forehead. It took a few moments before she could think clearly again. "The wagon belongs to the Little family and they were robbed yesterday by two men wearing Indian ceremonial masks. One of the men shot a child with a bow and arrow. The woman was pregnant and she went into labor and delivered a stillborn baby."

Storm's face contorted with rage and anguish before he spun away from Tess. He was dressed in fringed buckskin, stretched taut across his shoulders and back. She shivered in the dawn's cool air and wished for his arms to be around her again.

"Will the lies ever stop? I was nowhere near these white people, I swear it."

"You don't have to swear anything to me." Tess placed her hands on his shoulders and pressed her cheek against his back. He smelled of the outdoors, of pine and cedar and green grass. "I know you, Storm. You would never do such a hideous thing. It was the same men who attacked me. I'm sure of it."

He hung his head. "And the baby died. How is the other child, the one who was wounded?"

"She'll be fine. Her name is Cassie, and she saw that one of the robbers had blond hair. And he wore hair tonic."

"White eyes."

She winced inwardly and clutched at his shoulders, wanting his reassurance that he didn't lump all white people in with the robbing scum who hid behind Indian ceremonial masks and shot at defenseless children.

"I was hoping the trouble would be dying down."

"Me, too." She stepped around to face him. "Don't leave yet." Taking one of his hands, she pulled him into an empty horse stall and sat on a bale of fresh hay. "Sit down and let's talk. I want to hear your voice and feel you near me. I've missed you so."

He smiled and sat beside her. "Have you? I feel the same, although we've been apart for only a day."

"But it seems like a month."

He cupped the side of her face with his other hand. "Have we bewitched each other?"

"Maybe . . ." She averted her gaze. "Or maybe

we're in love with each other. Have you ever been in love before, Storm?''

''No. Have you?''

She shook her head. ''You weren't even in love with the girl you were supposed to marry?''

''I didn't know her very well. We were children.'' He pressed a soft kiss to her lips. ''I am selfish to come here. I place you in danger.''

''I don't care.''

''But I *do* care.''

Tess felt the tension in him and was afraid he might leave, so she decided to change the subject. ''Tell me what I can do to help. Should I speak to the marshall about my belief that you and Brown Otter are innocent?''

Some of the storm signals left his eyes and a smile poked at the corners of his wide mouth. ''You think the marshall would believe you?''

''Why shouldn't he? I know that the men who attacked me weren't Indians.''

''Stay out of it, Tess,'' he cautioned. ''This fight is mine.''

''But I could—''

He silenced her by kissing her soundly, his mouth opening over hers and chasing away her protests. When he leaned back away from her, his eyes were almost silver. ''You asked what you could do to help and I've told you.''

She frowned. ''But that's not helping.''

''Knowing you are back home, safe and happy, helps me.'' His gaze drifted over her hair, her dress, her polished shoes. ''I can see that you have picked up the reins of your life and are going forward again. That is good.''

''Is it? And am I going forward?'' She shook her head. ''Doesn't feel like it. I might be safe, but I'm not happy. I feel stuck. Stuck in the mud.''

He laughed softly and kissed her lips again. "You have important work here. Your brother is glad you're home?"

"I suppose, although he's not altogether pleased with me. He was so mad he was spitting lightning bolts yesterday when I told him that I hadn't been visiting relatives in the valley."

"Of course. You knew he would be angry with you."

She sighed. "Yes, but you know what?" Lifting her chin, she met his gaze. "I don't care anymore. I don't care if John is angry or upset with me. I used to try to please him and make his life run efficiently, effortlessly. But no more." She set her jaw stubbornly. "I've changed, and John doesn't like that, but I . . . *don't* . . . *care*," she finished, enunciating the last words to show her determination.

He raised his brows. "Tess, be careful. Your life is here and your work with your brother is—"

They both tensed when the rooster and hens squawked. A shadow fell across the ground. Tess looked at Storm and she widened her eyes, silently asking him what he wanted to do about the intruder.

"Miss Tess?"

Tess smiled at the sound of the small, breathy voice, and patted Storm's thigh. "It's all right," she whispered to him. "It's Cassie."

Cassie poked her head into the stall. "Miss Tess, is that you?" When she saw Storm, Cassie stumbled backward, her eyes huge with fear.

"Oh, dear." Tess reached for her, catching the girl by the arm. "Don't be afraid, Cassie. This is my friend. His name is Storm."

"He—he's an Indian!" Cassie's lower lip trembled.

"Yes, but he won't hurt you." Tess made a shooing motion behind her back, signaling for Storm to leave while she placated the girl. "Did you come out to help me gather eggs? Why don't you do that while I say good-bye to—"

"Are you the brave girl who was shot with an arrow?" Storm asked, moving to stand beside Tess.

Cassie tipped her head back to look into Storm's face. She swallowed hard and nodded, her eyes glimmering with unshed tears. Tess looked from Cassie to Storm, apprehensive with this direct approach. The girl had been shot yesterday and she was still afraid. Couldn't Storm see that? It would be better if he'd leave quietly and let her talk to Cassie.

Storm lifted the hem of his shirt and exposed his left side. He pointed out a white scar. "This is where an arrow went into me when I was about your age. My own brother shot me. He thought I was a deer. Do I look like a deer to you?"

Cassie's lips stopped trembling and curved into a grin. "No. Not a bit."

"You wouldn't have made that mistake. That's good. I can trust you." He settled on his haunches in front of her and spoke softly, calmly. "My name is Storm-In-His-Eyes, and I'm Blackfeet. I'm pleased to meet you, Cassie Little."

Tess watched the exchange and fell in love with Storm all over again. Examining Cassie's bright eyes and ready grin, she saw that Storm had won the girl's confidence.

Soft-pink color crept into Cassie's cheeks. "They said an Indian shot me, but they was wrong. It was a white man."

"So I've been told. If I had been there, I would have chased this white man and made him hurt the way he made you hurt."

"Would you have punched him?" Cassie asked,

her brown eyes round with excitement.

"Yes, of course," Storm agreed, appealing to the girl's sense of justice. "And I would have stomped him into the dust and blacked his eyes and bloodied his nose."

Cassie giggled. "Oh, I wish you had been there! I would have liked that!"

Storm laughed and glanced up at Tess. "I can see that your friend here hasn't suffered too much from her injury."

"She's bouncing back pretty good," Tess observed. "You're not frightened of Storm, are you, Cassie?"

"No." Cassie looked him over. "I guess not. But Indians kill people."

"Didn't your father try to protect you when the men attacked your wagon?" Storm asked.

"Yes."

"Then you can understand that our fathers and brothers are no different. If our people are attacked, they must fight and sometimes they must kill. But you said it wasn't Indians who robbed your family, but white men."

Cassie nodded. "One was. The one who shot me with an arrow." She stuck out her lip. "It hurt and I hate him!"

"And well you should." Storm stood up and looked at the sunlight falling across the yard. "I must go."

"Not yet," Tess said, emotion already clogging her throat. "We've barely talked to each other."

"You want me to gather the eggs?" Cassie asked, eyeing the bucket Tess had dropped.

"Yes, that would be nice of you. Don't let those fussy hens peck you."

"I won't." Cassie picked up the bucket and

glanced shyly at Storm. "I won't tell no one 'bout you being here, mister."

Storm smiled. "Thank you."

Tess stared after Cassie, surprised that the girl had accepted the furtiveness of the meeting. Taking Storm by the hand, Tess pulled him with her into the seclusion of the stall. Before he could protest, she placed her hands at the back of his head and brought his mouth down to hers.

He groaned and his arms tightened around her, crushing her to his chest until she could feel the thundering of his heart.

"When will I see you again?" Tess asked, rubbing her thumb across his glistening lower lip and stroking his long, ebony hair with her other hand.

"I don't know. Not until I get the marshall off my tail."

The answer didn't lift her spirits. "That long? Meet me out here at dawn, say, in three days?"

"No, Tess." He put her away from him firmly. "I shouldn't have come here, but I had to see you—"

"And I wanted to see you," she interrupted. "Why should we stay away from each other when we—"

"Why?" he demanded, his voice suddenly harsh. "Why, you ask? Because I am a wanted man, and one woman I love has already died because of me, that's why."

His reasoning sobered her. "Yes, but we'll be careful."

He nodded. "Yes, we will be. We'll stay away from each other until this trouble is past."

Tess sighed. "But will it ever be past?"

"Yes." His eyes suddenly turned to stone. "I will make it so."

Tess shivered, not liking his hard expression or

his flinty tone. "Storm, please, just lay low. This will all die down and the marshall will be concerned with other outlaws."

"*Other* outlaws?" He jerked a thumb at his chest. "I am not an outlaw, Tess, and *that* is why I can't lay low like some guilty yellow-belly. I have done nothing wrong. My sister was murdered by your marshall. Am I to turn my back on that and forget it?"

"No, of course not . . ." She sighed again, seeing no way out without resorting to violence. But what if that violence took this man from her? She closed her eyes, unable to consider that possibility. "I'm afraid." The words slipped out before she could stop them.

He cursed softly and pulled her back into the security of his embrace. "I know, I know," he whispered, stroking her hair and massaging the small of her back. "But don't be. I will settle this feud and then . . ."

"Then?" Tess tipped back her head to look into his face. She prayed for a spark of hope.

"Then I won't have to sneak around anymore," he finished. He kissed her forehead, his lips lingering as if he were loathe to remove them from the patch of skin. "May the Great Spirit watch over you," he whispered, and then he turned quickly and was gone before Tess could even release the sob building in her throat.

Later that morning Tess tied on her bonnet and pulled on her street gloves. She headed for the front door, her mind on her shopping list, when a small voice stopped her in her tracks.

"Where you going?"

Tess turned back to face Cassie. The girl looked lost and forlorn with her pale-blond hair tangled, and in a brown sack dress and bare feet. "I'm going out for just a bit to do some shopping."

"Can I come? Please?"

Tess started to refuse, but Cassie's big brown eyes speared her heart. Besides, Cassie had kept mum about Storm's visit so far, and for that Tess owed her a debt of gratitude. "Oh, I suppose so. But wouldn't you rather stay close to your mama?" Tess directed her gaze to the back room where Mrs. Little recuperated.

"My big sister's sitting with her."

"Very well. Come, if you want."

Cassie skipped beside Tess along the boardwalk that fronted the buildings on Main Street. Only a few people loitered outside the businesses. False Hope was not, and hadn't been for years, a bustling enterprise. Several buildings were boarded up, signs that the town's heyday had passed.

Tess glanced at Cassie and saw that she was being thoroughly examined by the youngster. Was she wondering what Tess had been doing hidden away with a Blackfeet brave?

"When do you think we'll be leaving here?" Cassie asked.

"From what your father said this morning, I'd say tomorrow." But if Tess had been asked, she would have told Mr. Little he should think twice before resuming his journey to California. His wife had delivered a stillborn and was depressed and listless, but the man seemed determined to get back on the trail. He honestly thought that he'd become a rich man overnight, and all his troubles would dissolve once he touched California soil.

"Do all ladies wear hats?" Cassie asked, eyeing Tess's brown-and-gold bonnet.

"Yes, they do. And gloves, whenever possible." Hadn't Cassie's mother taught her this?

Cassie examined Tess's tan gloves. "I don't have a pair of those."

"You're not quite old enough to worry about such things. In a few years you'll get your first pair of grown-up ladies' gloves. Here's the store. Now don't touch anything and stay close to me. Okay?"

"Yes'm."

The general store smelled of cinnamon and lemon oil, with a faint scent of vinegar. She hadn't actually needed anything urgently from the store, but Tess had wanted to escape the house for a while. With the Littles hanging around, all sad-faced and antsy to be on their way, the Summar home had become oppressive. Or maybe it wasn't all their fault, Tess thought. Maybe she found her life as John's sister and housekeeper oppressive. She couldn't keep herself from daydreaming about the Blackfeet, their way of life and how alive she felt when she was with Storm-In-His-Eyes . . . how lifeless she felt without him.

Selecting the items on her list—a new feather duster, a can of furniture polish, three rolls of bandages, a bar of Castille soap and a sack of tulip bulbs for the porch flower box—Tess kept one eye on Cassie, but the girl was well-behaved and even seemed hesitant to get near anything, much less touch it.

The jumble of purchases in her shopping basket drew her attention, and Tess found herself thinking how she wouldn't need any of them, except maybe the bandages, if she were a Blackfeet bride. Certainly there would be no use for a duster or furniture polish—tulip bulbs, when nature provided an abundance of wild flowers? Soap, yes, but she'd probably make her own. She could remember years ago when she and her mother had made lye soap.

". . . living with those Indians, I hear."

"No! She was? Really? Good Lord. What was she thinking of, a lady of her caliber!"

Tess stiffened and peered between stacks of tea cloths and aprons to see who was gossiping about her. How dare they! They didn't know Storm, and obviously didn't know that he'd saved her life. Her ire spiked, and she decided to confront the gossiping biddies, but when she moved quickly down the aisle and around to the next row, she confronted only the broad chest of a man. Rough hands closed on her upper arms to steady her.

"Excuse me . . ." She started to move around him, but he blocked her way.

"Howdy, ma'am. I don't think we've been properly introduced. I'm Buck Wilhite. Deputy Buck Wilhite."

Tess stared at the brother of the man Storm had killed in a gunfight. "Oh, hello."

He reached down to retrieve the feather duster that had fallen from her basket. "You dropped this, I believe, Miss Tess."

"Yes, thanks." When she took it from him, his fingers brushed against hers, and she noticed a particular glint in his eyes. Oh, dear. He was flirting. And she wasn't the least bit interested. She eyed his pale complexion and sniffed at the overly sweet cologne he must have bathed in. She noted with disapproval that he hadn't bothered to remove his hat when he'd entered the building.

"Who you got with you today?" He looked past her to Cassie.

She smiled, having nearly forgotten about her tag-along. "This is Cassie Little. She and her family are staying with us while they recuperate. Their wagon was attacked by—"

"Indians," Buck finished. "Yeah, I heard."

"No, not—" Tess began.

"Hey, there, honey lamb," Buck said, placing a hand on Cassie's small shoulder. "You're a pretty one."

Honey lamb. That endearment sent a cold finger of uneasiness down Tess's spine. She shook off the odd feeling. "Cassie was shot with an arrow by one of the—"

"Did that old stinkin' Indian shoot you, honey lamb?" Buck asked, bending closer to Cassie until the girl wrinkled her nose, obviously not liking his cologne either.

"My mama's baby died," Cassie offered, stepping away from him. "But I'm all better."

"If you'll excuse us, Mr. Wilhite..." Tess snagged the sleeve of Cassie's dress and pulled her around behind her, shielding the girl from the deputy. The man set her nerves on edge.

"Those Indians didn't hurt you, did they, Miss Tess?" he asked, his face drawn with worry.

"No, they saved my life."

"Oh, yeah?" One corner of his mouth tilted up, slanting his wispy mustache. "Better watch out there, Miss Tess. When you lie down with dogs, you get fleas." He leaned closer, lowering his voice to a hissing whisper. "You ain't itching anywhere, are you?"

Tess shoved him away, anger shooting through her. "Get out of my face and out of my way!"

"What you getting all uppity for?" He splayed a hand across his chest and widened his eyes, striving for a look of innocence. "I was only giving you some advice."

"I'd sooner go to the village idiot for advice."

"Hey, now." He gripped her upper arm when she would have darted past him, and all innocence, feigned or otherwise, vanished from his sharp features. He was thin, but he had incredible strength.

"Don't you flounce away from me. You aren't too good for me, you know. Why, you're nothing but a spinster who should be talking sweet to any bachelor she is lucky enough to meet."

Tess yanked her arm from his grasp and tried not to let him see that he'd unnerved her, even frightened her. "And you should remove yourself from my path before I slap your face."

"Leave her alone!"

Much to Tess's shock, Cassie swung back one bare foot and slammed it smartly into Buck's shin. The man let out a soft oath and rubbed his leg. Seizing the opportunity for escape, Tess grabbed Cassie by the hand and hauled her to the front counter, where the owner waited for them.

"Hello, Mr. Dawson," she said breathlessly as she set her basket on the counter. "Will you put these things on John's bill?"

"Sure. Be glad to."

She noticed that Cassie was staring wide-eyed at the glass jars of candy. "And add a penny's worth of peppermint, if you please."

"Very well."

Cassie beamed. "For me?"

"Yes, for you." Tess leaned down and whispered in Cassie's ear, "For helping me back there with that rude man."

"I don't like him," Cassie whispered back, making a disagreeable face. When Mr. Dawson handed her the sack of candy, Cassie smiled at him. "Thank you, sir."

"Isn't she a polite child?" Mr. Dawson noted.

"Yes, she is." Tess glanced over her shoulder and was disconcerted to find Buck Wilhite lounging by the door. She'd have to pass him when she left. Why wouldn't he leave her alone?

"I'm going to be a fine lady when I grow up,"

Cassie announced. "Just like Miss Tess."

Inexplicably, Tess wanted to cry. Looking into the girl's innocent eyes, she wondered if many in the town of False Hope would agree with Cassie. Having heard the whispered gossip and seen the insulting glint in Buck's eyes, she realized the rumor mill was active and people looked at her differently now.

Anger mixed with her distress, and she felt that odd restlessness again, a need to break out, to speak out, to be free of all bonds.

Let them talk! The town gossips would never tarnish one memory she treasured of Storm and the Blackfeet. And they would never understand the Blackfeet either, because they were too narrow-minded, too full of hate and fear to—

"Deputy Wilhite!" A shrill voice shattered Tess's thoughts, and she spun around to see a wild-eyed young man stumble into the general store. "Deputy Wilhite." He bent at the waist and struggled for breath. Tess thought she'd seen him hanging around the marshall's office, sweeping floors and burning trash.

"What is it, Jeb?" Wilhite drawled. "You got ants in your pants?"

"Red and Marshall Long sent me to get you. They done tracked down them thieving redskins."

Everything in Tess went cold. Cold to the bone.

"They have, have they?" Buck's eyes slid sideways, and he grinned at Tess. "Where are they?"

"In jail," Jeb said. "They throwed them in jail."

"Good." Wilhite tugged on the brim of his hat in an insolent salute to Tess, then he draped an arm around the messenger's shoulders. "Come on, boy. Looks like there might be a hanging today—if we're lucky."

Chapter 14

With Cassie in tow, Tess left the general store and crossed the street, unmindful of the dirt and patches of mud through which she dragged her skirt hem. Cassie jumped over puddles and giggled when her bare toes squished in the mud.

"Where we goin'?" Cassie asked.

"The jail," Tess answered, staring at the marshall's office into which Buck Wilhite and Jeb had disappeared.

"Goody! I've always wanted to see one!"

Tess glanced at the girl, then smiled in spite of herself at Cassie's burgeoning excitement. She admired the youngster's sense of adventure, and she wished she could share it, but she was quaking with fear and anger. Approaching the office, she prayed Storm was still alive.

Wilhite stood beside the marshall's desk, and Marshall Long and his son were lounging in chairs, when Tess entered the room. The lawmen slowly rose to their feet. Jeb, wet mop in hand, scooted past her and Cassie and began cleaning the boardwalk. Glancing down, Tess gasped when she saw smears of blood on the floor and on the planks outside.

"What have you done to him?" she demanded of the marshall. "I swear, if you've . . ."

"Ladies shouldn't swear, Miss Tess. You *are* still a lady, aren't you?" Marshall Long drawled, an unpleasant grin stretching his lips.

Tess bristled. Gently pushing Cassie into a chair, Tess gestured for her to stay put. She moved briskly toward the jail door, but Red Long stepped into her path. A cheroot stuck from one corner of his mouth, and the smoke curled out to choke her.

"Where you think you're going?" Red asked.

"I know you've arrested Storm." She was proud of herself for sounding stern while her insides quaked. "I want to see him, so move out of my way."

"Storm?" Red snickered and shared a chuckle with his father and Buck Wilhite. "Who the hell is that? We've arrested two thieving Indians. Don't know nothing about no Storm. Do you, Pa?"

"Nope," Marshall Long said with a laugh. "Never heard of no Storm."

"Get out of my way," she ordered, hating the men for finding sport in her distress.

"You're not going anywhere," Red told her. "This here is a jailhouse, not a social club. Now go on home before you make an even bigger fool of yourself."

Fury swallowed her up. Snatching the smoking cheroot from his mouth, Tess pressed the tip of it against Red's shoulder. He yelped with pain and hopped sideways.

"Why, you little bitch!"

But Tess was already past him and had swung open the door. She hurried into the darkness and blinked frantically, forcing her eyes to adjust. Shadows took shape and she saw that she stood between two jail cells.

"Tess!"

She whirled about and grabbed the cold bars. Storm's face, bloody and battered, came into view. "Oh, my God. Storm, are you all right?"

His hands closed over hers. "Yes. You shouldn't be here. Go home. Go home now."

"No." She shook her head. "Not unless I can leave here with you beside me." She squinted into the darkness. "Is Brown Otter in there with you?"

"Yes, I think some of his ribs are broken."

A heavy hand landed on her shoulder and pulled her away from the bars. Storm snarled like an animal at Marshall Long, who held Tess away from him.

"Let go!" Tess wrenched from the marshall's grip. "You can't treat these men like this, and you can't lock them up without any proof."

"I'm the law. I got suspicions and that's proof enough. Besides, we followed tracks that led us right to these two coyotes. They attacked those people you got at your house. They shot that little girl."

"You're wrong. Cassie says it was white men who shot her. The same white men who attacked me."

"White men?" The marshall set his hands at his waist and reared back to laugh, the robust guffaws bouncing off the walls until Tess cringed. He grabbed her by the sleeve. "Come on outta here now."

"No!" Tess jerked away from him and her sleeve ripped. "Look what you've done!"

"Don't touch her," Storm growled. He shot out a hand through the bars and tried to grasp the marshall by the throat.

Marshall Long seized Storm's arm and bent it at

an awkward angle. Afraid he might break Storm's bones, Tess used all her strength to shove the lawman backward and away from the bars.

"You watch yourself, missy, or I'll throw you in that other cell," the marshall roared, giving Tess a shove that sent her stumbling and falling against the wall. "Why I ought to—" He raised a hand and evil blazed in his piggish eyes.

"Just *what* is going on here?" John stood in the doorway and took in the scene. Tess smothered a sob of relief as a tense silence played out. "Marshall Long, I'm waiting for an answer."

Tess moved toward her brother, at once thankful for and aggravated by his intrusion. "Marshall Long and his deputies have arrested Storm and Brown Otter for crimes they didn't commit. Make him release them."

Marshall Long gave a short laugh. *"Him* make me? That's a hoot. Ain't that a hoot, Red?"

Red chuckled, but his eyes were burning with hatred. "Sure is, Pa." He rubbed his shoulder where the cheroot had burned a hole in his shirt. "Doc, you better take your sister home before she gets hurt."

"Let's go in the office and discuss this rationally," John suggested.

Casting a glance toward Storm, Tess nodded, realizing that their best bet was to prove to the marshall he had the wrong men. She couldn't do that by yelling and screaming and pushing and shoving. John was right. *Be rational.*

She straightened her dress and examined her torn sleeve as she walked back into the office. Jeb was mopping and casting furtive glances at her. Tess figured that Jeb had fetched John when she'd bullied her way past Red to see Storm. Buck Wilhite leaned negligently against a wall full of

WANTED posters. Cassie was still sitting in the chair, her feet dangling inches from the floor. She was small for her age, but her spirit made up for her slight stature. She grinned mischievously at Tess, clearly enjoying the fireworks. Marshall Long sat behind his desk, and Red stood beside him like a brooding sentinel.

"What are the Blackfeet charged with?" John asked. He frowned, noticing Tess's torn sleeve.

"Stealing horses and robbing people. They shot that child there. Yeah, that's right. They robbed that family."

John stared at Tess. "How can you defend them? They've nearly destroyed the Little family!"

"They didn't do it. Cassie told you it was a white man wearing an Indian mask who shot her," Tess reminded him, exasperated. "You want them to be guilty, but they're not."

"Why would white men go around wearing Indian masks?" Marshall Long asked with a spate of incredulous laughter.

"Why, indeed?" Tess challenged. "Maybe because they want the law to *think* that Indians are committing these crimes?"

"They *are*," Red asserted. "No matter how many wild tales you tell, we know them Blackfeet are nothing but trouble. Especially that one you call Storm. He's nothin' but a cold-blooded killer."

Tess turned toward Cassie. "Didn't you tell us that it was a white man who shot you?"

"Uh-huh." Cassie nodded her head vigorously.

"She's just a kid," Buck said. "She was so scared, she probably didn't know which end was up."

"She's not stupid like some people in this room." Tess stared pointedly at Buck, then Red, then the marshall. "What color hair did the man have, Cassie?"

"Blond. Slicked back with grease." Cassie grinned. "His hat blowed off and I saw."

"And then he shot you."

Cassie nodded. "He did. Right here." She pointed to her shoulder.

"I'm sure he wasn't aiming at you, honey lamb," Buck said. "Nobody would want to hurt a pretty, little thing like you. Why, you're going to have hairy-legged boys lined up soon just to get a little old kiss from you."

Cassie wrinkled her nose and looked at Buck as if he were completely insane. "Anybody tries to kiss me, I'll knock his teeth out."

Buck grinned. "She'll do it, too. She gave me a swift kick in the shin, didn't you, honey lamb? It's a good thing I'm a nice man or you might have gotten your butt whipped for that."

"Don't threaten the child," John warned, and Tess edged closer to him, proud that he was beginning to see the evil intent in the other men.

"I'm not," Buck said, his eyes wide. "I was just saying—"

"I heard what you said and you heard what I said," John cut in before turning back to the marshall. "Cassie Little is a witness, Marshall. She ought to know better than anybody who shot her. Wouldn't you agree?"

"Well . . ." Marshall Long rubbed his mustache. "I reckon. But that don't cancel out the horses them boys took last Friday night. A dozen brands from the Circle Four Ranch out by—"

"Last Friday, you say?" Tess interrupted, her mind whirring. Storm couldn't have . . . impossible! She glanced toward the jail door, anxious to get Storm out of that pit.

"That's right," the marshall assured her. "And folks ain't too happy about it. I'm trying to wait for the district judge to get here before I hang 'em as horse thieves, but I don't know—"

"We ain't gonna wait," Red said, hooking his thumbs in his gun belt. "Ain't no reason to wait. They're guilty as sin, the both of them."

"They aren't guilty," Tess said, glaring at Red. "And you shouldn't be wearing a badge if you don't think every man deserves a fair trial."

"I've had about enough of your mouth," Red said, his face almost as crimson as his hair. "You're just like my sister. Millie don't know when to keep her trap shut and her skirt down either."

A roar of anger exploded from the jail room, making everyone jerk and stare at the partially open door. The rattle of bars clanged loudly. Tess knew the bellow had come from Storm, and that he was trying to yank the cell door open with his bare hands. He must have heard Red and had reacted violently. A little thrill fluttered through her.

"Listen to that, will you?" Buck said. "They're nothing but animals."

"As I was saying," Marshall Long said, "me and Red followed them Indian scum's tracks and found the horses they'd stolen penned up a few miles from the Blackfeet camp."

Tess shook her head. "And what about the men who attacked me on the road? What have you done about them?"

"Haven't seen hide nor hair of any white men dressed like Indians," Marshall Long told her. "I think maybe you scrambled your brain when you hit your head."

"I think you haven't even looked for those men." Tess inched closer to the jail door. She could hear Storm's labored breathing and knew he must be nearly out of his mind with rage. She yearned to hold him, to soothe him.

"I gotta solve one crime at a time." Marshall Long stood up. "Me and my son tracked 'em down, didn't we, Red?"

"Sure did, Pa."

"Alred is a regular bloodhound. Why, he sniffed out them tracks . . . tracks I couldn't even see most of the time!"

"Isn't that amazing?" Buck asked, grinning like a drunk monkey. Something about him made Tess's skin crawl.

"Gotta have young eyes," Red said.

"Marshall, I want those men released. They're innocent," Tess insisted. John gave a sigh and a look that made her realize he wasn't exactly in her corner.

"You better check her ears, doc," Marshall Long told John. "She don't hear so good."

"Maybe he should check yours first . . . and your eyes!" She matched glares with Red, letting him know through her smoking anger that she didn't believe he had such miraculous tracking abilities. "I told you Storm could not have stolen those horses."

"And what makes you so sure?" Marshall Long asked, squinting at her.

Tess drew in a deep breath and her heartbeat thundered in her head. She felt everyone's intense stares, but especially Cassie's. Would the girl understand what she was about to say? She hated to sully Cassie's high opinion of her, but the moment of truth had arrived and Tess prayed for courage. "I'm sure because last Friday night Storm was with me."

John shouldered her aside. "What she means is that she was at the Blackfeet camp last Friday. She assumes that this Indian outlaw was there, too, but of course, she couldn't know for certain if—"

"I can speak for myself, John," Tess said, stepping in front of him. "And I *can* be certain that Storm did not leave the camp all night long." There. It was out. Almost. She glanced at John and saw his stricken expression. Cassie's mouth hung open, and her eyes were wide with curiosity. Tess lowered her gaze and stared at her muddy shoes. Lord, could she do it? Could she say the words and damn her reputation forever in this town and in her brother's eyes? She swung her chin up. "Storm was with me, by my side, all night long."

John moaned behind her and a deeper moan floated from inside the jail. Tess closed her eyes, amazed that she didn't feel defeated, but rather light-headed.

"You mean, you was sleeping with him?" Marshall Long asked, voicing the question Tess knew they all wanted her to answer—all except John. Poor big brother John.

Tess faced the marshall squarely. "Yes, that's right."

"Good God, Tess," John said, his voice broken. "Mama and Papa are turning over in their graves."

"Release them, Marshall Long." Tears collected in her throat and behind her eyes. She hadn't thought about how her parents might have reacted to such news, but she hoped John was wrong. She hoped she'd inherited her open mind from them. "Release Storm and Brown Otter," she repeated. "You have nothing to hold them on now."

Tess stayed in the saddle atop Cameo, but Storm and Brown Otter slipped off their ponies and dropped to their knees beside the stream. They dipped their heads and arms into the rushing water, washing away dirt and caked blood.

Surveying the area around them, Tess could see

no one and she hoped the marshall or his deputies had not followed them. The marshall had reluctantly released Storm and Brown Otter from the jail, but had sworn that he would eventually hang them. Tess's muscles tightened and her nerves screamed. She felt trapped, unable to shape her life or carve out her own destiny. If only she and Storm could leave, go up into the mountains and live in peace. But the law would probably track him there, too. Looking constantly over her shoulder was no way to live.

She'd insisted on riding with them out of town, afraid the marshall or someone else might try to shoot them. Not that she could stop them, but at least she'd be a witness. They weren't such fools that they'd do something like that right in front of her. Of course, they could stage an ambush. . . . She looked around again, nervous as a mouse caught out in the open.

"Are you going to be all right?" she called to Storm. "I have bandages and some medicine here in my saddle bag."

"You should have gone home with your brother and the girl," Storm said, rising to his feet and turning toward her.

Tess's heart sang sweetly. He was handsome even with wet hair, a swollen lip, and a blood-caked eyebrow.

"We're fine. Go back to town."

"You're not mad at me, are you?"

He ran a hand over his dripping hair and walked toward her, his shoulders wide, his gait that of a confident predator. "You shouldn't have sacrificed so much for me. You must go back home and tell your brother it is all a lie, that you were not with me all night."

She shook her head and slid down from the saddle. Storm's hands closed around her waist to help her, and stayed there when she was firmly on the ground. "I won't recant. It happened. I'm not ashamed."

"But you must hold your head up and—"

"I will," she insisted, although she already dreaded the whispered words behind her back, the furtive glances. "Don't worry about me. The marshall is determined to hang you, Storm. What were you and Brown Otter doing when he caught you?"

"Following the same tracks he was following. I was trying to find the men who attacked you."

"Oh, Storm." She placed a hand on his chest. His buckskin shirt was ripped, almost shredded. The marshall had roped him and dragged him some distance behind his horse. Red had done the same to Brown Otter, which had broken a couple of Brown Otter's ribs. "I hate what is happening, but what can I do to stop it?"

"Nothing. You can do nothing." He captured her hand and brought her palm to his lips. His kiss sent a tingling up her arm and straight to her heart. "You have done more than enough."

Tess looked toward the stream where Brown Otter sat and squeezed water from his long braids. "Maybe I could bind his broken ribs—"

"Minipoka will see to him." Storm tightened his hands on her waist and lifted her up and onto the saddle again. "You go on."

Tess frowned down at him. "I'm being dismissed, I take it."

"Yes."

"Without even a proper thank you?" She saw the flash of a grin race across his lips. "I shred my reputation and all you can say is, 'Go home, white woman?' I suppose you call every female

'AnadaAki,' and I'm a big fool to have thought that you—"

He pulled her from the saddle and ground his mouth against hers. She uttered a protest and his mouth gentled. Tess was adrift in the wonder of his kiss. She cleaved to him. His tongue mated lavishly with hers, and she felt his passion quicken. He moaned into her mouth and nudged himself against her. He was rock hard and she wanted him, wanted him desperately.

"Take me with you, Storm," she pleaded against his lips. "Take me back to the Blackfeet."

"No, I can't," he murmured, his hands roaming over her hips and then coming up to catch in her hair. "You must stay with your brother where you will be safe. If anything ever happened to you, I wouldn't want to live another moment."

A sob burned her throat and tears spilled from her eyes. "Please, Storm. I'll be safe with the Blackfeet and we can be together. I don't want to go back—"

"You must!" He set her away from him, agony clearly written on his face, in his eyes. Gritting his teeth, he caught her around the waist again and lifted her up and onto the saddle. "Don't argue with me, Tess. Go. Go now." He raised his hand to slap the horse across the rump.

Tess grabbed his wrist. "Be careful, my love," she whispered.

He rested his hand softly on Cameo's rump, and his eyes glistened with emotion. "Thank you for what you've done." A smile, incredibly tender, curved his mouth. "AnadaAki."

Tess managed to return his smile, although her lips trembled and his face blurred with her tears. She kicked Cameo and the horse surged forward. She didn't look back, couldn't bear to look back and think that it might be the last time she'd see him.

Chapter 15

Her lonely ride back to town was a revelation to Tess. That she desperately wanted to be reunited with Storm was no surprise, but that she was willing to turn her back on her life in False Hope gave her a start. Until that moment, she hadn't realized how starkly unhappy she'd become with her situation.

She, a white woman and circumspect friend of the Blackfeet, would rather live with them than in her family home. She closed her eyes for a second, overcome with the complete upheaval of her life. Her goals, her dreams, her security were suddenly gone, drastically altered to fit the woman she had become during the past few weeks.

Her mind felt full of fog, her heart full of woe. Nearing the house, Tess looked up to see Camilla standing in the doorway.

Oh, no, she thought. Lord, give me patience. If Camilla says one nasty thing about Storm ... but of course she would. Like John, Camilla thought all Indians were uncivilized heathens.

Tess took her time unsaddling and brushing Cameo. She was in no hurry as she dumped feed into the trough and filled Cameo's water bucket. But it was all to no avail. Camilla was waiting for her at the back door.

"John told me something I can't for the life of me believe," Camilla said. "He says you confessed in front of God and everyone that you spent the night with an Indian! What's gotten into you, Tess? Don't you know that what you say reflects on me and—"

"Camilla," Tess interrupted, holding a hand in front of Camilla's face, "I might endure such lectures from my brother, but pigs will fly before I take one from the likes of you. Now, excuse me. I'm going to my room and I don't want to be disturbed."

Camilla's teeth snapped together and hot-pink color crept over her face. "You can't speak to me that way in my own house."

"Your house?" Tess scoffed, moving past her and heading for the stairs.

"Yes, *my* house," Camilla called after her. "And if you're going to continue to stay here, I can't allow you to besmirch our good name."

Tess paused on the seventh stair and looked down at Camilla, a decision firming in her mind a second before she spoke. "For your information, I've had the Summar name all my life, and I value it much more than you. But don't worry. I'm moving out."

Camilla looked shocked for a moment, then she gave a mocking laugh. "You're moving? Where to, a tepee?"

Visions of Storm's tepee sent a weakness to her knees. Ah, wouldn't that be heaven on earth? She shook her head, dislodging the wishful thinking. "I'll move to a root cellar, if I must. I refuse to live in this house and be treated as a maid or as an inconvenience or as a disobedient child." Gathering her skirts in one hand, she ran the rest of the way up the stairs to her room, where she paced and tried to convince herself that the news of her indiscretion would die down after a few weeks, and her life would return to normal.

But all the while a little voice deep inside mocked her; she knew, in her heart of hearts, that her life would never, ever be the same again. A storm had blown into her quiet world and tossed everything hither and yon. She told herself it was for the best. Fingering the beads on the necklace around her neck, she drew strength from them as they fetched sweet memories of Storm. His sensuous voice, his tender touch, his soul-shaking kisses, all made her sigh with longing. Storm had touched her secret places and awakened in her a desire, a hunger so huge that even now she marveled at its immensity. In Storm's arms she had discovered sex, and the discovery had changed her forever. She couldn't imagine being satisfied by any other man, and she didn't want to even try.

She'd never regret her time with Storm, but was her time with him over? Did he ever wish he'd never met her? He said he'd brought trouble to her, but Tess saw it differently. Her confession had released him from jail, but she feared it might have also been a splash of kerosene on a fire that now raged out of control.

Sitting in the parlor on the horsehair sofa, which had been her father's favorite piece of furniture, Tess looked at John and felt sorry for him. He sat slumped in the matching chair across from her, drinking from a glass of whiskey, his eyes focused on the toes of his shiny boots. The grandfather clock ticked loudly. A floorboard overhead creaked and Tess glanced up, wondering if Camilla was walking the floor, waiting impatiently for John to come upstairs and tell her whether or not Tess had completely lost her mind.

"Mrs. Little says they'll be leaving before dawn," Tess said, unable to endure the silence another moment.

John blinked owlishly at her. "Hmm? Oh, yes. That's right."

"Is she well enough to travel?"

"Not really, but Ben is anxious to be underway again. He promised to travel half-days until his wife is stronger."

Tess frowned, wondering how long Ben would keep to that promise. He struck her as an impatient man.

Suddenly John stood up. "Tess, I thought I knew you."

Tess sighed, wishing she could avoid this particular discussion. "I know. We all change, John."

"Overnight?" He turned away as if he couldn't bear to look at her, then took another swallow of the whiskey. "I don't know if I can repair the damage to your reputation, Tess. I just don't know—"

"I don't expect you to."

"But I must. I'm your brother, your guardian. You're my responsibility."

"Piffle," she said, waving a hand in rebuke. "I'm a grown woman. I need no guardian."

"Obviously you do. What do you think Papa and Mama would say about this, Tess? You admit you've slept with an Indian . . . you, an unmarried white woman. The whole town is buzzing about it. How can you hope to be treated with an ounce of respect from anyone?"

Irritation made her squirm on the sofa cushion. "John, it's not as if I killed—"

"And am I supposed to fight everyone who talks badly about you? How am I to defend your honor?"

"I'm not asking you to—"

"And what about me and Camilla? We can't go anywhere now without hearing disparaging remarks about you. I thought you were a lady, Tess. I can't tell you how disappointed I am."

"Disappointed?" She tightened her hands into fists until her knuckles showed white. "What about Marshall Long? Are you disappointed in him, too?"

"He's not my responsibility."

"Yes, he is. He's the marshall in this town and he's corrupt. If you see yourself as a leader in False Hope, then you must share in the responsibility of supporting a lawman who kills innocent people in cold blood."

He whipped around to face her. "Innocent people? Who are you talking about now?"

"Willow-Bends-Woman. She was unarmed and the marshall shot her."

"Her brother shot her."

"No." Tess shook her head. "She told me Marshall Long turned his gun on her and shot her. Storm tells the same story."

"Well, what do you expect? They hate white people. It's easier to blame it on us than to admit they killed their own." He ran a hand through his blond hair, making it stand on end. "Sometimes, Tess, I wonder about your clarity of mind."

She saw the futility of trying to talk to him and stood up. He looked at her, one brow arching in inquiry. "I'm going to my room. Good night."

"Did that Indian rape you?"

"Good heavens, no!"

"Tess, you can confide in me. If you're trying to

deny what really happened, I can understand. But this isn't good, Tess. You must confront reality. If he forced himself on you, then you must tell—''

"We made love, John. He didn't force anything on me. He wouldn't do that."

"All right, then maybe you should reconsider, Tess. Honesty is not always the best avenue. If you say that you were forced, then people will look more kindly on you."

His suggestion filled her with hot, piercing contempt. She swallowed hard, afraid she might retch, and hugged herself until she was certain she could speak again. John was talking and his words didn't register in her mind. She heard his voice, but she'd stopped listening to him.

"I'm going to look for somewhere else to live tomorrow, John," she interrupted, chopping him off in mid-sentence. "As I've told Camilla, I've decided to move."

He finished his whiskey and set the empty glass on the sofa table. "Tess, be reasonable."

"I don't belong here, John. Not anymore. This is Camilla's house. Your house. Not my house."

"That's ridiculous, and there is nowhere for you to move to in False Hope. Besides, how will that look? People will think I've disowned you."

"I don't care how it looks, and I can't be concerned with what people think. I'm tired of trying to live up to other people's expectations of me—or to live down to them." She stood and moved to the cherry-wood cabinet where John kept the liquor. Opening the doors, she selected a bottle of gin, poured two fingers of it into a beveled glass, and replaced the bottle.

"What do you think you're doing?"

"You didn't offer me a drink, so I'm helping myself." She tipped the glass to her lips, but had barely gotten a taste of the liquor before John snatched it from her, sloshing gin on her hand.

"I've had about enough of you for one day, Tess," he said, his face red with anger. He set the glass on the sideboard. "I think you should take yourself upstairs and contemplate your actions today and how you are going to deal with the consequences tomorrow."

Tess regarded his stern, flushed countenance and shook her head, finding his attitude oddly amusing. "Are you sending me to my room as punishment, John?" She rested a hand on his sleeve and squeezed. "Poor John. I'm too much for you to handle, it seems. But that's perfectly all right, because I'm capable of taking care of myself."

"How, Tess? How will you do that?"

"Well, I know quite a bit about medicine, wouldn't you agree?"

"You're certainly not a doctor, if that's what you're getting at." His breath wafted over her face, smelling like whiskey. It was unlike John to drink in the evenings, and Tess knew she'd driven him to it.

"No, I'm not a doctor. But I am a housekeeper and a cook, aren't I? Even you can't deny that."

"You don't have to work outside this home. Just go to bed, and tomorrow I'll begin to salvage what I can of your reputation. Leave it to me."

"No, John." She seized the glass of gin before he could react and downed the contents in two quick swallows. Setting the glass on the sideboard again, she faced John's furious glare as the liquor spread fire in her stomach and sent fumes up through her head. "I'm not your responsibility or your ward or your problem. I will go to my room now, but I am planning to move, not because of anything you've done or not done. I'm grateful to you for standing beside me today at the marshall's. That meant a lot to me."

She was halfway across the parlor when he stopped her.

"Tess, that Indian outlaw probably cares nothing for you." He placed a hand on her shoulder in a fatherly fashion.

"Perhaps," Tess agreed softly, wondering if he was trying to help or hurt her now. "But I care very much for him. And he's not an outlaw. The marshall and his deputies are the outlaws, John. After what you witnessed today, I don't know how you can even doubt that."

She left the room. Halfway up the stairs, she wished she had thought to grab the gin bottle on her way out.

When she opened the bedroom door, Cassie sat up on the cot beside Tess's bed. Tess just managed not to groan aloud. She'd forgotten the girl was still sharing her room.

"I'm leaving tomorrow," Cassie announced.

"Yes, so I've heard. And you're leaving very early, so you'd better go to sleep." Tess stepped behind the dressing screen to remove her clothes and slip into her ivory nightgown.

"Mama still don't look good."

"She's ill, Cassie. And she's sad about losing the baby."

"Papa says she'll feel all better once we get to California."

"I hope he's right." But he's a damn fool, Tess thought, lumping him in with some other damn fools she'd wrestled with that day. She went to her dresser and removed the pins from her hair. Brushing out her long tresses, she caught Cassie's reflection in the oval mirror. "You aren't sleeping," Tess noted. "You're supposed to be sleeping."

"I'm not tired. I've been thinking about them Indians. Where'd you go with them?"

"Just outside of town." Tess pulled the brush through her hair, listening to the crackle and enjoying the tingling on her scalp.

"Miss Tess?"

"Hmmm?"

"Are you in love with the tall one?"

Tess laid the brush down and turned slowly to face the inquisitive youngster. "What do you know about such things, Cassie Little? Don't answer that. You snuggle down under the covers and go to sleep."

"Someday somebody is gonna love me and I'm gonna be a wife and momma."

Tess smiled and crossed the room to turn down the bed covers. "That's right, and you'll make a fine wife and momma, too, but don't be too impatient. There is plenty of time for you to find just the right man."

"Is that why you're not married? Did you wait to find the right one? Is *he* the one you want to marry?"

"So many questions!" Tess teased. She went to the bureau and opened the top drawer to remove a pair of gray gloves trimmed in black lace. "I have something for you."

"Really? What?" Cassie sat up on the cot, her brown eyes wide, her silky hair falling down her back.

"Your first pair of grown-up lady gloves." Tess handed them to her. "But you are only to wear them for special occasions."

"Oh!" Cassie slipped her small hands into the gloves, which were a loose fit. "They're beautiful!"

"You'll grow into them," Tess assured her. "But

from now on, Cassie, you conduct yourself with pride and ladylike decorum."

"With what?" Cassie asked.

"Be a lady," Tess explained with a smile. "A lady of your own making. As long as you behave with dignity and a pure heart, then you shouldn't give a moment's thought to what other people might be saying about you or thinking about you. Always be proud of yourself and be good to yourself, Cassie. When you wear these gloves, you remember that, okay?"

"Yes, ma'am!" Cassie wrapped her arms around Tess's neck and gave her a hug. "Thank you ever so much!"

"Take them off now and go to sleep," Tess told her, tucking her in when she was settled on the cot.

"Yes, ma'am. Miss Tess, is that Indian a gentleman? Are you two gonna get married?"

Tess slipped into her own bed and felt Cassie's bright eyes on her. She reached out to stroke a finger down Cassie's cheek. The girl had inched the cot closer to Tess's bed, and Tess wondered if she might be afraid in the strange surroundings. "A person might think you were nosy, Cassie Little."

"I was scared of him at first—the tall Indian—but he seems real nice."

"He is nice." She turned down the lamp. "Go to sleep now. You have a big day tomorrow."

"You think we'll run into Indians on the way to California?"

"You might."

"I hope they're all like your Indian. What's his name again?"

"Storm-In-His-Eyes."

"That's pretty."

Tess smiled and closed her eyes. Instantly Storm's face entered her mind and brought a lump to her throat. Her Indian. Would she ever see him again? Maybe it would be better if she didn't. Her association with him seemed to have made the marshall and his deputies hate Storm even more, and double their determination to hunt him down and hang him.

"Good night, Miss Tess," Cassie whispered.

"Good night, Cassie. Sweet dreams." She listened for a few minutes, wondering if Cassie would finally settle down. The girl tossed onto her side, then onto the other side before she grew still and her breathing deepened.

Tomorrow would be the beginning of a journey for both Cassie and herself, Tess thought. Cassie would resume chasing her father's dreams, and Tess would pursue a different dream by leaving this house. She planned to ask Mrs. Bishop if she could live with her in exchange for housekeeping and cooking. She fully expected the woman to agree to the arrangement.

Yes, tomorrow would be momentous. She had hoped that she would move out of this house and into the home she would make with her husband. It had never occurred to her that she might be leaving simply because she no longer felt comfortable or welcome. No matter that John and Camilla would protest and insist she should stay, that this house was her home as well as theirs. No matter. The dye had been cast.

Fighting off a wave of self-pity, she told herself that leaving was for the best. John and Camilla needed to have the place to themselves. Someday they would start a family and Tess's room would become a nursery. Yes, they'd have children and might eventually use all the rooms upstairs, moving their own bedroom downstairs the way Mama and Papa had when they'd all lived under this roof.

Happier times floated to her like half-remembered song lyrics. She floated in and out of them, smiling faintly at the childhood memories.

A wolf howled in the distance and Tess immediately thought of Storm. A deep yearning commenced, squeezing her heart and filling her with molten longing. She tossed restlessly in bed, finally lying on her back with her limbs sprawled, her breathing rapid, her eyes open and staring as his face burned in her mind.

Was he thinking of her? Had Minipoka treated his injuries? She wished for those uninterrupted hours again in the cave when it had been just the two of them against the world. Oh, she'd give almost anything for one more night alone with him. Just one more night.

She slid a hand down her stomach to her thigh. A thin veil of perspiration covered her flesh, spawned by passion's fever. The world without him was a lackluster place. She imagined herself traveling to the Blackfeet camp, begging him to let her stay. Yes, she would gladly swallow her pride if there was a chance she could be with him again.

Away from her he might decide that she was too much trouble, that his being with a white woman could only complicate his life even more, and he might very well be right. But that wouldn't stop her from wanting him or dreaming of him or praying for him to come back to her.

With her eyes closed she could feel the fire of his mouth on her skin, experience the tumultuous invasion of him. With a tortured moan, she pushed back the covers and went to sit on the window seat. She opened the window, letting in the cool mountain breeze. A quarter moon hung in the night sky. Blue light illuminated the earth. Timber wolves chorused far, far away.

"Storm," she whispered to the wind. Would he rescue her again, save her from the grip of unrequited passion, of undaunted desire? "Storm," she whispered again, willing the wind to carry the sound of her voice to his listening heart.

Chapter 16

Lying flat on his back, Storm stared up through the smoke hole of his lodge, up where the stars twinkled coldly. The deep abrasions and purpling bruises on his chest, stomach, and thighs throbbed and fired with pain, but he gave them little notice. They were but a flickering annoyance compared to the anger blazing in his gut.

He examined the anger because it was something he knew intimately, like the fury he now wrestled. Curling his hands into fists at his sides, he relived the ambush by the marshall and deputies, the valiant fight he and Brown Otter put up before the ropes tightened around them and they were jerked to their knees. White devils. They would pay, he vowed. He would not rest until he could reap his revenge.

Recalling how he had prayed that Tess would not see him, that she would not witness his defeat, he ground his teeth with frustration as he recalled her coming to his rescue and making him feel even less of a man. Of course, she couldn't know this and that hadn't been her intent, but his pride stung and he had never felt so impotent in his life.

Shame coated his heart and he muttered darkly, the curse words easing his burden and giving voice to his writhing anger.

She had sacrificed her honor for his. Damn her. He slammed his fists into the buffalo robe beneath him. He didn't like feeling beholden to her. He wasn't used to a woman who placed his honor before her own. She should have stayed away. It would have been better for both of them if he hadn't seen her again, if he hadn't slipped into town and sought her out. But he was weak where she was concerned. He could make iron-clad promises to himself and break every one when it came to Tess.

Ahhh, but she had been beautiful, standing tall and elegant, chin held high, a rebellious glint in her eyes. He'd seen her stare daggers at the marshall and spit disdain at the deputies. And he'd been proud, bursting with pride for her. Later by the stream he had wanted to make love to her and would have if Brown Otter hadn't been watching them. Brown Otter wanted him to stay far away from Tess, thinking she and all white people brought only grief to the Blackfeet. But Brown Otter couldn't know the power and passion of his AnadaAki. She was not just another white woman. She was brave and beautiful and she possessed great knowledge that she was willing to share. He loved the way her eyes sparkled with interest, and the seductive curve of her lips when desire wound around her heart. Brown Otter had not felt her magic.

Storm wanted her . . . now. He could feel himself growing hard with the wanting. Perhaps he should heed Brown Otter's words of warning. To be so devoted to a woman couldn't be a good thing. To feel such admiration for a woman could only bring a man to his knees. Was that where the white eyes' custom of proposing to a woman on bent knee had originated? Had the white men discovered long ago that some women deserved such deference? If so, then surely Tess was one of them. He was a man who would kneel for no one, yet he could see himself on one knee before her, asking for her hand, doing whatever was necessary to win her.

For she was a woman of heart. Pluck, he thought with a slow grin. He'd recognized that in her in the first few minutes. Should have run the other way right then. Would have if he'd been strong enough at the time.

He shoved up to his feet and took a cautious breath when his bruised ribs cried out. Gingerly, he touched them and waited for the pain to subside before pacing restlessly around the lodge. The lodge made him think of her. He could see her lying on the pallet, standing by the fire, sharing a long, speaking glance with him. He throbbed for her, and each beat of his heart seemed to call her name. But he had to get her out from under his skin, didn't he? There could be no future for them. A white woman and Blood. Never had worked.

Well, it had worked once, he amended. His grandfather, a Blood. His grandmother, a white. Yes, he knew about that union and how it was responsible for his lighter eyes, the hair that grew under his arms and on his legs. He had been told, but like the other Bloods, he had shoved it far, far back in his mind. Such a union was too risky, especially with the white eyes gaining more and more land, forcing the Bloods into battle. The climate was more hostile now than it had been in his grandfather's day.

He kept pacing, trying to walk off the yearning that had infused him. A life with Tess . . . children with AnadaAki. No. Wouldn't work. Wouldn't work. Wouldn't—

"Storm-In-His-Eyes?"

The soft voice speaking his name in lyrical Blackfeet spun him around and ended his mental chant. He pressed the heel of his hand against his screaming ribs. Slow-Riding-Woman stepped inside his lodge, her slender frame encased in a tight-fitting leather dress, fringed and beaded. A triangle decorated the skirt, down low between her knees and ankles. It was the symbol of womanhood, of the cradle of civilization every woman carried in her womb.

"Do I disturb you?"

He examined her, saw the glint of sexuality in her dark eyes. He shook his head. "No."

"How are your wounds?"

He shrugged. "They ache."

"Can I do anything to comfort you?"

He saw the glint in her eyes again and realized she was phrasing her questions carefully. She was a wolf in sheep's clothing. A very pretty wolf. His loins tingled, and his already hard man-root lengthened under his breechcloth. Even with this lovely woman standing before him, wanting him and willing him to want her, part of his mind clung to Tess. Could this be the kind of love he'd heard about from others, seen with his own eyes but never felt with his own heart—until now? Was he truly, deeply in love with Tess?

"Storm-In-His-Eyes? Are you feeling well?" Slow-Riding-Woman moved closer, her musky scent reaching out to him. "I couldn't sleep until I came here to see if I could ease your pain or make you forget for a few minutes . . . or a few hours . . . what the whites have done to you." She moved like a cloud, light and airy, her feet hardly touching earth. In a blink, she was standing before him, her eyes luminous, her lips glistening, her scent surrounding him.

"That's . . ." He found it difficult to speak. His mind and his body warred. His body wanted a woman—any woman—but his mind wanted Tess—only Tess. "That's thoughtful of you," he said, forcing each word out.

A faint smile flitted across her face. "Sometimes I feel we are joined, you and I. Not just by the promises made but by our spirits. You feel it, too?" One hand drifted up, paused in mid-air, then settled over his heart. Her skin was cool against his bare chest. He realized only then that he was burning up, inside and out, and he knew why.

The mating fever was keen in him, had been ever since he'd seen Tess again. She'd looked so different in her prim dress and with her hair skinned back from her face. Different, but no less desirable. His Tess, running to his side, fighting for his freedom.

He would honor her sacrifice, he thought. He would honor it by finding the men who preyed on the whites, who had tried to harm her, and he would kill them. Then he would be able to stand tall again.

"Storm-In-His-Eyes?"

The purring voice brought him back and he looked into eyes that weren't blue-green but jet-black.

"What can I do for you?" Her hand slipped lower to his stomach. "We are to wed, so nothing can be wrong between us." Her lips grazed his chin and her little tongue darted out to lick a path down the side of his neck. She touched him, pressed her palm against him. "Ahhh," she breathed. "You want me, too. I knew this in my heart."

The hand clamped around him, cut off his brain, and he ground his mouth against Slow-Riding-Woman's. She moaned, opening herself to him, and he plunged his tongue in deep. She tasted good, clean, womanly. But she didn't taste like Tess.

He shoved her away and gave her his back while he struggled with his own self-mocking demons. He couldn't go on like this, wanting a woman he shouldn't, pushing away a woman who was, by rights, his. But he couldn't see a way out of this sticky web spun by his heart, joining him tenuously to a white woman. She was out of reach, and Slow-Riding-Woman wasn't. No, he could feel her right behind him, sense her hovering hands, hear her rapid breathing, smell her heightened excitement.

"She is not for you," Slow-Riding-Woman said, her voice as cool as logic. "You know this. I have waited for you. I have kept myself pure for you. You will walk beside Chief Eagle Talon one day and you must have a Blackfeet wife with you. No Blood chief will have a white woman as his wife. It would dishonor the whole tribe."

"Blood chief?" He looked at her over his shoulder. "Chief Eagle Talon will never make me a chief. He is grooming his eldest son for that."

"He told my father that you're destined to be a leader."

"Maybe, but not a chief."

"One never knows what lies ahead."

"I know this."

She made a sound of exasperation. Her hands fluttered over his shoulders like persistent birds. The backs of her fingers glided down his spine.

"No one can know what fate has in store for us, my handsome brave. My sister was taken from us so that I would stand in her place, so that I would be your bride. The spirits have positioned us as they position the stars, the moon, the sun. We are meant to be one. Husband and wife."

Her words seduced, her language enticed. He turned slowly to face her and her proud carriage and winsome eyes brought his hand to her cheek, his mouth to hers once more for another taste. No, not Tess, but woman. Blackfeet woman. A woman promised to him long ago.

With her body bowing into his and her arms stealing around him, she tangled her tongue with his. Passion surged through him and he cupped her backside in his hands and lifted her up so that he could nibble her neck, her shoulder.

"Take me tonight and make me your bride tomorrow," she whispered, her legs sandwiching one of his. "I want no special ceremony. Simple tradition will bind me to you."

The wedding she was working up to doused the flames of his passion and he backed away from her. His breath sawed in his throat, and he knew he must look like a fuming beast to her with his body scarred and cut and bruised; his hair hanging over his shoulders, in his eyes; his mouth slick from her kiss. He shook his head to clear it and to stop her advance.

"No. I can't marry you."

"Can't?" She pinched her brows together. "But it is fated. You must marry me."

"No." Still shaking his head, he tried to walk off the steam left by his passion and escape the nagging ache filling his chest. "Another lives in my heart."

"Don't tell me you will make that white woman your wife!" Her eyes blazed with jealousy. "You would not spit in the face of your people."

"I have never accepted you as mine."

"No, but you have not released me either!" Her

chin bounced up and her eyes sparked twin flames. "Now you think you will cut me loose? Now that I am old and all the good young men have married or have selected their brides?"

He laughed at that, at the utter foolishness of it. Curling a finger under her jutting chin, he admired the sheen of her skin in the amber light. "You are not old, my blossom. And young men aren't good enough for you. What you need is a seasoned man."

"Like you." The soft light was back in her eyes, and her lips curved into a smile that shot fire to his groin again.

"My age, yes. And brothers my age will line up for you once it is known you are free to wed another."

"I want no other."

"Not now, but you will. You won't put yourself on a shelf and wait for me. You have too much pride for that."

"I won't be dishonored," she said, jerking her chin from his touch. "Everyone knows I am your intended, and when it is announced that I am free to find another, everyone will know I have been rejected by you." Her black eyes narrowed to slits. "Rejected so that you can pine for a white woman! I will not have this. You will not cast me aside. I am your blood and you will make me your Blood wife." Her hand arced toward his face, but he caught her wrist.

Storm yanked her against him. "And you forget yourself," he bit out. "I am not some *boy* you can order about at will. I am Storm-In-His-Eyes, from Tall-Walker and of Star-Falling-Woman. I was to marry your sister. My pledge was with her, not with you."

"But she died."

"Yes, and with her died my pledge."

"Not until you tell my father, my mother, and this you haven't done. You've kept silent, letting us all believe you would accept me as your wife. And I think you would have, if that white devil-woman hadn't poisoned your mind."

It was true—most of it—and the truth angered him. He pushed her away and reached for his shirt. "I'll tell them now."

She fell on him, her hands clutching, her dark eyes spilling over with tears. "No, please. I want you and you want me. I know it. I felt the fire in your kiss."

"I told you, the fire was put there by another, and I burn for another."

She stumbled back from him as if he'd slapped her. Her features hardened. "So, you mean to throw me aside for that white witch."

"That's what you don't like, isn't it? Not so much that I won't marry you, but that I want AnadaAki."

She laughed and it was a waterfall of ice. "How can you call her that? Her, with her colorless skin and her yellow hair and her spots like on a dog's muzzle!"

"Freckles, you mean." His lips curved as he pictured Tess in his mind and the sprinkling of freckles across her nose and cheeks, across the tops of her breasts . . . ah, he was aching again. Aching and burning. He jerked a shirt over his head and tugged at the laces. "I have waited too long. I will settle this tonight. You're right to be angry that I haven't been clear about what I want."

"You can't want her!"

"But I do," he said firmly, his gaze sparking against hers, flint against flint.

"But you will not marry her."

"No. I couldn't do that to her. This would be no

life for a white woman, and I have tried to live in the white man's world and failed." The impossible dream of being with Tess bedeviled him and squeezed his heart like a fist.

"Then why do you deny me?" She gripped his sleeve, her small fingers burying into the soft leather.

"Because it is clear that you were hoping I would be a chief and you would be a chief's wife. That won't happen." He removed her hand from his sleeve, her fingers unresisting, her eyes dulling.

"Chief Eagle Talon told my father that your time among the whites makes you important."

"Yes, but he has sons to follow him. He would not have let me leave if he thought I might be chief one day. You and your father have built a dream out of dust."

"This isn't so."

"It is so. Believe me. If you want a chief, you should swing your hips at the chief's sons, not at me. I don't even want to be a leader. What I want is peace. Here." He rested a hand over his heart, then made a sweeping gesture meant to encompass the Blackfeet settlement. "And here."

"You lie." Her mouth fell open for a moment. "Every brave wants to be a leader of his people. Why, this is like saying you don't want to defeat your enemies or embrace your friends. You fool yourself."

"I do want to defeat my enemies and I will. Only then can I embrace my friends." He thought of the marshall and the deputies, and hatred flared in him again. It felt good, making him focus on his inner path. Realizing that Slow-Riding-Woman had not moved to leave his tepee, he laid a hand on her shoulder, admiring her ambition. "You are free now to find another. I'll take the news to your family. Do you want to come along or should I do this alone?"

She measured him with eyes that were hard and unrelenting, then she tossed her braids over her shoulders. "I will come, so they will know I am not being thrown aside, but I am *stepping* aside to allow greater things to come my way."

Ah, yes, the woman brimmed with ambition, but he doubted it would bring her complete happiness. Only love could do that and Slow-Riding-Woman was too willing to sacrifice love for a position of honor in the tribe.

He gave her a slow wink and took her hand within his. "Good thinking. And tomorrow, will you be my friend even though you think I'm a fool?"

She glanced at him in quick judgment. "Yes. You are a Blood. All Bloods are my friends."

He bussed her cheek. "That's exactly what the wife of a chief would say." He chuckled when she fashioned a preening smile.

Storm-In-His-Eyes sat at the council fire and smoked the pipe. The fumes drifted over his mind, twisting and turning. He passed the warm pipe to Brown Otter. The stars overhead began to swirl into patterns—a tree, a buffalo. His heartbeat slowed and his blood thickened. Leaning his head back, he watched the heavens perform.

"Your wounds trouble you little?" Eagle Talon asked. He sat across the fire from Storm and Brown Otter.

"My wife rubbed oil deep into my muscles, and the aching eased," Brown Otter said, his voice rumbling up from his barrel-shaped chest. "Once my wounds are closed, I will go to the sweat lodge and cleanse myself of the white man's poison."

Eagle Talon grunted. "What about you, my son? You have no wife to tend to you and it seems you want none. Brown Otter, did you know that your brother told Slow-Riding-Woman's family to find her another mate?"

The lazy haziness cleared from Storm's body as if scattered by a mighty wind. He felt Brown Otter's keen glare, sharp as a knife between tender ribs. He pressed a hand to his side, sheltering himself. His body was hot from bruises and scrapes and from his ever-present manly needs. He had come to the council fire to smoke the pipe and make his body forget that it had not been satisfied. He wanted no more talk of wives or mates.

"Is this so?" Brown Otter asked. "You would turn aside a beauty like Slow-Riding-Woman? What's wrong with you, my brother?"

"She's not for me. It's time for her to find herself a husband."

"She *is* for you," Brown Otter insisted. "Her family and your family agreed—"

"I gave my oath to her sister," Storm interrupted, although he knew everyone around the fire was aware of this. He closed his eyes, tamping down his irritation, cautioning himself to speak wisdom not anger.

"Your oath extended to Slow-Riding-Woman," Eagle Talon said, but then he gave a wide shrug. "But if you think she's not good enough for your seed—"

"This is not the reason." Storm opened his eyes to find that Brown Otter was holding the pipe out to him. He took it but passed it on without smoking. "It's because I think so much of Slow-Riding-Woman that I decided to let her family find her a better mate than I could be for her."

"There is time for you and for her," Eagle Talon

said, speaking in his slow, even tones. "I did not take my first wife until I was into my thirty-first summer. My wife was much younger, and I would be with her still, but she took the fever the white man brought with him and she died. I am a better husband to my second wife, my sits-beside-me wife, because I have learned and am wiser to the ways of men and women."

Storm blew out a steady breath, glad to have someone on his side for a change.

"You took a Blood wife, my chief," Brown Otter said. "Always a Blood, and there was no doubt. With my brother here, it is not so certain."

"What?" Eagle Talon shook himself like a big dog. "What is this talk?"

Storm remained stoically silent, but he cursed Brown Otter for thrusting him into this trap.

"Storm-In-His-Eyes, I speak to you. Will you not answer your chief?"

"I've had visions of marriage," he said, hoping against hope that would satisfy. But he knew it wouldn't. It didn't even satisfy him. Questions persisted. Images of Tess flew through his mind and stirred the fire of his passion. He wanted more than visions, but he knew he couldn't have more. Shouldn't have more. He and Tess together were too dangerous.

"You need no visions, no guidance from beyond, to know it will be a Blood wife you will take into your lodge," the chief told him. "There is no doubt. In these times, *there should be no doubt.*"

The other men around the council fire murmured in agreement and all eyes focused on Storm. His skin tingled, burned, irritating the abrasions. He felt each cut keenly now, and each bruise seemed to develop its own pulse.

"I am like you and not like you," he ventured.

"I am Blood, born and raised, but these eyes remind me every day that at least one of my ancestors veered from the chosen path. I can't deny what courses through my veins, what is reflected in my eyes and the hair on my skin. No one here can. I have felt a kinship to the whites, although I spent most of my life fighting it. But it exists in me, this calling, this blending of blood with blood."

As he spoke the words, a dawning occurred within him, and he saw clearly that his life had been a divided one. He had been attracted to white women, attracted to the white life because it was a part of him that was a mystery. Exploring the white man's life, he found it wasn't for him, but the beauty he found in white women had not diminished. Even now his heart filled with sweetness when he thought of Tess, and he wondered what she was doing, if she was thinking of him on this night, at this moment.

"You have decided to choose a wife," Eagle Talon intoned. "I ask if you have decided to choose a wife among the Bloods."

"I haven't decided . . ." He couldn't finish, couldn't force the words out. His heart constricted painfully, and he was suddenly hot and sweaty. "If I choose a wife you don't like, will you cast me out?"

"No." Eagle Talon's face set in a deep frown. "But I will not invite you to sit at my council fire, to stand at my ready."

"This is a sacrifice I can endure," Storm said, adding a smile to his pronouncement.

The chief backed his head up an inch and his dark eyes widened, then narrowed slowly. The others around him watched, waited, tried to decipher his mood, his reaction. Storm saw the smile twinkle in his eyes before it appeared on his mouth. The men around the fire smiled, too. All except for Brown Otter.

"You are sly," Eagle Talon said, closing his eyes in satisfaction.

The fire crackled and sent up a pyramid of sparks, climbing to join the stars. The pipe was passed around again. Storm took his turn this time, drawing the smoke deep into his lungs and releasing it in a thin stream.

"I will wait," Eagle Talon announced. "I have learned not to let go too soon. Sometimes you think a buck has fallen, never to rise again. But when you bend over his body to skin him, he gores you with his antlers."

The elders nodded, smiled.

"So I will keep a hand on your shoulder, my son, to guide you, to make it known you are part of this circle. I will trust that you will choose wisely and make us all proud and pleased." He sought Storm's gaze through the dancing flames, flying sparks, and gray smoke, found it and held it long enough to make Storm wish to escape.

Shifting uncomfortably, Storm set his hands flat on the earth and pushed himself to his feet. "My wounds burn and itch. I'm going to my lodge."

Smiles and twinkling eyes shone through the night. All except for Brown Otter. His lips were drawn into a tight line and his eyes smoldered with banked anger. Storm decided he didn't care, couldn't let Brown Otter's opinion weigh on his heart. His heart had enough weight crushing it already.

His lodge was warm and blissfully quiet. He undressed and lay naked on his pallet of blankets and buffalo robes. But after a few moments, he moaned.

He ached. Oh, he ached. And not from any wounds inflicted on him by white *men*.

Tess. AnadaAki. Would he ever be able to forget her smile, the brightness of her eyes, the rich gold of her hair? He could feel her skin upon him, sliding like satin, whispering like silk.

He cursed, he moaned, he tossed onto his side. His manhood throbbed, alive and turgid. Storm shut his eyes and tried to think of anything but her, but it was no use. Her face, her freckled breasts, her rosy cheeks all swam behind his eyelids and burned a hole in his mind.

With a bitter oath, he stood, feet braced apart, his fingers splayed wide, his face tilted up to the moonbeam that stroked over his body through the opening above.

"Tess," he groaned. Ahhh, it felt better just to say her name aloud. "AnadaAki." Yes, better, better. The ache was diminishing. "I want you."

There. Better. Sweet relief. He shuddered and his hips bucked, his seed spilled. Gritting his teeth, he rode out the release and was left with a dull, lifeless void where his heart used to be.

He opened his eyes and stared up through dancing ashes in the moonlight. He knew he could live without her. What he was beginning to understand, what his poor, battered heart was trying to tell him, was that he didn't want to.

He dropped his head forward and his knees gave way. Kneeling in the lodge, he in the milky moonlight, his body achy and sweaty, bruised and bloodied, he felt better than he had since he'd seen Tess's sweet face in that dirty, filthy hole that False Hope called a jail.

"I'll come for you," he whispered. "I must come for you."

And somehow he knew she'd be waiting.

Chapter 17

The porch swing squeaked pleasantly as Tess set it in motion. Sitting beside Mrs. Bishop, she listened to the bird calls and reflected on how uncomfortable she'd felt in the house she'd left yesterday, and how peaceful she now felt in Mrs. Bishop's simple one-story home.

But the ache in her heart was ever-present. She could move to the moon and it would still be there, that aching pain of a broken heart.

Storm. His name burned in her mind, branded her soul and heart. When would she see him again? Did he want to see her or had he decided that they were star-crossed? Last night she'd dreamed of him, of tracking him though dark forests and over high mountains, of seeing him in the dim distance but never being able to catch up with him. Was he running away from her? Is that what her dream had been trying to convey to her stubborn mind and heart, that she should let him go before her relationship with him ended in his death? She shivered uncontrollably and made herself think of more pleasurable things—the shape of his mouth; the tenderness of his hands on her body, molding her breasts, her waist, her hips. No man would ever equal him and certainly no man would ever best him.

"What are you ruminating about, dear?" Mrs. Bishop asked, placing a warm hand on Tess's arm. "Are you homesick already?"

"No." Tess felt warm color creep into her cheeks. She couldn't very well tell the woman the truth, that she had been wishing for Storm to make love to her again. She cleared her throat and fashioned a half-truth. "Actually, I was thinking how nice it is to be here with you. John and Camilla are so unhappy with me . . ." Shrugging, she told herself that some day they would heal the rift between them. However, it might take some time. "I never believed my family home could feel so cold, so like a prison."

"I'm glad you feel at home with me. It's good for me and good for you."

"You're very understanding." Tess smiled at the small-boned, white-haired woman, who always smelled of lilacs and was usually dressed in a shade of purple. Today she wore a deep-violet dress with a white collar and cuffs. "I imagine most people in town think I'm a scandalous woman. I appreciate that you haven't peppered me with questions."

Mrs. Bishop pursed her lips and her blue eyes sparkled with mischief. "Can't say I don't have a few questions, my dear. I'm only human."

"It's like I told you, it's time for me to fly from the nest. John is married now, and I feel like a third wheel. He and Camilla need to be alone in their home to start a family."

"What about you?" Mrs. Bishop asked. "When will *you* start a family?"

"Me?" Tess laughed, although she felt sad inside. Images of brown-skinned children with blue eyes teased her. To have Storm's children ... ah, that would be heaven. She smiled at Mrs. Bishop. "First I must secure a husband, don't you agree?"

"What about that Blackfeet man you've been with?"

Tess stared at the older woman, surprised she'd asked the question so innocently, as if there was no scandal attached to it. Was she so easy to read that this woman could see that she was consumed with thoughts and feelings for Storm-In-His-Eyes? Tess laid a hand alongside her own cheek and felt the telling warmth.

"You do love him, don't you?" Mrs. Bishop peered at her through thick glasses that made her blue eyes huge and blurry looking. "You aren't the sort of woman to sleep with a man unless you'd given your heart to him."

Tess bit her lower lip to keep it from trembling. The woman's understanding and insight were just the tonic Tess needed. She placed an arm around Mrs. Bishop's narrow shoulders and gave her a companionable hug. "You're right about that, but it's not so simple, is it? He's from a whole other world, and he's never invited me into it ... permanently, at least."

"You're talking about the Indian village?" Mrs. Bishop's eyes widened even more. "Tell me what it was like. I've always wondered how those people live."

Tess laughed softly, realizing the older woman had a streak of the adventurer in her. "The village is like a small town, but with skin lodges instead of houses. The lodges are quite comfortable, actually." Her thoughts traveled higher into the mountains where the Blackfeet camp nestled against the banks of a sparkling stream. "People there care for each other. Everyone has a job to do, a duty to perform. Even the children. And the women are important, not just as mothers but as healers and leaders."

"Oh, how exciting!" Mrs. Bishop stared across the land, her eyes bright. "I wish I could have been there with you."

"You . . . like Indians?"

"Oh, some of them." She bobbed her shoulders, then she craned her neck and her eyes narrowed. "You see what I see?"

"What? Where?" Tess scanned the area.

"Over there . . . that clump of evergreens and cypress. Looks like a man on horseback in that deep shade. Guess my eyes are playing tricks on me. . . . I thought for sure it was an Indian."

"An Indian?" Tess searched the area but saw nothing. "Did he ride away?"

"Maybe I didn't see anything at all. Wouldn't be the first time these old eyes have failed me." Mrs. Bishop placed her hands on her knees. "Well, will you go to your brother's today and work?"

"No. I . . . I'll wait until he sends for me."

"Is it that bad between you and him?"

"I think it's best if we spend a few days away from each other and let our tempers cool and our feelings mend."

"You *will* continue to work with him, won't you?"

"I hope so, but I don't know. John is disappointed in me. He . . . he worries about what people think, and he's sure they all believe I'm an incorrigible tart now."

"Next week they'll all be talking about someone else, and Dr. John will be asking you to come back to work," Mrs. Bishop predicted with a firm nod. "As for being a tart, why, Millie Long has you beat by a mile. I swear, that little lady has inspected the privates of nearly every full-grown man in town. I do believe she and that new deputy, Buck Wilhite, will be the next couple folks gossip about."

Tess stood up and helped Mrs. Bishop out of the swing. "What makes you say that?"

"When I was in town a few days ago I heard Millie tell Buck that she didn't like kissing a man with a mustache. I saw him yesterday and noticed he'd shaved his off." Mrs. Bishop's brows lifted and she drew her mouth into a circle. "He was right proud of that little old mustache, but it's gone. I figure Millie will have to show her appreciation to him right soon."

"Nothing gets past you, does it, Mrs. Bishop?"

"It's a wonder what a person will see sitting right here on this porch." She shuffled to the front door. "Guess I'll can those tomatoes—"

"Oh, no, you don't." Tess held open the screen door for her. "I'll can them and you can keep me entertained. . . . Where did you meet Mr. Bishop?"

"Sidney? Why, I met him when I was six and he was sixteen. I thought he had the biggest ears I ever laid eyes on, and I sure didn't think I'd end up married to him and all my kids would be stuck with those ears."

Laughing, Tess linked arms with Mrs. Bishop, and the two women made their way to the sunny kitchen at the back of the house.

Outside, a horse and rider emerged from the black shade afforded by a copse of evergreen, pine, and cypress trees. One moment he was shadow, an apparition, and in the next he was flesh and blood.

The rider stared at the house for long minutes, then reined the chestnut around and headed for higher ground, his black hair wind-tossed, his teak-colored skin burnished by the sun. A single eagle feather fluttered near his left temple, caught in a narrow braid.

That night the rider returned. He left his horse in the thick shelter of trees and moved on silent feet toward the house. The moon spilled ivory light on the ground. Shadows danced ahead of him. Wolves howled in the distance, and his loins tightened in response.

He knew the loneliness of the wolf, and he knew their yearning for companionship. That was why he'd come, why he'd left the safety of his pack to sate his hunger.

Slipping from window to window and peering inside the house, he finally found the one he sought. The window slid up easily, quietly, and within a minute he was inside, standing by her bed, gazing at her.

She looked like a moon maiden, Storm-In-His-Eyes thought. A moon maiden with golden hair spilling over a pillow and alabaster skin kissed here and there by the sun and stroked by lunar light.

His need for her had been so consuming, he'd ignored the advice of the elders and the admonishments of Brown Otter. He'd decided he would sneak into town after dark and try to climb into her bedroom window, but then he'd heard her laughter on the wind. Following the sound, he'd seen her sitting on a porch with an older woman and realized she no longer lived at her brother's house, but had moved in with the other woman.

Because of him? he wondered, gazing at her sleeping form, the shape of her body beneath the sheet. Had he destroyed her life? Should he have stayed away?

She shifted restlessly, rubbing her cheek against

the pillowcase and making a little smacking sound with her mouth. He could smell her: warm, clean, faintly floral. His gaze drifted to the front of her nightgown where the buds of her nipples pressed against the white fabric.

Blood flowed to his loins and he throbbed. He removed his leggings, his moccasins, his shirt, and breechclout. Catching the corner of the sheet, he lifted it and slipped naked into bed with her. She awakened with a jerk and would have screamed if he hadn't stopped her by clapping a hand against her mouth. She tried to bite him and he grinned.

"It's me. It's Storm-In-His-Eyes." He inched back his head so she could get a good look at him. When he felt her relax, he replaced his hand with his mouth. Her lips parted and she moaned, the sound vibrating in his head. He spread his hands over her head, his fingertips combing through the strands of her hair. "I missed you ... I missed you ..." he said again and again, so happy to be with her once more that his heart seemed to sing.

"Storm, is it you? Is it really you?" Her fingertips danced across his cheekbones, played upon the corners of his mouth, stroked the bruised skin beneath his eyes.

She sighed. "My brave warrior. My foolish, brave warrior." Pulling away from him, she stared at him, her eyes growing wide. "How did you know I was here? Did you talk to John?"

"No. I came upon you earlier today while you sat in the porch swing. I was heading for your brother's house when I saw you."

"Mrs. Bishop thought she spotted an Indian."

"She did. Your Indian." He kissed her forehead, the tip of her nose, her smiling lips. "Did your brother make you leave your home because of me?"

"No, I left because I wanted to." She placed her hands on either side of his neck, and her eyes shone like jewels. "I'm so glad you're here. I was afraid—"

"Afraid of what?"

"Afraid I would never see you again."

"Others told me to stay away from you, but I couldn't. Was your heart calling to my heart?"

"Yes." She lay back, her hands now in his hair, her thighs parting for him. "Oh, yes."

He reached down to find the hem of her night-gown and brought it up and over her head. Then she was naked beneath him: his stomach pressed against hers, his chest touching the soft globes of her breasts. Her satiny skin tempted him and he dropped kisses across her shoulders, down her throat, and on the fragrant skin between her breasts. Her nipples gathered into hard, pink stones, and he took one into his mouth and drew hard on it. She arched her back and a mewling sound purred from her throat. He palmed her other breast, feeling the quickening of her body, the building of her passion.

He had thought of no one else during his time apart from her and he could hardly believe this was real and not another dream from which he would awaken, drenched in his own sweat and sticky with his own seed. He tongued her other nipple, tasting her skin, breathing in her aroma, wondering what it was about her he couldn't shake, couldn't escape from, couldn't keep shoved deep down within him. No, she bubbled to his surface—her laugh, her sultry whispers, the way her eyes glowed when she smiled and sparked when she was angry. She even felt different, he thought, running his hands from her shoulders to her hips.

As he drove himself into her, he felt a pang of

guilt; but then his own white-hot passion superseded, and he rode out his desire while she breathed his name like a chant and her body gripped him tightly, wholly.

After a few minutes, after he had burst within her like a shooting star, he felt her stir. Storm lifted himself off her, slid to one side to drape a leg over hers and an arm across her waist.

"How is the little girl? Cassie?"

"Gone. She left with her family for California. But she will be fine, I suppose."

"She touched my heart. Yours too?"

Tess smiled. "Yes, mine too."

"I never thought a child—or a beautiful woman—would save me from a hangman's noose."

Tess gave him a loving look for the compliment. "I hope things work out for them, but I wish Cassie's father could have put his dream aside for a few more months. His wife was deeply sad about losing the baby . . . and Cassie and her brothers and sister . . ." She shrugged. "They should have a roof over their heads and proper schooling."

"Dreams can rob a man of his common sense," Storm murmured, one corner of his mouth tipping up as he traced circles around her nipples with his forefinger. "I'm weak for you," he told her. "I tell myself I must be strong, I must stay away from you, but I'm weak. Here I am, where I shouldn't be."

"Don't say that." Her eyes were sad, her lips plump from his kisses. "You should be here. I'm glad you're here. You aren't trouble to me, Storm. You're—you're . . ." She bit her lower lip and turned her eyes from him. Pink dotted her cheeks.

"What?" he asked, crooking a finger under her

chin and bringing her face to his once more. "What am I?"

"Have you made love to other white women?"

He scowled at her. "Why do you ask that?"

"I want to know."

"Not since I met you."

"But before?"

He trailed a finger between her breasts. "Yes, while I was away from the Blackfeet there were white women."

"I see."

He saw the shadows in her eyes. "No, you don't." He lay on his back and placed his forearm across his eyes. "They were nice, pretty, but their faces don't haunt me every night. The face that haunts me is yours. The other women were flickering, feeble, inconstant flames, and you are my sun." He turned his head on the pillow to catch Tess's expression of pleasure, radiant and pure. He felt himself stiffen again.

"I hope you're not just flattering this gullible spinster."

Not liking the words she used, he caught a strand of her dark-gold hair and wound it around his forefinger, then gave it a gentle tug. "If all I wanted was to bury myself in something warm and giving, I could have a woman back at the camp—"

"Slow-Riding-Woman?"

"Yes, but I choose to be here with you."

"Will you marry her, Storm? She's your intended, isn't she?"

He drew his brows together in a scowl. "No. I won't marry her."

"Why not?"

"I don't love her."

"But the Blackfeet expect you to marry her."

"I've told her parents she is free to find another man."

"When? When did you do this?"

He gave her a quick grin. "Yesterday."

"But does she want to find another?"

"She will now."

"I think she will wait for you. She's staked her claim on you."

"So have you in your own way." He spread his hand under her chin and brought her mouth to his. He outlined her lips with the tip of his tongue and sucked gently on the lower one. "You branded me when I wasn't looking, didn't you? You slipped into me like a potion and fogged my brain, made me hard only for you. You are cunning like the fox and as dangerous as a rattlesnake." The mention of the snake reminded him of the vision and brought worry to his heart again.

"What's wrong?" Tess asked.

"Nothing . . . I was thinking of a dream I had."

"A bad dream?"

"It could be. I don't know yet."

"I've had bad dreams lately. I had a nightmare about Marshall Long and his deputies and John and . . . and they shot you. Killed you." She shuddered.

Storm gathered her into his arms and pulled her against him to ward off her shivers. "They are enemies but not powerful enough to defeat me."

She kissed his shoulder. "How can you be so certain?"

He wasn't, but he didn't want her to waste any more tears on him; he wanted to vanquish her bad dreams. "I know because I've had visions. Remember when I went to the sweat lodge? I came away knowing I should not fear the marshall." Part of that was true. He didn't fear the marshall or his son. His only fear was that he wouldn't be successful in making them both pay—especially the marshall—for what they'd done to him and his loved ones. They had taken his freedom, his sister, and now they threatened to deny him this woman—this magical medicine woman—and the happiness that only she could bring him.

"I had a dream about you," Tess said, her voice small and hesitant. "I dreamed that you were running away from me. It was a horrible dream."

"And only a dream, for I am here with you. I ran into your arms, not away from you."

After a minute he felt her relax against him. Holding her close, he kissed her forehead and stroked her hair and thought of the vision of the two-headed snake. Was it her? If the vision were true, then she would die to save him. He shut his eyes tightly, willing away that possibility. Often visions came to pass in ways no one could predict, and it would be so with this one. Any white person could be the snake. It didn't have to be his Tess. It wouldn't be his Tess.

He tightened his arms around her and pledged that after tonight, he'd stay away from her until his trouble with the law was finished. Only then would he see her again, hold her again. He looked down at her face and realized she was sleeping peacefully in his arms.

Tess awakened to the stirring sensation of soft lips stroking her inner thigh. She smiled, and like a woman who knows what she wants, opened her legs wider to his satiny lips and agile tongue. Within minutes Storm had brought her to a shivering, quivering pinnacle, and before she could alight on earth again, sent her soaring up into the clouds by filling her with his hard, pulsing shaft.

Clinging to him, she met his thrusts, letting him go deeper until he was buried to the hilt, his stomach rubbing against hers, his hips undulating against her hands. He tongued her stiff nipples and kissed the soft skin around them.

She would have released a sharp, piercing cry of fulfillment if his mouth hadn't covered hers to take in the sound and give it back. They moaned into each other's mouths, breathed each other's breaths. Their bodies grew slippery with perspiration as he continued to surge and retreat, rocking against her, making every inch of himself known within her. When he stilled and she could feel him straining for every passing second, she tightened her inner muscles around his throbbing organ. His eyes opened wide and then closed slowly, slowly.

"Ahhh, you make me weak," he murmured, and then he bucked inside her, his hips driving one more time, hard enough to lift her backside up off the mattress.

The world seemed to spin away from her like a top. Tess savored the pleasure that teetered near the edge of exquisite pain. When she came back to herself, she was biting Storm's shoulder and clutching his back as if he were the only solid thing in a world gone gloriously mad.

She lifted her mouth from his skin and saw the slight indentations left by her teeth. "I bit you. Sorry."

He chuckled and nipped playfully, carefully at her pouting nipples. She arched her back, her body responding to him in a blatant, hungry way that made her blush.

"Storm, I was wondering . . ."

He studied her, his dark brows looking like wings. "You are wondering if every man and every woman knows what we have known tonight with each other?"

She nodded, and he shook his head.

"No, Tess. It isn't always like this." Pressing his forehead to hers, he grinned. "There is no need to test this. You must take my word for it."

She giggled and inched out her lips to meet his. "I'll be glad to take your word for it."

He kissed her thoroughly, his lips warm and seeking every nuance of hers. She wound her arms around his neck and ran her heels up and down his legs. She wanted to tell him she loved him, but she held back because his kiss, while magical and wondrous, also felt faintly of farewell.

He smoothed his hands over her head. "I'm a hunted man."

"I know." She swallowed. Yes, this was farewell.

"I can't be yours until my troubles are behind me."

She nodded, tears clogging her throat.

He kissed her eyebrows, the side of her nose. "I'm going to find those men who attacked you, who dress up like the Bloods to make the white eyes hate us even more."

"How will you catch them?"

"They've been attacking ranches in Pleasant Valley, and I've seen their tracks there. Brown Otter and I think we will be able to find them soon. They're getting reckless. They'll strike again and we'll be ready."

"Pleasant Valley? My aunt and uncle have a ranch there."

"I believe the thieves keep their stolen horses in the valley. Out by the forked creek."

"That's right near my aunt and uncle's ranch." Tess gripped his shoulders. "You're going there now, aren't you?"

He nodded. "I have to go before light. I can't be seen anywhere near here."

"I know, I know." She kissed him, clinging and unable to keep the tears from spilling. "Take me with you."

"No, Tess. No."

"Just see me to their ranch, Storm. Let me warn them to be careful. They're isolated. They might not know about the horse thieves."

"No, Tess."

"Listen to me," she argued, giving his shoulders a shake. "Take me there, let me talk to them, and then you can see me back to False Hope. I swear, I won't put up a fight." She wiped away her tears with the heels of her hands. "Please, Storm? They're so sweet. I couldn't live with myself if something happened to them, if they weren't warned of the danger and I could have prevented—"

"All right," he said with a long suffering sigh. "You wear a man down, woman."

Smiling, she hugged him to her. "You're weak for me, Storm-In-His-Eyes."

He pulled her hands and arms away from him and held them against her sides. "Listen to me, Tess. I want no argument with you. I will take you to the ranch and you can speak to your people, and then we will return here by tomorrow night. I will be gone from your life until these men are captured. This is how it must be."

"Are you sure we can make it back here by tomorrow?"

"I'm sure."

She nodded, happy to have him for a few more hours. "I'll have to tell Mrs. Bishop so she won't worry needlessly. She's been so good to me, I have to explain where I'm going."

"What will you tell her?"

"I'll tell her that she did see an Indian, after all, and that I'll be with him."

Storm's brows lowered over his gray eyes. "She will send for your brother or the marshall."

"No, she won't. She's not like John and Camilla. She'll understand. She gets up with the chickens, so let's wait a few more hours and I'll tell her I'm leaving." She grasped his fingers and kissed one wide palm, then the other. "I'll assure her I'll be in good hands." Guiding them to her breasts, she sighed when his fingers kneaded her soft flesh. "Ahhh," she breathed, "such good hands."

Chapter 18

~~~⌒⌒⌒~~~

Topping a rise, Tess reined in her horse to appreciate the sight of the Blackfeet village spread before her. The conical-shaped homes were grouped on the south side of a mountain stream, far enough away so as not to be flooded, but close enough for bathing and washing and drinking. A cloudy sky turned the stream to gun-metal gray and gave the breeze a sharp bite.

A herd of horses mingled in a corral, tended by several long-limbed boys. Women and girls worked in groups beside the stream, at the cook fires, around Minipoka's large lodge, which was eclipsed only by Chief Eagle Talon's grander, more colorful tepee with its symbolic otters scampering around it and big sun painted above the flapping door.

Taking it all in, Tess yearned to belong to it. Why she should feel such a kinship, she didn't know. But it was there. Even though she was a white eyes to them, she longed to live among them, to know their ways, to live close to the earth and be useful and respected.

Feeling Storm's keen regard, she nodded at the

village. "I was thinking how peculiar it is that I should feel so close to the Blackfeet and want to be counted as their friend." She looked at him and smiled. "I was never particularly interested in Indians, you see. But while I was with your people I felt . . . well, free to be myself."

"I understand. When I was with the white people I felt bound by convention, by rules of conduct that made no sense to me. Sometimes I felt that the women did not want me as much as they wanted to be like me."

"Like you, how?"

"Since they saw me as an animal, I was not expected to follow all their rules. I spoke my mind and they allowed this since I was nothing but an ignorant savage. I set up my own tepee, away from the others because no one really trusted me. But that was good. I had my privacy."

"Sounds terrible to me. I'm ashamed of my own people for how they treated you."

He stared toward the village, his features set in a mask of indifference. "Maybe these things will change in time." He glanced at her and his features softened. "White people expect their women to be too many things, follow too many rules. If I felt tied to foolish notions, they must surely have felt like prisoners."

Tess shifted in the saddle and placed a hand to the small of her back. "Being a lady is sometimes a hardship," she allowed. "With the Blackfeet I didn't worry about stepping out of line."

"Women and men have their places even among the Blackfeet."

"But your women are allowed to be leaders, aren't they? You have medicine *women* and holy *women*."

"Yes, but I met a medicine woman among the

white people once. She was in Texas, but she had come from Boston."

"Oh, yes, there are a few, but none in False Hope."

"You could leave False Hope."

"Yes." She sighed, hating the sense of rootlessness that had plagued her for months. "I'm a woman who needs to belong, Storm. Setting off for parts unknown obviously appealed to you, but it holds no interest for me. If I leave False Hope, I must have a firm destination in mind."

He urged his horse down the rise toward the village. Tess followed him, smiling when children called out greetings, tensing when Brown Otter rode toward them, his eyes flashing angrily when he looked at her.

Somewhere along the way Brown Otter had decided she was not a friend, but she couldn't figure out when that had happened. He'd kidnapped her, brought her to Storm, convinced her that she must treat Storm's wounds, and then had decided to dislike her for it. His attitude astounded and confused her.

Storm and Brown Otter spoke in cryptic Blackfeet before Brown Otter wheeled his horse around and rode back to the village, leaving Storm and Tess in his dust.

"I take it, he's not pleased to see me," Tess quipped.

"He had asked me not to seek you out, to leave you be."

"Why?"

"You know why."

"He's the one who brought us together."

"Yes, but Brown Otter thinks we are bad medicine together." He stroked the mane of the big chestnut he rode. "Mixing with the whites has not been good for me."

"I hope you reminded him that he'd still be in jail—or worse—if it weren't for me."

"He means well, Tess."

"Is he coming with' us to my aunt and uncle's?"

"Yes." He rode ahead of her, guiding his horse toward laughing boys and girls and reaching down to haul three giggling girls onto the horse with him.

Tess rode behind him, watching the joyful home-coming, enjoying his easy way with the children, how they trusted him, laughed with him, vied for his attention and his tickling fingers. Nobody paid her any heed. She was a stranger, not to be trusted. Feeling bereft and friendless, she heard someone call her name and caught sight of Many-Smiles-Woman.

Reining her horse, Tess slid to the ground and laughed when Many Smiles embraced her.

"I'm glad you came," Many Smiles said, still squeezing her. "Thank you, thank you for what you did for my brothers. You made the white marshall let them go." Many Smiles held Tess at arm's length, her dark eyes glistening with tears. "For this, our chief wants to talk to you."

"To me? He wants to talk to me?" Tess drew back from the idea of being summoned by Chief Eagle Talon. "That's not necessary."

Many Smiles grabbed Tess by the arm and pulled her along with her. "Come. Make speed."

"B-but I've only dropped by because Storm wanted Brown Otter to ride with us to my aunt and uncle's ranch in the valley. I want to make sure they take precautions against these crazy men who are stealing..." Tess stopped babbling, noticing that Many Smiles was paying her no attention whatsoever. The young woman was intent on dragging Tess toward the chief's lodge. Casting around for Storm, Tess realized she'd completely lost sight of him. Where the devil had he gone? They were supposed to meet up with Brown Otter and be on their way. He'd said nothing about an audience with the chief.

As they neared Minipoka's lodge, the old woman stepped outside and intercepted them, much to Tess's relief.

"Minipoka!" Tess grasped the old woman's hands. "It's so good to see you again." She looked around. "I seem to have lost Storm-In-His-Eyes. . . . "

"In here."

"Oh. Is he inside your lodge?" Tess asked, already ducking inside. Straightening, she was brought up short when the man staring at her wasn't Storm but the chief himself. "Chief Eagle Talon! I . . . that is, I thought . . ." She looked over her shoulder at Minipoka, who had come inside, and wondered what she was supposed to do, if she should sit, stand, bow . . .

"When the scouts told me you were riding here with Storm-In-His-Eyes, I told them I wanted to speak to you," the chief said, folding his arms against his chest and standing with his feet braced apart. "When you were here before, you were a guest. You return, a friend."

Some of the nervous knots in Tess's stomach loosened and she released a long breath. She realized she'd been afraid of the chief. Every time she'd seen him, she'd been impressed with his physical prowess and the hard glint in his deeply set eyes. Today he wasn't wearing his huge headdress, for which she was thankful, since it was quite grand and intimidating. Even without it, the chief seemed larger than life and made Tess feel small and insignificant.

Dressed in dark-brown leather shirt and pants, his black hair shot through with white and braided into two thick ropes, the chief turned his wide, square face toward her. He was quite handsome, despite his rather flat nose. Tess suspected it had been broken several times and had never been properly set.

"We will sit and smoke."

"Smoke." Tess's gaze fell on the cushions near the center pole and a beautifully carved pipe lying to one side of them. "The pipe? But I—I've never."

He shrugged. "You won't say that after today." He motioned with a ham-sided hand to the cushions. "Minipoka will join us."

"Well . . ." Tess glanced toward the open flap. "Where's Storm? Maybe I should fetch—"

"He is with his brothers. You are with me and Minipoka."

Tess resigned herself to her fate. "So I am," she said, agreeing to the obvious. Oh, well, one puff wouldn't kill her, and then she'd be done with this distasteful custom. Sometimes John smoked a pipe and she never liked it. The smell lingered for days in the draperies, even after she threw open all the windows for a good airing. She'd envied men many things—their freedom, their positions in society, even their more comfortable clothing—but she'd never envied their smoking or—God, forbid—tobacco chewing.

"You will sit here, on the south, beside me." Eagle Talon sat cross-legged on a cushion and patted the one to his right. "It is a place of honor. Minipoka will sit on your other side."

"Thank you." Suddenly the seriousness of this ritual struck Tess. A place of honor. That's what he'd said, and Minipoka, revered by the tribe, would not sit there. Tess would sit there for this visit.

Before taking her place beside the chief, Tess helped Minipoka sit down on the thick mat. Sitting between the chief and the medicine woman, Tess was careful to tuck her legs to one side in proper ladylike fashion. The chief began packing the pipe with greenish tobacco.

"Minipoka tells me you are a wise one with medicine."

"She's kind. Compared to her, I'm a novice. A student."

"Do you use your medicine among your people?"

"No. My brother is a doctor."

"And you?"

"I—I help him."

"He teaches you?"

"Well, not really. I've learned a lot by watching him."

The chief paused in his preparation of the pipe to study her. His heavily lidded eyes seemed to pierce clear through to her heart.

"Among the Bloods it is different," he said, picking up the pipe again to tamp down the tobacco.

The pipe was a thing of beauty; stained red, the bowl was carved in the shape of a bird, a firebird. The stem was etched to look like connecting feathers.

"Here the work of the women is as respected as the work of the men. It is a great honor for women to carry and give birth to children so that our people will continue. And if a woman takes it upon herself to learn the ways of medicine or the ways of hunting or of fighting, then we honor this. All of us." He raised his hands and looked up. "The

Creator hands us gifts. How we use them is the gift we give to ourselves and to our people."

Tess glanced at Minipoka for guidance, but the old woman's eyes were closed and Tess wasn't sure she even heard the conversation.

"You have proven yourself a friend to the Blood," the chief said. He picked up a fire stick and lit the tip of it in the cooking fire. Placing the stem of the pipe in his mouth, he fired the tobacco and drew deeply, making a whistling noise as he sucked in air. Smoke rose, billowed, curled toward the patch of sky overhead. "Some think you mean well, but you are bad medicine."

"I'm not," Tess assured him. "I don't want to hurt the Blackfeet. Everything I've done is to help them. Why Brown Otter is being so unpleasant makes no—"

"You listen," Minipoka said, giving Tess a start. "He brought you here to listen, not to talk." Minipoka never opened her eyes.

"Oh, sorry." Tess faced the chief again. "This is all new to me. I don't know what I'm expected to do or say. I hope I haven't offended you in—"

"You got rocks in your ears?" Minipoka asked, her aged voice cracking.

Tess thought she saw a hint of a smile on the old woman's lips.

"Here." Chief Eagle Talon held the pipe out to her. "Smoke." He pulled it away when she reached for it. "But not too much at first. It is strong and will fog your head."

Tess nodded, thinking she had no intention of drawing any of the smoke into her lungs. Gingerly, she took the beautiful pipe from him and touched her lips to the stem. She sipped carefully, but found the pipe hard to draw on. Trying again, she inhaled deeply—too deeply. Smoke curled down her throat and clouded her lungs. Tess coughed violently, her throat burning, a foul taste bursting in her mouth.

Minipoka pounded her back and the chief took the pipe from her and watched the spectacle with open amusement. When Tess had recovered, she wiped her eyes and found that both the chief and Minipoka were sharing a chuckle at her expense.

"You should listen," Minipoka said, her eyes dancing. "Chief Eagle Talon told you the smoke is powerful."

The chief sucked on the pipe again and passed it to Minipoka. The old woman's cheeks caved in as she drew hard and long on the pipe. Tess shook her head, gladly bowing to her superior.

Settling back on his elbows, Eagle Talon stretched his feet to the fire. "When he was born, he was brought to me and I saw white blood running through his veins, mixing with the People's blood; and I saw clouds in his eyes. I said, 'This boy-child will be a brave warrior, but his path will have many forks in it and the sky over his head will be like his eyes—stormy, full of thunder and rain.' And so I gave him the name and it has not changed. It is a good name for him."

Storm-In-His-Eyes, Tess thought, her mind sharpening and her senses alert. So, the chief wanted to talk about Storm. Why? To warn her to stay away or to see if she was worthy of him?

"The white blood in him calls out. That is why he left us to live with the white eyes. That is why he went searching for you even after I told him it would be wise if he never saw you again."

"You—you told him that?" Tess asked, her heart heavy. So, the chief was against her. What about Minipoka? She'd thought that the old woman was in her corner, but perhaps that had changed.

The chief extended the pipe to her. Tess shook

her head. The chief jiggled the pipe, silently insisting she take it and draw upon it once more.

Gritting her teeth, Tess accepted the pipe. The bowl was hot to the touch and the smoke curled up, stinging her nose and eyes. With steely resolve, she inhaled the smelly fumes, but didn't swallow them. She blew out, and the gray smoke billowed around her face. She waved her hand in front of her nose, dispersing the cloud. Minipoka took the pipe from her, a chuckle rattling in her throat.

"He has never disobeyed me before," the chief said. "Minipoka tells me his head is full of you, and he has told Slow-Riding-Woman's family that she is free to marry someone else."

Tess felt dizzy for a few moments. Colors spun before her eyes and she seemed to float. Did Storm love her? Could it be? Is that why the chief wanted to talk to her?

"I wondered why he would disobey this one time." The chief stared at Tess, unblinking. "If he is to be a leader of the Bloods, he must take a Blood wife. He knows this. We have talked of this many times. I have always seen greatness in him, and I have let him answer the strange callings of his heart because I knew he would come back to us stronger, wiser, and more able to show us how to defeat the white eyes, who would kill us or chase us from our hunting grounds."

Her heart stumbled and Tess curled her hands in the folds of her skirt, suddenly cold with dread. He wasn't going to give her his blessing or welcome her into his Blackfeet family. She was a fool to think the chief would encourage Storm to take a white wife.

"Minipoka says you are honorable, you are brave." He shrugged his broad shoulders. "Storm-In-His-Eyes has always found his own path. His heart has gathered hatred and woe and has become like stone. But you have found a crack in the stone." He sat up and put aside the pipe. "Will you take him from us?"

Startled by the question, Tess looked from him to Minipoka. The old woman rocked back and forth and opened her eyes, but they were unfocused.

"I could never do that," Tess told the chief. "He's happy here. He doesn't want to leave."

"Then will you tell him you can't walk the path with him?"

"I can't . . ." Tess closed her eyes, her head spinning, her heart thudding dully in her chest. She felt sick, as if she'd eaten something spoiled. The tobacco? Was it working its evil spell on her?

Suddenly the air changed in the lodge. Tess felt something powerful ripple through the space like a lightning charge. She opened her eyes to stare up into Storm's angry face. He reached down, grabbed her by the wrist, and yanked her to her feet. In his native tongue he spoke heatedly to the chief, and the chief bellowed back. Tess pressed her hands to her ears, feeling as if she were caught between claps of thunder.

The next thing she knew she was being pulled outside the lodge, and the brisk breeze was like a splash of water on her face. She blinked, coughed, felt her stomach shift.

Moaning, she jerked free of Storm's hold and turned away from him just as her gut heaved. Falling to her knees in the dirt, she gave up the contents of her stomach.

Sitting by the stream with the wind caressing her face, cooling her brow, sweeping away the sudden sickness that had overtaken her, Tess leaned back on stiff arms and turned her face to the sun.

"I don't know what came over me," she said, eyes closed, sensing Storm's gaze on her.

"I do. You aren't used to smoking the chief's special tobacco blend. It's guaranteed to make you either sick, crazy, or sane, depending on how you were before you smoked it."

Tess smiled weakly. "He said it was an honor."

"That's true, but from what I heard before I came inside, he was not so much honoring as he was accusing you."

"No, he wasn't unpleasant. He's concerned, Storm." She opened her eyes. Storm sat with his knees bent and his arms looped loosely around them. He stared gloomily at the fast-moving water. "Storm, why didn't you tell me that you are in line to be chief?"

He whipped his gaze around to hers. "He told you *that*?"

"Isn't it true?"

"No."

"He said you were expected to be a leader—"

"Ah, yes. A leader." A humorless smile curled his lips. "Our chief has many sons." Waving a hand, he indicated the boys splashing in the stream, the others racing each other on horseback. "All the males are his sons, and he tells each of us that someday, if we are obedient and courageous, we will be leaders. He expects every Blackfeet brave to be responsible to the People. This way he keeps us close to him, doing his bidding, seeking his favor, and he keeps us close to the Blackfeet. Only if we band together can we keep what is ours from falling into the hands of our enemies."

Tess lay back in the grass and stared up at sky the color of Storm's eyes. "So you aren't in line to be chief?"

"No. The council of elders will choose the chief

when it's time, and I won't be the one they choose."

"Why not?"

"Because my destiny lies elsewhere."

"How do you know?"

"I've had visions. The spirits guide me and point me in a different direction."

"Which direction?"

"I'm not sure. I only know that I'm not to lead my people. Even Chief Eagle Talon knows this, but he turns a blind eye to it. He doesn't know that the spirits have shown me another path, and my heart answers another calling."

"So does mine, I think." She sat up and pulled grass and leaves from the ends of her hair. "I was talking with Mrs. Bishop yesterday while we were canning tomatoes and you know what she told me?"

"To be sure and cut out the bad spots?"

Tess wrinkled her nose at his jest and slapped at his shoulder. "Very funny. No, she told me that I am the most independent woman in False Hope now. And she's right. My reputation is blown to bits, I've moved out of my family home, and I have no husband or father to grind me under his thumb. She made me see that I've gotten what I have been praying for—a way out."

He twisted around to face her, bracing an arm on either side of her outstretched legs. "But this is not good, is it? How could you have been praying to be shunned by your people?"

"I wasn't praying for that," she admitted, "but it's as my father used to say, 'Be careful what you pray for; you just might get it.' I've wanted independence. I've wanted a way out of my brother's home, a chance to prove myself. I've prayed for these things and my prayers have been answered.

Not as I'd dreamed, of course, but answered all the same. Like any woman, I had hoped to move out of my brother's house and into the house I would make with my husband." She found his gaze too intense and her feelings too tender. Looking away from him, Tess wished she could see into his heart to find if she had a place there.

"I can't live beyond today. Do you understand?" He raised one hand to stroke her cheek softly. "I would like to talk of tomorrow, but I can't because there is too much evil nipping at my heels. I have to slay my enemies before I can embrace my friends. Embracing anyone now would only place them in my enemies' sights."

She nodded, rubbing her cheek against his fingers. "I understand. It's the same with me. Everything is in turmoil." Capturing his hand, she pressed a kiss into his warm palm, then curled his fingers around it.

He moved to sit behind her. "You have leaves in your hair." He plucked them from the gold curls. "Let me braid it for you."

Tess sighed as he dragged his fingers through her hair, loosening tangles and making her scalp tingle.

"We should be moving on soon. Brown Otter says he'll go with us. He and I will make camp near the ranch and come back for you in the morning when—"

"What do you mean? Why aren't you going to stay at the ranch with me?"

"Tess, you can't expect your people to open their home to two Blackfeet strangers."

"I certainly can, and I do!" She looked over her shoulder at him. "You don't know my aunt and uncle. They're the salt of the earth. Why, they'll be terribly hurt if you don't accept their hospitality.

They aren't like John, Storm. Actually, I think if anyone puts up a fuss about staying at the ranch it will be Brown Otter. He doesn't like me, and I'm sure he won't want to have anything to do with my relatives either. I swear, he's the most disagreeable, sullen—"

"Tess, he is my closest brother," Storm reminded her gently. "And he isn't the only one here who thinks I am crazy to have ridden to town and brought you back here with me. They think I am throwing stones at the grizzly instead of hiding in the bushes until he goes away."

She smiled at the analogy. Reaching back, she felt the long rope of hair he'd plaited, then tipped back her head and kissed his chin, his cheek. "I'm glad you came for me, Storm. Every moment I can spend with you is a treasure. I was feeling so alone and afraid that I was only a passing fancy for you. I had convinced myself that you never spent a moment of thought on me."

His arms stole around her waist and he pulled her up against his chest and stomach, in between his spread legs. His lips touched her temple where a pulse beat wildly. "And I was afraid you were wishing you had never seen me, had let me die in that cave."

She kissed the side of his neck. "I'll never regret what we've been to each other. Never, Storm," she swore before his lips touched hers like a spark that soon became a flame.

When she opened her eyes again, and Storm straightened from her, she saw Brown Otter standing nearby, a dark scowl on his face. He spun around and stomped back toward the lodges.

"We should go," Tess said, sitting up.

"Yes, but is something wrong?" Storm asked, his eyes seeking hers, his brows drawn together.

"No. I feel fine now, and you said you wanted to reach the ranch before nightfall."

He rose to his feet and helped her to hers. Hand in hand, they strolled back toward the camp, and Tess wondered if it would be the last time she saw the colorful tepees, smelled the aroma of the cook fires, heard the laughter of Blackfeet children hop-scotching on the wind. She savored it all, just in case.

Chapter 19

~~~~~○○○~~~~~

Furious activity around one of the lodges lengthened Storm's strides. He gripped Tess's hand more firmly, urging her into a trot to keep up with him.

"What's wrong?"

He nodded ahead of them, his eyes piercing and hooded like an eagle's. "That's Brown Otter's lodge. Something's wrong."

"Brown Otter? I saw him . . . he's right over there." She pointed ahead to where Brown Otter stood motionless beneath a spreading oak. He hadn't moved and still didn't, but as they approached Tess sensed he was coiled as tightly as a rattlesnake getting ready to strike.

"What's wrong?" Storm called ahead.

Brown Otter turned slightly to look back at his lodge. He spoke in Blackfeet, which irritated Tess, especially since she knew he did so just to aggravate her and to shut her out.

Folding her arms against her midsection, Tess waited for Storm to interpret for her, all the while staring rebelliously at Brown Otter.

After a quick exchange with Storm, Brown Otter

272

turned on his heel and jogged toward his lodge.

"What's going on?" Tess asked. "Is he mad because he caught us kissing and holding hands?"

"It's his wife. She is trying to pass a babe into the world. It's not going well. Brown Otter says he must stay here until the baby is born."

"Wife? I didn't even know he had a wife!"

"Yes, he took one while I was with the white eyes."

Her irritation toward Brown Otter dissolved. "How long has his wife been in labor?"

"The pains started last night."

"Is this her first child?"

"No. They have two sons."

Her mind whirred, formulating, calculating. "Will he let me see her? I might be able to help."

"I don't know. Minipoka's with her now."

"Then ask Minipoka if I can help. She'll let me, and Brown Otter won't go against her."

He thought for a moment before nodding. "I'll speak to Brown Otter first. If he is stubborn, I'll go to Minipoka."

Storm ran to the lodge and Tess approached more cautiously. Brown Otter stood outside like a sentry. A young woman burst from the lodge, carrying bloody rags and an empty pot. Tess remained a discrete distance away from Storm and Brown Otter while they conversed. She could tell by Brown Otter's frown that he didn't want her near his wife. The hypocrite! She treated his cousin, so why not his wife? She had a good mind to—

Storm signaled for her and Tess's heart lurched. Hurrying forward, she tried to read something in the men's expressions. Worry and desperation, she thought. Brown Otter was swallowing his stubborn pride to allow her near his wife, so he had to be losing hope.

"He says you can go in if Minipoka allows it," Storm said. "You ask her. They want no men inside the lodge."

The young woman who had left a minute ago came back, having disposed of the blood-soaked rags and filled the pot with steaming water. She went inside and Tess followed her.

Heat hit her in the face, although the fire in the lodge was banked. It was human heat, fed by pain and fear. The smell of blood and tears hung in the air like a vapor. Three women were in the center of the lodge, directly under the apex. Minipoka, the young woman who had fetched the water, and another woman, naked and squatting, her belly swollen with child, her brown skin gleaming with sweat. Blood and other fluids pooled between her spread feet. Her face was contorted with agony, and she breathed raggedly as she struggled to expel the child from her weary, torn body.

Minipoka's glance toward Tess was sharp, but she motioned her closer.

"Bad medicine is working on this one," Minipoka said. "I have done what I can, but still the babe won't come. I don't want to take a knife to her, but . . ." Minipoka shrugged helplessly. "Both will die if something isn't done quick."

Tess assessed the situation, noting the woman's writhing belly, the amount of fluid she'd expelled, and the lack of progress she'd made.

"Can I try my medicine on her? If it doesn't work, I'll help you cut her to take the baby."

Minipoka nodded. "Go ahead."

"I need for her to lie flat on her back."

"Lie flat? How will the baby come out that way?"

"I'll help it. Will you tell her?"

With a befuddled scowl, Minipoka spoke to the

woman and pressed a hand to her shoulder, urging to her lie flat. Tess rolled up her own sleeves and dipped her elbow into the steaming water to test the temperature. Hot, but bearable, she thought. Immersing her hands, she washed them and her arms up to her elbows.

"Minipoka, I need for you and this other woman to hold her down. Get on either side of her ... that's right ... and is there something she can bite down on? That leather belt? Yes, that's good. Give that to her."

As she gave directions, she pushed up the woman's feet, bending her knees, and leaned down to see what progress had been made. The passage was wide—at its widest, probably—but there was no sight of the baby's head. Grabbing one of the lamps, Tess brought it closer. The woman screamed as another pain hit her. Tess watched and saw exactly what she'd feared; a shiny butt and a couple of tiny toes.

Sitting back on her heels, Tess closed her eyes and readied herself for battle. "It's breach," she said, mostly to herself.

"Dead? It's dead?" Minipoka asked.

"No." Tess opened her eyes, realizing the old woman didn't know the medical term. "The baby is coming out the wrong way. It needs to arrive headfirst, not tail-first. If we can't turn it around, we'll have to cut her open and take the child that way." She glanced around at the lack of instruments, the dirt floor, the poor lighting. She'd have to turn that baby, she thought. She sure didn't want to operate under these conditions.

The laboring woman released another scream of misery and clutched desperately at Minipoka's bony arm.

"She asks me to kill her," Minipoka said. "She says she can stand it no longer."

Bracing herself, Tess locked gazes with Minipoka. "Hold her tight and don't let go. I'm going to reach inside her and see if I can turn the baby around."

Minipoka's eyes widened. "You will kill her *and* the baby!"

"Not if I can help it," Tess assured her. Bending lower, she took a deep breath and pushed her hand slowly into the woman.

The woman's muscles barely tensed. She was so exhausted from her hours of labor that she had no strength left to resist any invasion. Tess heard her grunt, but she concentrated only on the baby her fingers had located and now explored.

Yes, there's the rear and bowed back, she thought, closing her eyes to eliminate one sense and enhance another. What's that? A knee . . . no, elbow. Okay, then up here should be—yes! A shoulder and . . . there's the head.

"Not much room in here," she muttered. Another contraction seized the woman and Tess felt the muscles squeeze together. She waited for the wave to pass before she gently began pushing the infant in a clockwise direction. The woman screamed again and again, the sound sending chills up Tess's spine, but she kept pushing, hoping to turn the baby before the next contraction.

"Take out your hand," Minipoka ordered, her voice shaking with fear. "You are killing her. It's not right for you to do this. Her body does not want your hand in it!"

"Hold on . . . just a minute . . ." Tess let her breath out in a soft whoosh. She extracted her hand slowly, carefully. "Got it. The baby's head is right here. I can see it." She placed a hand on the woman's hard abdomen and pressed down. "Tell her to push, Minipoka. Tell her to push with everything she has left in her. Hurry! The cord might be wrapped around the baby's neck. We've got to get it out of her before it is strangled."

The old woman barked an order at the sweat-soaked woman, and she bore down, her teeth sinking into the leather belt, her body shaking with the exertion.

And slowly the baby's head emerged, then the shoulders. Tess stared, aghast at the cord wrapped twice around the baby's neck. "Push! Tell her to push!"

With another scream and surge of pain and fear and sheer desperation, the new mother ejected the baby from the passageway.

Tess wasted no time. She grabbed up the infant and unwound the cord, tied it off, then cut it with Minipoka's knife. Catching the baby by the heels, she held it aloft and smacked its backside with her palm. The infant didn't move or utter a sound. Tess's insides froze solid.

"Oh, God, oh, God." Tess pinched the baby's butt-cheek, tickled the soles of its tiny feet, gave its backside another sharp pat.

Nothing. No sign of life.

"It's dead," Minipoka announced. "I was afraid of this."

"No." Tess shook her head, then pushed her damp hair away from her hot face. "No, I'm not giving up on this little life yet."

Lying the baby on the mother's stomach, Tess poked a finger into the tiny baby's mouth to clear it of blood and mucus. As she bent over the infant, she caught sight of the mother's face, full of terror and anguish.

Have to make this baby breathe, she thought,

pinching the button nose shut and placing her lips against the tender mouth. She blew gently, feeling the baby's lungs inflate. Repeating the process, she continued to breathe for the baby, hoping against hope that life would catch, like a spark fed by a puff of air. Against her fingers she felt a thump. She paused, staring at her hand resting on the baby's chest. There! Another thump against her index finger. Tess forced oxygen into the baby's lungs again . . . again . . . again. The thump hit once more and then continued. *Thudump-thudump-thudump.*

Tess raised her head and looked down into the round, blue face. "Breathe, sugar. Breathe." She pinched the fat cheek—hard.

Brows knitted above the button nose and then a sound emerged. A funny, sweet, kittenish cry that would have made Satan himself weep. And then the cry increased to an honest-to-goodness bellow.

"The babe lives!" Minipoka said, her voice full of awe. "You have sucked death from the baby's body and breathed life back into it. You have great powers."

The mother began to cry softly, and the other young woman, who had been helping to hold her still, jumped up and danced around the room, giggles and laughter bubbling from her. The baby's *waa-waa-waahing* jolted Tess back to the business at hand. Lifting the baby into her arms, she laid it in her lap and reached for a wet rag.

"It's a girl," she said, wiping away the slippery fluids. "A beautiful girl. Tell her, Minipoka. Tell her how beautiful her daughter is. And send the other woman outside to tell Brown Otter. He's worried sick, although he's too much of a bear to show it."

The baby waved walnut-sized fists and cried lustily while Tess finished washing her skin and observing the blue color give way to beautiful brown and healthy pink.

"Yes, yes, you go ahead and cry," Tess told the newborn. "Cry loud and long, little one. Tell God how grateful you are to be a part of this world."

Batting aside her own tears of joy, Tess lifted the baby from her lap and placed her in the mother's arms. The woman's black eyes shone with gratitude and tears filled them and spilled over. Tess patted her shoulder and smoothed her dark brown hair from her wet face.

"You did fine," she told her, although she knew the woman didn't understand English. "And your baby seems to be healthy. You rest." She closed her eyes for a moment to illustrate. "You need to rest. Minipoka will wrap your baby in a warm blanket, won't you, Minipoka?"

The old woman smiled and reached for a blanket. "I know what to do for her now. You have done enough."

Tess sat on the ground and leaned back against the lodge wall. Fatigue buzzed lazily in her head and swam through her veins. She closed her eyes, listening to the baby cry and Minipoka sing softly.

The wonder of life stole over her and she felt tears roll down her cheeks. Thinking of the Little baby that could not be saved, Tess once again mourned for Cassie's mother. Every life was precious. A woman might have two children or twenty or none. Didn't matter. The loss of one tore a chunk from every woman's heart. She listened to her own heartbeat, glad to be alive to witness this every day miracle and to usher a new soul into the world.

Minipoka stuck her head out of the lodge and motioned for Brown Otter.

"Come see your daughter."

"Daughter!" Brown Otter beamed. "At last, a girl. I have prayed for a daughter for years."

Minipoka grinned. "She was taken from us, but the white medicine woman breathed life back into her. If it weren't for her powerful medicine, your child and your wife would be in the spirit world." Her beady eyes crinkled at the corners. "You come inside, too, Storm-in-His-Eyes. Your woman did good work, but she needs her man now to lend her strength."

He started to correct her, to tell her that he had no claim on Tess, but he bit back the words. He could see the mischievous sparkles in the old grandmother's eyes and knew she was goading him, getting under his skin.

Minipoka ducked back inside and Brown Otter rushed in past her. Storm followed more slowly, his eyes smarting from the sting of burning herbs and incense. Far-Off-Fawn-Woman, one of Minipoka's great-granddaughters, waltzed around the lodge and held aloft a smoking cache of herbal grasses that would cleanse the lodge of the pain, the letting of blood, and any evil spirits that might have hovered like vultures, waiting for life to expire.

Brown Otter's wife lay on a bed of clean blankets. She held a squirming, fretting babe in her arms and smiled at her husband as he approached on hesitant feet.

"Look, my husband. Look what the Creator has given us."

"A daughter," Brown Otter whispered, grinning from ear to ear. "We are blessed."

Turning away from the touching scene, Storm looked for Tess and found her sitting with her back against the wall and her legs outstretched. Her limbs were relaxed and limp, reminding him of a rag doll his sister had carried everywhere when she was a toddling child. The hair he had so carefully plaited hung loose around Tess's face, some of it clinging to her damp forehead and curling at her temples. Dark smudges beneath her eyes gave her a bruised look that squeezed his heart.

She didn't stir when he squatted beside her. His woman. Minipoka had called her that, and he wanted it to be true. This brave, beautiful woman would make any man proud. She was a match for any warrior. A man who had such a woman at his side could accomplish great things.

Her sable lashes twitched, and she wrinkled her nose and wiggled it like a bunny. Raising a hand as if it weighed a ton, she rubbed the tip of her nose with the back of her wrist. The itch scratched, her arm fell like a lead weight back along her side. He noticed the flecks of red under her fingernails. Blood, he realized. She had engaged in a bloody battle with death and had won. Just as she had won the fight for his own life after the marshall had shot him and again when the marshall had wanted to hang him. Yes, this woman brimmed with miracles.

Unable to resist her any longer, Storm braced a hand behind her head and kissed her parted lips. "Tess," he whispered against her mouth. "AnadaAki."

Her lips curved into a smile against his and her breath floated out of her and into him. Drawing back from her, he admired the blue-green color of her sleepy eyes. He caressed one side of her face, his thumb following the delicate lines of brow, cheek, and chin.

"The baby is alive," she said, her voice weak and wavering.

"Yes. Minipoka says it lives because of you."

"It's a girl." She closed her eyes again. "I was so

afraid. . . . The mother had used up all her strength, and I was afraid she wouldn't have any left to force the baby out once I got her turned in the right direction."

"She is Brown Otter's first girl-child. He is bursting with pride."

"He should be. She's a beautiful baby and a fighter. So is his wife. What's her name?"

"Morning Star."

"That's a pretty name." Giving a little sigh, she propped herself up higher, her spine lengthening, her proud carriage returning. "I need some fresh air, I think."

"Come. I'll help you up." He stood, and taking her hands in his, pulled her to her feet. With an arm around her waist, he guided her from the lodge and out where the air was brisk and mountain-clear.

She stretched her arms above her head and swayed from side to side, a smile giving her face a heart-wrenching beauty. Her blouse molded to her high breasts, and the wind bound her skirt tightly against her shapely hips and legs.

"You are a miracle-maker," Storm said, speaking before he could ponder the wisdom of such a compliment.

Tess lowered her arms slowly. "Not really. I just did what I'd seen John do before. I believe even he would be patting me on the back."

Storm took a step toward her, wanting to haul her into his arms and kiss her until she was limp again, but he quelled that notion when he spotted Chief Eagle Talon heading their way, in the company of young sons and daughters and a few of the tribal elders.

"Tess, look who's coming," Storm whispered

close to her ear. "He must have heard about the birth and your part in it."

"Uh-oh." Tess tipped up her chin at a spunky angle. "The baby is fine and Brown Otter's wife is resting, Chief Eagle Talon. Morning Star will be up and about in a few days, I hope."

The chief afforded them hardly a glance before slipping inside Brown Otter's lodge. The others milled outside with Storm and Tess. Storm could hear the chief talking with Brown Otter, but he couldn't make out the words over the crying of the infant. A minute later, the chief, Minipoka and Far-Off-Fawn-Woman came out of the lodge, all looking pleased. Chief Eagle Talon stood before Tess, and Storm was struck by how delicate she seemed, like a reed confronting a mighty gust of wind.

The chief lifted a hand and touched the bead necklace around Tess's slender neck.

"Storm gave it to me," she told the chief.

"I know." Chief Eagle Talon glanced at Storm, then returned his full attention to Tess. "You have shown valor and wisdom. Minipoka tells me that her medicine could not have given the child life, but yours did."

Tess averted her gaze shyly. "I'm glad I was able to help the baby and her mother."

Brown Otter came out of the lodge and stood next to Storm, his arms folded, his expression giving away none of his thoughts. But Storm had known the man all his life, and he sensed in him great joy and burgeoning pride.

"You have proven yourself once again a friend of the Bloods." The chief removed a necklace of black beads and white elk's teeth from around his own neck and put it around Tess's. "I give you this to wear with the beads my son has given you. I would be honored if you would accept it."

"Of course. Thank you, the honor is mine."

"If anyone asks how you came by this necklace, you tell them that it was given to you by the great Chief Eagle Talon, my white daughter."

Surprise punched Storm, and he glanced at Brown Otter in time to catch the twinkle of pleasure in his eyes. The chief wore a hint of a smile as he gauged Tess's reaction. She seemed startled for a few moments, and then her eyes glimmered with tears and her lower lip trembled.

"Thank you," she said, her voice husky with emotion. "I shall always treasure this necklace, Chief Eagle Talon, and the sentiments behind it." She knitted her brows in a moment of indecision, then raised on tiptoe and bestowed a quick kiss on the chief's leathery cheek.

Storm winced, worried that the chief would not find the kiss appropriate. Chief Eagle Talon scrutinized Tess, squinted one eye, then grinned. The other Blackfeet sighed and laughed in relief. Giving a quick nod, the chief turned and walked back to his lodge, taking everyone with him except for Storm, Tess, and Brown Otter.

Tess sent an idle glance toward Brown Otter. "What about you? Have I earned my way into your good graces? Are you going to be nice to me from now on, Brown Otter?" She jutted out a hip and tapped her foot. "I certainly hope so, because I've had about enough of your surliness."

"You are a good woman," Brown Otter said, his words slow in coming. "And I am beholden to you. I wish happiness and health for you and your people, and when you return to the white eyes, I hope you find an honorable man and are blessed with many children. I will say my farewell to my wife and then join you and my brother for the trip to the valley." He essayed a brief bow and stepped back into the lodge.

Storm wished he could kick his cousin all the way to False Hope. How could he slash through Tess's hopes like that, after what she'd done? He directed his gaze away from Tess's hurt, stricken expression to study the pearly gray horizon, and sought words to lessen her disappointment. "Don't let him bother you, Tess. He holds to the belief that mingling with whites isn't good." Shaking his head at his inadequate apology, he reached for her hand. "We should be going. It's getting late."

Tess cleared her throat. "Too late?" she whispered, her tone yearning, melancholy.

He looked at her, saw the shadows in her eyes, felt the rain clouds in her heart. She knows, he thought. She feels the weight of the odds stacked against us and the wicked uncertainty of the world.

He knew she wasn't talking about their trip to Pleasant Valley, but he didn't want to discuss the obstacles in their path or the unlikelihood that theirs would be a vow of forever. So he lifted her fine-boned hand to his lips and kissed her fingers, her thumb, her wrist.

"Wash up in my lodge," he said, letting her go, "and then we'll be on our way."

The sadness of her smile ripped at his heart. He watched her walk toward his lodge, her steps slow and measured.

"I love you," he whispered, and the truth and power of those words struck him like a coup stick and made his knees wobble and his heart tremble. "By all that is holy, I do."

Chapter 20

A pproaching Elmer and Mattie Summar's ranch, Tess felt the tension in the two men flanking her. Glancing at each, she surveyed their stony expressions, watchful eyes, and sternly set lips and jaws. Obviously they expected anything but a warm welcome.

Tess tapped her heels against her mount and took the winding road that led to the house at a gallop. As she cleared the last gate, she spotted her uncle out by the barn and her aunt bent over pumpkin vines in the garden. Flinging an arm over her head, she fashioned a broad, rambunctious wave and received the same from them.

Laughing, she barely gave her horse time enough to stop before she was out of the saddle and into her aunt's welcoming embrace.

"Lordy, lordy, if this ain't a wonderful surprise!" Aunt Mattie squeezed her tightly before letting go. "What in the world are you doing riding with the Blackfeet?" Aunt Mattie turned toward the two men still on horseback and gave them a big, wide grin. "Well, climb on down off them ponies, boys. You speak English, don't you? I hope so, 'cause I

286

can count on one hand the number of Blackfeet words I know."

` "They speak English," Tess assured her. "The one getting off his horse is Storm-In-His-Eyes, and the one who is being mule-headed and looking like he swallowed a horny toad is Brown Otter."

"Hey, there!" Uncle Elmer hurried to them on stubby legs. "Is that the prettiest girl in False Hope? Where's that brother of yours?"

"Back home. I've brought some friends with me." Tess hugged the short, wiry man. "Hello, Uncle Elmer. Everything okay around here?"

"Everything's fit as a fiddle." He nodded at the two Blackfeet. "How do. I'm Elmer Summar." Holding up one hand, Indian style, he greeted the visitors. "You boys part of Eagle Talon's tribe? And did I hear right? Did you say this here is Storm-In-His-Eyes?"

"Yes, I'm Storm-In-His-Eyes."

"Well, well. If it isn't the famous Indian outlaw." Uncle Elmer slapped his thigh and let out a lusty chuckle. "I been hearing about you, son. You shot Marshall Long's deputy, didn't you?"

"Uncle Elmer, he was forced into that gunfight," Tess said, jumping to his defense.

"How long are you staying?" Aunt Mattie asked, slipping an arm around Tess's shoulders.

"Only overnight. I just came to warn you."

"About what?" Aunt Mattie asked.

"There are some bad men dressing up like Indians and stealing horses around here."

Aunt Mattie nodded. "Yes, we know. They hit the Johnson's place. Took twenty of their best horses and burned down their barn. Happened a couple of weeks ago. I went over there to be with Cora Johnson. She had a spell with her heart over it, but she's fine now."

"Mattie, what are you going to rustle up for supper? What do you boys like to eat?" Uncle Elmer pulled on his work gloves. "Hey, I could use some strong backs. You boys mind giving me a hand with some fence posts? I'm replacing some rotted ones."

"Why, Elmer, that's the rudest thing I've ever heard. Who taught you manners? These are guests, not ranch hands."

"That's okay," Storm said. "We're glad to help."

Tess sent Storm a grateful smile. He looked relieved and pleased that he and Brown Otter had been accepted by the couple so easily.

"Tess, let's you and me throw together something lip-smacking in the kitchen while these men work up an appetite."

"Okay, Aunt Mattie." Tess let herself be guided away from the men and into the homey ranch house. The last glimpse she had of Storm, he and Brown Otter were walking with her uncle toward the corral behind the barn.

Aunt Mattie's kitchen was warm and pungent with the aroma of baking bread.

"Honey wheat loaves," Aunt Mattie said, answering Tess's question before she could voice it. "They ought to be ready to take out of the oven by now. You think your friends would like some pork chops and white beans?"

"I'm sure they would." Spotting pie pans lined up on the window sill, Tess went to inspect them. "Hmm. Are these sweet potato pies?"

"Two of them are. The other is strawberry-rhubarb."

"You've been busy today."

"So have you." Aunt Mattie pulled two loaves of bread from the oven, set them on the table to cool, and faced Tess. "Since when do you run with Indians?"

"I've moved out of John's house, Aunt Mattie."

Her aunt sat heavily in one of the chairs situated around the long table. "John's house? It's your house, too, Tess."

"No, it hasn't been ever since John married Camilla." Tess strolled to the window again and looked out, but she couldn't see Storm. "Things change, Aunt Mattie. I've been feeling this change coming for a long time. In John's house I'm a cook, a maid, an assistant, and sometimes a nuisance. If I continue to stay there, I will eventually be an old-maid aunt to his children. That's a life I can't bear any longer, so I moved to Mrs. Bishop's house. You remember her, don't you? She's a sweet lady."

"Yes, I know her." Aunt Mattie fanned her round, ruddy face. She outweighed her husband by about a hundred pounds, but Uncle Elmer still referred to her as "the little woman." Puffing her gray and black bangs off her forehead, she clucked her tongue. "Lordy, lordy, I can't even ponder how John will get along without you, Tess. That wife of his is good for looking at, but you know as well as I do that she don't know spit about keeping a house clean and a man fed."

"She can learn."

Aunt Mattie made a disparaging sound. "She won't. You know it and I know it. The day John married her, I told Elmer I was afraid John had driven his cattle to a bad market."

Tess laughed. "I never heard it put that way before. Oh, Camilla's not so bad. She's just lazy, and John pets her too much. He doesn't want her to ruin her lily-white hands in dishwater. I think he even finds it charming that she can't cook."

"We'll see how long it takes before the bloom is

off that rose. I give him a month before he either hires a cook or tells his wife she'd better learn how to boil water and quick." Aunt Mattie pushed herself up from the chair. "Or he'll come crawling to you and beg you to come back home—where you rightly belong."

Tess shook her head. "No, Aunt Mattie, he'd be wasting his breath. I don't belong there anymore, and I think even John would agree with me." Clasping her hands tightly in front of her, she faced her aunt. "I've brought shame on the family, so I guess you should know what I've done. The taller Blackfeet out there ... I ... we ..."

"Me and Elmer already heard about it."

"You did?" Tess gulped air and swallowed it. "H-how?"

"One of them deputies ... Buck? ... he was out here yesterday. Said he was keeping an eye peeled for some thieving Indians. He told us that you said you was sleeping with one of them Blackfeet. Elmer 'bout keeled over."

A sharp thorn of hatred pricked Tess. Buck Wilhite. That loud-mouthed snake! "I'm sorry you had to hear it from a stranger, Aunt Mattie."

"So, it's true."

"Yes."

"Tell me it's the tallest one out there."

"It is."

Aunt Mattie nodded. "The handsome outlaw. Did John make you leave, Tess?"

"No, but he's very disappointed in me. He's convinced that I've lost my mind."

"Hmmm. Well, having knowed you since you was a sprout, I say it's not your mind you've lost, but your heart."

Tess turned away and smiled, then felt herself blush. "I didn't set out to make everyone hopping mad. I never even thought I'd feel this way about him—or about any man. I always wanted to fall in love, of course, but this is more than I ever imagined."

"Does he love you?"

"I don't know. He won't say because he's in trouble. The marshall is bound and determined to watch him swing from a rope. But he's a good man, Aunt Mattie. He's made mistakes and he's been a bit of a renegade, but I know he's honest and honorable."

"You thinking of living with him or moving him into town with you?"

"I don't know. Like I said, we haven't talked about that. Until his name is cleared, until these bad men are caught, we can't speak of such things." She frowned, trying to picture Storm living in a house in False Hope. "He won't live in town. I wouldn't want him to. He's tried living like a white man and he didn't like it."

Aunt Mattie placed two skillets on top of the stove. "Can't imagine you living with the Blackfeet."

"I can."

Aunt Mattie peered at her, completely confounded. "Say again?"

Tess forced her gaze up and across the room to her aunt. "I've been to the Blackfeet village. I like it there. The Blackfeet appreciate my knowledge of medicine, Aunt Mattie. Their most important medical person is a woman named Minipoka. She is a remarkable healer. I could learn so much from her." Encouraged by her aunt's respect for the Blackfeet, she approached her at the stove. "She used porcupine quills to lower Storm's fever and ease the pain of his wounds."

"Wounds?"

"He was shot by the marshall."

"What for?"

"The marshall says he steals horses and robs people, but that's not true." She lowered her voice and leaned closer to her aunt. "Marshall Long shot Storm's sister in cold blood."

"Doesn't surprise me none. I've known Chester Long for twenty years, and he was never what I'd call trustworthy. Only reason he's a marshall is because he's a big bully." She used a wooden spoon to stir a pot of beans simmering on the stove. "But, honey, living like an Indian ain't no adventure. Those folks don't even have land to claim. When the army says they got to move, then they got to move. And come winter, they nearly starve to death. Me and Elmer have seen them out hunting, their ribs showing and their guts sunk in. You'd better think long and hard before you talk about joining up with the Blackfeet."

Tess spotted the chops lying on a sideboard. Picking up cans of salt and pepper, she sprinkled the meat with the spices and rolled the pork in flour.

Aunt Mattie was right, she knew. The Blackfeet lived close to the earth, and their larder was often nearly empty. Winters were harsh in Montana; and much of the game left the mountains for the valleys, where they hid or died, buried under snow and ice.

"You're not afraid of the Blackfeet, are you, Aunt Mattie? I mean, they've never given you any trouble, have they?"

"No. Me and Elmer made peace with their chief years ago. In fact, we've been known to trade meat for skins and furs come winter, just so's their people could eat proper. We'd give them some food, being the Christians we are, but Chief Eagle Talon won't take something for nothing. He always wants to trade." She handed Tess a bucket of potatoes. "Peel some of them for me. I hope you told Mrs. Bishop you were coming here for a visit."

"Yes, and she knows I left with Storm."

"Honey, you sure you ain't biting off more grief than you can swaller?"

"Mrs. Bishop understands. She knows I've been unhappy, and she says I should do what my heart tells me to do. If John goes to her house looking for me, she said she'll tell him I'm here, but she won't say that Storm is with me. I don't want John to jump to the wrong conclusion."

"Poor John. You're going to make him old before his time."

"He's not my keeper, Aunt Mattie. It's time he understood that."

"He loves you, Tess. You can't slap his face for that."

"And I love him." She sat at the table to peel the spuds. "He thinks I'm too picky, too romantic, and now just plumb crazy. He doesn't understand that I'm of an age that I ache for a home of my own. I don't want to take care of his children, I want babies of my own. I want a husband to cook for and clean for and curl up with at night. John thinks I should grab any old bachelor or widower and hope love enters into it some day. But I can't do that, Aunt Mattie. Don't I deserve to fall madly in love with someone just as John fell madly in love with Camilla?"

"Of course, you do, honey." Her aunt bowed her head for a moment, and when she looked up her eyes were moist with tears. "Well, then, you got to do what Mrs. Bishop says, I reckon. You got to follow your heart." She turned to the stove and dropped the first chops into the hot grease in the skillet.

"Aunt Mattie, I knew I could count on you," Tess said, rising up from the chair to go to her aunt and give her a hug. She leaned her head on Aunt Mattie's shoulder, accepting the comfort and the connection of family ties. "But I didn't come here just to lean on you, although it sure feels good."

Aunt Mattie laughed and turned back to the popping grease and frying meat. "Feels good to me, too."

"Aunt Mattie, you and Uncle Elmer have to be real careful. The men who are stealing horses around here are animals. I know, firsthand."

"What do you mean?" her aunt asked.

"You didn't know?"

"Know what?" Worry pinched Aunt Mattie's lined face.

"They attacked me, and if it hadn't been for Storm and Brown Otter, they would have raped and killed me."

"Lord have mercy, child!" Aunt Mattie's eyes widened with stark fear. "I didn't know a thing about this. That deputy didn't say nothing about you being attacked when he was flapping his gums at us."

Tess gathered in a deep breath as fear crouched in her chest. "I haven't said much about this to anyone, but those men—those devils—they said they know me. I think they must live in False Hope."

After a hearty dinner they all gathered in the front room around the fireplace. Uncle Elmer regaled them with tales of how he kept his land in Pleasant Valley—of fighting wolves, coyotes, bears, deserters, and thieves.

Tess had been so absorbed in the stories of derring-do she wasn't aware when Brown Otter left the room. She only noticed Brown Otter's absence when Uncle Elmer paused in his narrative to throw some logs on the fire.

"What happened to Brown Otter?" she asked, looking around the room.

"He slipped out awhile back," Aunt Mattie said from her rocker. She didn't even look up from the trousers she was mending. "I thought maybe he was answering the call of nature, but he's been gone a good spell now. Your uncle's stories must have driven him into the woods." She smiled, still not looking up from her sewing.

"Did you know he'd left?" Tess asked Storm, who was sitting next to her on the floor near the hearth.

He nodded. "He's restless, and he's not used to places like this." He glanced around the cheery room, crowded with furniture and family heirlooms. "Neither am I."

Feeling his uneasiness, Tess stood up and reached out a hand to him. "Let's go for a walk."

Without a moment's hesitation, Storm grasped her hand and stood beside her. "Yes, I'd like that."

"I'll show Storm your prize bull, Uncle Elmer." With that, Tess led Storm out into the breezy night.

Storm lifted his nose into the air. "I smell rain."

"Do you?" Tess sniffed, but could only discern the dusky aroma of geraniums and the faint odor of livestock. "How do you like my aunt and uncle?"

"They're good people. Salt of the earth, as you said."

"See? White people can be nice and kind and good-hearted."

He turned to her, placing a hand along her

cheek. "I already knew that. You taught me that."

Tess stood on tiptoe and kissed his mouth. "You have reason to hate certain people, but do be careful. Nothing is so important that you should lose your life over it."

He ran the backs of his fingers lightly down the side of her face. "You're wrong. I would rather die than live as a hunted animal. And I can find no peace until the man who killed my sister is dead."

A chill stole over her heart. "Don't talk like that. You scare me."

"What should scare you is that the men who attacked you, who hurt you, are running free while I am a hunted man. Until they are stopped, we can't talk of tomorrow. That is what angers me the most."

"Let's not dwell on it," she said, moving away from him toward the sturdy pen behind the barn where her uncle kept Hercules, his bull. She broke into a run, laughing when Storm caught up with her and grabbed her around the waist. "I've caught you, but can I keep you?" he asked, smiling.

"I'm not going anywhere." She placed her hands at the back of his head and brought his mouth down to hers.

His hands were big and gentle upon her back as he pressed her closer. Her lips parted, and his tongue thrust deep, sliding against her own. Tess clutched his hair and opened her mouth wider as hot shivers raced through her.

It was always this way when she was with him, this quick, total surrender to his mastery. She gave as good as she got, driving her tongue into his mouth, her strokes light and teasing. He groaned and tore his lips from hers to kiss the curve of her neck while his hands moved lower to massage her hips. She felt his hardness. His eyes sought hers and were full of storm warnings.

"I want you."

The simple request filled her with intense longing. She glanced around. "Not here. . . ."

"Where?"

She smiled, eager and willing to sneak into the night with him. "The barn? We could go up into the loft—"

Thudding footsteps broke them apart. Brown Otter jogged toward the house, spotted them, and headed in their direction. Storm cursed softly.

"What now?" he muttered, squeezing Tess's hand.

Stopping in front of them, his chest heaving and his eyes glistening with banked excitement, Brown Otter rested a hand on Storm's shoulder. He spoke quickly in Blackfeet and Storm bunched his hands into fists.

"What? What's he saying?" Tess asked, sensing the tension and the danger.

"He says he's found where the thieves are corralling the stolen horses before taking them to market," Storm said before turning back to Brown Otter. "Are you sure? Are there horses there now?"

The stocky Indian shook his head. "But there were some there no more than a day or two ago. The droppings are still fresh. Come with me. I'll show you. The trail away from the corral can be seen, followed."

"Is it far from here?" Tess asked.

"No."

"So that's where you've been," Tess said. "Are they on Uncle Elmer's land?"

"They are up higher. About a mile from here as the eagle flies and to the east. It's a natural corral, bound on three sides by rock and the fourth by a gate they have made from logs and wire."

"Let's go." Storm turned to Tess. "Don't wait up for us. We'll bed down in the barn."

"The barn!" Tess grabbed his sleeve. "Wait until morning. You can't see anything in the dark."

"Yes, I can. The moon is nearly full tonight." He touched the side of her face with his fingertips. "Don't worry. I won't be gone long." He nodded toward her aunt and uncle's house. "Tell them we thank them for everything."

"You can tell them yourself. Aunt Mattie will expect you at the breakfast table in the morning. You, too, Brown Otter. And don't argue or you'll hurt my feelings."

"I mean you no dishonor," Brown Otter explained, his face set in its usual serious lines.

"Okay, so go." Tess released Storm's sleeve. "Maybe the tracks will lead you to their hideout."

Brown Otter and Storm went toward their horses, which were tethered in front of the house. Both ponies were saddled and ready to ride. Brown Otter's horse was already lathered.

"Why don't I come with you?" Tess suggested, afraid to let Storm out of her sight. "I can saddle up in no time and—"

Storm caught her hand before she could head back to the barn. "No, Tess. Go back inside." His eyes darkened to match his somber expression.

Tess knew that look and realized it was pointless to argue with him. "Be careful. I don't want to doctor you again." She rested a hand on his chest where the marshall's bullet had lodged. "You have enough scars on this body, enough wounds that need to heal."

He lifted her hand to his lips. "Go back inside." He kissed each fingertip and the back of her hand. "Please."

Her heart hammered frantically, and she wanted

to fling herself into his arms and hold on to him forever. Instead she managed to smile and step away from him. "I'll be waiting for you, Storm."

She retreated toward the house, holding his gaze as long as possible. She wanted to tell him she loved him, but she bit her tongue. Not in front of Brown Otter, she thought. Such an admission should be for Storm's ears only, and the time had to be right.

Storm grabbed some of the stallion's mane, gave a little hop, and swung up onto the horse's back. Moonlight painted his hair with silver and drew dark shadows under his slashing cheekbones. He raised a hand in a silent farewell. Tess mirrored the gesture and watched Storm and Brown Otter ride to the east.

The sky rumbled overhead and flashes of lightning lit up clouds banked in the north. Now she, too, could smell the rain. It wouldn't be long before clouds rolled in and covered the moon, making it dark as pitch. The rain would wash away the tracks left by the horse thieves.

Thinking of the robbers, of their hands on her, of their voices and how they'd acted as if they knew her, sent a cold chill through Tess. Those voices had been familiar, but she couldn't for the life of her place them. She'd gone over and over in her mind what they'd said to her, the inflections in their voices and the tones. Sometimes she felt as if she were on the verge of recognizing the men, but then the images faded like a dream.

Like a dream . . . something about a dream she'd had. A dream about Storm and the marshall and John. But it was all too hazy and unformed for her to grasp. Sometimes she thought that her mind was closing her off from the truth, keeping her away from discovering the faces beneath those hideous masks. But that was silly. She *wanted* to know the truth, and she *would* know eventually. Maybe even tonight. Storm and Brown Otter might track down the varmints before the clouds could hide them and the rain could wash away the proof of their sins.

Thunder boomed like a cannon blast, making her jerk all over. She glanced up and saw that there were fewer stars as the clouds raced in. Another clap of thunder sent her back inside where it was warm and bright and safe.

Chapter 21

"**S**o you delivered a baby all by yourself— and a breach baby, too. Sounds like you're giving John a run for his money." Aunt Mattie rocked back in the chair with a hearty laugh. "I'd like to see his face when he hears about this. Poor John. I shouldn't be laughing, I reckon."

Tess smothered her own giggles. "You're right. He's a good man, but he *is* rather pompous."

"Don't surprise me none that you can deliver babies and heal up gunshot wounds," Uncle Elmer announced as the rocker he sat in squeaked on its runners. "You've been lending a hand to doctors since you was in pinafores. It's natural you'd pick up some of that know-how."

"John doesn't see it that way." Tess pulled her feet up onto the sofa and tucked them under her. "I understand that he went to school to learn his doctoring, and I only know what I've cribbed from him and his books, but . . . I *do* know something about doctoring, and I wish he'd at least acknowledge that. Sometimes I think he would be happier with me if I'd be more like Camilla."

"Oh, no, he wouldn't," Aunt Mattie disagreed.

"Lordy, honey, what he *doesn't* need is another Camilla in his household. Maybe he believes that, but it sure isn't what that man needs. No sirree."

Uncle Elmer spit tobacco into a tin can and wiped his mouth on a stained handkerchief. "I think it's right interesting how the Blackfeet chief gave you that there necklace. Sort of makes you one of them, doesn't it?"

Tess fingered the chain of beads and elk's teeth. "Not really. I'm not sure that's possible. . . . "

"Why, of course it is. Look at Storm-In-His-Eyes."

Tess angled her head sideways. "What about him?"

Uncle Elmer raised the cup and spit. *Ping!* "His grandpappy had him a white wife. How do you think he got them gray eyes of his?"

"His grandfather? How do you know that?"

"The chief told me hisself, that his uncle—and I believe he said that was Storm's grandpappy Roaming Stag—had took hisself a white woman as a wife. He already had a Blackfeet wife, but she was sickly. This here white woman, the chief told me, was married to a man who ran a trading post. Seems like this old boy beat her pretty regular and Roaming Stag struck a trade for her. She went along without so much as a tear. Guess she figured Roaming Stag couldn't be much worse than her husband." He chuckled to himself and chewed tobacco. "Anyhoo, they got along like a house afire and had themselves a few children before they got killed in a cavalry raid."

"I was told that no one knew which of Storm's ancestors were white," Tess said, lost in thought. Why had Slow-Riding-Woman lied to her? And why hadn't Storm told her about this mixed marriage? Surely he knew. She could think of only one reason, and it pained her. They didn't want her to hope for a happy union like Storm's Blackfeet grandfather and white grandmother.

"Say, have you and Storm-In-His-Eyes decided to wear a double yoke?" Uncle Elmer gave her a wink. "Where do you think you'd live with him?"

"Not in False Hope," Tess said, jumping to the logical answer. "But double yokes haven't been discussed, Uncle Elmer."

"Maybe he ain't talked about it with his mouth, but he's done a peck of talking with his eyes."

"You two are already married in the eyes of most decent folk," Aunt Mattie reminded her. "If I was you, I'd mention that to him and ask him what he intends to do about it. If he cares anything for you, he'll do the right thing."

"Marshall Long is out for his blood, Aunt Mattie. He can't promise anyone anything until he shakes the law off his tail."

"You think the Blackfeet would let you live with them?" Uncle Elmer asked.

"I don't know." A ball of frustration unraveled inside Tess, and she rose up from the sofa and shoved her feet back into her shoes and laced them. "All I know is that I can't read this man like I would a book. I don't know what's in his heart or his head. I'm praying that he cares for me, and that he'll ask me to be his as soon as Marshall Long and his mad-dog henchmen are muzzled. I know that sometimes I'm glad I gave myself to Storm, and sometimes I feel like the town tart because of what happened between us. And I know that when I'm with him I stop thinking altogether."

"Oh, honey," Aunt Mattie crooned. "You got it bad."

"Yep." Uncle Elmer deposited another juicy

morsel into the tin can. "Love done jumped up and bit her on the butt."

"Elmer! Watch your mouth," Aunt Mattie admonished.

Struck by the awful truth of it, Tess laughed, bending over at the waist, weak with giggles. After a moment her aunt and uncle joined in until they were all hooting.

"Uncle Elmer, you're a treasure," Tess told him, her laughter dwindling to a chuckle.

A horse whinnied outside, catching Tess's attention and tempting her. "I'm restless. I'm going outside for a stroll."

"Honey, it's dark out there—and cold. You shouldn't go alone."

"I'll be fine, and I'll wear my shawl." She plucked it off the hook by the door and draped the wool covering around her shoulders. "I won't stay out long. I just want to stretch my legs and commune with the stars."

"Okay, honey." Aunt Mattie picked up her handwork again. "But stay close to the house."

"I will."

Outside there were no stars with which to commune. Gray clouds smothered the starlight and the moon, throwing the valley into a thick darkness. Waiting just outside the door for a few minutes to allow her eyes to adjust, Tess pulled the shawl more tightly around her shoulders. A swift breeze that held the perfume of rain swept through the valley, kicking up Tess's skirts and tossing her hair. The shuffling of hooves and another sharp whinny drew her from the house toward the corral. She rested a hand on one of the new posts Storm and Brown Otter had helped her uncle drive in and watched the dozen or so horses inside the corral shift and dance. She could hear Hercules in the back pen pawing and huffing and pacing. Everyone was restless tonight it seemed.

The coming storm has them in a stir, she thought, catching sight of a wild eye, a flashing hoof, and clacking, square teeth.

"Easy, easy," she crooned, but the crack of thunder drowned out her puny voice.

She stood on the lower rail and folded her arms on the top one. The wind blew her hair back from her face and made a sail of her skirt. Tess closed her eyes and enjoyed the cool caress. She felt a raindrop fall on her cheek, another on her eyelid.

Oh, she wanted it to rain. She wanted it to thunder and lightning and release torrents. The world seemed primed for a good, hard cry, a glorious release, a shout and a shaking fist aimed at the devil.

"I love Storm-In-His-Eyes," she whispered, and the thunder came rolling in again. Lightning split the sky open and threw bright, blinding light across the valley floor. Tess flung back her head as the thunder growled and howled overhead. "I love him!" she yelled, and it felt oh-so-good, oh-so-right. Right as rain.

Laughing, she held on to the top rail and leaned back, letting her head loll and her hair swing free. Raindrops wet her face and she closed her eyes and let the rain wash away her doubts, her fears.

She heard the crunch of a boot on gravel and was about to turn around when her shawl was suddenly snatched from her shoulders and flung over her head. Tess raised her hands, grabbing at the wool and trying to pull it away from her face. Hard, callused hands grabbed her wrists and yanked her hands down and behind her. She cried out as pain burned in her shoulder sockets.

"Who . . . stop it!" Drawing in a deep breath, she was ready to scream when something rock-hard rammed into her chin with a sharp crack that spun her in a circle. A groan was all she could muster. Blood pooled in her mouth. The world dropped away from her feet and she fell into the devil's arms.

"Helloooo! Yo-hoooo!" *Snap. Snap.* "Now don't you play 'possum with me. Open up them eyes. I didn't hit you that hard, darlin'. Yo-hooo!"

The sing-song voice wafted through Tess like a bad omen. Although her eyelids felt as if they were weighted, she lifted them somehow and stared at a blurred face, six eyes, three hats, three noses, a monstrously wide grinning mouth. She shivered and a pain sliced through her head. She closed her eyes again, not wanting to see or feel or hear.

"Put on your mask, stupid."

"Oh, yeah. That damned thing is so hot. Makes my skin crawl."

"You want her recognizing you?"

Something pinched her cheek and gave it a tortuous twist that popped her eyes open again. She emitted a squeak of protest, but the sound came out muffled. With a jolt of alarm, she realized she was gagged . . . and bound!

Forcing clarity to her mind, she surmised that she was sitting on the ground, her legs outstretched. She rubbed her back against a rough, hard surface and ropes bit into her wrists. Her shoulders burned from the strain of having her arms pulled back and her hands shackled together. Ropes circled her knees and ankles and waist, and one scratched against her throat. She was so tightly bound to the tree, she could hardly move a muscle without the ropes burning and biting and rubbing her skin raw.

The face swam back into focus, jeering and toothy. She shivered, repulsed by the sinister presence emanating from the visage. It wasn't a face anymore. And the hat was gone. A mask . . . with big, pointy teeth. She'd seen it before. Another shiver scampered through her.

"She's coming 'round," the man said, in the tone of voice used to address a child. "Hi, there, redskin lover. You're so pretty, you ought to be able to do better than mess with a dirty Indian."

"We'll have to kill her."

Everything went still inside Tess. She cut her eyes sideways, trying to see the other man who had spoken that death sentence. All she could see were fancy-stitched boots, sharp-pointed star spurs, and brown trousers. He was sitting nearby, his legs stuck out, his ankles crossed.

"What do you mean?" The man leaning into her face directed his attention to his partner. "Why kill her? She don't know nothing."

"She saw your face before you put that mask on, stupid."

"I don't think so. She was woozy. Hell, her eyes were crossed and only half-open." He looked at her again, the white mask almost glowing in the darkness. "You don't know me, do you, honey-lamb?"

Honey-lamb. I'm your man, honey-lamb. Where had she heard that before?

"Keep talking to her and she'll for sure know you, if she doesn't already. We get rid of her, then we don't have to worry that she'll flap her jaws in town."

The masked man straightened away from her and moved out of her vision. She released her breath through her nostrils and tried to move her tongue, but it was shoved up against the cloth in her mouth. She swallowed. Her throat was dry and chalky. How long had she been tied up? Where was she? What she could see around her triggered no memories. She smelled rain and felt dampness under her backside. It had rained. Her clothes smelled of it and stuck to her skin in wrinkles. She'd been soaked and now she was damp. Hours, she thought with a twist of despair. She'd been unconscious for hours. Glancing up, she saw a few faint stars, but the sky was beginning to lighten. Dawn couldn't be more than an hour away.

"The only ones I'm interested in killing is them Indians, and that one in particular. We don't need to kill everyone who looks cross-eyed at us."

"You turning yellow on me?"

"No, but we started out to stir up trouble for the stinking Blackfeet and to make up for Jake's death."

Jake? Jake Wilhite. They were talking about that deputy and the way this man had said Jake's name . . . it was personal. Could it be . . . ?

"Don't forget my sister."

Sister? Tess's mind whirled helplessly. Whose sister?

"Okay, and for what he did to your sister. Now you're talking about killing white folks?"

"We've already done that. Remember that farmer who came at us with a pitchfork."

"Yeah, but I—"

"Besides, I'm not the one who shot a kid."

"You know that was an accident."

A kid . . . shot a kid. Cassie. Tess wished she could free her hands long enough to scratch the man's eyes out.

"I say you're gun-happy," he said to his partner.

"And I say if you can't handle a man's job, step out of the way and I'll do it."

"Look here, just because your pappy is the— hey!"

The two men stumbled into Tess's view as one grabbed the other by the throat and danced him backward. They both wore Indian masks, but the one with his back to her and his hand on the other's throat had red hair. And what had the other been about to say . . . something about someone's father.

Red hair. His sister.

Tess sucked in a breath. Sweet Jesus, it was Alred Long, the marshall's son! And the other man . . . honey-lamb. The dream! They had both been in the strange dream. A mustache that looked like a caterpillar. But he'd shaved it off . . . because Millie Long didn't like mustaches!

Buck Wilhite.

She closed her eyes, limp from piecing together the puzzle and the import of what it meant. She felt stupid for not guessing it all before now. If she'd looked more carefully at who would be Storm's most rabid enemies, Red and Buck would figure at the top of the list. Storm had killed Buck's brother, Jake, in a gunfight and he'd been caught spooning with Red's sister, Millie. And the two men hated Indians of all tribes, but especially the Blackfeet, who claimed the area around False Hope as their hunting grounds, their tribal lands.

So obvious, she thought. The badges had blinded her. She had known of their narrow minds, but hadn't thought they would tread so boldly on the other side of the law. Why hadn't she stopped to think about it, to put it all together? Might have saved herself and Storm and . . . What had happened to Aunt Mattie and Uncle Elmer? Had these men hurt them, murdered them? No, not murdered. They hadn't mentioned that . . . only a farmer with a pitchfork.

Beating down the panic that threatened to rise in her and cloud her judgment, she concentrated on saving herself and getting back to the ranch to check on her aunt and uncle. They might not have been hurt, she reasoned. She'd been outside when these two had pounced on her and knocked her senseless. Aunt Mattie and Uncle Elmer wouldn't have even known anything about it until they'd started worrying about her staying outside so long. Then they'd go looking for her, not find her, and Uncle Elmer would saddle a horse and start searching the area while Aunt Mattie stayed at the house and waited for Storm and Brown Otter to return.

Yes, that's how it would have happened, she told herself. And Red and Buck were still seeking their revenge, so that meant that Storm and Brown Otter were out there somewhere, probably looking for her.

They'll be here in no time, she thought, clutching at any scrap of comfort she could find. And these two weasels will be no match for them.

A gurgling noise emitted by Buck, whose throat was being closed off by Red, snagged her drifting attention. With a burst of panic-driven strength, Buck threw Red off him and sucked in air like a man who had been held underwater. He massaged his throat and retreated from Red.

"You're crazy, man," Buck said, his voice a rasp. "You got blood on your hands, and now you want to take a bath in it. Crazy."

"You watch your mouth. You almost let something slip, you ignorant jackass." Red flung a finger at her. "You think she ain't sharp as a whip? Hell, she already knows too much, I tell you. She's sitting there right this minute memorizing the sound of our voices and next time we talk to her on the street, she'll go running to my—the marshall."

The two masks turned in her direction and Tess could feel the intense stares behind them. She tried to look innocent, as innocent as one could look trussed up to a tree with a filthy gag in her mouth. Averting her gaze, she strove for an appearance of distraction. If they thought she had recognized them, they'd kill her for sure.

"She's pretty," Red murmured. "I tried to start something up with her, but she never would give me the time of day."

"Now who's talking too much?"

Red laughed behind the mask. "You think every man in False Hope ain't tried to catch her eye? Hell, she and Millie are the only good-looking single women around."

"Yeah, and that dung-heap of an Indian has had them both," Buck said, his hands curling into fists at his sides. "He's ruined them for decent men like you and me."

Tess wished she could laugh, but she closed her throat to it. Lord, did they actually think *they* were decent? Murdering, lying, thieving dogs like them?

She tested the ropes around her wrists, hoping to find a loose knot. Any bit of encouragement would be welcome, she thought, but then Red took a step in her direction and she froze. Fear washed over her like a wave of ice water and the hairs at the back of her neck lifted.

"Yeah, she's a looker." Another step. Spurs jingled. Hands flexed. "You know what her problem is? She ain't never had a white man, so she don't know what she's missing. She thinks that filthy redskin has the only stiff one in the Rockies, that's her problem." His hand moved to cup himself. "But I got a cure for that, uh-huh. I surely do."

"Hey, there, partner," Buck said, his voice taking on a whining plea. "We got other fish to fry."

"I got me a hankering." The hand cupping his privates swung out to grab hold of Tess's tangled hair. He gave it a yank, tilting her face up. The toe of his boot inched up under the hem of her skirt and petticoats, moved on to her calf, to her knee, the spur leaving long, bleeding scratches. "Um-um-um. You got good legs, gal. Bet your titties are right nice, too. Did that Indian scum suck on them? Huh? Did you like it? Oh, baby, you'll like it a heap more when I'm on top of you and inside you."

Tess began to tremble, and she couldn't stop herself. Sweat beaded on her upper lip, her forehead, and ran between her breasts. She wished she could faint.

"Partner, don't get all worked up," Buck cautioned. "We can have our fun later."

"I'll have mine now."

Red knelt on one knee and ran a hand over Tess's hair, along the side of her neck, over her shoulder. He palmed her left breast and rubbed it, over and over again. Tess struggled against the ropes, not caring that she was sheering off pieces of skin and making herself bleed. Red chuckled inside the mask and caught her nipple between his fingers through the layers of her clothing, giving it a painful tweak. She wriggled and tried to scream, but only a gurgling noise emerged.

"Hey, there now," Buck whined. "You don't want to do that to her."

"Yes, I do." He massaged her other breast while he continued to pinch her left nipple. "Oh, yeah. I like this."

His hand slid from her breast and over her quivering stomach, down, down, between her legs. When she tried to squeeze her thighs more tightly together, he laughed, clamped his hands on her knees, and forced them apart, but only the couple of inches allowed by the ropes. Frowning, he studied the bonds.

Yes, yes! Untie me. Tess held her breath, hoping, praying.

His hands moved to a knot, tested it.

"We ought to keep our eyes peeled, don't you think?" Buck asked, moving with mincing steps toward his partner.

"She's tied up so tight, I can't get at her," Red observed.

Untie me. Hurry. Do it, you sack of horse manure. And then I'll kick what little brains you've got right out your ears.

Did Millie know? Did she know what an insane, violent, demented brother she had? And what about Marshall Long? Did he realize that his own twisted teachings had created a son who couldn't see right from wrong anymore? Was the marshall in on this plot? Maybe he had decided to turn a blind eye on his son and his deputy and their lawless deeds.

"So leave her be. We got other things to be concerned about." Buck whirled around. "You hear something?"

Red stood up. Tess closed her eyes, half-relieved, half-disappointed. If only he'd untie her . . .

"I don't hear nothing and neither do you. You're just trying to get my mind off this little whore here. What's the matter? You don't like women? You don't want to take a turn with her?"

"Sure I like the looks of her, but we didn't take her just to have a poke at her, did we?" Buck tipped his head sideways. "Don't you hear that? Sounded like a rustling." He sniffed the air like a dog after a scent. "Might be them."

Them? Tess shifted her eyes frantically from side to side, trying to see for herself if help had arrived.

Red stood over her, planting a foot on either side

of her hips. Looking up fearfully, she found herself staring at a bulge between his legs.

"I could take that gag out of her mouth, I reckon, and make her suck me dry." Red chuckled. "What you bugging your eyes out for, Injun lover? You'd like it, and even if you didn't, you'd do it or I'd break your pretty neck."

"You don't want them to come up on us and find you with your pants around your ankles, do you?" Buck moved farther away and sniffed again. "I smell Injun."

"Bull," Red growled. "They ain't gonna get here until after daybreak, I tell you. They'll be chasing our old tracks all night before they go back to the Summar Ranch. Then they'll spot the fresh tracks we made."

"I hate to tell you this, but it's daybreak."

Red looked up at pale golden bars of light falling through the tree branches. "Aw, hell."

"So they're coming, right?"

"Yeah, shouldn't be long now." Red stepped over Tess and his spurs jingled as he strode out of her sight. "Better check your weapon and make sure the powder's dry."

Blood tickled her legs where Red's spurs had torn through her stockings and broken the skin. She tried to form a plan in her mind in case Storm and Brown Otter showed up to help. But what could she do? Futility battered her, mocked her. She jerked at the ropes binding her wrists and got another flash of pain for her efforts.

An owl hooted and bird songs filtered through the forest with the advancing dawn. Mist rose in pockets. Bugs stirred in thick carpets of leaves and pine needles and grass. A twig snapped.

"You hear that?" Buck whispered.

"Get in place," Red commanded.

Tess shut her eyes and writhed in frustration. She couldn't see them but sensed that Red and Buck had darted somewhere behind her. What had they heard?

A rustling noise straight ahead made Tess focus her attention on the spot from where the sounds seemed to originate. Someone was coming!

Wriggling and making desperate noises in her throat, she tried to make herself conspicuous. She heard a husky chuckle behind her. What were they laughing about?

Ahead of her, branches parted and Storm stepped into the small clearing. Her eyes smarted with sudden, gushing tears even as his widened at the sight of her. Brown Otter appeared behind him. They came forward, eager to untie her. Tess sobbed in utter relief.

Red. Buck. Where were they? What were they doing? Oh, God. Was she bait . . . was she leading Storm and Brown Otter into a trap? She tried to shake her head, frantic to convey the danger they were walking toward.

Storm was only a step away from her when the first gunshot rent the air and threw him backward.

Chapter 22

Before he hit the ground, Storm was rolling and scrambling and ducking behind a boulder. His neck stung and he glanced at where his shirt was torn away and blood-splattered. He touched his neck and felt ragged flesh, then examined his shoulder. Didn't feel like a bullet was in there, so he figured he'd received only a flesh wound. Lucky. He hadn't seen or heard his attacker until it was too late.

Catching sight of Brown Otter no more than twenty feet from him and well hidden behind a massive oak, he nodded and lifted a hand to signal that he was all right. Brown Otter made a circle in the air with his forefinger, and Storm nodded again, telling him to go ahead and circle around to get a jump on whoever had fired on them.

Storm surveyed the area and saw a rustling in the bushes behind where Tess was bound.

Tess. Storm's heart froze for an instant, then shuddered in his chest. She looked so frightened, so alone. Her eyes were wild and unfocused, and she was trussed so tightly to the tree that she could barely move. Her hair fell, damp and tangled. Her skirt and shirtwaist were muddy and torn. For a few crazy moments, he was sorely tempted to run into the clearing and slice the ropes from around her body. Damn the bullets. But then logic struck his mind like a shower of ice, and he took a deep breath and concentrated on a realistic plan of action.

"Hey, redskin! Got your white woman tied up here. Got my rifle aimed at the back of her pretty head, too. You'd better show yourself or I'll blow a hole through her."

Redskin. Maybe the man didn't know about Brown Otter, Storm thought. Good. He started moving by inches in the opposite direction Brown Otter had taken. He'd circle, too, toward the voice. Another shot rang out. Storm dove for a clump of bushes and heard a bullet zing over his head. Crouching, he ran from the bramble bushes and found better shelter behind a massive tree trunk. Reaching back, he eased his revolver out from under his belt where it pressed against his spine. In his mind's eye, he visualized the area where the voice had emerged. With a quick, hitching breath, he stepped out from behind the tree, aimed and fired off a shot. Leaves burst from the bushes and he heard a startled oath, then fire and smoke bloomed from a rifle.

The shots were wide and Storm used the next seconds to cover more ground and find another hiding place behind a moss-covered swell of land. He lay flat and peered over the top at Tess. He could see the whites of her eyes as she tried to look around her. She squirmed in her bindings. He was close enough now to see thin lines of blood on her wrists and legs. Her skirt was hiked up to past her knees and he didn't want to think about how it might have gotten that way.

She'd been here for hours. When he and Brown Otter had returned to the ranch, her aunt and uncle had been frantic. She'd gone out for a breath of air and had never returned. Her uncle had saddled up a horse and gone looking for her, but it was dark and rainy and he'd been unable to find any tracks. But when the sky had lightened and dawn had slipped closer, Storm and Brown Otter had located a trail and had followed it to this place.

Seemed as if that's exactly what had been expected. He'd walked into a trap and Tess was the bait. So her kidnapper was someone who knew of his involvement with her. Someone who knew both her and him.

Another shot took out a piece of mossy ground, inches from his nose. Storm ducked lower, gauged his next spurt and the boulder in the near distance. Could he make it? Every muscle bunched, and he readied to spring into the open and make a mad dash—

Click.

Centuries of collective instinct and years of survival skills kicked in, and Storm rolled across the ground before his mind could catch up. A bullet dug into the earth right where he'd been lying and another missed his knee by inches. But by then Storm could see his attacker, and he charged through the underbrush, past trees and rocks, and plowed into the man who aimed the rifle at him. The rifle tilted up and the next bullet soared through the tree branches.

The two men hit the ground with Storm on top. He grabbed the rifle in one hand and wrenched it from the man's grasp, then shoved a fist into his face. But it wasn't a face. A mask. A corner of his mind registered that it was not a Blackfeet mask, but Hunkpapa Sioux. He sent his fist into the mask again, cracking it down the center so that it split in half and fell away. The face beneath was familiar . . .

A fist came up and struck Storm in the jaw, jarring him, making him see double for a moment. With grim determination, Storm pressed the tip of his revolver between the man's eyes and the fight went out of him. The man tensed and his pale-blue eyes bulged in their sockets. Grabbing a fistful of his shirt, Storm stood up and hauled his prey up with him. He shoved him back against a tree and leaned into him. The features triggered a memory . . . then dropped into place.

"The deputy," Storm growled. "That means your partner is the marshall's son."

"Don't kill me."

"Why not?" He pulled back the trigger. "You're trying to kill me."

"You killed my brother."

"In a fair gunfight. I didn't want to face him off, but he forced it. I went back to my people to live in peace, but you wouldn't let me alone. And now you've dragged Tess into it. If you've hurt her, I'll—"

"That was Red's idea. But you shoulda kept your hands off her. She was a respected lady until—"

A gunshot rang out, followed by a wild thrashing, grunting and thudding. Another man wearing a Sioux spirit mask staggered backward into the clearing and Brown Otter leapt after him. Storm saw them from the corner of his eye, and in the second his attention was divided, the deputy he held at gunpoint shoved a knee up into his groin and bit a plug out of the back of his hand.

The spasms of pain loosened his hold and his attention, and the deputy seized the moment to slam Storm's gun-toting hand back against the tree.

A mad fight for the Colt had them gnashing teeth and trading punches. The gun skittered from Storm's hand and across a carpet of leaves. Before Storm could retrieve it, a knife blade flashed past his eyes. He retreated, crouched and winded, as he faced the deputy, who waved a long-bladed knife at him. The man passed the weapon from hand to hand, grinning like a drunken cat, bouncing on the balls of his feet.

"Come on, Injun. Come and get me now, why doncha? I'll slice you up for dog meat, I will. I'm right handy with a knife, you know. I can slit your throat, neat as can be."

From the direction of the clearing came thuds and thumps and grunting moans as the fight between Brown Otter and the other deputy continued. Storm bent his knees and slipped a hand down to his knee-length moccasin to withdraw his own knife, short-bladed and deadly sharp. He grinned when his opponent's pale eyes narrowed.

"You don't much like a fair fight, do you, Wilhite?" Storm jeered.

He made the first swipe, anxious to be done with the wiry man so he could help Brown Otter defeat Red. A niggling fear for Tess's safety kept buzzing in his brain. The men were fighting near her. What if a knife were thrown, a weapon fired . . . in her direction?

Wilhite's knife flashed and the tip ripped a two-inch tear in Storm's shirt. Storm lunged once, twice, missing both times. The deputy danced out of range, his eyes glassy, spittle foaming at the corners of his mouth. For all his bravado, Storm could smell fear on him.

Wilhite sprang forward, slashing up and down and sideways. Storm circled out of his way, chose his moment, and aimed for Wilhite's neck with his own knife. But the deputy anticipated and jumped out of range. Storm's forward momentum sent him past the deputy. His foot struck a rock and he fell forward, landing hard on his knees.

His hackles rose and he felt the man's charge behind him, felt danger crack around him like a thousand whips. In a split-second he flipped the knife in his hand and swept his arm up and back just as Wilhite shouted triumphantly of his premature victory.

The blade of Storm's knife found a target and sliced Wilhite's face. The victory shout became a screeching howl. Wilhite kicked out blindly, and his boot heel struck Storm in the head, shoving him forward, over the rise of land and tumbling like a rock to the edge of the clearing. As he fell, Storm glimpsed Wilhite, his hands clutching his face and blood dripping between his fingers.

"My eye . . . My eye . . . !" Wilhite cried.

His hands and feet gained purchase again, and Storm started to climb back up to the man and finish him off, but a gunshot spun him around.

Brown Otter staggered, clutching his chest. His knees gave way and he fell. Red, no longer masked, aimed his revolver again, this time at Brown Otter's head.

Howling with rage, Storm flew across the ground and into Red. The two fell and the gun rattled from Red's hand. Rolling and punching and kicking, the fight raged, both men baring their teeth and using all their strength. Red's hand shot up and grasped Storm's throat, squeezing until Storm thought he'd crush his windpipe. Gasping for breath, he shoved the heel of his hand against Red's chin and jammed his knee into Red's stomach.

They rolled again. Punches were landed. Storm's

knuckles stung. Blood ran from his nose, from inside his mouth. He gained leverage and swung hard, driving his fist into the side of Red's face. The blow was sufficient to spin the man and make him stagger. Cocking back his fist again, Storm aimed for Red's nose.

Tess made a squeaking sound of panic and in the next moment another gunshot rang out and a bullet grazed Storm's cheek. He spun about, his eyes filled with burning tears, his face feeling as if it were on fire. The stench of gunpowder and blood stung his nostrils. Another bullet plowed into the dirt at Red's feet. The man jumped back and glared at the hillside.

"Buck, you damned idiot!"

Buck Wilhite staggered on the hillock, his boots slipping on loose rocks and moss. One bloody hand covered the right side of his face, and in his left hand he tried to aim his rifle at Storm to fire off another shot.

"I can't see! All this damned blood." The rifle wavered, swinging between Storm and Red. "Which one are you, Buck?"

"Here!" Storm shouted.

The rifle swung away from Storm. Red raised his hands, realizing too late that Storm had out-foxed him.

"Noooo!"

The rifle kicked and Red grunted and grabbed at his chest. His eyeballs protruded from their sockets, and his lips moved, but no sound came out. He fell to his knees and turned his head to glare at Storm.

"Stinking Injun—" Red sucked in a final, shuddering breath and crumbled sideways.

"Red? Did I get him?" Buck called, the rifle wavering toward Storm again. "Red? Aw, damn . . ."

Ducking to make himself a smaller target, Storm started to take the hill and the wounded man on it. He sensed movement . . . not Tess . . . another. Whirling, he saw that Brown Otter had his revolver in one hand. Still stretched out on the ground, his shirt wet with blood, Brown Otter aimed and fired. Fired true.

Buck squealed when the bullet bit him and fell backward out of sight. Storm knelt beside his cousin and turned him onto his back.

"How bad?" he asked in Blackfeet.

"Missed my heart."

"Good."

"Got one of my lungs, I think."

"Hang on, my brother." He grabbed Brown Otter's knife and looked at the crest of land but saw no sign of Buck, so he scrambled toward Tess and jerked the gag from her mouth. She sucked in air and released a sob.

"Storm . . . oh, God. Storm."

He duck-walked around her, slipped the blade under the ropes and sawed at them, cutting her free. She wrapped her arms around his neck and pressed her wet face against the side of his stinging neck. Her sobs tore chunks from his heart, and he grappled with emotions so intense they scared him. He stroked her hair and gave thanks to the Creator for sparing her life.

"Th-they were after y-you," she said, sobs chopping up her words.

"Did they—hurt you?" He couldn't ask what he wanted to know. She was too fragile, and he was afraid she'd fly into pieces if he asked and she had to answer with danger still chilling the air.

"No. I'm just so s-scared. I th-thought . . . Oh, Storm."

She'd thought she would die, he finished for her.

Thought that her life was over because he had placed her in the path of death.

"If they harmed you . . . if they had—" He bit off the rest and held her tightly against him. "Come on. We have to leave here. Brown Otter is injured. He's losing blood."

"Oh, no." She stirred, lifting her tear-streaked face from his shoulder. "Brown Otter . . ." Easing herself from Storm's arms, she stood up and the ropes fell away from her. "Let me look at him."

Her steps were void of her usual grace as she traversed the clearing and knelt beside Brown Otter. Storm glanced at the swell of land again, waiting for the other deputy to reappear. He listened, but heard nothing other than Tess's soft voice comforting Brown Otter while she examined the wound. She tore off a big piece of her petticoat and wrapped it around Brown Otter.

"You're right," she said to Storm. "We have to get him back to the ranch where I can work on him. The bullet is lodged near his lung, I think."

"In my lung," Brown Otter said, coughing up red liquid.

"No, I don't think so. But your lungs are bruised. Help me get him on his feet, Storm. Those men have horses tied up back there. . . ." She pointed south, behind the tree where she'd been tied.

"We have horses, too." Storm nodded in the opposite direction. "That way." He grabbed one of Brown Otter's arms and placed it around his shoulders, then hauled his cousin to his feet. Brown Otter moaned, and his eyes rolled back in his head. His eyelids fluttered and drooped.

"He's out," Tess observed.

Storm bent down and shoved Brown Otter up and over his uninjured shoulder. He was heavy, but carrying him like a sack of potatoes would be easier than trying to drag him through the woods to their horses.

"You were shot." Tess placed a hand on his bloody shoulder, his stinging cheek.

"The bullets just took some skin."

Her cool fingertips caressed a swelling bruise beneath his right eye and a throbbing cut on his lower lip.

"Storm, it's over, isn't it? These were the men who were trying to harm you, to brand you and Brown Otter as horse thieves." Her eyes widened and she gasped. "Aunt Mattie and Uncle Elmer!"

"They're fine," he assured her. "They weren't harmed." Taking her by the hand, he started for the horses, his knees and thighs trembling with the exertion. He knew they'd staked the horses only a short distance away, but the trip felt like a mile. He almost shouted for joy when he spotted the two horses ahead of them.

Using the last of his strength, he slung Brown Otter over the back of one and helped Tess up on the other. He pointed to the narrow trail that led down from the higher ground toward the valley.

"Go that way."

"What do you mean?" She stared down at him as if he'd lost his senses. "I'm not going anywhere without you."

"Yes, you go. I'll catch up." He laid a hand on her thigh, calming her. "I'm going to get the white men's horses and their bodies. I'll be right behind you. But don't wait. Brown Otter is dying. You have to get him to the ranch and use your medicine on him." He squeezed her thigh through her skirt. "Do this for me, Tess."

She clamped her lips together in a stubborn line, then heaved a sigh. "All right." Her eyes narrowed. "But you'd better be right behind us, or I'll track you down and make you sorry."

He grinned. "Pluck."

"Wh-what?" She blinked her blue-green eyes at him.

Grabbing the halter, he turned her horse in the right direction. "Never mind." After tying the reins of Brown Otter's horse to the saddle beneath Tess's shapely rump, he whacked the side of the horse with the flat of his hand. The horses set off at a trot.

"Hurry up!" Tess shouted back at him. "And be careful!"

Tramping through the woods again, Storm located the other two horses easily. He brought them to the clearing and heaved Red's body up on one. After scrambling up the hill to collect the other body, he was confused when all he found was blood. He thrashed around, looking under bushes and behind rocks before noticing the faint trail of blood droppings leading into the denser woods. He followed them a ways. Some places the blood was more than drops, staining the leaves and grasses liberally. Looking ahead at the thick woods, he felt his legs tremble with weakness. His breath soughed past his swollen lips, and the pain in his shoulder streaked down his side and into his hip.

The man was dead in there somewhere, he thought. He saw the glimmer of more blood ahead. Yes, dead. Storm considered going back for the horses and trailing Wilhite on horseback until he finally found his body to take back to False Hope, but weariness overtook him.

Let the white eyes worry about this one, an inner voice suggested, and he was more than willing to listen. He was tired, exhausted, and he wanted to return to the ranch to check on Tess and Brown Otter. Those were the people he needed to track, not Buck Wilhite.

Thrashing through the woods again, he retraced his steps and groaned mightily as he heaved himself up onto the back of the other horse. He bent over the animal's neck, resting for a few moments, his cheek pressed against warm horse flesh and coarse mane. He counted his heartbeats and the corresponding throb in his shoulder and the other cheek.

Finally gaining a second wind, he straightened and dug his heels into the horse's flanks. He snagged the dangling reins of the other horse and jerked them to get the blaze-faced mare moving.

The gray he was riding was strong and sure-footed. Storm let the reins go slack, giving the steed his head. He glanced back at the mare, making sure Red's body hadn't slipped off.

A ray of morning sun speared through the tree branches to find him. Sighing, Storm turned his face up to the light and recited a prayer for his people to the Sun God.

Behind him in the tall grass Buck Wilhite, bloody and nearly mad with pain, breathed a sigh of relief. With gritty determination, he heaved himself to his feet and headed for the stream to wash his wounds. Just to spite those redskinned sons of bitches, he'd live to see another dawn.

Lying on the living-room sofa of Elmer and Mattie Summar's log farm house, Storm let his eyes fill with the vision of the white, two-headed snake. It had come to pass. The snake had bitten him on the neck and then it had bitten itself, thus saving him.

That's not how Buck had planned it or what he'd been trying to do, but that had been the result. Buck had killed his own partner, sparing Storm's life. The mystery of it all startled him, humbled him. He felt the wolf inside stirring, whining, stretching. Wanting a mate, he thought, and sighed with a keen yearning for Tess. A dark cloud seemed to hover in his mind whenever he thought of taking Tess as his mate. Was he asking too much, accepting too much risk, placing his happiness above hers? Ah, if only the answers came as easily as the questions . . .

Mattie peered over the back of the sofa at him.

"You dying, too?"

"I don't think so."

"Tess sent me for more warm water. You gonna be okay or should I send her out here to you after she's done with your cousin?"

"I will live. How's Brown Otter?"

The old woman chewed on her lower lip. "She got the bullet out, but he's still bleeding something bad, and his lungs are rattling like they're full of bones."

A moan floated down from upstairs.

"I gotta go." She rushed upstairs with the bucket, water sloshing over the sides.

Storm struggled up on one elbow and his shoulder screamed. He lay back in quick apology. The front door opened, and sunlight and Uncle Elmer rushed inside. The short man shut the door with a bang and pulled off his gloves and hat.

"Got the horses seen to, and I sent one of my ranch hands to town to tell Marshall Long to come and collect his son." He shook his balding head. "Damn shame, but I can't say I'm surprised. That Red always was too big for his britches."

"He wouldn't rest until he killed us both— maybe even Tess, too."

"Well, he's getting a good rest now." The old rancher sat in the padded chair across from the sofa. "We couldn't find that other feller, but we seen his trail. He might still be alive."

Storm shrugged. "Then he'll turn up. He better hope he doesn't turn up where I can get at him."

The older man chuckled. "You feeling well enough to answer a couple of questions for me?"

Storm nodded, shifting on the sofa to confront the other man.

"You love my niece?"

Storm must have looked as if he'd been socked in the gut, because the old man's lips twitched before he finally gave in to the grin.

"The reason I ask is because I love her, you see. I set quite a store on her. After what you two have been through, it's only natural that you cling to each other. But I want to know if you love her."

Storm found he couldn't look the man in the eye when he answered. He stared at the beamed ceiling. "Yes." It cost him, that one word. In saying it, he revealed his heart and ignored the common sense he valued. The easy thing would have been to deny his love.

"That's what I figured." The old man was quiet for a minute or two. "Got one more question for you, if you're up to it."

The urge to tell him that he was too tired to answer was great, but he nodded again and braced himself.

"Where you planning to live with her? False Hope? You see yourself getting a job there, do you?"

Storm cut his eyes sideways. "That's more than one question."

"Answer whichever you're a mind to."

Storm ran a hand down the front of his sticky, dirty, tattered shirt. Something thumped to the floor upstairs and Storm held his breath and gazed up, listening. He could hear Tess talking and Mattie saying something back to her, but the words were muffled.

"They'll be down in a bit. I told the ranch hand to tell John to come on out, too, but I imagine Tess will have your cousin fixed up long before John gets here."

"She's a good medicine woman."

"I figured her to be right smart."

"She saved my life." Not Minipoka. Not the Creator. Tess. Tess had saved him, brought him back to life as she had done the dead baby of Brown Otter's wife.

"You gonna live in town then. Gonna work somewhere there. What kind of work do you do? I know you used to do some jobs for white men, didn't you?"

"I was a guide for a while."

"Not much call for guides in False Hope."

Storm swung his feet to the floor and sat up. "I won't live in town. I won't go back to living in the white world."

"Oh, so Tess is going to become a Blackfeet." Uncle Elmer scratched at his whiskers. "Reckon she'll fit in among your people?"

"I know what you are really asking, and I have no answers. You think I haven't asked the same questions? I have tried to see ahead, to reach out to our tomorrows and shape them into days of love and peace. All I know is that I won't live in town, and I would not ask Tess to live among the Blackfeet."

"How come?"

He glanced sharply at the old man. "Because I would be asking too much."

"How you see that?"

Biting back his irritation, he managed to answer patiently, "She would have to uproot her whole life. Her family—at least her brother and sister-in-law—would not approve. They would part from her, and this would break Tess's heart. I won't do that to her."

"Hmmm." The rancher pulled a leather pouch from his pocket and pinched from it a plug of tobacco, which he stuck into a pocket of his inner cheek. "If I were you, I'd ruminate some more on this. I get the feeling you don't know Tess as well as you think you do. She's always been headstrong—more like, strong in the head. You understand my meaning?"

Storm shook his head, losing track of the old man's words.

"What I'm trying to get across is . . ." He paused and spit tobacco juice into a tin can at his feet. Leaning back in his chair, he grinned. "She's partial to thinking for herself. Been doing it most of her life." He chuckled and glanced up when a door hinge squeaked. "Here they come."

Chapter 23

Upstairs, Tess moved away from where Brown Otter slept in her aunt's big, four-poster bed and crossed the room to the window.

Aunt Mattie opened the bedroom door and the hinges creaked. "Let's leave him be, honey. He won't be coming around for an hour or so. You done good, Tess. John couldn't have done any better getting that bullet out and stitching him up."

"Thanks." Tess rolled down her sleeves and stared at the two puffs of tan dust bouncing along the road leading to the ranch house. "Somebody's coming. . . . " The dust separated like a cloud scattered by the wind, and she could make out a rider in front and a horse and buggy following at a distance. Squinting, she focused on the rider for a few moments before she could see any features. A ruddy face. White mustache. "Oh, it's Marshall Long. I guess that's John bringing up the rear in the buggy. The marshall's riding all-out."

"Sure. His boy's been killed and he's frantic, I reckon."

Brown Otter stirred and grunted. Tess dashed back to his bedside, but he slept soundly, his color not as richly bronze as usual. He'd lost so much blood, it would be weeks or months before his full strength returned. The bullet had nicked his lung, bruising it, and had buried deep in his chest. Tess had begun to think she wouldn't be able to extract it without killing him. But patience and steady hands had served her well.

Aunt Mattie picked up a basin of bloody water and rags and left the room. Tess checked her reflection in the full-length mirror and shuddered. *My stars and gold bars!* She looked like a spook with her hair flying in all directions, and her skirt and blouse were as dirty and torn as a scarecrow's. *Why, they ought to stake her out in the cornfield.*

Smiling ruefully, she glanced out the window again and her heart stuttered. Marshall Long swung a leg over his horse and stared at the house as if he despised the very sight of it. She'd never seen such stark hatred on a face before, except on Storm's when he'd confronted Marshall Long in the jail. Tess opened the window to let in a chilly breeze. John stopped the buggy and leaped out of it, rushed to the marshall, and grabbed him by the arm.

"Marshall, please. Let's hear what they have to say first."

"Get off me." With a vicious swipe, the marshall caught John in the jaw and sent him sprawling to the ground. "Stay out of my way unless you want to end up like my son."

"Oh, no . . ." Tess spun from the window and ran out of the room and down the stairs. "Storm, Uncle Elmer, the marshall's outside and he's—"

"Redskin!" The marshall's voice cut through the door and rang like a warning bell. "Get your filthy hide out here!"

Having stopped half-way down the stairs, Tess

gripped the banister and her gaze clung to Storm's. "Don't go out there, Storm. He's crazy. I saw him hit John just now."

"I'm coming inside if I have to, Injun!" the marshall yelled. "One way or the other, you're dying today."

Uncle Elmer peered out the window. "Yup. He looks crazy as a loon."

"Do you see John?"

"Yup. He's standing way off to one side, clear of the marshall, which is a good place to be." Uncle Elmer eyed Storm. "What you gonna do?"

"Go out there."

"No!" Tess ran down the steps and stationed herself in front of the door. "You can't. He—he'll kill you."

"Maybe. Or maybe I'll kill him." Storm reached back and removed his Colt from under his belt. "I'm glad I found my gun when I was looking for Wilhite's body. Looks like it's going to come in handy." He checked his ammunition and pushed the gun back under his beaded belt, against his backbone. "Move out of the way, Tess. This isn't your fight. It's mine."

She shook her head.

"Tess," Uncle Elmer said, his tone gruff. "Do as the man says. Step aside."

She couldn't fight them both. Looking from her uncle to Storm, she knew she was no match for this bristling male determination. Holding Storm's gaze, she moved away from the door and hoped he could see in her eyes all the things he was to her.

"How is Brown Otter?"

Brown Otter. She drew in a quick breath. Lord, she'd clean forgot about him. "He's resting. I got the bullet out and I believe he'll mend."

"I knew you'd pull him through."

"Injun!" A fist pounded on the door, making Tess jump and Aunt Mattie screech like an owl.

Storm's eyes went as cold and hard as granite, and he moved with the swiftness of a river. Flinging open the door, he filled the entrance, startling the marshall enough to send the man stumbling backward. Righting himself and gaining his balance again, the marshall sneered under his bushy, white mustache.

"About time you slinked out here, you skunk."

Tess flew to the window to look out. Shoving open the two glass panels, she stuck out her head. John was no more than three feet from her, edging toward the porch. She could see the marshall, then she saw Storm as he walked out of the house and off the porch.

The marshall retreated. Good, Tess thought. Go away. Take your son and go.

But when the marshall stopped, she realized he had paced off the traditional twenty. His gun hand hovered above a silver-handled butt. Storm's hands were slightly out from his sides, too, as though he wore a gun belt. Only he didn't. Couldn't the marshall see that? Or didn't he care?

"He's unarmed, marshall," John shouted before ducking behind a wash pot full of red geraniums.

"He doesn't care," Storm said, his tone deathly in its deep-throated monotone. "He shot my sister when she was unarmed, didn't you, lawman?"

Marshall Long's mustache twitched and his eyes narrowed and widened and narrowed again. "That's right, Injun. She spoiled my aim and I shot her. If she hadn't gotten in the way, you'd be dead and buried now and my boy would be alive."

"Red kidnapped me," Tess shouted out the window. "He would have raped and killed me if it weren't for Storm."

"You shut your trap, you Injun's whore," Marshall Long growled back at her, never taking his gaze from Storm. "My boy was only using you as bait to draw out this stinking coyote."

Uncle Elmer came to stand behind Tess. "What's this about him killing Storm's sister?"

"The marshall shot her," Tess told him. "His sister told me herself what happened before she died."

"Well, hell's fire, girl, why didn't you say something? I wouldn't have sent for the marshall if I'd known."

"I didn't know you'd sent for him," she hissed back. "I was upstairs tending to Brown Otter."

Uncle Elmer's small eyes tracked to the open door and the man-sized shadow falling onto the floor. "But Storm knew I sent for him and he let me do it."

A cold draft poured through her. Marshall Long wasn't the only one spoiling for a fight, and he wasn't the only one who had been baited either. Storm wanted this deadly confrontation. Tension built inside her, and she told herself to look away, to refuse to witness this insane battle of wills, but she couldn't. She was riveted.

Aunt Mattie came to stand with them at the window and spotted John.

"You stay right there, John Summar," Aunt Mattie whispered urgently to him. "Don't you try to be a hero."

John darted a look at the window. "He's crazy. The marshall has lost his mind."

"He never had a mind to lose," Tess shot back.

"Did you kill Buck, too?" the marshall asked.

"I tried. I hope he's dead up there in the mountains somewhere," Storm answered evenly. "I pray that the death birds are picking at his carcass while his soul turns to dust."

"Why, you . . ." The marshall sucked in a breath, expanding his chest, and the fingers of his gun hand quivered. "You've killed your last man, you son of a bitch."

He made his move, the gun appearing in his hand like magic, and fired. Tess screamed before she even knew the sound had come from her. The shot went wide, digging into a porch post and splintering wood. But before the marshall could squeeze off another shot, Storm had whipped his own gun out from under his belt, and in the next second Tess saw the marshall's eyes widen as he stared at the last mistake he'd ever make. He had believed that Storm was without a weapon, and his face reflected shock and horror. Tess saw a flickering smile cross Storm's face, then the gun bucked in his hand and the marshall grunted and pitched backward into the dirt. His body jerked once. That was all.

John stood up slowly from behind the flower pot. "You killed him."

"Damn right, he did," Uncle Elmer said. "Killed him before gettin' killed."

Storm walked smoothly toward the body and stood over it, staring at the twisted death mask, the glazed eyes. He pursed his lips and spit.

Tess gasped and covered her gaping mouth with her hand. Looking at him, she could see savagery glinting in his turbulent eyes, pride in the width of his shoulders, and sadness in the tense line of his lips. He was not a perfect man, but he was an honorable one.

She went to him, taking him by the hand. He lifted his gaze to hers, but his eyes were glassy, cold. Tess pulled gently, leading him away from the man he'd killed. Embracing him, she laid her cheek against his chest and listened to his steady heartbeat. The pungent smell of blood was on his shirt, and she remembered that he'd been wounded in the earlier gunfight.

She hugged him tighter, sensing that he was far away, that his emotions had been sent to a remote place and he had not—could not—summon them yet.

"Storm, come back to me," she whispered, turning her lips toward him and kissing his throat. "Please, Storm. I need you."

He swallowed, drew in a jerky breath as if it were his first in a long time, and released it on a tortured sigh. His arms came around her and he buried his face in the curve of her neck. She felt a shudder course through him.

"It's over," he murmured against her skin. "I am free of my burdens."

"Yes, yes." Tess ran her fingers through his hair and lifted his head to look at his face. "You can braid your hair again. Your mourning is over now that your sister's spirit can rest in peace."

His eyes glimmered, and she saw his heart and soul in them again. She stroked her fingertips over his torn, bloody shirt.

"They will never touch you again, AnadaAki."

She realized that one of his burdens had been to protect her from the men in masks, to make them regret ever laying a hand on her. Tears burned her eyes, and she knew she could never find words to express what he meant to her.

"Thank you, my brave Blackfeet." She laced her fingers with his. "You've avenged your sister's death and made the world safe for me again. You have cared for me as no man has ever cared for me. Come inside now and let me care for you."

Lifting a hand, he smoothed back her hair. "You've done enough for me."

"I don't think that's possible." She slipped her arm around his waist and made him walk with her to the house, glad when he didn't resist. For once he didn't seem to have any fight left in him.

"You think the law will be making more trouble for Storm?" Aunt Mattie asked when they were all sitting around her kitchen table, all except for Storm and Brown Otter, who were upstairs recuperating in the bedroom.

Tess had rested but had been unable to sleep, and had joined the others downstairs for a late breakfast.

"If they do, we were all witnesses to the shoot-out and can vouch for Storm," Uncle Elmer noted, staring intently at his nephew. "Ain't that right, John?"

John held his coffee cup in both hands and gazed broodingly into it. "The marshall was out of his head with grief, that's all."

"That's *not* all." Tess let her knife and fork clatter to her plate. "Can't you admit you're wrong about Storm and the other Blackfeet, John? The marshall wasn't grieving when he shot Storm's sister in cold blood."

John frowned. "What could he have been thinking?"

"He was thinking the same way lots of people in False Hope think," Tess said. "When the marshall and Red and Buck looked at Indians, all they saw were animals. Something less than human. So why not shoot them? *That's* what he was thinking."

John heaved a sigh and his face registered fatigue and confusion. "You loaded the bodies in your wagon, didn't you?"

Uncle Elmer nodded. "Sure did."

"I'll take it back to town and Tess can follow in the buggy. We'll bring the wagon back as soon as we can." He glanced at Tess. "Millie Long will have to be told."

"I'll help her through it," Tess said. "She'll probably feel guilty about all of this."

"Why?" Uncle Elmer asked.

"She was . . . well, she and Storm courted a little. The marshall caught them."

"That's why the marshall hated him so much?" John asked.

"Yes, and because Storm shot Deputy Jake Wilhite, Buck's brother, and because the marshall was a mean, gutless—" Tess looked past John at the two men who had entered the room. "Just what do you two think you're doing?"

"We're leaving. We have to go back to our people," Storm explained and Brown Otter nodded.

"No, Storm. Brown Otter's not fit to ride yet."

"I can ride. It is a short distance," Brown Otter informed her, but his face was pale and his limbs trembled.

"Let them go, Tess," John said.

"You stay out of this," Tess shot back with more venom than she'd intended.

John blinked in surprise, and his teeth clicked together.

"Storm, please stay the night. After what we've all been through—"

"You stay, Tess, but we're going home." The stubborn streak in Storm's voice was about a mile wide.

Her nerves, already stretched, snapped. She stood up and glared at him. "Yes, you go ahead. Pay me no mind. After all, I'm just a woman, so what do I know? Ignore me. I'm used to it." She marched past him, outside into the sunlight, out to the porch. Hens scattered, frightened by her sudden appearance. A squirrel sat on the bannister and scolded her. "Oh, shut up!" The rodent flipped its tail and skedaddled.

Big, gentle hands closed on her shoulders and forced her around. Storm dipped his head to catch her smoking gaze.

"You are not *just* a woman. You *are* woman, brave and strong and wise. And because you are all these things you understand that Brown Otter will rest easier in his own lodge, surrounded by his family. His wife and children and newborn babe will rest easier with him there, too. It's a short ride and he will make it without too much discomfort. And Minipoka will greet us and make a great fuss over him."

"You mean, her medicine will heal him," Tess said, knowing she was pouting, but not caring. If anyone deserved to pout, she did!

He cupped one side of her face in his hand and the contact of his skin on hers was like a magic potion. She felt her nerves settle and peace stole over her.

"Your medicine gave him back his life, Tess, as it gave me back mine. Minipoka's medicine will help him mend now that you have chased the curse of death from his body." He unfastened the top button of her blouse and nudged aside the material so he could touch the necklaces—one from him, one from his chief. "You and I have forged a bond that will never be broken."

Her heart flew to her throat and fluttered there.

"But it's time for me to return to my people. You are safe now among your family, so I won't worry about you, and you don't have to worry about me either."

Her lower lip trembled and she pulled it between her teeth to stop it. "You don't mind if I miss you, do you?"

He grazed her other cheek with his lips and then kissed the shell of her ear. His warm breath tingled, tickled. "I would have it no other way." As he drew back from her, his gray eyes were misty. "Do you think bad of me for killing those men?"

"No. Why would I? They were trying to kill us."

"Yes, but you are a healer and I . . ." His lips quirked. "I'm an Indian outlaw."

"Not anymore. We'll all tell the people in False Hope what happened, and you know what?"

"What?" He smoothed a hand over the top of her head and his eyes tracked it, eyes that were glowing and gentle and smoky-gray.

"Then you'll be an *Indian hero*." She pressed closer to him, her arms circling his waist. "You already are one to me."

He dipped his head and she lifted up on tiptoes. Their mouths met like lightning striking earth. Tess moaned and hugged him tighter. His lips and her lips opened like flowers seeking sun, and their tongues rejoiced together. His kiss became divine ravishment, and Tess's bones melted and a fevered heat raced beneath her skin.

Oh, how she wanted him, how she loved him. He was fire and wind, rock and wave. He was everything essential and beautiful, and she wanted to be part of him, not just for now but forever.

His hands moved over her, stroking and kneading and letting her know that he loved her body and knew it intimately. Everywhere he touched seemed to burn, to singe, to sizzle.

She didn't know she was crying until she tasted

the salty tears on her tongue. When he tasted them, he ended the ferocious kiss and drew his brows together in puzzlement.

"I don't want you to go," she admitted, her heart beginning to break. She buried her hands in his hair, clinging to the long, silky strands. Suddenly her pride seemed as insignificant as a gnat. "Take me with you back to the Blackfeet."

Sadness colored his eyes charcoal. "Tess, think of your family."

"I don't care about them."

"Yes, you do." He held her chin between his thumb and finger and tilted it up until her gaze met his again. "You must go back and sing my praises. How else will I become an Indian hero?"

She wanted to beat him with her fists and scream at him for being heartless, but she had given him her pride and all she had left was her courage. She'd need that in the weeks, the months, the years to come without him. Tess stepped out of his arms, out of his life.

Brown Otter leaned in the doorway and spoke in Blackfeet to Storm. Tearing his gaze from Tess, Storm looked at his cousin and answered with a grunt and a nod.

"If you're leaving, you'll want your horses," Uncle Elmer said, sliding past Brown Otter. "Come on, Storm. They're in the turnout. I'll help you saddle them."

Brown Otter sat heavily in the porch rocker. "I'll wait here," he said in English.

"I guess I'll bring the wagon around," John announced, sending a questioning glance toward Tess. "I wouldn't be in such a hurry, but I feel I should get the bodies back to town and notify Millie Long."

"Yes." Tess lifted her chin along with her spirits.

"I'll go with you, John. I should be the one to tell Millie."

John extended a grateful smile. "I'm sure it would be better coming from you." He strode in the direction of the barn where the wagon had been left in the shade.

"So, y'all are leaving us," Aunt Mattie said, coming out on the porch.

"Looks that way."

"Hold up, Tess. Let me run into the root cellar and fetch a couple of jars of that cucumber salad you and John love so much. Oh, and I'll send along a jar of my honey butter for Camilla." Aunt Mattie was already moving around to the back of the house and the root cellar before she'd finished the last sentence.

Left alone with Brown Otter, Tess felt awkward. Storm's cousin had been nearly hostile to her at times, and she knew he resented her involvement with Storm. After a few moments she decided to go inside the house until John arrived with the wagon.

"I must thank you for what you did for me," Brown Otter said before she could escape indoors.

Tess huffed out a breath. "*Must* you?" She shook her head. "I know you don't like me, but I have nothing against you, Brown Otter."

"It's not that I don't like . . ." He pressed his lips together and focused his dark eyes on the horizon. "Your medicine has given miracles to me and my family."

"But?" Tess asked, propping one hand on her hip and waiting for him to speak his mind. "You don't want me in your family, right? Well, it looks like you win, Brown Otter. Storm is going back to the Blackfeet, and he's not taking me with him, even though I asked him to."

Brown Otter turned his head slowly to look at her. "You would live with the Blackfeet?"

She looked down at her scuffed shoes, her throat tightening and tears stinging the back of her eyes. "Yes. I would live anywhere with Storm."

"What of your family and your life among them?"

Tess lifted a shoulder in a half-hearted shrug. "You'll laugh when I tell you this. . . . "

"No. I will not laugh."

She glanced at his impassive face. "Yes, I guess you won't." Resuming the study of her dirty shoes, she fought back tears of self-pity. "Among the people of False Hope, I'm Doc Summar's spinster sister; but among the Blackfeet people I'm AnadaAki, the white medicine woman." Although her eyes were full of tears, she lifted them to confront the Blackfeet warrior. "If you were me, Brown Otter, which would you rather be?"

Moments passed before Brown Otter gave an almost imperceptible nod and faced the horizon again.

When John brought the wagon around, Tess scrambled up into the buggy and took up the reins. Aunt Mattie ran around from the back of the house and handed up the glass jars of cucumbers and honey butter.

"Do you want to wait and say good-bye to Uncle Elmer and Storm?" John asked.

"No." Tess slapped the reins against the horse's back. "I've said all the good-byes I want to say for a while."

She sat bolt upright on the springboard seat and didn't even look back to make sure John was following her in the wagon or when Aunt Mattie called out a farewell to them.

*　　*　　*

Standing in the turnout while Elmer rounded up the pad saddles and halters, Storm watched the buggy and wagon roll away, his heart atremble.

A single tear tracked down his cheek before he brushed it away with a muttered curse.

Chapter 24

"**T**ess? Oh, Te-esss."

Blinking away the shroud of melancholy drooping around her mind, Tess stared blankly at Camilla before her sister-in-law's bemused smile registered and time resumed. Tess lifted her hands from the dishwater and stared at her wrinkled, white fingers.

"I'm sorry, Camilla, what were you saying?" Tess dried her hands on her apron and wondered how long she'd been standing at the sideboard with her hands plunged into a basin of soapy water. From the tepid temperature of the water, she guessed she'd been woolgathering for nigh on half an hour.

"Sit down, sit down. Let's talk, shall we?"

With growing suspicion, Tess sat at the table with Camilla.

Camilla grinned. "Do I look different?"

Tess scrutinized her, taking in her flushed cheeks and glowing eyes.

"I should look different," Camillia insisted.

Tess played out a hunch. "When are you due?"

"You guessed!" Camilla giggled again. "Yes, I'm

in a family way. John says our baby will likely be born in the early spring." She sighed and fell back in the chair. "You'll help me with it, won't you?"

Two days of being back with John and Camilla had only made Tess more determined to move out again and stay out. "John will help you. He knows all about babies."

Camilla was quiet for a few ticks of the clock. "You're leaving again, aren't you?"

Tess nodded.

"I was afraid of that. You've been moping about and—well, *you* look different, too."

"I look different?" Tess glanced down at her dark-blue dress, one she'd owned for a couple of years and often wore. "How so?" Good Lord, Camilla wasn't implying that she was pregnant, too!

Camilla's eyes moved, taking in Tess's features. "The way you're wearing your hair, for one thing."

Tess's hands flew up instinctively. She touched the wisps of curling hair at the nape and in front of her ears.

"You used to pile your hair up on your head real tight. Now you're pinning it sort of loose-like. Makes you look younger and fresher. And then there are those necklaces you've taken to wearing."

Tess touched them, her fingertips stroking the beads, the elk's teeth and the silver arrowhead. "I like them."

"And you love him, don't you?"

Tess's mouth opened, but she couldn't make the words come out. She'd meant to scoff and deny such a silly notion, but she found the lie too sticky and foul. Noticing her inability to answer, Camilla smiled with understanding and grasped Tess' hands in her own.

"It's all right, Tess. I don't know near as much as you do about the world, but I do know love when I see it. Oh, I don't understand it and I don't imagine many people do, but I know it when I see it and when I feel it. You're in love with him. That's what's different about you."

John cleared his throat and both women jumped. He smiled, standing in the doorway and rolling his shirtsleeves up to his elbows. His blond hair was tousled, and Tess could smell the outdoors on him.

"Back from your rounds, darling?" Camilla asked. "Me and Tess were having us a good, long talk."

"Tess, I think you'd better come outside."

"Why? Is something wrong?"

John crooked a finger mysteriously. "Just come outside, please. You, too, Cammie. You'll want to see this."

Curious, Tess stood up and went past John through the house and out onto the porch. Camilla and John joined her, and John pointed down the street. Looking in that direction, Tess gasped and Camilla followed suit.

"My stars and gold bars," Tess whispered, staring with wide-eyed wonder at the unusual procession heading her way.

Three riders, all on flashy Indian ponies, advanced slowly down the middle of False Hope's main street. People on the boardwalks stopped in their tracks to gawk. Wagons and buggies and horses and riders pulled off to one side to give the three colorful Indians plenty of room.

Eagle Talon, in full Blackfeet chief regalia, commanded the lead. His magnificent headdress proclaimed his high status, and his proud carriage vanquished any doubt of it. His spotted pony's mane and tail were braided, and he sat on a thick, white wolf hide and a multi-colored Indian blanket. He carried a painted hide shield in one hand and a decorated lance in the other.

Behind him rode Brown Otter on his liver-and-white-spotted horse, its white mane and tail curly and flowing. Luxurious furs draped his lap, spilling white and gold and red. Wearing a fancy-beaded chest-piece and silver-studded leggings, he had obviously dressed with care. He'd braided his hair and had stuck feathers in it. A number of necklaces swung from around his neck, and gold and silver studs flashed in his earlobes.

Bringing up the rear was a man who made Tess dizzy just to look at him. Storm-In-His-Eyes had never been more handsome than he was astride his chestnut stallion with its white-blazed face and socks. Feathers and braids fluttered in the horse's mane and tail, and a leather headstall was peppered with red and green beads, the forehead piece lined in beads and covered with red trade cloth.

Storm wore fringed leggings, a quill vest, and a fringed jacket, all in white. Even his moccasins and breechcloth were white, and all were trimmed in red and green beads to match the tack and saddle. His coal-black hair fell to his shoulders. He'd tied a red cloth in a band around his head. A mound of colorful blankets fell across his lap, and he held the halter ropes of four sturdy horses that pranced behind him.

The procession lined up in front of Dr. John Summar's house, pretty as you please. Tess, along with John and Camilla, could only gaze in stupefaction.

Chief Eagle Talon raised one hand in greeting, then lowered it, resting his big hands on a wooden box in front of him. "You are John Summar?"

John blinked rapidly in surprise. "I-I am."

"I am Eagle Talon, chief of the Blackfeet."

"Yes, I remember you from before, when you collected your daughter's body. How can I help you, sir?"

"Are you the head of this family?"

John looked at the two women flanking him before nodding. "Yes, I suppose I am."

"Then I offer you these things, John Summar." He extended the wooden box, and when John didn't move, he shook it impatiently. "Take it."

John leaped forward and grabbed the box. "W-what is it?"

"Herbs and medicine from our great medicine woman, Minipoka. She shares her powerful medicine with few. This is a great honor for you to receive her offering."

"Ah . . . well, thank you very much." John exchanged befuddled glances with Tess and Camilla.

Tess could hardly take her eyes off Storm, but he resolutely avoided hers. Staring straight ahead, his back as stiff as a board, he fixed a taciturn expression on his handsome face and kept her completely in a stew about what this all meant. Moving closer in an attempt to snag his attention, she did manage to catch Brown Otter's eye and was dumbfounded when he grinned at her.

What was going on here?

A tingle scurried up her back and over her shoulders. Whatever was happening, she had a feeling it was good and that she was somehow, someway going to be rejoicing soon.

"We have furs," Eagle Talon intoned. "Many fine furs."

Brown Otter lifted one, then another and another from his lap, holding them for a moment for John and Tess and Camilla to see before dropping them in a growing mound on the porch steps. He pealed off five more before his lap was empty.

"And we have four young horses, three mares,

and a gelding. The white mare is with foal." Storm slipped from his pad saddle and tied the halters to the porch railing, then hopped back up on his beautiful chestnut.

"Also, we have blankets from the trading post," Eagle Talon continued. "All good. No holes."

Storm dumped several blankets onto the porch.

"Very nice," John said, when it seemed something else was required of him. "Forgive me, but I'm a bit confused."

"All this"— Eagle Talon extended an arm in a sweep to take in the gifts—"is given by me, head of my family, for a trade. These gifts for Tess Summar. Storm-In-His-Eyes wants her for his sits-beside-him-wife, his only wife."

For a moment Tess thought she'd fainted. The world was reduced to a pinprick of black, and she thought her feet had risen off the ground and that she floated. But in the next few moments the world came back to her, and she found that she had, at last, captured Storm's attention. His eyes glimmered with banked fire, and although he didn't smile, she felt it.

"I-I don't know what to say," John stammered.

"Say it's okay," Camilla whispered, grabbing one of his hands in a tight squeeze.

"But this is so . . . so unconventional," John argued. "Trading furs and livestock for Tess? Why, it's—it's—"

Tess drew back her shoe and aimed it at John's shin. When it connected, John let out a yowl and tears sprang to his eyes. One look at Tess's smoldering glare and he faced Eagle Talon, red-faced and massaging his shin.

"It's okay," he said. "We'll accept the gifts." John turned to Tess, frowning at her ear-splitting grin. "Are you sure about this?"

"Yes, yes!" It was all she could do not to dance happily around him and Camilla.

"But where will you live?" John insisted.

"With the Blackfeet," Eagle Talon answered. "It has been discussed by the council. The wedding will be held in two days' time at sunrise at our camp up by Two Forks Creek. She is to bring herself and her treasured belongings. All else will be provided for her." The chief's eyes were warm and his lips curved in a slight smile when he looked at Tess. "She will be a beautiful bride, a good wife, and a friend to our people."

"Yes, she will be a favored sister," Brown Otter agreed.

Joy bubbled in Tess's heart, and with sudden clarity she knew that she owed much of this moment not only to Storm but also to Eagle Talon and Brown Otter. Evidently both of them had spoken to Storm, given him their blessings, and encouraged him to ask for her hand and make her part of the Blackfeet community.

"Sunrise? You want us to bring her to your camp at sunrise?" John repeated.

"Before sunrise," Eagle Talon corrected. "The ceremony to join them as husband and wife will take place when the first rays are given to the earth by the sun god." He held up his hand, signaling that he was finished talking. "We go now."

"We're invited to this ceremony, aren't we?" Camilla asked, her voice small as if she were reluctant to draw attention to herself.

"You are family of Tess Summar," Brown Otter told her. "All family must rejoice and take part. It is a good match, one that will bring great pleasure, many children, and much goodwill."

Almost in unison, the three turned their ponies around and headed back the way they'd come, but not before Storm could sneak a slow, heart-stealing wink to Tess. His lips twitched into a quick smile before he put on his solemn face again, his noble Blackfeet visage that made Tess's pulses thunder and her knees shake.

When the horsemen disappeared around a curve, Tess let go of a trembling laugh.

"Are you sure this is what you want?" John asked. "It's not too late to change your mind."

"Johnny, dear, open your eyes," Camilla scolded him with a smile. "Your sister is madly in love! It's as plain as the nose on your handsome face. Why, she's near to bursting with happiness. How can you ask her such a silly question?"

Catching Tess by the shoulders, John took a moment to scrutinize her high color and smiling mouth. "Good lord, you're right. You *do* love him, don't you?"

Tess nodded, finding it hard to stand still when all she wanted to do was shout and laugh and dance in circles.

"And you want to live with the Blackfeet, don't you?"

Again, she nodded.

"But why?"

"Because I love who I am there, who they let me be," Tess told him, wishing she could give him a more thorough explanation, but unsure he would ever truly understand.

Tears built in his eyes, and then he snatched her to him, hugging her tightly and kissing her hair.

"All right then," he whispered hoarsely. "I want you to be happy and Cammie is right. You are clearly more happy at this moment than I've ever seen you."

"Then you'll come to my wedding?" Tess asked, hugging him back.

"Sister dear, I shall not only come, I shall dance at your wedding." His heart thumped against her ear. "I won't have to paint my face, will I?"

Laughing, Tess tipped back her head to share a grin with him. "I don't think so, John. Dancing should be enough."

She wore a white dress of calfskin studded with fifty elk's teeth. Many-Smiles-Woman said the dress was highly prized among the Blackfeet and fit for a princess. Tess left her hair loose and wore a crown of flowers. She carried a bouquet of sage and lavender. White shells, painted with a sunburst design, dangled from her ears, and ropes of beads hung around her neck, all given to her by Eagle Talon and her husband-to-be.

John and Camilla, Uncle Elmer and Aunt Mattie stood near her as the ceremony commenced while the sun slowly lit the world. They fidgeted, feeling out of place and conspicuous among the Blackfeet, although they were treated as honored guests.

When Tess had emerged from Minipoka's lodge and walked with Many-Smiles-Woman toward the arbor where the ceremony would take place, her family members had dropped their jaws and blinked in amazement. She'd smiled at them, serene in her mode of dress and her place among the Blood.

Storm awaited her under the arbor. Brown Otter stood at his side and held his new daughter, the child Eagle Talon had named Born-Again-Woman.

Tall and lean, Storm was dressed in the white garments he'd worn into town to ask for Tess's hand. He'd gathered his hair into two long braids, abandoning his show of mourning for his sister on this day of great joy.

He trembled at the sight of Tess, and during

most of the ceremony he heard only his own heart-beat thundering in his ears and making him dizzy. His gaze strayed to Tess, and he continued to re-mind himself that this was real, that she had con-sented to be his wife, that she would sit and stand beside him from this day forward.

When the ceremony was complete and the great fire was lit and the men and women sent up cheers and shot arrows into the sky, Storm took Tess's hands and led her to the marriage lodge, which he and Brown Otter had painstakingly prepared.

"Shouldn't we stay and dance and eat and make merry with everyone else?" Tess asked.

He smiled and lifted her hand to his lips for a kiss. "No, my wife. They will celebrate for us all day and all night. The celebrating will not stop un-til the next sunrise. But we must embark on our own celebration, and we must be alone to do this. It's the traditional way."

"Oh, well, if it's tradition . . ."

Lying back, on a bed of soft furs, Tess stretched and watched shadows dance across the skin-lodge walls. Storm, naked and virile, returned to her and slipped beneath the buffalo robe. He hooked an arm at her waist and pulled her flush against him, skin to skin. Although they had made love several times since they'd entered this marriage lodge, she felt him stir and lengthen. Soon he would seek her warmth again and take her to that special, mindless place.

"Am I Mrs. Storm-In-His-Eyes now?" she teased, unbraiding his hair to run her fingers through its inky silkiness.

Chuckling, he trailed a finger down the valley of her breasts. "If you want, yes."

"And I'm also White-Medicine-Woman," she

said, liking the sound of it. The Blackfeet had given her the name and used it during the wedding ceremony that had joined her to Storm-In-His-Eyes.

"The council chose that name for you," Storm explained. "It is hoped that you will add Minipoka's knowledge of medicine to your own, that you will be a bridge between the white eyes and the Blackfeet."

"Whew!" Tess breathed. "That's a tall order."

"But not beyond your capabilities," he assured her.

Tess dragged a finger down his cheek. "I appreciate the confidence you have in me."

"I have seen your courage and I have known your wisdom."

She brought his mouth to hers and nibbled hungrily at his lips, suckled greedily on his tongue. When the kiss ended, he was breathing heavily and his eyes were smoky and turbulent with desire. He kissed her breasts and his tongue circled her nipples until she writhed and moaned and wrapped her legs around him.

"You make me so happy," he whispered against her lips. "And it will always be so. My heart tells me this. I am wolf and I have found my mate. I will want no other."

The words sang to her, and she smiled and stroked his shoulders. Her fingers traced the scars on his back, on his chest. Her warrior. Her hero. Her husband.

He drove into her with a swift thrust that lifted her hips off the furs and brought a cry from her throat. She clung to his shoulders, passion building with each stroke, with each parry of his tongue in her mouth. She moaned and he moaned back, filling her head with sound.

As her body began to tremble, he lifted his

mouth from hers to watch her shattering fulfillment and experience every quiver, every spasm of
passion.

"You are so beautiful," he whispered, his voice
soft with love. He ran a hand over her golden hair,
and his smile was tender, his touch reverent. "My
wife."

"My husband," she whispered back, moving
gently against him, rocking on the hardness that
still filled her. "Oh, how I love you."

"To my people you will be White-Medicine-
Woman, but to me you will always be my
AnadaAki."

Tears spilled from the corners of her eyes. "And
you will always be my daring, darling renegade."

Holding her fast, he took her with him once
again to the fiery realm of the sun—hand in hand,
heart to heart, soul to soul.

And outside the marriage lodge of Storm-In-His-
Eyes and White-Medicine-Woman, the Blood and
their honored guests danced in celebration of the
bridge that love had built.

Avon Romances—
the best in exceptional authors and unforgettable novels!

America Loves Lindsey!

The Timeless Romances
of #1 Bestselling Author

KEEPER OF THE HEART	77493-3/$5.99 US/$6.99 Can
THE MAGIC OF YOU	75629-3/$5.99 US/$6.99 Can
ANGEL	75628-5/$5.99 US/$6.99 Can
PRISONER OF MY DESIRE	75627-7/$6.50 US/$8.50 Can
ONCE A PRINCESS	75625-0/$6.50 US/$8.50 Can
WARRIOR'S WOMAN	75301-4/$5.99 US/$6.99 Can
MAN OF MY DREAMS	75626-9/$5.99 US/$6.99 Can
SURRENDER MY LOVE	76256-0/$6.50 US/$7.50 Can
YOU BELONG TO ME	76258-7/$6.50 US/$7.50 Can
UNTIL FOREVER	76259-5/$6.50 US/$8.50 Can

And Now in Hardcover
LOVE ME FOREVER